WANTED

Dead or Alive

REWARD $50,000

Other Sapphic Pixie Tales By Cassandra Duffy:

The Last Best Tip

Astral Liaisons: Lesbians in Space!

Demons of Paradise

Demons of Paradise 2

An Undead Grift for Christmas

The Vampires of Vigil's Sorrow

Divine Touched

The Eternal Autumn

The Steam-Powered Sniper in the City of Broken Bridges

The Gunfighter's Gambit

The Gunfighter & The Gear-Head

Cassandra Duffy

Day Moon Press
2011

Day Moon Press

This is a work of fiction. Names, characters, locations, and events are meant to be fictitious. Any similarity between any persons living, dead, or undead is completely coincidental. The version of Tombstone, Las Vegas, and any other location are fictionalized renditions.

ISBN-13: 978-1475110227
ISBN-10: 1475110227

4th Print Edition
Cover Design and Interior Artwork by Katiie Kissglosse
Edited by Nichole Mauer

For Nikki,
the Gunfighter to my Gear-Head
the love of my life
and
my partner in mischief!

Chapter 1

Short flights cut shorter

"Coming up on the teeth of the line now," Ramen's voice buzzed through the static-riddled intercom.

The dirigible thrummed and breathed like a living thing. Hot air pumped from the boiler into the zeppelin's cylinder and beat with the thumping of turbines engines providing the forward thrust. Both mechanisms created an unimaginable din, preventing direct communication between the pilot and the automaton running the major systems without the intercom. Along the underside, between the ribs of the armor plates, a walkway ran the entire length of the airship from the boiler in the back to the primary weapon in the front. Gieo scampered down the narrow walkway, using the handrails to keep upright as the airship swayed and jolted in its flight path.

Tamping her leather top hat down on the four, purple braids at the four corners of her head, she lowered her green-tinted goggles over her eyes. The hat didn't fit right, leaving her with three options as she saw it: find a new hat, fix a chinstrap, or wear her hair in the four thick braids. It was an easy decision as far as she was concerned. Sliding down the ladder into the ball-turret on the nose of the great, sturgeon-shaped airship, her riding boots hissed against the copper piping.

"Go serpentine, Ramen," she shouted into the intercom cup next to the base of the ladder.

"Aye, aye, ma'am," the automaton's voice crackled back.

The immense gears of the airship's bat-like wings engaged with a squeaking, rumbling cacophony. Gieo strapped herself into the reclined seat of the ball-turret, affixing the leather belts across her chest and, clipping the metal tongs onto the lapels of her tailed tuxedo jacket that held tight against the brown, leather corset she wore beneath. As the chair lowered into the Plexiglas turret, she hooked the rubber hose from the air-hydraulic feed into the leather and chain choker she wore. Fresh air pumped up around her head to cool her and aid in breathing.

With the wings flapping in machinated patterns, the great airship took on a wide swing to its flight, shooting back and forth in as athletic of zigzags as a fifty-meter long blimp could manage. Gieo spun the handles on the weapon system's hydraulic feeds, sending steam power into the four guns positioned in a box around her. The desert floor, thousands of feet below, rolled back and forth beneath her, held at bay only by the glass ball she sat in.

"Leveling the outcropping at the precise center of our undulations," Ramen's voice crackled through the com speaker in the ball-turret.

"Have the smoke-screen loaded and ready."

"Aye, aye, ma'am."

"Disengaging now." Gieo pulled the pins on the ball-turret's gyroscope arm. The entire turret, with her inside, dropped down off the bottom of the armored airship, dangling by a ten meter, articulated metal arm and a dozen hydraulic tubes and hoses. She slipped her feet into the leather straps of the turret and took control of the swaying arm. All around her the hisses of steam and clanking of gears let her know the gyroscopes were functioning as intended.

Puffs of white smoke from the ground erupted out of an underbrush canopy nestled between the furthest most rocks of the outcropping. Shells whistled up toward the zeppelin, followed by explosions, and the clanking of flack bouncing off the airship's armor.

Gieo leveled the gyroscopes to steady her gun platform even as the airship swayed in evasive maneuvers. She brought the targeting reticule of a large, copper hoop with four smaller hoops arranged in the center to indicate the four guns, on the outcropping, and pushed the two trigger handles forward.

"I see your teeth," she growled, "now take a look at mine!"

The four guns around her erupted in steam-powered blasts, sending shells of explosive material down onto the antiaircraft battery four at a time. The shells exploded across the rocky surface in showers of white, magnesium fire. She saw a few of the scattering Slark trying to escape the kill zone, and she zeroed in on them to put the fire right across their path. She got some, more than some, several even, before a direct hit caught her dirigible on the port side, knocking free one of the wings with a shriek of metal and a resounding thump.

"Son-of-a…" Gieo kicked free the emergency hold on the main spring of the arm's gyroscope, pulling the entire swinging arm of the ball-turret back into the body of the blimp. The swaying of the ship was replaced by a long, descending spiral, as the wounded blimp fluttered toward the ground with a torn cylinder and only one functional wing. Gieo unhooked herself from the ball-turret and scrambled back up the ladder into the main body of the ship. "Launch the smoke-screen," she shouted into the intercom.

"On the way," Ramen replied.

Four quick pops were followed by four loud explosions as the outer plates on the boilers blew off and the water content dumped onto the stoking fires. White steam and smoke poured from the dirigible, obscuring even the vaguest outline of the ship as it began its slow, spiraling descent toward the ground. Gieo scrambled back down the walkway to the radio room, cranked the hand-wheel to extend the antenna, and tapped out the distress code for a languishing aircraft.

"This is Dirigible Purple 6, going down," Gieo shouted into the mouthpiece. "Do you copy, air-defense network?"

After a few minutes of trying and retrying the distress call, an old, familiar voice crackled back over the shortwave. "This is air-defense Tempe-2," the dithering old man said. "There hasn't been anything flying in years. My radio was buried under laundry."

"There has too," Gieo protested. "We went through this not six months ago."

A long stretch of radio silence followed.

"Are you sure it wasn't years ago?" Tempe-2 asked.

"Positive!" Gieo shrieked.

"Oh, well, I guess if you're positive," the old man said. "What's your situation and location?"

"Situation is stable, but crashing," Gieo said, "and location is sector 7-G."

"That's the Tombstone Three-Three-O," Tempe-2 said. "I'll see if I can get someone over there on the horn for a retrieval team, but don't expect much luxury. Those Tombstoners are hardscrabble from tip to toe."

"Whatever, it beats walking home," Gieo said. "Dirigible Purple 6, over and out."

This was her sixth crash in the last three years and the story was always the same. Tempe-2 was the only air defense network radioman left in the world as far as she knew, and he was half-gone most of the time. She suspected he was a methanol drinker, peyote user, or ether huffer. Every time she got shot down, it was like the first time for him. She was glad for his existence, as he always managed to get someone out from one of the free cities to pick her up, but he never remembered having done it.

"We're at 750 feet," Ramen's voice came through the com.

"Get back to the shop," Gieo replied. "Hopefully I'll see you in a couple days."

She heard her automaton's escape tube fire and the telltale thumping of his helicopter blades as he flitted away, too small and well below the notice of the antiaircraft batteries to be fired upon. She climbed up the ladder into the spider room. The spherical room, dead center in the zeppelin cylinder, comprised a network of rubber tubing with a harness in the middle. She shimmied into the harness, hooked herself in, including the neck brace, and waited for the ship to hit the desert floor.

Crashing was becoming routine. She was more curious about what kind of person might be sent from Tombstone than she was afraid of the impending impact. She'd never met anyone from the Tombstone hunting camp, although their reputation for being hardcore, psycho Slark-killers was well-traveled.

Her thoughts were interrupted by four concussive explosions slamming into the underside of the airship—shoulder-fired rockets. One must have snuck through a chink in the ship's defenses as the dirigible's descent took a violent shove from soft flutter into chaotic tumble.

"Oh, you guys are dickheads," Gieo growled. She reached into her pocket, thrust the mouth guard over her teeth, and braced herself for impact. The ship hit with an explosive crash as the blimp portion ruptured. The boiler launched itself away from the wreckage, and the pilot whipped around inside the spider room like whirling dervish.

Chapter 2
Taciturn retrieval

When Los Angeles fell, Fiona was twenty-one years old. She even still had a Lakers bumper sticker on the back of her car. The modified muscle car, more precisely two different American muscle cars melded together with a repurposed engine from a Slark fighter, cut a fiery streak across the Cochise badlands at over 100 mph. The car was a straight-line bullet of raw power with a spiked cattle-catcher on the front and a trail of fire and smoke behind. Fiona, who had lost her driver's license a full year before the Slark invaded, kept as trophies a few of her old speeding tickets on the dashboard to fade in the desert sun. Anyone trying to take away her right to drive now would have to make their case to the business end of her Colt Anaconda .44 Magnum.

Some insane, dirt-worshiper from the ruins of Tempe claimed to see an aircraft and called it in to the Tombstone defense grid. At least, that's what Zeke had radioed her to say. She was the closest, and he wanted to know for sure; not that he'd offered anything in return for her time or fuel.

It was a fool's errand. Nothing flew but birds, bugs, and bats. For awhile, after the cataclysm and the resulting great purge, both sides tried to regain the sky. Nothing stayed airborne for long as the antiaircraft guns far out-paced low-tech aircraft. Fiona suspected she wouldn't find anything, but, nearing the coordinate estimates radioed in, she spotted a smoke spire on the horizon. If there was an airship, the Slark had long since shot it down. It served the idiot right, whoever they were, but, if Fiona hurried, she might still catch the Slark recon team in their work and take a few heads.

The alleged aircraft, which looked to be nothing more than twisted metal, smashed wood, and billowing cloth, had crashed relatively close to the old 10 highway. The Slark recon team, four of the ugly lizards in all, was attempting to set up a perimeter around the crash site, partially on the patchy highway, covering their movements with shoulder-fired rocket tubes. Fiona yanked the emergency brake and spun the wheel to the right, sending the roaring beast of her car into a whirl. The resulting cloud of dust and exhaust smoke blew through the crash site, obscuring the direction she was coming from. Correcting her course, aided by the spinning compass on the dashboard, she gunned the engine, released the brake, and roared forward through the opaque dust cloud. Two loud clangs followed by meaty squish noises let her know her cattle-catcher had collected two of the Slark. She slammed on the brakes and came to a stop. As the cloud passed her by, she stepped from the car, jerked her Colt Anaconda from its hip holster, and scanned the area for the remaining two. Through the slowly clearing haze, she spotted them fleeing in their weird, sidling run. With her gun arm fully extended, she sighted in the first, fired, swung over to the other, sighted again, and fired. Both Slark hit the ground in quick succession with gaping bullet holes in their backs. Fiona twirled the massive, chrome-plated revolver a couple times before letting it settle back into the holster slung low on her slender hips.

A lanky goddess, a hair under six-feet tall, she moved with the practiced grace of a career predator on dusty cowboy boots. Scarce times had carved every drop of fat from her body, leaving only lean muscle on a willowy frame. She further accentuated the hard-edged, straight lines of her body with tan, skin-tight leather pants and a tight, denim jacket two sizes too small for her long torso, leaving ample space to easily get at the bandolier belt for her pistol. A wide-brimmed, russet cowboy hat kept the desert sun off her short-cropped red hair, while wrap around Oakley sunglasses shielded her blue eyes. Her heavily tanned skin, formerly from tanning beds, was now a natural product of her time spent in the desert.

“You may as well come out,” Fiona said to the smashed kindling of the crash site.

A curious leather top hat, pulled tight over four purple braids and brass goggles, poked out of the wreckage. "How did you know I wasn't another one of them?" the pilot peeped.

"You don't smell like fish barf," Fiona replied. She slid the Wakizashi, a much shorter katana, from its wooden scabbard along her back, and set to the task of cleaving the heads from the bodies, starting with the mangled, four-armed, two-legged, five-foot tall lizard men tangled in the spiked framework on the front of her car.

"Thank you, I try to practice good hygiene." The pilot extracted herself from the remains of her airship, dusting off her tailed tuxedo jacket and tight riding britches.

"I didn't say you smelled good," Fiona corrected her. "I said you didn't smell like fish barf." She punctuated the sentence with two quick slashes of the sword, decapitating the impaled bodies in twin sprays of green blood. It was a lucky hit, both heads were already impaled on spikes, and the severed bodies came away easily.

"My name is Gieo," she said. The pilot's clothing might have looked like a traditional English horseback riding outfit if not for all the buckles, leather straps, and brass gizmos adorning it. She trundled out of the scattered remains of her ship, hand extended, half-blind with her dusty, pilot goggles still over her eyes. She blundered past the two dead Slark on her way toward Fiona.

"Yo?" Fiona asked, raising a curious eyebrow at the small, strange pilot.

"Gieo," she repeated, slower this time. "There's a 'G' on the front. It's Korean—I'm Korean, from Orange County." When Fiona didn't shake the offered hand, Gieo pulled it back and used it to pull the goggles onto their resting place along the front of her leather top hat. "So, how long until the rescue crew gets here to help me salvage my airship?"

"Probably never." Fiona walked around Gieo, to claim the heads of the two Slark she'd shot. "Don't even think of asking for half the bounties on these guys either."

"No, no, those are all yours." Gieo nearly threw up when Fiona hacked off the triangular heads of the dead Slark. "I'll just get my things and we can be on our way."

"Whatever," Fiona said.

The little pilot scampered past her back into the wreckage. Fiona wiped her blade clean with a scrap of cloth from one of the Slark and re-sheathed it. She finished mounting the other two heads, in much better condition than the first couple, on the spikes along the front of her bullet-shaped, silver car. Her hand instantly jumped to the butt of her gun when she heard the pilot shriek.

"It's broken!" Gieo stumbled back out of the airship crash with a cornucopia of devices cradled in her arms, discarding most of them as she went, finally filtering down to one specific machine, no bigger than a television remote, hemorrhaging copper wires.

"What is it?" Fiona asked, hoping it wasn't something useful she might later steal.

"It's a Sapphic Intimate-Encounter Reciprocity Concluder," Gieo said glumly.

"Um…okay…what does it do?"

"Only let's a lesbian couple know when they're done having sex, duh," Gieo said. "Without it, girl-girl sex could hypothetically go on indefinitely. I mean, how else would you know when you were done?"

"Usually when everyone's happy or my jaw starts hurting."

"You've clearly had better lovers than me." Gieo tossed the broken device over her shoulder, searched the scattered items on the ground around her, and retrieved a leather tool-kit. "Okay, let's go."

"You're over it, just like that?"

"Catastrophe breeds necessity, which is the mother of invention." Gieo circled around to the passenger side of Fiona's car and waited to be let in. "My entire airship just got blasted out of the sky—a little perspective here, please. Besides, I stayed up two hours this time—a personal best!"

"You do this a lot?" Fiona slid into the driver seat and unlocked the passenger door.

Gieo hopped in and situated herself on the hot, vinyl seat. "If you know a better way to test whether something will keep flying after being shot, I'd like to hear it."

With a whiplash inducing jolt, Fiona's car spun back in the direction it had come and fired out in a straight line across the desert, leaving scorched earth and a smoke trail hundreds of yards long in its wake.

"Is it always this loud?" Gieo shouted over the thundering of the car. "Is this a Slark fighter engine? Where did you get it? How did you make it compatible with a 2009 Allison transmission? Why does your car look like a Challenger fucked a Mustang? Can I take it apart? Why do you even have a passenger seat if you don't want to talk to passengers?"

"I didn't have a compelling reason to take out the passenger seat until now," Fiona grumbled.

"Hey, I know you!" Gieo shouted, oblivious to the barb.

"I'm sure you don't…"

"Yeah-huh, you're Fiona Bishop," Gieo said. She snatched one of the speeding tickets from the dashboard to confirm the name. "You're the Victoria's Secret model that stabbed the paparazzi guy in the mouth with a penknife at LAX. What did he even say to you?"

"He wasn't real paparazzi, just some freelancer, and I don't remember what he said."

"Uh-huh, sure, are you still crazy? I read on Perez, back when there was an internet that you plead insanity."

"I was crazy back when the world fancied itself sane. Now that the world has gone insane, I like to think I'm just a little more colorful than most. Besides, that was all a long time ago."

"It wasn't that long ago…like six years," Gieo said. "I had the hugest crush on you in high school." Fiona became uncomfortably aware that the purple-haired pilot was sliding closer, leaning over the edge of the center console. "I used to touch myself watching the Angel series video on your website. I got kicked out of a SAT prep program for writing inappropriate essays about you."

"What are you doing?" Fiona asked quickly.

"Nothing, shut up, keep your eyes on the road, we're going like a hundred or something." Gieo's hand found its way onto Fiona's thigh, gripping the tight, muscular quad meaningfully. "I heard the model-turned-talk-show-host went all stalker over you and tried to break into your house. What was her name?"

"Tyr..." Fiona squirmed when Gieo's hand pressed into the crotch of her leather pants, cutting off the rest of her answer. "What if I'm not…"

"…into girls? Into me? Whatever, it's just a hand either way, right? Don't look down or over and I'm whoever you want me to be." Gieo's deft fingers unbuttoned, unclasped, and unbuckled everything in her way with remarkable alacrity.

"What are you…?" Fiona muttered, feeling the soft, talented fingers make their way down the top of her unzipped pants.

"I'm the last scientist on earth, the airship pilot extraordinaire, the three-time Junior Aerodynamic Expo of Laguna Beach winner, but you can call Gieo or 'oh baby'."

The pilot was flippant, sarcastic, arrogant, unflappable, and most likely full of shit, but it had been so long since Fiona had let anyone even come within arms length of her, let alone touch her, that she thought she might go with it to pass the three hour drive back to Tombstone. Gieo's fingers froze before touching anything of much interest. Fiona turned to find the pilot frowning.

"What?"

"You're not wearing underwear."

"I never really liked underwear."

"But you were an underwear model."

"Is any of this a problem?"

"No, I can pretend, I guess."

"Fuck off." Fiona grabbed Gieo's hand by the wrist, pulled it from her pants, and tossed it back to the pilot. "My reality doesn't have to match up with your fantasy. The person you thought I was died years ago if she ever really existed at all."

Gieo laughed and bit her thumbnail around a coquettish grin. "Oh, I like you," she said. "You're prickly in some delightful ways."

"Whatever." Fiona stomped the accelerator to the floor, rocketing the car up over 200 mph. The desert flew by in a blur. The thunder of the engine and the enormous, solid-form rubber tires roaring along the worn asphalt prevented any further conversation for the rest of the ride. Fiona backed off the throttle as they rumbled into the outer limits of Tombstone. A faded, wooden sign on the outskirts informed them they were entering the town "too tough to die" with a population of 1,500 badasses. The population and motto were original to the sign, but the "badasses" part had been added with a can of orange spray-paint. On the main thoroughfare, Fiona brought her muscle car to a dusty stop in front of the Slarkhead Saloon. She buckled her belts and zipped her pants, remaining in the car for an awkward moment after.

"I should find a way to thank you for the ride," Gieo said.

Fiona rolled her eyes and stepped from the car. She'd barely closed the door when she heard a slow, sarcastic, clichéd clapping from across the street on the balcony of the town hall.

"Only four heads," the one man audience said through a chuckle. "Did you at least get a balloon ride, Red?" The man wore authority with a distinctive largeness. He wasn't specifically muscular or particularly fat, but a mix of both that gave a brawny, powerful quality to him. He wore Slark-skin overalls without a shirt underneath. The gray, scales of Slark pelts were hardly the toughest looking leather on him as his weathered skin had long since turned into elephant hide from a lifetime in the desert. With a gray, handlebar moustache and eyes narrowed to slits from squinting into the Arizona sun his entire life, he had the look of a cunning land walrus, which was precisely how Fiona always pictured him, although she would never dare say so.

"Zeke, I can't help but notice your bumper is empty, clean even." Fiona nodded in the direction of the modified El Camino parked across the street and the empty spikes on the front.

"Mathematically speaking, four is infinity percent larger than zero," Gieo said.

"Technically, so is one," Zeke said, the smile never leaving his face, "but fact remains, the quota to get fuel is six."

"Then I guess you better get hunting." Fiona passed around the back of the car, taking Gieo by the arm to lead her into the saloon.

"I'm surprised he knew enough math to understand that," Gieo whispered.

"He only looks dumb," Fiona replied.

The interior of the saloon reeked of unwashed human flesh, tobacco spit, cheap tequila, and burned food. A haze of dust and cigar smoke hung in the air of the vaulted ceilings, almost obscuring the walkway around the second floor in the dimly lit bar. Fiona's boots thumped across the wooden floor, casting silence in their wake through the dozen or so dirty denizens occupying the handful of gaming tables turned into a restaurant dining area.

"Who's your friend there?" The bartender didn't look up from the ancient newspaper he was reading.

Gieo stepped right up to the bar, hopped onto an unoccupied stool, and stuck out her hand to be shaken. "Gieo—airship pilot, steam compression scientist, and mathematician extraordinaire, pleased to meet you."

"Scientist, huh?" The bartender let out a low, sarcastic whistle. "We don't get many of those in here, what with them all getting wiped out by their own EMP pulses. Got any tech to trade?"

"She had a device that let you know when you were done having sex," Fiona said, "but it broke in the crash."

"Shit, Fiona, you'd need to start getting laid before you would need to know when to stop." The bartender set down his paper and smiled to Fiona. A short, stocky man with a receding hairline of greased back black hair and matching, whisper thin moustache, he struck a far more jovial figure than might be expected of such a position in such a town.

"Why would she have a hard time getting laid?" Gieo asked.

"You aren't from around here, are you?" the bartender asked. "Aside from the wagon train of prostitutes out of Juarez that rolls through every few months, she's it for women in this town, and she's made it abundantly clear to all the men that she's only interested in ladies. Female gunfighters tend to be rare and short-lived in the free cities." The bartender pulled a bottle from below the bar and poured two shots, placing one in front of each woman. "What makes a good gunfighter is a lack of hesitation. Fast hands are important, but there's always a hesitation in taking a life that can slow even the quickest draw when it comes to pulling the trigger. The less conscience a gunfighter has about killing, the faster they'll be. Fiona here is the only one, male or female, I've ever met without even a fraction of a second's worth of hesitation. Most women have too much to be any good at the killing trade."

"That's sexist," Gieo said.

"I'll be dipped, you're right! I'll make sure to turn myself in to the ACLU when they get back on their feet." The bartender went back to reading his old newspaper.

"Got a room for her?" Fiona asked.

"Colorado hunting party in town," the bartender said. "We're booked to overflowing. I wouldn't recommend leaving her to her own devices with that bunch around. They've been drinking hard and haven't found enough Slark to vent on."

"Fine, she can stay with me." Fiona downed her shot, took Gieo's shot, and drank it too. "I need a nap before I go back out."

Fiona wandered away from the bar with little more than a grunt of acknowledgement from the bartender. Gieo fell in behind her, following her up the stairs, around the walkway, until they reached one of the largest rooms in the far, back corner. The room was once a slightly-modernized replica of Old West accommodations for tourists, but had since become genuine accommodations of the post-apocalypse west when the tourist trap section of the town turned into the most functional part. Fiona flopped onto the bed, metal springs creaking in protest. Her long legs stretched out to hook the heels of her boots on the metal footboard. She slid her hat down until the brim rested across her face, blocking out the bright, afternoon sun flowing in through the two windows.

"The train to Vegas comes through every few weeks," Fiona said. "You can stay with me until then."

"What if I don't want to leave?" Gieo took off her top hat, releasing the four braids of her purple hair to bounce around her head.

She unbuttoned her jacket the rest of the way and tossed it aside as well.

Fiona raised the brim of her hat with two fingers to expose one eye enough to watch what Gieo was doing. “Why would you want to stay around here?”

“Shits and giggles.”

“Fine, but you’ll have to earn your keep somehow.”

“I’ve got a few skills…”

“Good.” Fiona let the brim of her hat drop. “Let’s hope shutting up for an hour is one of them.”

The two shots of tequila combined with the warmth of the sun to make sleep an easy proposition despite the presence of the flighty pilot, and soon Fiona was comfortably snoozing.

Chapter 3
Thanks a truckload

Fiona awoke from her nap to find her room alarmingly empty. A strange sense of concern, odd in its very existence, settled over her at not seeing the diminutive pilot. She leapt from the bed, and, on her way to the door, checked her reflection in the dusty mirror above her vanity, which typically served as her casing reloading and gun cleaning station. She'd obviously looked in the mirror before, but this was the first time in years she'd actually used it to check her appearance. Her hand froze on the doorknob. She could hear Gieo's voice through the thin walls. The pilot was chattering away with several people downstairs, talking tech, and seemingly having a good time of it.

Fiona returned to the mirror. She'd slept in her hat and sunglasses, leaving large dents on the sides of her long, slender nose and a distinctive rim indentation in her hair. The reflection, familiar in its former unimportance, suddenly mocked her by showing the rust on the beauty she'd once prized. Before she fully understood what she was doing, she'd poured water in the basin from a pitcher, dipped a hand towel in it, and cleaned the grit from her face and neck. The shine came back to her diamond without a great deal of polish, and soon she was looking at the angularly beautiful face that had once adorned magazine and catalogue covers with her high cheek bones, delicately tapered jaw, and pert chin with a tiny cleft. Why she should care what the pilot thought of her, she couldn't quite piece together, but she rationalized it by telling herself she needed a good face washing regardless.

Armed with a clean face, she replaced her sunglasses over her eyes and headed downstairs. The bar was full, far fuller than Fiona could remember it ever being. Two dozen men were milling about in something of a loosely organized line. The bartender trundled amidst the clientele, carrying a serving tray in one hand and a sack in the other. The patrons took drinks from the tray and dropped payment into the sack; when the tray was empty or the sack full, the bartender headed back to the bar to reload one and unpack the other. Fiona leaned over the railing to find where the line ended. In the middle of three tables arranged around her, Gieo was seeing customers in a slapdash repair shop. Included in the pile of payments on one of the tables were two dusty Slark heads.

Fiona made her way downstairs, catching the bartender by the arm as he passed. "What's going on here?"

"Gieo's fixing tech," the bartender said.

"Yeah, I gathered that," Fiona snarled. "Why is she fixing tech?"

"Says she's got a plan," the bartender said with a shrug. "What do I care why? She's got the bar full of happy, entertained, paying customers. Nobody breaking anything, everyone getting along, it's a goddamn dream come true." The bartender pulled away from Fiona to return to his customers.

Fiona strode over to Gieo's station and slapped her palms against the table making the first four customers in line jump, but not drawing so much as a blink out of Gieo. "What are you doing?"

"Making this pressure cooker pressurize and cook," Gieo said as she popped open the thermostat to replace the spring.

"I said I was taking a nap," Fiona said.

"Yep, did you sleep well?"

"I mean, why did you come down here when I said I was taking a nap?"

Gieo finally pulled her attention from the pressure cooker she was working on. At least, she pulled her eyes away, but Fiona noticed with a twinge of impressed surprise that the pilot's hands were still working of their own accord. "That's kind of a silly question," Gieo said.

"Why do you have Slark heads?" Fiona asked.

"That's a better question. Eddie paid me to affix calculator solar panels on his iPod to make it run without batteries."

"Who the fuck is Eddie?" Fiona demanded, her voice becoming a little shrill.

"You know Eddie." Gieo pointed to a grizzled, bearded man near the front windows with ear buds in his ears, listening to the newly solar-powered iPod. Eddie waved and Gieo waved back. Fiona vaguely recognized the man as someone she'd seen around town, but had never bothered asking his name. "He runs the hothouse farms on the outskirts. He wanted to listen to Miles Davis while he worked."

"But how…?"

"Come on, we're in Arizona," Gieo said, returning her full attention to the pressure cooker in front of her. "Enough sun hits this state every day to run a fleet of battleships. I'm sure there's more than enough to let a tomato farmer listen to some jazz during peak farming hours."

"That's not what I…"

"The Slark heads are for you, silly," Gieo said. "You needed six to get fuel, so I got you the two you were short."

"I appreciate it, but I can…"

"Don't go thinking this makes us even." Gieo turned her screwdriver on Fiona with an accusatory poke before immediately launching back into the work of repairing the cooker. "I'm still going to think of a way to make things up to you. But, in the mean time, since you don't have to go out hunting again today, I thought we could take a ride with Mitch to the crash site. He said he has a truck and there're a few things I could use off the dirigible."

"Who is Mitch?" Fiona asked, glad to finally get a full expression out.

Gieo and the entire line of customers pointed at the bartender.

"Seriously, you didn't know his name? How long have you lived here?" Gieo asked.

"A couple years, I guess."

"Manners aren't your thing, huh?" Gieo said with a low whistle.

"Manners don't count for much in Tombstone," Fiona said defensively.

"Here you go, Cutter." Gieo pushed the finished pressure cooker to the mountain of a man covered in black leather and knives at the front of the line. "You'll be enjoying your grandmother's award winning goulash again in no time."

"Thank you, Gieo," Cutter said. "I'll bring a batch by tomorrow if you like."

"I *would* like that, and you're welcome." Gieo smiled to him. Cutter smiled back with a mouthful of gleaming golden teeth.

"Can I borrow you for a minute?" Fiona grabbed Gieo by the hand and dragged her out from behind her tables. The line let out a collective groan as Fiona pulled the pilot to a more secluded corner. When they had managed the iota of privacy Fiona felt she needed, she leaned down far enough to whisper, "Are you crazy?"

"Considering I've never stabbed a man in the mouth for asking a question that's a hell of a thing for *you* to ask *me*," Gieo said with a little giggle. "What color are your eyes under those glasses?"

"These people are insane killers operating in a largely lawless town."

"Have you ever tried being nice to them? Most are just regular people trying to make the best of things," Gieo said. "Can you even see in here with sunglasses on?"

"You don't know them the way I do."

"You don't even know their names!" Gieo exclaimed. "Did you know Eddie was a florist? Cutter was a mobile locksmith for AAA. Mitch ran a landscaping company that specialized in low water need vegetation. These people aren't monsters."

"They're not the only ones here." Fiona took off her glasses to look Gieo directly in the eyes. "There are plenty of dangerous people in Tombstone with life stories that include prison, gangs, rape, and mental institutions."

"Oh, your eyes really are blue," Gieo said with the most adorable little 'oh' sound on the front. "I love red hair and blue eyes. With all the digital editing in magazines and internet photos, I just assumed they changed your eyes to blue in post."

"Are you even listening to me?"

"Are you worried about me?" Gieo offered her a demure smile that was a loaded gun pointed at Fiona's heart.

Fiona quickly put her sunglasses back on. "This conversation is over." Fiona spun on her heels and began walking toward the bar.

"Does this mean we're going to the wreck site?" Gieo called after her.

"Fine," Fiona said. "Finish with your line. I'm going to go exchange the heads for fuel." Fiona changed her trajectory away from the stairs to head back to the repair station to collect the two dusty Slark heads. They looked desiccated, more than usual even for lizards; they'd likely been hauled out of traps around some farmer's land. Fiona detested the creeping sense that she was taking charity for work she should have done herself. If anyone in the bar shared in her humiliating take on the situation, none of them voiced their opinion. In fact, the people milling about the saloon were either paying attention to Gieo or themselves.

Back on the street the hot, dry air, remarkably fresh compared to the interior of the saloon, hit Fiona like a moving wall. She ambled to her car and slid the heads onto the brush-guard's spikes. The heads, dry as mummified jerky, slid onto the sharpened metal without an ounce of protest. The heads-on-bumper-pikes system was Zeke's idea. Fiona couldn't readily think of another way to indicate a Slark bounty had been collected, and she didn't particularly mind driving a car with the heads of her kills lined up on the bumper in such a gruesome fashion, so she'd never really questioned the logic of it. Settling into the inferno of her car's interior, she rolled down the windows and rumbled through the dusty streets at a crawl with her kills on full display. The car, like most hunter vehicles, had two speeds: ludicrously fast and stopped. Driving through town required her to leave the accelerator alone entirely while finessing the brake.

Zeke was the one with the Slark engine fuel, the Midwestern contacts that kept the town fed, and controlled the water supply through wells, so he decided what was valuable, which was Slark heads. There were rumors, more than rumors really, that Zeke ate the flesh of his kills. Fiona had knocked a Slark into a fire at one point. The smell that resulted turned her stomach in ways that even bad sushi and raw eggs couldn't. If Zeke did eat the green, alien meat of dead Slark, Fiona sincerely hoped he didn't cook it beforehand. She knew the man to have a sadistic streak and a fiery grudge against the aliens, but she hadn't the faintest idea why. There were ample reasons for all of humanity to hate the invaders, but Zeke seemed hell-bent on making them suffer.

The devil himself stood large next to his modified El Camino at the fueling station. He beckoned Fiona over to the front of the line when he saw her approach. She pulled into the slot of the converted old gas station that he motioned her toward. Before she was even free of her car, he'd begun collecting the heads from her spikes.

"You're in a rare mood," Fiona said.

"Bagged me eight today," Zeke replied. "Up-close and personal with a shotgun and a baseball bat always elevates my mood."

A few of Zeke's pump jockeys set about the work of fueling up, lubricating, and removing of grit for Fiona's car. Aside from the strange, glowing, yellow fuel salvaged from Slark tankers, the hunting cars of Tombstone required ridiculous amounts of lubricant for the turbines and daily scrubbing of sand from the massive air intake filters. Fiona's car, one of the fastest and best balanced, required less than most, but it would still strangle and seize up without the daily care of the pump jockeys. She pulled a pack of ancient Mentos from her jacket and tossed it to one of the greasy, skinny teenagers working the pumps. The mints were dried to solid little rocks, but she knew the orphaned scarecrows that worked the fueling depot didn't have teeth anymore anyway and preferred candy they could suck on. The other pump jockeys, greasy and non-descript, gathered around the one who had accepted the tip to claim their share of the reward.

"I've got a proposition for you, Red," Zeke said, drawing Fiona's attention back to him.

Propositions from most in Tombstone meant sex, but Fiona knew Zeke didn't have any interest in sex; he wanted power and the only reason he wanted it was to cause more pain to the Slark. Since she'd already brought him six heads, she doubted his proposition would have much to do with the latter.

"I'm listening." She leaned against her car with her arms folded over her chest.

"The Hawkins House is getting too large again," Zeke said. "After the last culling, they're also better armed. I need someone with some skills at creeping about to spike their methanol."

"Poison doesn't sound like your style," Fiona said.

"It's not, but I'm not going to risk my men against a bunch of half-blind crazies if I don't have to." Zeke moseyed over to his El Camino, his Slark-skin overalls hissing with every step. He reached into the bed and pulled out an old milk jug with cloudy liquid inside. "They don't know about your little pilot friend yet, but you can imagine what they'll say when they find out about her. If you're planning on keeping her, this would be in your best interest."

He had a point. The methanol drinking cult had it in their minds that the devil was a woman. They already had their wary, barely functioning eyes on Fiona as the one, and she'd shot half a dozen of them before they stopped coming after her with truncheons and knives. She didn't really want to risk their zealotry against Gieo, but poisoning them felt a touch too cowardly for her taste.

"What are you offering?" Fiona asked, hoping it was something easy to reject.

"A month of free fuel and cuts in line until it needs to be done again." Zeke held out the jug of poison and shook it as if that would somehow make it more appealing.

"I'll think about it." Fiona pulled herself from her leaned position against her car and walked back around to the door.

"Offer's got an expiration date on it," Zeke said.

"Don't they all?" Fiona slid into her car and slowly crept away from the fueling depot.

As far as she knew, the Hawkins House cultists had existed somewhere in Texas before the Slark invasion, but she figured they only started drinking methanol as communion after. They were a blight on the town, screaming dire prophecies in the streets, stealing wood to smoke into methanol to drink, and breeding like insane rabbits on the edge of town. The old church at the end of Fitch Street, surrounded by trailers and mobile homes, marked out their district, but they hardly kept to themselves. The last time their numbers had grown too large, mostly through conversion, Zeke had firebombed their camp with Molotovs. Fiona doubted it would be so easy this time; however, she had no interest in poisoning women and children, which would likely be a requisite of the job. With a prize as good as the one offered, Zeke would find someone to do it, and Fiona would be the primary beneficiary of the act, but she wasn't interested in Zeke's dirty work.

Without hunting to do, Fiona decided it might not be the worst idea to actually take Gieo up on the trip into the desert for tech salvage. Judging from the pilot's skill with gizmos of all shapes and sizes, it stood to reason there would be some pretty valuable goods if they got to the wreck before another Slark recon team did.

Pulling around the front of the saloon off old Freemont Street, the first thing she noticed was Gieo and Mitch standing on the back of a massive Chevy Kodiak C7000 flatbed. Where Mitch had been hiding away such a monstrosity, Fiona wasn't sure, but now that the secret was out, it had attracted more than passing attention. A mob of twenty or so people swamped in the street side of the truck and didn't seem interested in letting Mitch or Gieo get down. As Fiona crawled closer, her engine noise caught the attention of the crowd.

"Methanol drinkers," Fiona grumbled when twenty pairs of milky, half-blind eyes turned toward her. They were still brandishing their crudely drawn signs depicting her, which were as artistically devoid and inaccurate as one might expect from a mostly-blind cult of mental patients. They abandoned their shouting match with Gieo and

Mitch at the sight of the silver tornado that was Fiona's car and began advancing on her instead. She revved the engine several times, threatening the spikes of her brush guard on them, but being mostly blind, they paid the deadly cattle-catcher only token attention. She let out the clutch just enough to make the car jump forward about ten feet in a single lurch. The cultist's broke ranks and scattered from the street. Fiona wasn't entirely sure what might happen if she drove her car at full speed through a crowd of twenty people, although she was certain she wouldn't be able to eat for a week after.

Pulling up alongside the truck, she rolled down her window and stuck her head out. "You two okay?"

"Yeah," Mitch grumbled, "they had some choice words for Gieo."

"If they come back around, I'll put some choice bullets in them," Fiona said. "If you're ready to roll, I'll lead you out."

Mitch nodded once, grabbed the handle along the truck's side, and slung himself into the driver's seat with surprising agility. Gieo hopped out off the bed of the truck instead and scampered around to the passenger side of Fiona's car. Before Fiona could protest, Gieo was in the passenger seat.

She leaned over, kissed Fiona softly on the neck, and whispered against her ear, "Keep making a habit of saving me and see what happens."

Chapter 4
Unreasonable aspirations

As they drove, Gieo rested her left hand on the top of Fiona's right thigh. The positioning of the hand was a simple draping in a comfortable state for both, but sans anything active or directed. Fiona's mind kept retuning to the drive earlier that day where Gieo's hand had been a lot more aggressive, and she wished it would be again.

"This cult, the methanol drinkers, how did that happen?" Gieo asked, picking the most distasteful topic Fiona could imagine to spoil the sexual tension.

"The Slark have a superstitious aversion for blindness," Fiona replied. "The Hawkins House was a cult from Texas that took the natural defense mechanism people were trying with methanol blindness and turned it into a religion with methanol as their holy communion. They imagine they'll sweep away the Slark with an army of the blind. I don't know how they'll know if they succeeded or not since most of them can't see more than a few, blurry feet."

"Leave it to Texans to turn stupidity into a religion," Gieo mused.

"Speaking of stupidity, how many times have you been shot down?"

"Touché," Gieo said. "I've mapped the Slark defense line and now I'm trying to break it. Sure I crash, but each crash teaches me something."

"It teaches them something too—they are smarter than us."

"Correction, they *were* smarter than us." Gieo pulled her hand from Fiona's thigh to draw a little diagram in the dust on the dashboard. "Their technology started here, thousands of years ahead of ours, but that doesn't mean they're smarter, just that they started developing earlier." Gieo drew out the Slark timeline in the dust. "When our scientists wiped out their mother ship and effectively caged them with the bear that is humanity, we all leveled out. The best and the brightest on both sides were killed, all the technology was dropped to the same archaic point on both sides, and now it's just a question of who is going to recover faster." Gieo swiped her hand through the dust cutting both the shorter human line even shorter, but also the Slark line to match. "We're physically bigger, stronger, and tougher, but we can't win based solely on that. We need to win the arms race and that means flying."

A slow dawning overcame Fiona—Gieo was likely the smartest person she'd ever met, and might be the smartest person left alive. This realization carried with it a strange, inherent preciousness to Gieo's life that Fiona found herself more than a little territorial and protective of. If the pilot was right, and humanity couldn't brutalize their way to victory as Zeke claimed, the world needed her more than a thousand Tombstones.

"Let's say that's an accurate assessment, and I'm not conceding it is, won't the Slark be developing their own aircraft?"

"Exactly! Our technologies flip-flopped, which gives them the advantage," Gieo said. "They have the oil fields of California. They're running internal combustion while we're plunking along with repurposed Slark tech and salvaged Slark fuel. Eventually we're going to run out of their fuel, since we have no idea how they made it, and they'll still have all the fossil fuels they need to crush us. Slark fuel and engines are better, but finite, and we don't have the infrastructure to return to the fossil fuels we used to use. When all our cars grind to a halt, it won't matter that the Slark crawlers get four miles to the gallon, they'll be the only thing running."

"So we're screwed?"

"Hardly," Gieo said. "We can't figure out how to make more Slark fuel, but we can switch to solar, bio-diesel, and steam, which is exactly what I plan on doing to Mitch's truck. I'm going to tear out the Slark engine and replace it with the boiler from my dirigible. It's been running on used fryer oil at an incredibly inefficient pace. I think I can fix that."

"Is Mitch aware you're planning on doing this?"

"Aware? He volunteered his truck for the experiment!"

"Zeke won't like it; you're chipping away at his stranglehold on the town."

"Maybe Zeke doesn't need to keep his stranglehold much longer."

A second, colder realization followed, and Fiona knew, with dread certainty, she would have to kill people to keep Gieo alive. The inevitability didn't actually sound all that bad; she hoped the pilot would ultimately be worth it.

The sun was setting when they arrived at the crash site. Fiona was a little disappointed the Slark hadn't sent a second recon team. She could always use the easy heads as she'd fully decided to reject Zeke's proposition. Tracking down the boiler, which Gieo explained jettisoned from the aircraft on impact, as it was designed to, rather than explode and blow up the entire crash site, took close to an hour, but eventually they found the hulking black tank. Mitch's truck, which apparently had served as a classic car hauler in a former life, easily winched the boiler up onto the flatbed where it was secured with heavy chains. Back at the primary crash site, Fiona kicked her way through the discarded piles of tech in the sand, unsure of what might be valuable and what was junk.

A clanking of metallic legs, not unlike a Slark crawler, drew her attention to the large boulder the crashed dirigible was listing against. Her gun was instantly in her hand with the hammer thumbed back. She couldn't smell anything out of place, but the sound of Slark crawler legs was unmistakable. She nearly fired out of simply being startled when an upside down crescent, not unlike an overturned wok, peeked around the edge of the boulder, inspecting her with glowing green eyes.

"What the hell is that?" Fiona muttered to herself.

"Ramen," the little mechanical chirped. He emerged entirely from behind the boulder, walking his mostly spring and solar panel body on two little Slark crawler legs, very similar to a crab's, flitting twin helicopter props on his back to keep himself upright.

"Like the noodles?"

"More like Range Activated Mechanical … um … something … fuck it, yes, like the noodles."

Gieo overheard the conversation and came running from her duties of securing the main gun pod of the airship to the back of Mitch's truck. "Ramen, why aren't you at the lab?"

"I lost primary coordinates and tried to recalibrate from the…"

"…bullshit?" Gieo finished for him.

"I was worried about you," he admitted.

"Wait, he lies?" Fiona asked. "Why would you teach a robot how to lie?"

"The challenge, of course," Gieo said. "Do you have any idea how difficult and complex it was to create subterfuge and nuance in an artificial intelligence program? Some of my earliest attempts lied all the time or lied indiscriminately, but Ramen knows exactly how and when a lie should be used. He's better than many people in that regard."

"I can also fly," Ramen added with a little buzz of his propellers.

Mitch came thundering over, shotgun in hand, stopping short when he saw Gieo hugging what looked like a mechanical dragonfly. "What the hell is that thing?"

"Ramen," Fiona explained.

"Like the soup?" Mitch asked.

"Can we not go over this again?" Ramen asked. "My batteries are low and I'd just like a quiet place to rest and recharge."

"We've got what we came for," Gieo said, hugging her arms around herself to fight the encroaching cold of the desert twilight.

Fiona fought the urge to put her arm around the pilot. Instead, she agreed they were done, and guided the lot back to the vehicles.

Back in Tombstone, with Mitch's truck hidden away again along with the incredible haul of tech, they placed Ramen on the roof of the saloon to await the morning sun, before retiring to their respective rooms. Fiona pulled the paper-thin curtains closed over the windows while Gieo set about lighting the candles and lamps. The domesticity of the shared chores carried a familiarity, warm and comfortable, that Fiona found strange, but inviting, considering she'd only met Gieo earlier that morning.

Fiona slung her lanky form down the middle of the bed, letting the metal, rail headboard push her hat over her eyes. She wasn't particularly tired, but always took rest when and where she could get it, much like any other predatory cat.

"Have you thought about what I said earlier?" Gieo asked.

"Nope," Fiona lied.

"Maybe I can convince Zeke to change course."

"He doesn't like risk, doesn't care for tech, and he's more interested in making the Slark suffer than actually getting rid of them," Fiona said.

"Maybe Tombstone needs a new potentate." Gieo slid across Fiona's lap, straddling her waist. "This is our world. It's time we took it back and became what we were before."

"What if I don't like what we were before?" Fiona tossed aside her hat, grasped Gieo by the shoulders and threw her onto the bed beside her. Before Gieo could react, Fiona was on top of her, straddling her waist. She grabbed Gieo's hands and pinned them above her head. "I like this world, like my place in it. I don't want to go back to being a pampered coke-fiend flouncing around in my underwear."

"Then at least rule your world." Gieo was smiling, clearly enjoying the rough treatment, which irritated Fiona more than a little bit.

"Maybe I start with you," Fiona hissed.

"Maybe I don't believe you could."

Fiona let go of Gieo's hands and sat back a little on her lap. "You don't even know me."

Gieo reached up, grabbed Fiona's hands, and replaced them in the pinning position above her head. "I do too," she protested. "I wrote an unofficial biography of you; sure, nobody wanted to publish it, but I did all the research."

Fiona restrained herself from pointing out how crazy Gieo sounded; the phrase, 'takes one to know one' prevented her. "Okay, fine, you know me, but I don't know you."

"I'm a Leo, I liked Korean boy bands when they still existed, my favorite food is sushi, my favorite sushi is yellow-tail, and I used to have a pug named Gizmo," Gieo rattled off quickly. "See, now you know me as well as anyone."

Fiona slid off Gieo's lap and sat on the edge of the bed. The pilot was confusing, paroxysmal, and irritating—all of which would have been fine, if she also wasn't attractive. Fiona couldn't rationalize her desire for Gieo as anything other than her being the first woman she'd seen in ages that wasn't both a prostitute and straight; of course, there was a great deal more to it that Fiona didn't want to admit to herself regardless of how aware of it she was.

"But seriously, was being rich and famous actually that bad?" Gieo asked.

The part of Fiona's brain most in charge of impulse control never functioned correctly. Things easily jumped from being thought about to being done. She called them chaos tics, and she had been more than a little surprised to find most people had them; the only difference was, most people didn't scream "FIRE!" in a crowded movie theater, shove people off curbs, or throw drinks in peoples' faces just because the thought occurred to them. Fiona did all these things. More often than not, a chaos tic of sorts passed through her mind and her body opted to carry it out. She grabbed Gieo's hand, flipped the pilot over onto her stomach and straddled her lower back from behind. She deftly removed her belt and bound Gieo's hands to the wrought iron headboard piping with it. When Gieo began to voice her objection, Fiona shoved her face into the pillow resulting in a muffled stream of what she guessed to be Korean swear words.

Dodging Gieo's clumsily kicked legs, Fiona yanked down the back of the pilot's riding pants to mid-thigh, exposing her taut, pert behind, lovely in black, cotton panties with little cherries on them. Fiona marveled, if only for a moment, how clean all of Gieo's clothing was.

Fiona brought her hand down hard on Gieo's behind with a resounding slap. Gieo's kicking ceased. Fiona swatted her again and again with her left hand, still holding Gieo's face into the pillow with her right. All the fight immediately drained from the little pilot. Red, angry hand prints rose on the soft curve of her flesh around the black edges of her underwear. Fiona, thinking she'd taught Gieo a proper lesson, released the pilot's purple hair.

Gieo's head rolled far enough to the side for her to look up at Fiona through sparkling eyes. She began to squirm a little against the belt holding her hands, making the leather creak. It took a few moments for Fiona to realize it wasn't actual struggling against bonds, but something far more sexual.

"Fuck me, please," Gieo whispered.

Fiona glanced from Gieo's pleading eyes to her behind, writhing against the pants pulled partially down, lewdly pushing up for attention. She couldn't take her eyes off the beautifully curved ass. She was breathing heavily, her heart pounding, and, for some strange reason, her mouth began watering. She brought her gun hand down hard on Gieo's right butt cheek with a loud, satisfying thwack.

"Or you can keep spanking me," Gieo moaned. "That works for me too."

"Is there anything you're not going to enjoy?" Fiona grumbled.

"I'm not sure. Why don't you start doing things to me, and I'll let you know when I don't like one of them?"

"You're infuriating!"

"Look, you can keep doing what you're doing, alone, trying to hide your past while slipping under everyone's radar, or you can try something worthwhile, find someone to care about you, and become something great," Gieo said. "Remember what we talked about earlier? Whoever adapts and recovers the fastest survives."

Fiona hated when other people started making sense.

"I don't like being told what to do!" Fiona punctuated each worth with a hard slap of her open palm against Gieo's already red behind. As much as she intended the swats to hurt, the pilot still seemed more aroused by them than anything else.

"Fair enough," Gieo moaned. "You can tell me what to do."

Fiona left her hand on the warm curve of Gieo's behind; the heat rising off the spanked portions thrilled her far more than she expected. The possessiveness she felt regarding the pilot was manifesting itself in some peculiar ways, and Fiona believed, on a very instinctive level, that what was beneath her hand was not only hers to protect, but hers to do with as she pleased, and not just because Gieo all but said as much.

"I don't know what I want," Fiona murmured.

"No kidding." Gieo made quick work of the belt around her wrists, undoing the bonds from the inside out, retrieving her hands easily. She rolled across the bed away from Fiona toward the opposite edge. Hooking the heels of her boots on the footboard, she pulled her feet from them and inched her pants the rest of the way down to toss them off the bed as well.

"How do you keep your clothes so clean?" Fiona asked.

"I have these incredible machines that do it for me," Gieo snarled. "I'm thinking of calling them a washing machine and a dryer." Gieo rolled onto her side, facing the wall, with her back to Fiona.

Fiona couldn't keep from staring at the delicate curve of Gieo's hips, the slender waist hugged by the jacket, and the artistic line where her shapely, legs met the round swell of her ass. Something long dormant tried to claw its way out of the darkest recesses that Fiona had banished it to; she wanted Gieo, not just sexually, although, at the moment, carnal lust dominated her thoughts about the purple-haired pilot, but wanted to be around her, to listen to her talk, to have Gieo's hand resting on her thigh when she drove. It was difficult to admit how lonely she'd been, and even more difficult considering the first person who might quell the loneliness was exotic, intriguing, and hotter than the Arizona sun.

"Do you want to make out?" Fiona asked and nearly pistol-whipped herself immediately after for how astoundingly stupid and childish the words sounded when left to hang in the air.

Gieo rolled over onto her back with a grin that looked to be comprised of equal parts delight, disbelief, and sarcasm. Fiona felt her cheeks warm with a furious blush. She couldn't remember the last time anyone or anything had made her blush, let alone something as innocuous as a grin. Every second Gieo went without actually saying yes or no to the request compounded the embarrassment until Fiona was on the edge of jumping out of her own skin.

"Sure," Gieo finally said. She reached up with both hands, grabbed the front of Fiona's denim jacket, and pulled her down until their lips met.

What Fiona perceived as her relative sexual inexperience, compounded by years of rust, left her breathless and stunned by the pilot's verve. Her primary concern, aside from figuring out how to breathe effectively without actually letting her lips part from Gieo's for one second, was to get more skin-on-skin contact. Gieo seemed to sense Fiona's desire, and teased to stoke the fire. She squirmed coquettishly away from Fiona's touches, refused to relinquish her hold on the jacket Fiona desperately wanted to be rid of, and put her own weight into the balancing act required of Fiona's arms to maintain the kiss.

Without another option left to her, Fiona broke the kiss long enough to hiss the single word on her mind, "Evil." In a surprisingly strong move, Gieo used Fiona's bodyweight against her, knocked out one of her support arms, and flipped the much taller woman onto her back, rolling easily on top to pin her.

Gieo's bare leg thrust its way up between Fiona's, rubbing her knee meaningfully into the crotch of Fiona's leather pants. "You passed on fucking me," Gieo whispered, her lips flickering over the tip of Fiona's nose as she spoke, "but you can dry hump my leg since you've clearly changed your mind."

Fiona hated the change in power dynamic. She held stock still, refusing to give an inch. She couldn't shoot the pilot, which was usually how she brought power struggles to a close, but she couldn't give in either. Gieo made Fiona's decision not to accept the offer all the more difficult by leaning down to begin kissing her again. Fiona closed her eyes, thrilling at the sensation of the pilot's insanely soft lips, the teasing of the talented, darting tongue against hers, and the tickle of Gieo's braids along the sides of her face. With little more thought than is given to breathing, Fiona's body responded of its own accord, and she began writhing against Gieo's leg in slow gyrations.

Chapter 5
A spiritual education

Nearly a week's time passed in a strange haze of what might be considered a courtship in the peculiar terms Fiona understood. They shared a bed, shared meals, and shared free time talking about everything under the sun. Gieo only ever let Fiona do as she'd done the first night with heavy making out until Gieo allowed Fiona the chance to rub herself lewdly on the pilot's leg, always to climax, and never with skin against skin contact. The good news, if there was any, was that Fiona was getting exceptionally good at the dry humping act; the bad news, which was all Fiona could focus on, was that Gieo had taken complete sexual control of her.

Every morning Ramen flitted away to Gieo's workshop to retrieve clothing and other necessary items until the roof of the saloon looked like a proper tent-city workshop. While Fiona hunted, Gieo busied herself on converting Mitch's truck to the new power source with the help of the items retrieved by Ramen. Every evening when Fiona returned, Gieo took her up to their shared room for another leg rubbing. In a strange, Pavlovian twist, Fiona began finding herself aroused at just seeing or thinking about Gieo's right leg.

Fiona considered this peculiar conditioning she'd undergone on Sunday morning as she watched Gieo get dressed before breakfast. The pilot wore a brown, leather pencil skirt, matching knee-high boots, and a white, lace Lolita blouse. Fiona couldn't help but watch

Gieo's legs hungrily when she planted one foot on the desk chair to zip up the back of one of her boots.

"I'm sick of eating in the room," Gieo said. "Let's go downstairs for breakfast."

Fiona was in no position to argue or otherwise find fault with the plan. She followed the pilot downstairs to the busy saloon floor; two dozen of the rougher looking customers of Tombstone gathered around the tables. The grizzled men sat hunched over their respective plates, shoveling food into open mouths with forks or bare hands. When they spotted Gieo and Fiona at the top of the stairs, table manners suddenly rippled through the room, straightening backs and adjusting utensil use. Mitch cleared a table as a group of three bikers left.

Once they were settled at the table, Mitch brought two metallic plates of what had likely been eggs, potatoes, bacon grease, and tomatoes before it was all stewed together.

"The truck's looking great, Gieo," Mitch said.

"Thank you." Gieo settled a scrap of cloth over her lap as a napkin. "It's going to run even better."

Fiona paid little attention to Mitch, keeping her eyes roving across the room as she carefully brought tiny bites to her mouth.

"It looks…good," Gieo said of the food before Mitch took his leave.

They ate in silence for a short time before Gieo pieced together what was oddly mechanical about Fiona's fork use—she was eating left-handed. Craning her neck to see around to Fiona's right side, Gieo spotted the reason: Fiona had her right hand on the butt of her pistol.

"So…did your mom ever cook you breakfast?" Gieo asked. "I had a tiger mom. She would make me breakfast, but then would drill me on differential equations when I tried to eat until I didn't feel hungry anymore."

"My mom was a fame whore who tried to take my success for her own," Fiona said without pulling her eyes from the room. "She used to call me her chubby little sister and seldom woke up before noon. So, no, breakfast wasn't really a priority growing up."

"Wow, that's fucked up," Gieo said. "Where was your dad?"

"Sperm donor," Fiona corrected her. "Dad would imply he did something beyond shoot his genes into my mom and then start sending child support payments through an intermediary."

"Yeah, well my dad was a robot," Gieo said. "He was only programmed with three English statements: Stacy, do homework! Stacy, practice piano, now! Stacy, stop all you weird being! And volume was stuck at eleven. He was a little more articulate in Korean, but only a little."

"Yeah, that sounds pretty…wait, who is Stacy?"

"Me," Gieo said. "I never liked it though, so I changed it to Gieo when everyone who knew my real name was killed by the Slark."

"I kind of like Stacy," Fiona muttered.

"Aw, I kind of like you too, sugar." Gieo leaned over and kissed Fiona on the nose.

"Why Gieo?" Fiona asked, a little flustered by the public display of affection.

"It's Korean for…"

A loud throat clearing on the other side of the table cut Gieo's explanation short. They both looked over to find an enormous rectangle of a man, right down to his flattop hair cut, standing with a plate of food in hand and expectant expression painted across his moon pie face. What looked like baby fat had followed the man into adulthood, giving him a youthful appearance along with something of a doughy physique despite his obvious attempts at building as much muscle as possible. The man's affected jovial demeanor came complete with a grin that gave him something of a simple quality.

"What do you want, Rawlins?" Fiona snarled.

"Officer Rawlins." The man offered the meaty palm not holding a plate of food to Gieo as if to shake.

"Officer of what?" Gieo asked, shaking the offered hand.

"California Highway Patrol," Rawlins explained, his chest puffing out in the process.

"Like Paunch and John?" Gieo asked.

"Nope," Fiona said, returning her attention to her food. "He was the car kind."

"This seat taken?" Rawlins asked, pointing to one of the empty chairs.

Fiona stretched her long legs out under the table and gave the chair a hard enough kick to send it tumbling backward at Rawlins' feet. "Take it," she said.

Rawlins carefully righted the chair and sat in it, scooting up to the table.

"No, I meant pick the thing up and take it to your own fucking table," Fiona said.

"There aren't any more tables," Rawlins explained.

"Then shove it up your..." Fiona began.

"What do you do now, Officer Rawlins?" Gieo interrupted.

"I'm Zeke's executive officer," Rawlins explained, "which is why I kept the title."

"He means secretary," Fiona said.

"Say, are you a church going lady?" Rawlins asked of Gieo, although it was clear Fiona's barb had found a soft spot from the flash of anger in his blue eyes.

"I'm a Buddhist," Gieo said. "Are you talking about the Hawkins House church?"

"No, not those heretics," Rawlins said. "We've got a little congregation that meets in the old credit union. We're nice folk with a little singing of hymns and bible study most Sunday afternoons. You should come by and check it out, both of you."

"What part of Buddhist didn't you understand?" Fiona snapped.

"She's a rattlesnake, isn't she?" Gieo leaned over, wrapped an arm around Fiona's shoulder, and gave her a soft kiss on the cheek.

"Could you stop that?" Rawlins jovial demeanor dropped in a stern attempt at authoritarianism.

Fiona's eyes flashed with trouble, catching on the opportunity. "Stop what? Oh, you mean stop *this*?" Fiona took Gieo's face in her hands and kissed her deeply. The pilot allowed herself to be drawn into the kiss, playing an equal role in the making out. Officer Rawlins stormed out of the saloon in a huff, leaving his steaming plate of food untouched at their table. Gieo broke the kiss and gave Fiona a hard slap across the cheek.

"Whoa, what was that for?" Fiona asked.

"Using me to make that guy jealous."

"Okay, firstly, it's not like you weren't enjoying yourself; secondly, I wasn't using you to make him jealous; and thirdly, ouch." Fiona reluctantly turned her attention back to her food with her left cheek still stinging.

"What was his deal anyway?"

"He's asked me to marry him a half-dozen times," Fiona said.

"And you told him?"

"Go away or I'll shoot you."

Gieo gave her a look that just screamed, *aaaaaaannnd*?

"How much more evidence do you need that I'm a lesbian?" Fiona dropped her fork onto her plate with a loud clank. The entire saloon quieted around them.

"I'm going to church this afternoon," Gieo said.

"Fine, I'm going hunting." Fiona stood, put on her cowboy hat, and walked to the door. "If you get lynched for being a scientist, Buddhist, lesbian, witch, don't blame me."

Gieo sat on the roof of the saloon beneath her beach umbrella watching the feeds from the security cameras Ramen had installed all around town for her. The outing to the church was as productive as she'd hoped. An old Jewish couple, who only went to the church for the same networking opportunities Gieo was there for, happened to have a few industrial washers and dryers; they had a notion of getting out of the leather tanning business to open a laundry if the machines could be fixed. They'd given her a down payment of three jugs of agave white lightning for her to start work later that week.

Of course, the biggest deal she'd managed to broker was with Zeke. Somehow he had it in his head that Fiona should poison the Hawkins House, and he tried his best to put it in Gieo's head that she should convince the gunfighter to do it. Gieo offered to do him one better, cut out the middle woman as it were, and do the job herself. Zeke was disinterested in how it got done so long as it got done.

On the flattop roof of the saloon, warm beyond reason even in the shade of the umbrella, Gieo sat with her four jugs acquired at church: three filled with cactus moonshine and one of strychnine. Ramen had easily infiltrated the Hawkins House compound while they were busying themselves about the weekly communion of wood alcohol. The cameras he'd set up were dusty, scratched, and gave off a poor signal, but the receiver Gieo had for them, powered by a solar panel ripped off a cattle gate outside Phoenix, boosted the reception enough for Gieo to make out what was important: where the defenses were, and how she might infiltrate the compound.

She didn't know what she was going to do with the poison just yet, but there was no real reason to waste it—something as valuable as a gallon of raccoon poison could have any number of uses, even if it didn't fit into her immediate plans. As she watched the feed, she made notes in her Hello Kitty notepad, sketched a vague map, and listed possible uses for the poison.

Ramen clattered around the roof between their many projects in various states of completion, whistling a jaunty tune. He was making remarkable progress in cataloguing the incoming tech from various jobs, the payments Gieo hadn't quite figured out what to do with yet, and assessing the prices things might fetch once repaired.

"We should have done this years ago, ma'am," Ramen said.

"Opportunities arise when they are meant to," Gieo replied. "Everything happens as it should and when it should."

"So you're Buddhist again now?" Ramen asked.

She'd leaned forward, almost involuntarily, to peer at the fuzzy picture on the LCD screen. Children, none older than four or five, were being given doses of methanol from a colossal tank in the middle of the compound. From what she could tell, the largest tank likely also carried the highest concentration. The smaller tank, the one garden-variety cultists weren't supposed to know about, appeared to be the gas tank on a scuttled Dodge pickup. The mucky-mucks of the cult, easily identifiable by their orange parking-cone hats, snuck over and took a drink from a hose running out of the gas cap when they thought no one was looking.

"Right now, I'm planning on being the angel of mischief and mercy," Gieo murmured.

The roar of Fiona's engine encroached on the peace of the town like rolling thunder. Gieo had begun to look forward to hearing the engine as it meant the redheaded gunfighter was almost home; unfortunately, she wasn't all that happy to hear it after that morning.

She leaned on the two-foot tall lip running around the edge of the roof, watching the silver car pull up in front of the saloon. Four fresh Slark heads lined the spikes on the grill. She'd had a good day. When Fiona stepped from the car, Gieo placed two fingers in her mouth and let out a loud, sharp whistle. Fiona snapped her head up.

"I want to talk to you," Gieo shouted.

"So talk," Fiona shouted back.

"I said talk, not shout."

Fiona stomped up into the saloon with her head down. Gieo could hear her petulantly clomping all the way up the stairs and finally bursting onto the roof. Gieo hated to admit it, but Fiona was unreasonably attractive when fuming mad. When Fiona folded her arms over her chest, cocked her hips to one side, and jutted out her lower lip until a little glisten was showing she created a sexiness that Gieo couldn't quite put her finger on. After studying Fiona's pout for awhile, she decided it was remarkably similar to one of the poses she often used in the catalogue; other models usually looked spaced out and dead behind the eyes, but Fiona always seemed lively and perturbed.

"Did you have fun at church?" Fiona asked.

"I had productive at church," Gieo said. "But that's not what I wanted to talk to you about. I want to apologize for earlier."

Fiona's entire demeanor softened at the mere mention of apology. Gieo noted the smoldering, angry sexiness softened as well; she resolved, no matter how difficult it might be, to not make Fiona angry just for sexual purposes…at least, not very often.

"Could you take the goggles off?" Fiona walked over to Gieo, standing just outside the ring of shade provided by the beach umbrella.

"Oh, sure," Gieo said. She'd forgotten she was even wearing them. She pulled the green tinted goggles off and reached out to set them on the lip of the roof next to her chair. Fiona's eyes followed them instinctively, but immediately refocused on something below at street level. "I'm really sorry for…um…what are you doing?"

Fiona yanked her gun from its holster, took two steps past Gieo to the edge of the roof, and fired once down into the street. When the ringing cleared from Gieo's ears following the explosive .44 magnum round being fired right in front of her, she heard a man groaning in the street. She jumped to the edge of the roof and looked down to find Jackson Roy, the hunter who had asked her to keep an eye out for a power drill, bleeding in the street, desperately trying to hold his right forearm together.

"You stay where you are, Jackson," Fiona shouted down.

Fiona turned on her heels and was running back for the roof access ladder before Gieo could even ask what was going on. Gieo jumped up to follow but struggled to keep pace, losing track of Fiona before she could even get to the saloon's main floor. Gieo ran out between the saloon's swinging doors, and nearly got her head blown off when a spray of bullets passed at Fiona's height across the plank front of the building. Gieo ducked, even though the shots were intended for someone six inches taller than her, and barely caught a glimpse of Jackson standing in front of Fiona's car with a steaming Mac-10 in his good hand. Another report of Fiona's Anaconda echoed through the street and Jackson's right knee exploded in blood and bone fragments. Fiona emerged from the alleyway on the side of the saloon with her pistol trained on Jackson's downed form.

In a daze, Gieo plucked several splinters from her hair, and began walking toward the scene of carnage. Fiona had her Wakizashi out and was demanding that Jackson tie it off. *Tie what off*, Gieo wondered. She couldn't see exactly what Jackson was doing in front of the car, but he seemed to be working a leather strap with his teeth. Fiona lifted her sword. Time finally caught up with Gieo's mind.

"Wait!" Gieo screamed and ran to intercept Fiona's sword arm.

Fiona stopped with her sword raised, clearly aimed at taking off Jackson's wounded arm. Gieo hadn't really expected Fiona to stop simply because she'd shouted it, and wasn't really sure what else to say once she did.

"Why are you chopping off his arm?" she asked.

"Do you think I should take his head instead?" Fiona answered by way of question.

"What!? No!" Gieo said. "Why did you shoot him in the first place?"

"He was trying to steal my heads." Before Gieo could protest further, Fiona's sword fell, hacking off Jackson's arm at the elbow. The tourniquet, which was apparently what Fiona had demanded Jackson tie off, stemmed much of the blood loss, but Gieo still nearly vomited from the sight. Fiona slid her gun back into its holster, picked up the hand, and swatted it down on one of the spikes along her grill, impaling it next to the four Slark heads. After seeing that, Gieo did go ahead and throw up next to Fiona's front wheel well.

"Man's dead anyway," Zeke said from across the street, standing out on his balcony to watch the entire show. "You ought to take his head."

Fiona sheathed her Wakizashi and picked up Jackson's discarded Mac-10. She slid the clip from the hand-held machinegun, and judged it to be about half-full by the weight. "You've got to the count of ten to get out of my sight before I cut you in half with your own gun," Fiona said.

Jackson tried to stand, stumbled, tried again, stumbled again, and finally made it up onto his one good leg before passing out, falling flat at Fiona's feet. She dropped the gun on his back and flipped the bullets out of the clip like rain over his downed form.

"Rawlins!" Zeke bellowed. Officer Rawlins blundered out of the front door of the old city hall beneath Zeke's balcony, whipping his head around wildly to find the source of his boss's voice. "Get that thieving piece of shit out of Red's way." Rawlins jumped to the task and went about hauling what was left of Jackson back into the city hall. Zeke looked down at Fiona for a moment and nodded with something akin to grim respect. "I'll have Rawlins deliver Jackson's car by sundown tomorrow. I believe he has two heads on his grill;

that'll settle you up for the week." Zeke disappeared back into the dark recesses of the city hall as the sun began to set.

Gieo wiped her mouth with the back of her hand when she was quite certain she'd thrown up all she had in her. With a stabilizing hand on the fender of Fiona's car, she looked up at the gunfighter as though seeing her for the first time. Fiona seemed contemplative, almost melancholy.

"It's been almost two years since someone tried to steal from me," Fiona said, barely above a whisper. "I've gone soft because of you and people know it."

"That was soft?" Gieo asked.

"If you weren't here, I would have cut his head off and dragged his body through town behind my car as a message to the other hunters." Fiona brushed past Gieo on her way back into the saloon, sending one final remark over her shoulder before stepping through the double doors. "Welcome to the real Tombstone, Stacy."

Chapter 6
Aggravated mischief

Gieo returned to her rooftop perch with a head full of concerns and a stomach full of butterflies. She'd had a serious lapse in judgment—an unpleasant mistake with potentially catastrophic consequences. How she saw Fiona made a drastic transformation after seeing her gun down a man, whose name they both knew, with the cannon she kept on her hip and then dismember him using a sword she kept on her back according to some draconian code of the fucked up post-apocalyptic, new Old West. Even for the new world order, this was bizarre. Fiona was absolutely right when she claimed Gieo didn't know her. Whatever remained of the fashion model, traumatized girl, and probable cocaine addict had been completely burned out by the desert sun, replaced by a hardened gunfighter with psychotic tendencies.

Gieo took failure well though; her parents had pretty much insisted on it. Failures and lapses in judgment were opportunities to learn, change, grow, and come back with a better plan. She needed data, information, and a removed perspective to formulate new thoughts and opinions.

Firstly, she had to stop sleeping in Fiona's bed. Whatever else was going on between them, the sexual teasing she was giving the gunfighter might have added to the volatility. Besides, when the fun of sexually topping Fiona wore off, the charade always left Gieo with a ridiculous case of the hornies that she hadn't remotely started to deal with yet.

Secondly, she would need to learn a lot more about the town, which would be easily accomplished with a telescope and time spent observing. She set up a low-power telescope she'd acquired in a trade with someone for something—she really couldn't remember how she'd come by it as more and more stuff kept coming in and going out. It was easily fixed by repositioning the internal mirrors, but she hadn't figured out what to do with it until that point. From her perch on the front edge of the hotel, using the telescope, she could see much of the town as no building was taller than a couple stories. She'd misjudged Tombstone to be similar to the other scattered pockets of humanity she'd come across when it was clearly playing by a whole other set of rules.

Thirdly, and lastly, she needed a stiff drink to get the image of Fiona cutting off Jackson's arm out of her head. Unlike most survivors of the Slark invasion, Gieo hadn't really seen or encountered much violence. Her parents had done a masterful job of shielding her, which she had to offer up a whispered prayer to whoever was listening to thank them. They'd died, just like most people's parents, in one of the many gas attacks the Slark made on relocation colonies set too close to the frontlines. But even this was without violence as the gas simply put people into a sleep they didn't wake up from. Gieo dipped into one of the jugs of cactus white-lightning with the goal in mind of taking the shake out of her hand. Drinking the clear liquid from a tin cup, she decided it tasted like a mixture of tequila, agave tea, and gasoline. In addition to the stomach churning taste, horrible burning sensation it made all the way down her throat, and mind-numbing properties, she also suspected it might be hallucinogenic.

She sat at her telescope, observing the comings and goings of the night denizens of Tombstone to deduce their behaviors, rules, and purposes. After an hour or so, two occurrences confirmed her suspicions that there was peyote mixed into the alcohol. The first was an extreme nausea followed by glimmering lights appearing where no glimmering lights should be. Hallucinating was going to make any further observations she made completely worthless, so she abandoned the telescope and laid out on the lawn chair to look up at the stars. Eventually, she couldn't really tell how long, the nausea subsided and the hallucinations intensified.

The desert night, alone on the roof since Ramen had long shut down to conserve battery power, was cold and uncomfortable. Aside from the companionship of sharing a bed with Fiona, there was the warmth of another body and a mattress beneath her. She had a hammock and a sleeping bag somewhere in the tangled mess of bartered items on the roof, but she doubted she could find or operate either while tripping and drunk.

Fiona had seemed prickly and truculent, which Gieo simply thought made her more interesting, but somehow adding violent and dangerous to the mix didn't do much to dampen Gieo's desire for the gunfighter. It was an odd notion, which she attributed to the booze and drugs, that she would be able to get past Fiona shooting people and hacking off their limbs. Of course, her sexual frustration might have been partly to blame for the crazy thoughts. She didn't have a specific timeline in her head for how long she would tease Fiona sexually before finally letting the gunfighter tear her clothes off and ravish her, but she'd suspected it was on the soon-ish side, at least, until Fiona went nuts.

Gieo pulled her tailed tuxedo jacket over her like a blanket to hold out the chilly desert night. The bands of color and light that had danced across the sky shifted and started taking on shapes. Gieo watched with mild amusement, knowing they weren't really there on an intellectual level, but enjoying their beauty in an animalistic aesthetic way. After shifting through a few zodiac patterns, which Gieo didn't really care for as it seemed rather pedestrian to look up the stars and literally hallucinate crabs, archers, twins, and fish, the patterns began taking on familiar, human shapes—specifically, the shape of Fiona. Gieo was altered enough, horny enough, and had already abandoned her sexual plans with Fiona enough to go ahead and do some self-gratification since she didn't see anyone else satisfying her anytime soon. Her hands made their way down her stomach. Pulling up the leather pencil skirt wasn't a reasonable plan, so she unzipped the side and pressed her hands into the top as best she could. The writhing sky image of Fiona matched her movements, swirling a little more than Gieo might like, but still discernable in her shape and intent.

Gieo's own fingers were like old friends who hadn't been by nearly enough in the past few months. She teased the outside of her lips with soft fingers until she felt sufficiently warmed and relaxed. The sky image of Fiona winked to her. Gieo pressed down on her outer lips with both fingers, stroking up and down until she was able to add a light pinch around her clit between her knuckles. Using the middle finger of her other hand, she rubbed the length of it down over the tip of her clit, letting it curl into her at the end of each pass. She'd perfected the act in high school to the point where she could do it anywhere, at almost any state of dress or undress, and always achieve an orgasm. It had been so long since she'd even touched herself, or had any inspiration or desire to do so, that she was well past driving herself crazy after only a few passes of her middle finger. Moreover, the apparent teasing she'd been inflicting on Fiona had taken its toll on her as well. Being quiet in such a moment would have been difficult under the best of circumstances and was downright unfeasible while drunk and drugged. The sky version of Fiona told Gieo it was okay, nobody would mind, and so Gieo let her body make the noises it felt like making, which included unrestricted moans, whimpers, and gasps, all escaping her mouth in visible, colored letters.

Her eyelids opened and closed of their own accord, guided solely by her building pleasure. When they drifted shut, the backs of her eyelids swirled distracting lights and sounds, while she tried to focus on how amazing and necessary it all felt. When her eyes fluttered open, she watched the sky Fiona mirroring her actions. Even though the hallucination of the gunfighter kept shifting and morphing, Gieo thought she was beautiful, sexy, and desirable even though she had multiple arms, stretched out shapes, and hair made of flaming snakes. Gieo climaxed once, a shallow little tease that only made her thirstier. She redoubled her efforts, sliding two fingers down to press deep inside her while moving her wet middle finger to focus entirely on her clit. The sky Fiona seemed pleased by this plan.

Gieo couldn't be sure where sleep, hallucinations, dreams, and waking thought delineated anymore. She was fairly sure she was awake, fairly sure she was enjoying every second with herself, and knew, at least in small part, that what she saw in the sky wasn't real. The hands manipulating her clit and plunging fingers inside her became not hers; they were attached to her arms, which were anchored on her shoulders, but the hands themselves must have belonged to someone else. It made her feel a little naughty, dirty, slutty even to have someone else's hands doing these things to her—no, not that they were doing them, but that Gieo was enjoying it so much. Darkness swirled through the images painted across the sky, spoiling the shifting pornographic pictures. Gieo wished them back, but her will couldn't repaint the sky. In a flash of light, like morning coming on all at once, she exploded in an orgasm of surprising strength coming upon her as a creeping wave. With the sky white with light, she threw her head back and screamed in primal delight. For a second, the peyote fled from her mind. The small, quiet part that had known it all wasn't real, caught on an ingenious plan, rolled it around like a crab exploring a mussel shell, and found it liked what was inside.

♠♣♥♦

Waking up the next morning was a brutal proposition. Gieo managed to muddle her way through the hunters' cars starting and departing, returning to full sleep shortly after, but when the sun climbed toward its apex, the heat and light became almost unbearable, driving her from beneath her tuxedo coat, which had shifted from blanket to veil at some point in the night or early morning. She pulled her goggles over her eyes to block out some of the light before peering out from beneath the cover of her jacket. Ramen was busying himself in the junk piles again, seemingly unaware she'd been sleeping on the roof.

Gieo stumbled from her lawn chair, finally drawing Ramen's attention.

"Hey, Boss," Ramen chirped. "Had a hard night?"

"Something like that." Gieo fumbled through the nearest pile of bottles until she found the jug of water she was looking for. She spun off the cap and tilted it back, drinking greedily until the warm, dusty-tasting water glugged entirely down her throat. "Give me a hand setting up the hammock and a tent around it."

Ramen gave her a quizzical look, cocking his saucer head to one side. "That doesn't sound comfortable."

"I don't expect it will be," Gieo said, "but it's necessary."

The headache and stomach-churning vertigo that accompanied Gieo's hangover made sure she was helping Ramen more than vice-versa. It was well into the afternoon, with evening fast approaching, when they finally completed setting up Gieo's new bedroom. The canvas, military surplus supply tent around the hammock actually felt homier than Gieo had expected. Her self-satisfied inspection of her temporary quarters was cut short by the sound of a tow truck clanking up behind the saloon.

Rawlins stepped from the cab, and set to work lowering the faded yellow and black 1970s Jeep Wagoneer. Gieo placed two fingers in her mouth and let out a sharp whistle. She waved when

Rawlins looked up to find the source of the sound; he didn't wave back. She pulled her top hat on tight, and headed downstairs to question him about the vehicle. She caught him just as he was about to get back into his truck, door open, one foot on the side-step.

"Hey, what's with the Jeep?" she asked.

"It's Jackson's old rig," Rawlins explained, frozen in his half in, half out position on the side of the tow truck. "By hunter law, it's rightfully Fiona's after she took his hand."

"Oh…how is Jackson?"

"He died in the night," Rawlins said dispassionately. "The man was half-starved to begin with and two .44 magnum slugs didn't do him any good. Lopping off his hand was overkill if you ask me."

"Will my reward for the methanol spiking job work in this thing?" Gieo nodded in the direction of the Jeep.

"Sure, but it ain't your reward."

"What's that supposed to mean?"

"You're property of a hunter, which doesn't give you a hunter's rights." Rawlins finally stepped fully down from the tow truck and closed the door behind him. "When you finish the job, Fiona will have to collect for you."

"Zeke didn't mention anything about that."

"Why would he?" Rawlins spat on the dusty ground. The spit quickly congealed into a dusty scab on the earth. Gieo watched the spittle for a time, fuming mad. "She's the one he wanted to do the job in the first place and the one he wanted to reward. Now that her property has signed up for the deal, she's the one who'll default if it doesn't get done."

"That's bullshit," Gieo snarled. "I'm not anyone's property."

Rawlins snorted and shook his head, folding his brawny arms over his chest to complete the pose of disbelief. "You belong to whoever claims you and is strong enough to keep you. Laws around here only benefit hunters—everyone else is just paying their way to keep from becoming property. If Fiona hadn't laid claim to you, someone else would've."

"Fine, how do I stop being property?"

"Become a hunter," Rawlins said with a mocking chuckle, "but even then, you've still got to be able to defend yourself from being claimed, and you don't have it in you, kid. Fiona shot dead more than a dozen men when she came into town before people stopped trying, and then she shot a few more just to make sure. Think you could handle doing that?" He turned his back on her, threw open the tow truck door, and hauled his bulk into the cab. Before he closed the door, as a parting shot, he said, "If you don't like our laws or don't like Fiona killing in your name, I'd get the hell out of town before someone gets the drop on Fiona. You'd be quite the prize for most around here—a fuck doll that can fix tech."

Gieo glared at him the entire slow drive away, which didn't seem to bother him in the slightest. She hadn't really ever thought herself capable of killing someone, but she definitely thought she could maim Rawlins if push came to shove, and might just be mentally capable of crippling Zeke for tricking her into making Fiona beholden for a job she didn't want to do and Gieo wasn't really planning on taking seriously. Of course, she knew she wasn't actually a physical match for either man, but she thought it was an important step to get used to the idea of violence.

She was smarter than them though, and her drug trip from the night before had given her a deliciously devious plan to complete the job. She'd just have to dodge Fiona until it was done.

The black, spandex cat suit had actually been a cat costume for Halloween at one point, which was precisely why Gieo still had a fluffy black tail following her around. She suspected the cat suit might be overkill considering the guards looking for her were likely night blind in addition to being mostly blind all the time, but it also didn't have a lot, aside from the tail, that might get caught on wire traps, which she suspected would make up the majority of the Hawkins House compound defenses. She'd stuffed enough cotton into the jug in her backpack to prevent it from sloshing, even at a dead run. As stealth went, she was pretty well equipped. Despite the fact that it was an insanely stereotypical thing for a cute Asian girl to do, Gieo put on the accompanying kitty-ear headband to match the rest of the suit. It's not like anybody would see her if she did things right, and she liked wearing the ears, although she would never admit that to anyone out loud.

For all the threats leveled against the Hawkins House cult, their primary defense appeared to be their overall creepiness; Gieo had studied them carefully and had found half a dozen ways into the compound without the slightest difficulty. She crept under the barbed wire fence on the eastern slope, using a couple branches off a sagebrush bush to hold up the bottom wire. She proceeded at a slow,

low to the ground crawl, keeping a careful ear and eye out for rattlesnakes. Instead, her hand struck something metal, partially buried in the dusty ground. Suspiciously, she brushed away some of the dirt to find a coyote trap. Rather than jamming a stick into it to disarm it, she carefully flipped the trap over to point the pressure plate toward the ground so the jaws would close wrong-side down if stepped on. Her slow crawl revealed three more traps on her path; she flipped these over as well.

In the heart of the compound, she snuck between two scuttled school busses. Only a dozen or so paces in, something caught on the tips of her kitty ears, nearly pulling the headband off. She stopped, looked up, but couldn't see anything. Reaching up, she felt around until she found a tightly strung strand of piano wire across the gap at the perfect height to clothesline/garrote a full grown man. She had to hand it to them, for crazy blind people, they sure had a lot of tricks up their sleeves. Skulking her way through the maze of vehicles being used as apartments, she found several more of the piano wires, including a few strung much lower intended to trip intruders. The neck-height wires weren't a problem even if she had to run back the same way, but the trip wires needed to be dealt with. She hadn't brought wire cutters, something she was quickly regretting, but she had brought glow-sticks. She cracked, shook, and placed one of the glowing green tubes at the mounting point of the wire, faintly illuminating the length of each trip-line.

The vehicles turned into apartments gave way to open ground, a lot of open ground, at the center of the compound. She would have to cover sixty feet or so to reach the old Dodge acting as the mucky-muck's personal methanol stash. She took several calming breaths and scanned the area for any movement that might indicate a guard. The waxing moon lit the compound just enough to give vague outlines of where people were. She waited for her gap and made a mad dash for the middle ring of the inner-sanctum. One ring of benches away from the target pickup, she skittered to a stop, seeing a seated old man on one of the old park benches lined up like church pews. With nowhere to run and nowhere to hide, she crouched as low to the ground as possible, and prayed he wouldn't see her.

The man cocked his head to her side, listening intently for the sounds she'd made when she'd slid to a stop. When no further noise followed, he glanced over to where she was crouched, his milky old eyes clearly unable to make out much in the low light.

"Oh, good evening, Miss Kitty," he said.

Gieo's heart leapt into her throat.

"Are you out on your nightly hunt?" he asked.

Gieo made her best 'meow' noise and began rubbing her side along the bench like a cat. The old man squinted to make out what she was doing, and seemed satisfied that the fuzzy black figure was close enough to cat size and shape.

"I won't frighten away your prey then," the old man said. Under great protest from his arthritic joints, the old man managed to pull himself from the bench and tottered back up toward the main church, tapping with a knotted cane.

Gieo struggled not to burst into nervous laughter. After regaining her composure, she skulked on hands and knees the rest of the way to the Dodge pickup, careful to still look like a cat to any mostly-blind passerby. She slipped easily under the propped up truck. Little remained of the inner-workings of the vehicle. A garden hose ran from the gas cap along where the pipe had rusted through, and into a hastily cut gap in the gas tank. Gieo carefully unzipped her backpack. The sound of the zipper was deafening in the silence of the compound. Once the bag was open, she waited with bated breath for any noise that might indicate she'd been heard. When she was certain she'd gone undetected, she slid the jug between the leaf-springs, unscrewed the cap, and slid the hose from the methanol-filled gas tank into the jug instead. With her work done, she carefully zipped up her backpack and slipped out from beneath the pickup on the opposite side from which she'd come.

She turned to flee and immediately bumped right into a soft, warm wall. Rebounding back a little, she glanced up to what she'd run into, and ended up looking right into the face of Yahweh Hawkins himself.

"*Ay shibal!*" she cursed in Korean.

"Demon speech from a half-cat, half-woman succubus!" Hawkins shouted in alarm. Wild eyed with a matching wild, wiry gray beard and head of hair, he looked more like a garden variety homeless man than a high priest of a holy order, but Gieo knew from watching the video feeds that he was revered to a godlike level within the cult. His startled utterance immediately jumped the entire compound to attention, and she heard the tapping of dozens of canes closing in on her from all sides. The old cult patriarch lifted his hands to make a grab for her, which she easily ducked under. Slipping around behind him, she swung her foot up between his legs as hard as she could, feeling the satisfying thump of his testicles against the top of her shin. Yahweh Hawkins dropped like a groaning scarecrow cut from its posts.

"*Shibal nom, Geseki,*" Gieo hissed at him. "Blinding children in the name of your made up god…you're lucky I didn't kill you like Zeke wanted." With that, she ran. There were subtler, less testicle-crushing and obvious ways to implicate Zeke in what was about to happen to the cult, but she didn't have time for any of those anymore, and there was a very slim chance, she hoped, that Hawkins might believe Zeke was summoning demons to attack him, which would be a fantastic and hilarious accusation for the despotic mayor to have to address.

Gieo split between two guards, who barely saw her racing past, on her way into the gap between busses that she'd come through. They altered course and gave chase, but she was already down the corridor, leaping over the lighted trip-lines and passing beneath the neck-cutters. At the far end of the bus, she spotted a man's shadow cast from where he was waiting in ambush for her across the path she wanted to take through the overturned traps. She almost giggled at the blind-man's blunder; just because he couldn't see his own shadow didn't mean she couldn't. She ducked into a baseball slide at the end of the corridor, easily passing under a cane swung at head height. As she was scrambling to her feet on the other side, she heard something metallic snap closed and felt an enormous tugging weight on the back of her suit. She glanced back to find her fluffy kitty tail, dusty from the slide, caught in a smaller trap that she hadn't overturned. She grabbed the tail and trap and yanked, pulling the mounting stake from the ground. Reasonably free, she resumed her run for the gap in the fence that she'd entered through, jangling the trap from her tail as she ran.

She ducked under the barbed wire propped up by sticks and wriggled most of the way through before the trap, still dangling from her tail, knocked out both the twigs, snapping the wire down on the backs of her thighs. She felt the barbs press against her skin, embedding themselves in the spandex, but not in her yet. She knew, if she struggled, she ran the risk of tetanus or worse, but the panic began to rise when she heard the tapping canes closing in on her. She tried to roll to her side, tried to restore the sticks holding up the wire, but to no avail. Failing that, she tried to pry the trap from her tail or break the tail off to extricate her from the trap, but the trap's teeth had bitten firmly into the wire running down the center of the tail, making it no easier to remove than the barbwire. She'd nearly given up on any option other than blindly thrashing her way free when she heard Ramen's whirring chopper blades.

"She's over here, tall boss," she heard him call. His head lamps flashed over her in friendly yellow light, illuminating her prone form pinned beneath the fence.

Before she could explain how happy she was to see him, the night exploded in thunder claps and muzzle flashes. Fiona stormed in behind Ramen, gun arm extended, firing the hand-cannon back into the compound. The massive slugs whirred a few feet above Gieo's head, sounding like angry hornets flying faster than the speed of sound. Screaming and bodies falling followed, but Gieo couldn't get her head around far enough to see how many of the cultists Fiona had shot. The remaining cane-tapping guards fled back into the relative safety of the vehicle cluster.

Ramen, using one of his omni-tool hands, quickly cut away both the barbed wire and the tail just above the trap, effectively freeing Gieo from the fence. Gieo scrambled to her feet and immediately ran to Fiona. She intended to say something witty, possibly flirty, and then kissing the lanky gunfighter, but she never got the chance.

Fiona slid her pistol back in its holster before Gieo got to her. She grabbed the pilot by the arm and roughly shoved her in the direction of the road where Fiona's car was still idling with the driver side door open. When Gieo was past her, Fiona gave the pilot a hard kick in the behind.

"Get in the fucking car, reckless bitch," Fiona growled.

Chapter 7
Collared and collected-on

The drive back to town took a looping, crawling course around the outskirts, keeping the engine low enough not to be easily heard or seen, so as not to let anyone know a hunter was involved in the sabotage of the Hawkins House. Gieo could tell from the white knuckles of Fiona's hand at the top of the steering wheel that she wasn't happy.

"Do you know what they would have done to you if they'd caught you?" Fiona finally spoke.

"Rape, torture, blinding, attempted conversion to their wacky ways," Gieo replied. "I knew the risks; I'm not stupid."

"Not stupid, but plenty reckless," Fiona snarled. The car nosed its way back into town finally, stalking through the empty streets like a prowling jungle cat. "How could you just poison people like that?"

"You don't really believe I used the poison, do you?"

Fiona looked over to Gieo for the first time since they'd left the compound. She could see true concern and hurt on the pilot's face. "No, but that'll piss off Zeke and make collecting on the bargain impossible."

"Not like I could collect anyway." Gieo flopped back into the seat in a huff and stared out the window up into the night sky. "Apparently, I'm your property."

"Who told you that?"

"Rawlins."

"That asshole," Fiona grumbled.

"Asshole or not, is it true?"

They pulled up in front of the saloon. Fiona took the car out of gear and slowly wound down the engine. The hot metal of the car ticked lightly as it cooled in the chilly desert night. They sat listening to the pings that interrupted the silence between them for a time before Fiona finally spoke. "In a sense, it is, but it's not what I want or believe."

"Great," Gieo grumbled. "So if I'm going to stay in this town, should I just wear a dog collar with your name on it to avoid confusion?"

"We could get you a leash too," Fiona chided. "It'll at least keep you from running off to do dangerous things without backup."

"Fuck you." Gieo made to open the door to escape the car, but the gunfighter grabbed her arm and pulled her back in.

"I'm sorry," Fiona said hastily. "I thought we were joking around."

Something strange and slightly unsettling occurred to Gieo in the moment after. It was a reprehensible thought on the surface, and her pride immediately wanted to reject it, but the taboo, twisted nature of it appealed to her on a sexual level in something of an unsettling way, while the practicality of it would solve a lot of the problems she'd created that night by not fully honoring the deal.

"Actually, that's a good idea," she said.

Fiona released Gieo's arm and gave her a perplexed look. "What is?"

"A leash and a collar, especially in public."

"Is this another sexual control thing?"

"No" Gieo knew it was a lie, but it was one she wanted to tell herself as well, at least, for the moment. The thought of being collared and led about on a leash by Fiona disgusted and thrilled her in confusing ways she wasn't remotely ready to discuss. "It'll show you've taken control of your property. Once the Hawkins House has their inevitable freak out and blames Zeke, it'll look like this was your plan all along."

Fiona had to admit, if people thought Gieo could do whatever she wanted, it would make them both vulnerable; it was a clever ruse, and one that would solve a lot of problems, but certainly not a serious suggestion Fiona could have put forth. "What did you do tonight? Ramen only told me you had a clever crab plan."

Gieo laughed. "I think I was still a little high when I told him. Anyway, I left Yahweh Hawkins with sore testicles and a distinct impression Zeke was summoning cat demons to fuck with him."

"But what about the poison?"

"Come up to the roof tomorrow and you can watch."

"Are you going to come to bed tonight?" Fiona asked in a small, nervous voice, so unlike the steely gunfighter tone she used in public.

"I still have some things I need to finish," Gieo replied. "I'll see you in the morning though." She leaned across the center console and kissed Fiona gently on the lips. "Thank you, yet again, for the timely rescue."

"Just my luck," Fiona whispered into the kiss. "The first woman I meet that I'm afraid to lose and she's reckless and crazy. This isn't doing my fear of abandonment issues any favors."

Gieo found her fingers playing with the collar of Fiona's denim jacket of their own volition. "I'm not going anywhere," Gieo said, although she wasn't entirely sure she meant it. "Plus, soon you'll be able to find me at the end of a leash." She'd intended it as a joke, but it passed her lips sounding earnest; moreover, her body reacted lustily to both the words she spoke and the mental picture they created. Gieo practically leapt from the car and ran for the front of the saloon, hoping Fiona didn't notice her nipples suddenly jumping to attention through the black, spandex cat suit.

The tent, sleeping bag, and hammock, along with the lack of peyote in her system, made sleeping on the roof almost a fun little excursion. Ramen, who had found his own way home after the debacle, awoke with the sunrise and decided to wake Gieo at the same time. She owed him for the heroic part he'd played in her rescue, and so didn't hold a grudge for waking her before her usual 9 AM start time.

"That was quite the night, eh, boss?" Ramen added a few excited clicks from his rotors to punctuate the comment.

"Exciting to say the least, but it's a shame Fiona had to shoot a few cultists in the process; it would have gone over a whole lot more smoothly without a body count for them to parade around." Gieo rifled half-heartedly through the crates of her acquired goods with her left hand while sipping her morning tea with her right. Things were organized for usefulness, which didn't have a filing for leash and collar.

"Oh, she didn't shoot them," Ramen corrected her. "She fired above them. They screamed because they couldn't see her. And then they dove onto the ground and covered their heads. I knew she was going to do it and the gun still scared me; I can't imagine what the mostly-blind weirdos must have thought."

Gieo abandoned her search for the moment, took a long drink of her tea, and gazed out over the town's rooftops to the Hawkins compound on the outskirts. She'd seen Fiona hit smaller targets from much farther away; if the gunfighter had meant to hit the cultists, she would have. Gieo couldn't make heads or tails of it. Fiona would shoot a man she knew for trying to steal from her, but wouldn't shoot cultists who hated her in the process of saving her girlfriend … friend … property … whatever. Gieo thoughtfully scratched the midline of her forehead with the back of her thumb—figuring out Fiona was going to be an ever evolving headache.

"Are you sure she didn't hit them?" she finally asked, knowing full well Ramen saw better at night than most people did during the day.

"Not a one, boss," Ramen said. "They all got up and ran, bumping into each other on the way, of course."

"Interesting…" Gieo polished off her tea and set aside her tin cup. She abandoned her sifting through the crates operation and decided she might make herself presentable for Fiona. "I'm going to get dressed. See if you can find a dog collar and a leash, will you?"

"You got it, boss." Ramen immediately fluttered down from his perch and headed for a group of crates that Gieo hadn't searched yet. "Are we getting a puppy?"

Gieo dressed quickly in her ruffled white skirt, matching high heel, knee high boots with tan spats, and her tan, leather matador jacket over a white, lace blouse. Ramen had made so many trips back and forth from the workshop she likely had more in Tombstone than she did at home. The outfit was demure in a way most of her clothing wasn't, but not without a hint of burlesque. She emerged from the tent, planted a foot on the edge of the roof, and quickly finished tying her boots.

"What's the word on the leash and collar?" she asked.

"Puppy?" Ramen asked hopefully, dropping a leather leash and spiked dog collar in Gieo's hand. His robotic little face dropped when Gieo promptly latched the collar around her own neck.

It was slightly uncomfortable and a little on the wide side for Gieo's taste, but it would serve the purpose, and miraculously, it sort of matched a lot of what she usually wore. She flipped over a metal pie tin with a shiny bottom to admire her reflection and how the collar complimented her slender neck.

"What? Oh, puppy, um, I'll think about it, I guess," Gieo said. Once she was certain the collar would work, she unbuckled it and wound it up with the leash. It was for show, a display to set the town at ease about Fiona's position of authority…so why did Gieo want Fiona to be the one to buckle it onto her so badly?

"No, I meant, is the collar for a puppy?" Ramen corrected her.

"Oh, no, the collar is for…something else. Where did we even pick this up? It doesn't smell like dog."

"I don't think it was ever worn by a dog. Remember the two guys who came in with the portable DVD player…?" Ramen was interrupted by the door to the roof creaking open in an almost apologetic way. They both looked over to see Fiona poking her head out of the slightly ajar door.

"Is everything okay up here?" Fiona asked.

"Sure, come on up," Gieo said. "The show should be starting soon."

Gieo noted, with more than passing interest, that Fiona was cleaner and more softly adorned than usual. Instead of her alternating three pairs of leather pants, she was wearing faded blue jeans with tan chaps, a white baby-tee, a leather vest buttoned halfway, and the gun belt with the Colt Anaconda strapped low on her right hip. Gieo pointed to the telescope by the lawn chair at the edge of the roof. She fell in a half-step behind Fiona on the walk over. She tilted her head just enough to get a good look at Fiona's backside; the jeans, which were practically painted onto the gunfighter's lanky form, hugged the contours of her pert little ass, aided by the buckles and lines of the chaps just below each cheek. Gieo hadn't even known something could look so appealing, and she had to fight an overwhelming urge to bite Fiona's behind.

Gieo repositioned the telescope, and motioned for Fiona to sit in the lawn chair. When she'd found the exact center of the Hawkins House compound, she stepped aside to let Fiona lean in closer to take a look. "I've been watching them," Gieo said. "The priesthood, for lack of a better word, drinks from a different well than the general population. You can spot them by the traffic cones they wear like miters."

Fiona leaned in, close enough for Gieo to catch a faint whiff of the soft, lavender soap she had used with an undertone of sweat and gun oil. Fiona looked through the telescope, watching the compound as she spoke, "Are they siphoning gas out of that truck or something?"

"That's where they keep their private stash of…who the fuck knows," Gieo said. "But they're not drinking their usual methanol concoction this morning. I changed the hose to a jug of agave white lightning with peyote in the mix."

"Why?" Fiona pulled away from the telescope, surprised, but not unhappily so, to find Gieo leaned in very close.

"Ethanol, alcohol that normal people drink in beer and whiskey, helps the body metabolize methanol to counteract methanol poisoning," Gieo said. "And the peyote…you know."

Fiona's beautiful blue eyes opened a hair wider. "So they're going to get very lucid and then trip balls?"

"Exactly!" Gieo said. "Hopefully, they'll mistake it for a religious experience, put that together with Zeke's demon-based attack on them, and *want* to leave Tombstone to follow whatever direction their trip guides them. If it doesn't work, no harm done; they'll just have some new material to write a Braille bible with."

Fiona returned her attention the telescope to watch with mounting morbid curiosity. The handful of men sneaking over to the Dodge pickup drank greedily and departed on wobbly legs. It became something of an exciting waiting game to see which cone-head would lose their shit first. Fiona reached over and grasped Gieo's knee in nervous anticipation, watching the priests stumble drunkenly for a short time before suddenly, Yahweh himself, had a colossal freak out.

She couldn't tell exactly what he said, due to the great distance, but it looked as though he were suddenly assaulted by something flying. Fiona couldn't fully read his lips, because of his crazy beard, but she could have sworn she saw his mouth form the words 'teddy bears' as he swatted at the empty air around him. The followers seemed perplexed by his new behavior, but soon picked up on the sufficiently direness of the situation when the rest of the priests joined in on the hallucination and began to have trips of their own.

"I was concerned peyote wouldn't work as well on blind people," Gieo said.

"You can stop worrying," Fiona replied with a little giggle. "Apparently they don't need fully functioning eyes to see things that aren't there." She pulled away from the telescope and leaned back in the lawn chair, obviously satisfied by the outcome. "So, what now?"

"Now we wait and see if they have a sufficiently moving religious experience," Gieo said. "Oh, I also found these." She produced the collar and leash, holding them out for Fiona, displayed across her open palms.

Fiona leaned forward a little to look them over and nodded noncommittally. "That should work." She began to lean back again.

"Can you put the collar on me?" Gieo blurted out. "I mean, it's like a necklace, but harder to get on, you know? I could use the help."

Fiona shrugged and took the offered collar. She started to reach up to put it on Gieo, who was sitting a little higher than her on the edge of the roof, but Gieo apparently had other ideas. The pilot knelt between Fiona's boots and tilted her head back to display her neck to Fiona.

"Um…okay." Fiona gently slipped the collar around Gieo's neck and buckled it into place.

Gieo's stomach did tiny somersaults through the entire collaring process and refused to calm down even after it was comfortably buckled. There wasn't any rationale to how good it made her feel, but she quickly listed it as one of the more important moments in their burgeoning relationship. When she opened her eyes to look up at Fiona, she found the gunfighter staring at her, confusion clearly painted across her face.

"There's a leash too." Gieo offered the wound leather strap to Fiona, who took it, a little begrudgingly.

She clipped the end to the loop on the collar and held the unfurled strap as though she weren't quite sure what to do with the five-feet of leather dangling from the front of Gieo's throat. "Um…what do I do with it?"

"You lead me over to Zeke's to collect your payment," Gieo said. "The other hunters should be just about ready to head out. They'll all see us and *know*."

"Okay, right, good idea," Fiona said, getting a little enthusiasm off of Gieo's infectious mood.

Gieo walked a few paces behind Fiona, with plenty of slack in the leash, as they made their way down into the saloon, through the main hall where all eyes were on them, and then out onto the thoroughfare. Gieo, who had planned on every level to act the subservient piece of property, actually strutted, head held high, almost preening with pride in being collared by Fiona. This seemed to confuse the other hunters more than anything; they watched the couple with slack jaws and some, quite-literally scratched their heads.

Out on the street in front of Zeke's community center, Fiona let out a sharp whistle. Slow, as if the morning held twice as many hours, Zeke ambled out of the dark interior to stand on the balcony. He glanced down to the duo with a little snort of amusement. Rawlins emerged from the front door of the building, directly beneath Zeke, leaning heavily against the door frame with a contemptuous glare leveled at Gieo and the leash. His angry eyes, tantrum-red face, and twitching jaw muscles were irrelevant to her—they both knew their position in relation to Fiona, and she knew he wished he was in her place, even if it meant being at the end of a leash.

"They're bugging out over there, but I don't see any of them dropping," Zeke growled. "The job was to thin the heard, not stir it up."

"The job was to spike their supply," Fiona corrected him, "and that's been done."

"We'll see if something comes of it." Zeke shrugged and snorted. "You're keeping your pet on a leash now?"

"Your houseboy mentioned there might be some question as to who she belongs to," Fiona said. "I didn't want to leave you shorthanded, but I also didn't want to leave any doubt in his mind."

Zeke stomped twice on the wooden slats of the balcony, dropping a shower of dust and sand across Rawlins. "You clear, down there?"

"Crystal, sir," Rawlins growled through clenched teeth.

"That's settled," Zeke grunted. He shifted his posture to lean his impressive bulk against the railing, which strained to contain him on the balcony. "Matter of the job is still on the table though. I can't pay you full price for a job half-done, but I don't expect there'd be much point in having you try the same trick twice. No cuts and half a week's ration of fuel."

"Two weeks," Fiona said, "and my pet will debrief your secretary on the defenses she saw inside the compound."

"Done. Good doing business with you, Red." Zeke turned to head back into the building, barking back over his shoulder as he ambled inside, "Rawlins, get your ass over to the saloon this evening with a notepad to take down what the pet saw."

Fiona's and Gieo's eyes tracked down to Rawlins; they both gave him a haughty smirk before turning on their heels to head back into the saloon. Gieo walked a little closer to Fiona on the way up the steps, close enough to pass a whisper between them. Her heart had leapt into her throat at being called 'pet', and the act of being led around by the willowy gunfighter with the perfect ass had set a fire between her legs that she had to have an answer for.

"Take me to your room," Gieo whispered.

"I'm holding the leash here," Fiona replied, her eyes never wavering from straight ahead. "I heard you screaming my name the other night." Gieo's cheeks flashed bright red. She fell back a few more paces, almost to the end of her slack. Fiona gave a light tug on the leash to pull her back in step. "It's not nice to have that much fun thinking about a person without inviting them to join."

Gieo could have died of embarrassment at that moment. She hadn't realized she was screaming, let alone anything as specific as Fiona's name. The crushingly mortified feeling lifted when Fiona turned left at the top of the stairs and led Gieo toward the bedroom.

Chapter 8
Cultists gone wild

They were barely in the room with the door closed behind them when Fiona walked her way up the leash, hand over hand, pulling Gieo in close. Her fingers made for the buckle on the collar, but Gieo shook her head. "Leave it on," she whispered.

Fiona moved on quickly from the instruction to let the collar alone, opting to kiss Gieo with a fierce intensity that made the pilot's knees weak. They staggered across the floor, refusing to break the kiss, groping each other with fumbling hands made clumsy by pent-up desire. Gieo finally got to grasp, fondle, and squeeze Fiona's behind in the tight jeans, reveling in the steely muscle of the thin-framed gunfighter. Fiona sat on the edge of the bed and dropped the handle loop of the leash over one of the posts on the footboard to get it out of the way. Gieo responded by flicking Fiona's hat off her head; she ran her fingers through the gunfighter's bright red hair, ruffling it out of the tamped down shape the hat had left.

Fiona's hands found their way up the back of Gieo's skirt, searching through the ruffles for the pilot's slender legs. Gieo batted away Fiona's hands and pushed the gunfighter back onto the bed. She hopped onto Fiona's waist, straddling her awkwardly at the edge. The pilot's talented fingers snaked their way up the bottom of Fiona's shirt, tickling her abs, intent on finally undressing the gunfighter.

A peculiar sound, one Gieo hadn't heard in ages, and didn't really recognize at first, echoed across the town. The rhythmic thrumming noise increased in intensity until it captured Fiona's attention. The gunfighter's eyes went wide, and she struggled to extricate herself from the many ruffled folds of Gieo's skirt. When Gieo finally placed the noise as a didgeridoo, she couldn't for the life of her think of a reason why someone would be playing one of the strange aboriginal instruments, or why Fiona would care so much.

Fiona raced to the window, took one glance down at the street, and sprinted for the door. Gieo grabbed the gunfighter's hat and started to follow before the leash, still attached to the footboard, yanked her back. She pulled the end of the leash free from the post and gave chase. The gunfighter, with her head start and long-legged strides, was already down the stairs and at the door of the saloon, gun in hand, sunglasses slipped on to conceal her eyes.

"You're awful far from home, Bill," Zeke bellowed from his perch across the street. He'd always used Yahweh Hawkins's given name, although, to Fiona's knowledge, he was the only one who did, and she had no idea how he knew it.

The didgeridoo never ceased playing, but was soon drowned out by several hunters' vehicles returning from all directions. When Gieo finally caught up to Fiona, she found herself pushed back away from the door by Fiona's free hand, barely able to see out the front doors of the saloon to the street beyond where it looked as though the entire Hawkins House cult had gathered to speak with Zeke.

"This town's wickedness has spilled over onto the sacrosanct ground of our sanctuary," Yahweh shouted back. "Demons have visited us in the night, assaulting the faithful and implicating you. The Lord our Father demands the blood of the she-devils who have vexed Tombstone for far too long. You will give them to us or feel the Lord's holy wrath."

"You'll get nothing and like it," Zeke bellowed. "I never took orders from any man and I'm not about to start with some blind old Jesus freak. Clear the street or I'll have my hunters clear it for you."

Fiona glanced around to the numbers of the returned hunters, judged the situation to have shifted toward favorable, and stepped through the saloon doors to stand on the plank sidewalk in front. She kicked the nearest cultist off the edge of the sidewalk with a cowboy boot between the shoulder blades. The wiry man she'd punted landed face-first in the dusty street with an audible grunt. The kicked man's two mates rushed Fiona. The first received a backhand from the long, heavy barrel of her Colt Anaconda, and the second stopped short when the same barrel was brought into pointed contact with the center of his forehead. Even the mostly blind man could see the massive blast door of the .44 magnum at point blank range; he held his hands up in surrender and backed away. Other hunters crept into position on rooftops and doorways around the gathered cultists, no less violent in their shepherding of the blind people into a single clump.

"The legions of heaven cannot be moved by guns, will not bow to the puppets of the she-devil whore, and walk in the light of the Savior!" Yahweh held his arms out to his sides, tilting his head back until the orange parking cone he wore as a hat nearly fell off. Cultists, families mostly, staggered out into the streets, milky eyes staring blankly ahead as they tapped their way into the town with long canes and eerie singing voices rising to join in a rousing chorus of "Take My Life and Let it Be" with the cultists that had already gathered. The arrival of the hymn, which was haunting and creepy all on its own without being sung in a toneless chant by a mob of milky-eyed cultists, had an unsettling effect on the gathered hunters with the exception of Fiona.

She strode through the cluster with murderous intent. When she reached Yahweh, she grasped him by the back of the shirt, spun him around to face her, and brought the butt of her gun along his jaw, knocking two teeth from his mouth in a spray of blood. The cult leader crumpled to the ground like a heap of laundry.

"You want me so bad?" Fiona snarled, swinging a boot hard to kick the downed man directly in the ribs. "Here I am!"

Yahweh laughed an insidious, wheezing chuckle, dripping dark blood on the dusty street with every shake of his frail frame. He regained his feet slowly without help. Before righting his posture entirely, he sought out and retrieved the parking cone hat he'd lost. "The great eye in the sky has told us you are not the she-devil who will lead this town into temptation." His voice took on a strangely powerful quality despite coming from such a desiccated old man. His finger, gnarled and twisted, shot out toward the front of the saloon to where Gieo stood, Fiona's hat in one hand and her leash in the other. "She is the true devil incarnate who will be the downfall of humanity and the damnation of all lost souls. Give her to us now, let us cleanse her by fire, and the world will be saved from the devil's treachery."

Fiona let loose with a growl more feral and jungle cat than Gieo would have thought a person could even manage. She swung her long, shapely leg in a wicked arc, kicking Yahweh's legs out from beneath him. The old man went airborne for what seemed like an eternity before landing flat on his back in the street. Two cultist men, armed with knives, lunged from the crowd, intent on grabbing Gieo. Fiona spun on her heels, leveled two, well-placed shots, and blew off one man's right hand while striking the other in the lower back. She spun back around to point the barrel of her gun at Yahweh's chest.

"You so much as look at her funny, and I'll send you to meet the god you won't shut up about," Fiona snarled.

"That's enough, Red," Zeke shouted. The street went deadly calm, hunters nervously made eye contact with one another, clearly outnumbered by the cultist families who had come to join the men. The milky-eyed men, women, and children, who had formerly walked the streets singing, stood silent, stock-still, staring straight ahead as if gazing into another dimension. "Well, Bill, it looks like you have your answer," Zeke said. "She doesn't want to give up her pet to be barbequed even if it means saving the world. You may as well head home and see if you can find some chickens to grill up in her place."

"He broke hunter law," Fiona shrieked. "He threatened my property and tried to have his men take what is rightfully mine. His head belongs to me."

"He's not a hunter, Red. Hunter law doesn't apply to him," Zeke said.

"He's less than a hunter, meaning I can do whatever he can't stop me from doing!"

"You'll die with your sins on your head." Yahweh growled and slowly regained his feet, yet again. "You're an unnatural abomination, disgusting in the Lord's eyes, and only hell awaits you."

"You didn't want to kill him before," Zeke snorted. "Why start now?"

Fiona, hand still shaking with rage, slipped her gun back into its holster. She loomed over the cult leader, casting a long shadow over him. "I could have poisoned your entire fucked up society and shot anyone the poison didn't do in," Fiona said, her voice even and calm with a spooky edge of detachment. "You're only alive right now because I felt sorry for you pathetic freaks. But my pity and patience is spent. Any of you cane-tappers cross my path, and I'll end you all."

Fiona turned and walked away. She grabbed her hat and the leash on the way past Gieo, leading the pilot back into the saloon. The street remained quiet for a time after Fiona had departed.

"We need to get you a weapon," Fiona said.

They paused outside Fiona's room. Gieo was visibly shaken and Fiona was still a fiddle string strung too tightly, threatening to snap and lash out violently at the slightest provocation. Gieo simultaneously wanted to soothe the gunfighter and wanted Fiona to comfort her; instead, she stood at the end of her leash trembling.

"I don't want to shoot anyone," Gieo whispered.

"I saw the giant gun pod we took from the crash site," Fiona said. "You've clearly shot Slark before."

"That's different. Slark aren't human. Isn't there a difference for you to hunt them versus shooting humans?"

Fiona shrugged and shook her head. "Why would there be?"

"You frighten me sometimes," Gieo said.

Fiona opened her mouth to respond, but the resumption of the haunting singing of hymns began again outside. They ran into Fiona's room and made for the window. Down on the streets, walking slowly in clumps of a half-dozen or so, the entire Hawkins House cult spread through the town, clogging the streets with their aimless march.

"What are they doing?" Gieo asked.

"Seeing if I was bluffing," Fiona replied.

Fiona stood at her window the rest of the day, watching the cultists marching around the streets, clogging any vehicular traffic, singing their dire hymns in eerily flat voices. The net effect on her was to make her antsy. Her skin was crawling with the need to be free, to rocket her car across the desert away from the blind masses. She'd seen a few other hunters walking the streets, unable to get their cars out either, and they looked as agitated as she felt.

"Rawlins is here," Gieo said, poking her head into Fiona's room.

Fiona pulled her attention away from the window. Rawlins would have word from Zeke and Zeke wouldn't be happy that the cultists, who were supposed to be poisoned and dead, were wandering the streets, en masse, preventing anyone from participating in the town's primary business of Slark hunting. Gieo blocked the door, the leash in her hand, held out for Fiona to take. The pilot's face was unreadable and blank. Fiona took the leash and tried to force a smile.

"I'm sorry," Gieo whispered.

"For what?"

"For the mess that's outside," she said. "If I hadn't taken the job, Zeke would have found someone willing to actually poison them, and this shutdown wouldn't have happened."

Fiona sighed and ran her free hand gently down Gieo's smooth cheek. "As big of a headache as this is, poisoning them would have gone too far, even by Tombstone standards," she said, a great deal of the tension draining from her in finally saying what everyone should have been thinking. "For what it's worth, I'm glad you took the job." Fiona pulled Gieo in close by the leash and kissed her full on the lips in a steamy embrace. Gieo's thumbs looped through the front of Fiona's gun belt and held her close. Their lips reluctantly parted and Gieo stepped aside to let Fiona pass.

"This leash is driving me nuts," Gieo whispered as Fiona led her toward the stairs.

"I'm sorry," Fiona replied, "maybe we can get by with just the collar."

Gieo closed the gap between them and gave Fiona's butt a meaningful squeeze. "That's not what I meant."

Fiona found herself flushed and excited when she came to the meeting table with Rawlins. The cultist protest had been bad for the saloon's business as most of the tables were empty, and the few patrons who had found their way to the watering hole spent most of their time at the windows. Rawlins was sitting at one of the center tables with his hands folded in front of him. Fiona sat across from him, guiding Gieo toward the chair to her right. Rather than sit in the chair, the pilot knelt at Fiona's side and sat back on her feet expectantly. Fiona had to bite her lip to keep from laughing.

"Zeke isn't happy," Rawlins said.

"Nobody is," Fiona corrected him.

"One of the methanol drinkers you shot has died and the other is circling the drain." Rawlins leaned his bulk back in the chair, trying to affect a casual posture; it looked a little forced to Fiona. "They've got the dead one dressed up like a saint; they're taking turns parading him around town like a goddamned beauty queen on tour. People are starting to say maybe you went too far."

"Makes me wonder what they'll say when I clear the streets with my car's cattle catcher," Fiona growled.

The comment, for all its pointed intent toward the cultists, actually seemed to make Rawlins uncomfortable as though it was leveled against him. A drip of sweat ran down his ruddy face.

"You don't think we should take this seriously?"

"What makes you think I'm joking?" Fiona narrowed her eyes at him to let him know she saw him acting suspicious. She really wished she was a more conniving thinker in moments like this. She was a hammer, a gun, a battering ram, which had been problematic in a world that hadn't cared for those traits in lingerie models, but had served her well after that world crumbled under the Slark invasion; on rare occasion, Tombstone abandoned its violent, straightforward tendencies to sit down and make a game of chess out of things. Fiona was at a distinct disadvantage when this happened.

Gieo tapped Fiona on the leg, and sat up far enough to whisper into the gunfighter's ear, "He's angling to have you give me up to the cultists for the sake of peace." The assessment didn't make sense; Zeke hated appeasement and never would suggest breaking hunter law, the laws he'd created, to coddle the cult he hated. Gieo divined the thoughtful look on Fiona's face and shook her head slowly, mouthing the words, "Not Zeke."

If Gieo's hadn't nuzzled under Fiona's gun hand in a submissive, kittenish act, Fiona knew she would have jerked her pistol and blown Rawlins out the back of his chair. Her vision flashed over in red. The worthless cuss was here without orders, trying to guilt her into giving up Gieo, for his own, self-serving ends. Fiona wondered if Rawlins knew that Gieo was the only reason he hadn't been shot dead in a blind rage.

"Mistress," Gieo whispered in a demure voice, almost entirely uncharacteristic of her, "I can tell the secretary what I know of the Hawkins compound while you get a drink. He has no other business here."

From a lifetime of being thrown out of bars by bouncers and managed out of volatile situations by her agent, Fiona recognized when she was being cut off. Whether it was at a bar or a paparazzi-surrounded red carpet, she knew she had a redline and she wasn't good for anything but violence when she passed over it. Somehow, the act of being pulled out of a situation she no longer could control herself in was a lot easier to take when it was done by Gieo in a loving voice; she'd never liked or appreciated it when bartenders or her agent did it. Fiona unhooked the leash, and slipped from the table without another word, storming to the bar intent on getting a proper buzz going.

Gieo pulled herself up from the floor and sat in Fiona's vacated chair. Rawlins went from jangled nerves to angry disdain in the span of a blink. His eyes shot daggers across the table at the collared pilot taking the seat vacated by the woman he longed for; Gieo knew the level of jealousy and rage storming its way through Rawlins—she smiled sweetly and fingered the collar.

"I'm wondering what your boss might think if he knew you were here bartering with authority you don't have to an end he wouldn't want," Gieo said. "I also wonder if you know exactly how close you came to dying just now."

"Fiona wouldn't shoot me," Rawlins said through clenched teeth.

Gieo couldn't tell if Rawlins meant she wouldn't shoot him because she cared for him or wouldn't shoot him because it was against a hunter law of some sort, regardless, it was obvious he fully believed the words, no matter how ludicrous Gieo knew them to be. It was interesting that Rawlins, who had apparently known Fiona for years, didn't actually seem to know the first thing about her.

"You're a poor judge of character, Officer Rawlins," Gieo said. "But it doesn't matter what you think. It only matters what you'll do to keep me from telling Zeke what you tried to do here."

"He wouldn't believe…"

"…wouldn't believe me? Because I'm not a hunter? I'll give you that." Gieo leaned forward across the table and produced a small, metal shard. It took a moment for Rawlins to recognize the device as a digital voice recorder. "Think he'd believe you?"

It was a bluff, the voice recorder not only hadn't been on, but didn't even work anymore. Gieo could tell from the way Rawlins' face drained entirely of blood that he didn't know that, and she didn't have any visible tells that might have given away her bluff. Her poker face was apparently ten times better than his. She settled back into her chair, leaving the voice recorder on the table, just out of his reach.

"Now that I have your undivided attention, get out your notepad," Gieo said. "You're going to take down what I know of the Hawkins House defenses and then you're going to use that information to do a little job for me."

Chapter 9

With a little help from blackmail and lies

After dinner, which was a little difficult to enjoy, what with all the disturbing singing of hymns by the passing clusters of blind people, Gieo and Fiona took a bottle of corn whiskey to the roof to see if they could settle themselves down.

Gieo sprawled on the lawn chair, in control of the bottle, while Fiona stalked the roof. Gieo considered it stalking as she was significantly more prowl than stroll in the way she moved. The whiskey bit like a rattlesnake, possessed the sickly yellow tint of stale urine, and had cost them some choice pieces of tech to acquire. All drawbacks aside, it was a necessity to dull the irritation of the singing. Gieo downed a shot out of the bottom of her tin mug and poured herself another. Fiona, having made her way around most of the roof, finally came to the little army tent with Gieo's hammock inside.

"You're pretty settled up here," Fiona said, her voice taking on a sullen edge no matter how hard she tried to be breezy about it.

"Nothing like sleeping in the open air for…um…some health benefit, I'm sure." Gieo downed the freshly poured shot and considered another. Nothing would be admissible in future relationship conversations if she could effectively blame anything stupid she said on corn whiskey.

Fiona seemed as eager to drop the topic as Gieo was to have it dropped. She continued walking on, becoming increasingly difficult to see in the gathering dark as she slid through Ramen's filing system.

She stopped when she finally reached Ramen's resting place; he had shut down for the night to conserve battery power. The little robot, with his arms, legs, and twin propellers pulled in, looked a little like a trumpet mute, albeit a trumpet mute for some sort of jazz playing giant. It would have been hard for Fiona to believe anyone could build something so remarkable if she hadn't seen it herself; of course, at one point, it would have been pretty hard to believe space lizards would make Los Angeles their new capital, but there they were.

"Jackson's truck is out back," Fiona said idly, glancing down to the Jeep in the ally below.

"I've been meaning to ask you about that." Gieo poured herself another shot. "Do you have plans for it, or do you mind if I break it down, use what I can, and part off the rest for profit?"

"Take, part, profit, whatever," Fiona said with a dismissive wave of her hand. "I never wanted it in the first place."

"Good, because I have a plan." Gieo motioned Fiona over with her cup, which she then realized contained a shot, which she drank. The effects of the whiskey were starting to become a little more apparent in her speech, and she guessed wasn't doing any favors for her walking, should she choose to try any of that. "Now, don't get mad…"

"Whenever people say that, my first inclination is to always get mad." Fiona walked over to pilot's perch, took the bottle from beside the lawn chair, and drank deeply of the noxious, yellow whiskey.

"…but I sent Rawlins on an errand." Gieo pulled up the monitor for her spy cameras around the Hawkins compound, waited for the slow software to load up, and then tabbed through the feeds until she found what she was looking for. "With all the cultists wandering the streets, it shouldn't be a problem for him to get in and get out without too much trouble."

"What did you give him?" Fiona knelt beside Gieo, leaning in close beside her to watch the grainy, black and white feed.

"Nothing," Gieo said. "I blackmailed him."

"That's my girl."

Gieo's heart fluttered at the gunfighter's words and her proximity.

"What's he doing?" Fiona asked, pointing at the feed with the lip of the whiskey bottle.

"That is a 1948 Indian Chief Roadmaster," Gieo said, "and he's stealing it for me. I spotted it when I was spying earlier and fell in love."

The dusty, barely recognizable motorcycle from just after World War II seemed to be fighting Rawlins every step of the way. Getting it up from the hard-baked ground that had practically grown around it was the first obstacle that nearly did him in. Rolling it on two flat tires that fell apart like dry coffeecake was the second. Pushing it up the ramp into the back of his tow truck that he'd somehow managed to pull right into the compound was the last. The whole thing looked like a comically angry Sisyphus who had traded in his boulder for a motorcycle.

"Feminism is all well and good," Gieo said, "but there was no way I was going to be able to haul that thing out of there myself. More importantly, I needed a distraction."

"You knew the cultists would flood into the city to be a pain in everyone's ass?" Fiona asked incredulously.

"Hell no!" Gieo grabbed the bottle from Fiona's hand and poured herself another shot, feeling loose and happy with her mounting buzz. She downed the drink and poured another. "My original plan involved setting a fire and stealing a forklift, but this worked out much better."

"What are you going to do with an antique motorcycle?"

Gieo leaned heavily against the arm of the lawn chair, placing her face inches from Fiona's. "You're cute when I'm drunk," she slurred. "Not that you aren't cute all the time, but when I'm drunk, your edges are all fuzzy." Gieo ran her finger along the outline of Fiona's face, down her jaw, ending with her index finger resting on Fiona's chin.

"I'm going to put you to bed." Fiona gently lifted Gieo from the lawn chair, sliding in under one of her arms to support the wobbly pilot.

"You should put me to the spurs, or your spurs should be put to me…hey, why don't you have spurs?" Before Fiona could answer, Gieo nearly spun out of her grasp to head back toward the edge of the saloon roof. "Hey! Shaddup you damn cane tappers!" She hoisted the nearly empty bottle by the neck and hurled it over the edge at one of the passing groups of cultists who were singing a toneless rendition of "Old Rugged Cross." The bottle sailed over their heads, and, remarkably, struck the dirty road without breaking, rolling across the street on its side to come to rest against a clump of weeds clinging to the base of the town hall. The cultists didn't appear to have noticed the bottle and thus made no move of response, continuing along their merry way without so much as a tilted head. "I'm not going to be able to sleep with all that racket," Gieo said, stumbling back into Fiona's arms.

"Oh, I expect you'll manage," Fiona said with a little laugh.

The laugh, brief, but genuine, stopped Gieo in her tracks. "You don't laugh enough."

"I haven't had much reason to."

"I'll invent a machine that will make you laugh and…yanno what? Fuck it, I'll make you laugh." Gieo allowed herself to be led toward the army tent while attempting knock-knock jokes, most of which ended in some sort of mathematical pun that Fiona didn't understand. Gieo forwent the sleeping bag, flopping onto the hammock and nearly spilling herself back onto the roof in the process.

Fiona leaned over the quickly fading pilot and brushed one of her purple braids from her face with gentle fingers. "Sweet dreams, Stacy."

"Normally I don't like people calling me by my real name," Gieo said dreamily, "but you can because I'm your collared little pet…" She might have had more to say or it might have been a yawn, but whatever followed failed to escape the fast approaching sleep.

Fiona tucked in Gieo as best she could and headed downstairs. Between the head full of confusing thoughts, stomach churning with bad whiskey, cultists singing in the streets, and nail-biting sexual frustration, Fiona struggled to find sleep as though sleep wanted nothing to do with her.

Fiona rolled out of bed much later than usual. The lousy night of sleep, combined with the alcohol and lack of necessity to get up early to go hunting, held her in bed until she naturally came to the day—something she never did. Despite the added hours, she wasn't any more rested than usual, and had a headache hitchhiker. She was barely dressed for the day when a harsh knock came at her door. Rawlins, no doubt grumpy from his long night of working for someone else's silence, barked at her through the door that there was a meeting in twenty minutes and her ass had better be there.

She put on another pair of blue jeans, skipped the chaps, strapped on her gun belt, and pulled on a black tank-top. With her hat and sunglasses on, she headed out to the meeting at the town hall. In all the time she'd lived in Tombstone, they'd only ever had a handful of meetings between the hunters, and those were in the very early days of the town to establish the order they would all live by. Since then, the hunters worked in a solitary fashion. If a new hunter came into town, Zeke or one of the veterans made sure they knew the score; if they didn't follow the rules, they didn't last long.

Out on the street, the cultists were beginning to show signs of wear but none of stopping. A full day and night had taken its toll. They were all sunburned, with chapped lips, and blisters rising on the areas hit hardest. Fiona walked calmly between the passing clusters; they neither avoided her nor acknowledged her presence.

The interior of the town hall was dark and cool, smelling dusty with a hint of leather, sagebrush, and gun oil. Forty or so men were milling about in the space meant for over a hundred, and they were all chaffing under the cramped accommodations being so used to elbow room for miles. Zeke took his sweet time getting to the podium after Rawlins ushered in the last few stragglers. Fiona found a spot against the wall with good visibility on the podium and the door. She fell into her pose of practice relaxation that set others at ease, but was so carefully planned to keep her at a state of readiness to strike at a moment's notice. Her back was leaned against the wall, one boot up flat to push off should she need to, and her thumbs tucked into her pockets, close enough to her pistol that she could jerk it faster than someone could drop a hat.

"We've got a problem…" Zeke began.

He only managed to get four words out before the crowd turned on him. "You're damn right we do!" "You're pro-rating the quota for days spent stuck in town." "You should have let the bitch kill the old fuck!" The last comment wasn't directed at Fiona, but she knew she was the 'bitch' in question. She had to wonder as well why Zeke had stopped her.

"Why don't you just give them the purple-haired whore and be done with it?"

Fiona lifted her eyes for that comment, scanned the crowd, and found the speaker to be Steve Olsen. She marked him off as someone she would have to shoot.

"That's a great plan, Steve," Zeke bellowed, silencing the murmurs of the assembled hunters. "While we're at it, why don't we just tell them anytime they want to fuck us, all they have to do is march around the streets singing and we'll bend right over? Better yet, how about you find old Bill and bend over for him yourself. I'm sure your crusty ass will be a welcome change from his harem of 12-year-old child brides. We're not giving them shit, and I'll personally castrate the next man who suggests it."

"Then why'd you stop Red from enforcing the law?" Danny O'Brien shouted from the back. If there was another hunter Fiona liked, or at the very least respected, it was Danny. He was easily the best driver among them, which was saying a lot, and he sought out clean kills for professional purposes. Of all of them, he was likely the only sane person in the room; she had no idea what he was doing as a Tombstone hunter. But she couldn't very well save a person's life only to tell them what to do with it…

"Bill's got a trump card," Zeke finally conceded. "I can't tell you what it is, but I know the cagey bastard would have a way of playing it even if he was gunned down in the street on a lark."

"So what are we supposed to do?" Fiona finally spoke. Her voice, feminine and powerful, cut through the room like lightning, and suddenly all eyes were on her.

"Of all the people to ask that question, I'm glad it was you, Red." Zeke had the look of a sleeping cat with yellow feathers stuck to his whiskers; Fiona didn't like it one bit. "I sent a messenger to Vegas on horseback. We'll finally be accepting the Lazy Ravens' invitation for a franchise, due to arrive on the train coming in Friday."

The collected hunters cheered. Even Danny, who should have known better, had his San Diego Padres cap off, waving it in the air like he, of all people, didn't know what it really meant. Fiona stormed from the town hall, burst out onto the street, and nearly knocked down a group of the singing cultists on her way back to the saloon.

The timing was bullshit. The train from Vegas would be in Tombstone no later than the day after tomorrow and there was no way a rider would even get to Vegas before the end of the week, let alone back in time to tell Zeke the response date. She knew the Lazy Ravens would send the cultists scurrying back to their bibles and methanol rituals faster than the threat of rolling Armageddon, but that wasn't the point. Fiona stomped through the saloon, up the stairs, and burst out onto the rooftop. Gieo was awake, more or less, still somewhat in her underthings, wearing only a white slip and the blouse from the day before, half her braids undone, with a dazed, groggy look about her. She tried quickly to straighten her hair and wipe the sleep from her eyes.

"Hey, sorry about last night," Gieo said quickly. "Things got out of hand, and, was it just me, or was that whiskey really strong for being made out of corn husks?"

Fiona ignored her comments, ignored her really, stormed to the edge of the roof where she'd seen the milk jug Zeke had tried to give her for the job to poison the cultists. She hoisted the jug, spun off the cap, and took a long pull of the cloudy liquid. She spit what was supposed to be poison out over the edge of the roof. Across the way, standing on his balcony, Zeke's look of gloating pride had only deepened. He knew that she knew, and he knew there was nothing she could do about it.

"Whoa," Gieo shouted and ran toward Fiona, nearly tripping over a pile of old desktop computer parts. "Don't drink that! It's poison!"

"No," Fiona said, "it's not."

Gieo, dressed in her leather blacksmith's apron, little brown corduroy shorts, and a leather vest, was torso deep in the bowels of Jackson's old Jeep Wagoneer, giving Fiona all the stretched legs and tight ass she could stand to look at in the fading, golden light of the day. Fiona was making a show of drinking a warm beer from a refilled bottle, although she was far more focused on the pilot's backside, waving back and forth as it was in the little shorts while Gieo worked under the hood.

"So, no matter how I did that job, the result was going to be the same?" Gieo asked.

"From what you told me about Yahweh showing up at just the right time," Fiona said, "I don't think you were supposed to get back out. Everything else though, was exactly what Zeke wanted."

"You think Zeke tipped off the cultists?"

"I think we have to assume this was something he's been planning for a long time."

Gieo finally pulled herself from beneath the hood. Her face was smudged with engine grease, her hands covered in heavy leather gloves that fanned out around her forearms, and her eyes were still covered with the green goggles, but she was easily the most beautiful grease monkey Fiona had ever laid eyes on.

"What are the Lazy Ravens anyway?"

"A Vegas-based brothel…corporation for lack of a better word," Fiona said. "They're part business, part crime syndicate, part government."

"That doesn't sound like the influence Zeke would want in Tombstone."

"It isn't, or, wasn't, anyway. This concocted nonsense with the cultists is far too elaborate to simply be a cover for a change of heart, so I don't really know why he bothered with it." Fiona finished off the last of her warm beer and set aside the bottle. The setting sun had moved just enough to put a backlight on Gieo, and she considered moving to keep her lovely view. "I can only assume they've offered him something worth giving up some power over or there's something else going on that is beyond my brain's figuring capacity. It's not dangerous that I know what I know. Zeke can outthink me, no problem, but I'd imagine he wouldn't want you looking into it."

"You're not stupid," Gieo said, "not by a long shot. So don't sell yourself short. Besides, I can't be that bright if I was the patsy for a job you turned down."

"Those two comments don't fit together in a flattering way from where I'm sitting," Fiona said with a smile.

"I'm sorry; I didn't mean it like that." Gieo set aside her wrench and pushed the goggles up away from her eyes. "I'm feeling foolish and you're looking damn clever from where I'm standing."

"Is that all I'm looking?" Fiona's smile passed from joking to coquettish in an alluring way Gieo could distinctly remember from the gunfighter's old modeling days. There was a very specific picture, a cover shot from the summer catalogue, which Gieo had carried with her in the clear, plastic cover of her binder through her entire senior year of high school, displaying that very smile; she loved the fact that it was something natural to Fiona, and not a product of a photographer's direction.

"Actually, you're looking hungry for something that I might be able to…" The rest of Gieo's comment was cut short by the sound of Rawlins' tow truck grinding its way around the saloon to the back.

Beside the main winch, hugged to the truck's frame with a dozen or so bungee cords, sat the skeletal remains of the 1948 Indian Chief. Gieo couldn't help but hop a little in excitement.

Rawlins, who seemed increasingly agitated since Gieo's arrival, slammed the truck door and stormed to the back to unload the goal of Gieo's blackmail scheme. It was a difficult proposition that neither Fiona nor Gieo offered to help with, and resulted in Rawlins barking his knuckles against the bike or his truck no less than a dozen times, and squashing any number of his limbs between the motorcycle and the railing nearly as many. He leaned the old hulk of the bike against the side of Jackson's Wagoneer, and began the weary walk back to his truck without so much as a word or glance directed at Gieo or Fiona.

"One more thing," Gieo called after him, stopping him dead in his tracks.

Rawlins looked angry, even from behind, lifting his hands to plant them on his hips with an exasperated sigh. "What now?"

"The collaring thing bugs you," Gieo said. "Are you mad because you want to wear Fiona's collar, or you'd want her to wear yours?"

The audacious temerity of it aside, Fiona thought the question was just about the funniest damn thing she'd ever heard. Moreover, Rawlins' slow, or absent really, response, left both gunfighter and pilot to wonder if it really was the former.

"Fuck you," Rawlins growled.

"Answer her question," Fiona said.

"Why are you doing this to me?" Rawlins finally turned, leveling his gaze directly on Fiona.

"Why do you think?"

Rawlins didn't bother answering the question or waiting for one to his. He stormed back to the truck, got in, slammed the door, and tore away from the scene in a spray of dust and gravel. When the cloud of his departure slowly drifted away on the breeze, Gieo and Fiona were left to giggle at what they could only assume was his admittance to wishing for a collar of his own from the gunfighter.

"Seriously, though," Fiona said when her laughter subsided, "what do you want that old thing for?"

"Ah, an astute question from an eager student of science." Gieo winked at her and tapped the Wagoneer with the socket wrench she'd lifted from her toolbox. "The power plant in Jackson's old ride is from a Slark hover thingy. You know, the ones they used before they figured out how good human snipers were? It's too small to really do much for this monstrosity, but it'll be perfect for a motorcycle, especially after I reclaim another one of our forgotten technologies."

"Which technology is that?"

"Internal combustion!" Gieo hopped off the footstool she'd been using to get into the Wagoneer's engine compartment and knelt on the dusty ground in front of Fiona's feet. She drew out a hasty diagram of a piston and cylinder in the sand with the handle of the socket wrench. "Basically, an internal combustion engine just harnesses the chemical kinetic energy of gas expansion, usually a small explosion, and transfers it to mechanical energy. The Slark engines use a similar technology, but work with torsion, like a jet engine. I'm going to combine what they know, with what we know, and make an engine that is steam-powered internal combustion powering a torsion turbine. Creating an ember that will flash-vaporize water using Slark fuel should make the engine 82% more efficient than anything on the planet. Think of it as a Harley-Davidson crossed with a steam engine made possible by Slark hardware and fuel."

"What about the boiler experiment with Mitch's Kodiak?"

"Complete failure, well, moderate failure anyway," Gieo grumbled. "On dirigibles the ship became light enough to haul the extra weight by using the heated air to help float it. The truck has no such capacity, and thus drives at about a snail's pace at peak efficiency. Call it a mathematically sound, but ultimately not a physically viable plan. It'll have to wait until I get the new engine type perfected, which means I need to get back to work." Gieo hopped up and walked back to the Wagoneer. "I'm sorry; this must all be really boring."

Fiona leaned back against the saloon wall, her eyes wandering up the pilot's legs as she tucked her upper body under the hood again. "Not in the slightest."

Chapter 10

The Ravens have landed!

Fiona awoke with a realization kicking her in the head from the fading dream world she was leaving. She'd heard of people sorting out complex problems in their sleep to awaken with the answer, but she hadn't actually experienced it until that morning. The payment, the thing Zeke was supposed to give over to the cultists for the singing protests in the streets, was the precise thing he was claiming he would not give them now. Fiona's instincts had been right all along. He'd set up Gieo to be caught so the cultists could have their female villain to burn. Zeke could have asked any of the hunters to do the job, but he'd come to her first and then sought out Gieo when Fiona turned him down. No wonder Yahweh was so agitated, and Fiona's pummeling of him in the street couldn't have helped.

The urge to kill Zeke was nearly overwhelming. One saving grace of being a practiced hunter was the ability to assess and weigh a situation; she couldn't beat Zeke in a fair fight and there was no way he would ever enter into a fair fight anyway. He was a thinker and she was a reactionary. No matter how fast she was, and she was damn fast, he would always be yards ahead of her because he knew how to plan and she only knew how to have fast hands.

She would need Gieo to plan, to think, to figure out why Zeke was conspiring with the cultists, to discover what trump card Yahweh might have, and for…other things. Regardless of what Zeke threatened or said, Fiona had a bad feeling about Steve Olsen. The man was a high quality moron with a drinking problem, cowardly tendencies, and a history of terrible judgment; moreover, Yahweh most likely saw it as a debt unpaid and would be looking for someone to finish paying it since Zeke clearly wasn't going to. Steve had thought enough of the idea to give Gieo over to the cultists to say it out loud in public, and there was no telling what he might try in private. Fiona made up her mind. She needed to kill Steve Olsen somewhere people would see her do it.

Fiona was dressed and ready by the time Gieo came down from the roof to meet her for breakfast. The pilot had somewhat gleaned what Fiona was doing when she was working beneath the hood of the Wagoneer, and started wearing revealing clothing on her lower half when she worked on the motorcycle, which was all the time. The current day's ensemble included skintight black leather pants that Fiona had never seen the pilot wear. She was also wearing the spiked leather collar, which she hadn't taken off once that Fiona had seen since it had been buckled around her neck.

"Hey, ready for cold mush and runny eggs?" Gieo asked with a little hop in her step.

"After." Fiona brushed passed her, gently grazing her hand over the pilot's exposed shoulders to feel something pleasant before an unpleasant task. Gieo fell in behind her, a little perplexed, but not overly so since cryptic was something Fiona excelled at.

"Is this going to be a long enough 'after' that I should go work on the bike a little before we eat?" Gieo asked as they descended the stairs.

"No, I don't imagine it'll take that long."

The saloon bustled with a breakfast rush as it had the past few days. Hunters had found their way into the mix as most still couldn't get their cars out of town without mowing down cultists to do so. The cultists started cycling their members, which thinned the ranks some, but still only allowed a few hunters from the outskirts to escape every day. The word was the lucky few to get to the desert were having a rough time with the Slark now that the numbers weren't even; a few hunters hadn't come back the day before, likely outnumbered and overwhelmed by would-be-prey.

Fiona scanned the crowd for Steve Olsen's trash bag coat. It wasn't really fair to call it that. She knew it was a rain slicker of some kind, but the black plastic looked exactly like a garbage bag to her. When she finally found him at a table of hunters, she shouted above the raucous din of conversation, "Steve Olsen, you and I have business outside." The room fell dead silent.

"This doesn't have to happen," Steve objected. "Zeke told me how it was, and I'm fine with the explanation."

"I say it does."

"What has to happen?" Gieo whispered to Fiona.

He couldn't back down and save face, not now, not in front of so many others like them. She'd laid out a challenge on fertile grounds for insult, and his reputation depended upon accepting. What's more, she could see in his face he was scared of her, and everyone could see on her face, the feeling wasn't mutual.

She began to get the adrenaline tingles in her fingers, ache in her stomach, and the pounding in her chest as her heart worked overtime to supply the fight response with blood enough to carry out the kill. Her senses sharpened as her brain sought to give her an edge by blocking out all but the most crucial information. Steve walked for the door; Fiona followed. Everyone in the room, save Gieo, knew what was about to happen, and they all gathered to watch the fight unfold.

Standing opposite each other in the street, twenty yards apart or so, even the cultists gave them room, although they couldn't even see the spectacle born of the Old West and revived by the hunter code. Gieo figured out what Fiona was planning far too late to voice her concerns, never mind try to talk Fiona out of it.

Steve's adrenaline response to the situation was clearly flight, rather than Fiona's fight, and he tried one more time to talk down the redheaded huntress who could claim his head for a public slight against her ownership of the pilot. "You can walk away," Steve hollered. A quake in his voice all but put the final nail in his coffin.

"You can't."

They drew with nothing more than a visual cue between them to start. Fiona pulled first by a country mile, pivoted in her draw of the weapon to put her entire body in profile, presenting a sliver of a target, partially obscured by the enormous gun at the end of her entirely extended arm. Steve's gun made it to his hip, far behind Fiona's draw, and he had to fire, knowing she had him sighted in with a much stronger position. His gun went off first, and Gieo's heart leapt into her throat at seeing the powder blast come from his side an instant before she heard the increasingly familiar thunder of Fiona's Colt Anaconda.

Fiona was nearly six feet tall and couldn't even break 130 while carrying her gun. Hitting her turned sideways was like trying to shoot a loose thread from a coat, and Steve wasn't a good enough shot to do either even without the duress of the duel and Fiona getting the drop on him. His shot sailed wide, well wide, nearly hitting a collection of cultists behind and to Fiona's left. Her shot struck home though, and planted a finger width hole in his upper chest and a grapefruit sized exit wound at the base of his neck on the back. Everything in his face said he was gone on to whatever comes next long before his slack body hit the ground.

The high that followed, the endorphin rush of killing, and the satisfying secondary jolt of adrenaline that came with being shot at combined in a delicious hormonal cocktail in Fiona's head. She hadn't had time enough to enjoy the rush when she'd killed Jackson, as she was still half-blind with rage. Steve's death she would savor along with the applause and respect granted by the collected peers and townspeople.

"What's mine can't be offered to the likes of them…" Fiona pointed to the cultists on 'them' before continuing. "…by the likes of him." She finished by leveling her gun once again at the downed form of Steve Olsen. She could see many of the other hunters nodding in the crowd, although nobody else seemed to share in the agreement.

"The man had it coming," Danny O'Brien spoke up from the assembled crowd. "We all heard him demand that we barter with what wasn't his to offer. Got a preference on what we do with his goods, Red?"

Fiona holstered her gun, and turned to scan the crowd, finally landing her gaze on Gieo. "Gift it all to my pet—just like Jackson's rig," Fiona said. "If the fools in this town keep up at this pace, she'll be a rich woman before summer is out." Fiona walked to the stunned pilot, who looked less likely to vomit than she had after the Jackson incident, grasped her by the collar and pulled her in for a fierce kiss. Part of Fiona, a very large and growing part, rather liked shooting men for the favor of the purple-haired pilot.

"Rawlins!" Zeke bellowed from his perch, finally making himself known in the conflict. "See to another transfer for Red."

♠♣♥♦

The bike, which was burning through Gieo's supplies quickly, both in items used to repair or build it, but also in barter for the things she needed but didn't yet have, came together slowly, far slower than she might have liked. She had lost yet another morning of work and didn't have much of an appetite, as she'd had to watch the woman she was quickly falling in love with challenge and gun down some random person on her behalf for completely unexplained reasons.

Her hand had shaken so much while they tried to eat breakfast, that she eventually excused herself to go work on the bike. Predictably, her hand was shaking too much to work a jackhammer let alone the delicate wiring needing to be done on the fuel injection system. She finally abandoned the project to sit in the front seat of the old Wagoneer, staring blankly ahead at the crack pattern in the windshield.

By her final tally and conclusion, Tombstone was a thoroughly fucked up place.

Ramen fluttered down from the roof to keep her company and help her on the bike, but stopped short when he noticed she wasn't doing much working and didn't seem in the mood for company. He skittered around to the passenger side of the Wagoneer where Gieo was sitting, and poked his upside-down Wok head around the open door.

"You okay in there, Boss?"

"Fiona shot another man."

"I saw," he replied. "She's fast."

"I don't even know why she shot this one."

"Have you asked her?"

"No, but the answer isn't going to make much sense anyway."

"She did tell you Tombstone was rough."

"Of the two dozen words she's spoken to me, it's funny that those were the ones I chose to ignore," Gieo said with a little sniffle. "Are we making a mistake by being here?"

Ramen clattered a little further out around the door to look Gieo dead on. "You were lonely, Boss. I think you needed a return to what passes for civilization regardless of the crash."

"Maybe," Gieo murmured, "but I hardly think Tombstone was the smartest choice."

"If you think Vegas would be better, the train is supposed to arrive today."

Gieo perked up at the mention of the train. "It is, and it's going to have the Lazy Ravens on it. Let's go check it out." She hopped out of the truck, nearly knocking Ramen over. She untied her leather apron, and did a quick check of her lace-lined corset and matching bowler hat.

"Shouldn't we wait and see if Fiona wants to come, Boss?"

"She won't, and it won't matter," Gieo said. "After today, I could walk the streets naked, spitting in people's faces, and nobody would do anything but smile and wish me a good afternoon for fear she would come after them next. Now, let's go meet some pimps and hoes."

The train was late, as it tended to be by all accounts. The schedule on the station wall indicated it had a window of several days, which was only narrowed down for this specific arrival based on the exciting nature of the cargo. Gieo found an honest-to-goodness shoe shine station, manned and stocked with everything, to get her black, leather riding boots polished for the occasion. The strange little man, with enormously thick glass goggles intended to correct a vision imbalance of epic proportions and two little tufts of white above his ears for hair, asked only for a sock or stocking in payment. Gieo said she didn't have a sock or stocking to spare. He countered with the offer to do both boots for free if she would step barefoot on his head and call him scum. As strange as the request was, Gieo didn't see the harm in it. She pulled off one of her riding boots, the little man laid down on the train platform, and she stepped on his head gently, and called him scum. He was giddy with excitement right up until she removed her foot, and then he immediately returned to a perfectly professional demeanor. He'd nearly finished shining her boots when the train finally rolled into the station with a billow of steam, smoke, and a strange undercurrent of dozens of mingled perfumes.

Gieo stood from the shoe shine station, accidentally stepping on one of the bootblack's hands in the process. He let out the same little trill of excitement he had when she'd tendered payment, and thanked her for the tip she hadn't realized she was bestowing.

In something of a haze, she walked toward the train, along with others who had come out to greet the Ravens, and waited at the front of the assembled dozen or so people, standing out starkly as both the only clean person in the bunch, but also because she was female and dressed entirely in form-fitted black clothing, which, she thought glumly, Fiona hadn't even commented on.

The Ravens departed the train more like peacocks, flamingos, or birds of paradise than something as provincial as a raven. They were all dressed like proper saloon girls of the true Old West with some strange elements of modern trappings in the mix like an occasional hula hoop, Rainbow Bright backpack, or Mickey Mouse ears. In a surprising twist that Gieo hadn't remotely expected from Fiona's description of them, she was shocked to find they were beautiful, refined, and not at all what one might expect from Las Vegas prostitutes of the new Old West. They also seemed to be coordinated in how they disembarked the train, walking out in a pattern that indicated some grander point of focus was still yet to come.

Gieo watched with building anticipation and delight as each woman made some motion of greeting or some signature flirty gesture before taking their spot in a slowly curving arch around the impromptu Tombstone welcoming committee. Finally, with more than thirty of the women off the train, the Madame was introduced. Gieo's jaw nearly hit the floor; the entertainers, enforcers, prostitutes, and even the boss were all women!

Madame Veronica Vegas, or VV as the pink embroidery on her parasol identified her, was young, remarkably young for her position. Gieo thought, without the pageantry, makeup, and outlandishly feathered costume, Veronica might actually have even been a little plain. She commanded attention through sheer presence though, and with the added theatrical spectacle of costumes and makeup, she held an undeniable allure. Her blond hair was a carefully planned puff of large spiral curls in a top-knot ponytail, her thin lips were perfectly pearled in pink gloss, and her hazel eyes sparkled with a feisty glimmer that came from far more than just the glitter-laden blue eye shadow she wore. When her multiple curtsies of welcome were concluded, which was a show in itself as the hem of her Can-Can skirt was lined in bright pink feathers, she thanked the dozen or so townies for the welcome, and then zeroed in entirely on Gieo.

"You have the look of someone important about you," Veronica purred. "Are you our official attaché from the mayor to guide us to our future lodgings?"

"Oh, no, I'm..." Gieo stuttered and stammered, searching for an explanation for what she was doing there. She'd never had a problem coming up with a witty title or list of accomplishments for herself. In fact, she'd actually enjoyed meeting new people in Tombstone for the sole purpose of being able to use all the titles she would like associated with her that couldn't be listed in a single introduction to just one person.

"I'm your attaché, Danny O'Brien," Danny said, stepping forth from the crowd like the soothing surfer he was. From a distance, he might seem as rugged an unkempt as all hunters, but up close, Danny wasn't just good-looking, he was downright handsome. His mop of sandy blond hair jutted from around the edges of his baseball cap. His sky-blue eyes twinkled like the open ocean on a sunny day. And his close-cropped beard let show just enough of his strong jaw and proud chin to let anyone know he had a pretty enough face that it wouldn't matter if he covered more than half of it with beard. Gieo was immediately jealous that he not only had the looks to command Veronica's attention, but also the penis she probably preferred.

"Quite charmed, Mr. O'Brien." Veronica took his hand, curtsied again, very deferentially, rising a step closer to him so he might catch a stronger whiff of her perfume and perhaps see a bit more cleavage. "But then who is this alluring creature?" Veronica pointed the handle of her parasol in Gieo's direction.

"She's actually a pet of one of our more prominent hunters," Danny explained in somewhat polite terms that seemed to make him a little uncomfortable. "I don't know her name."

"A hunter's pet, you say?" Veronica played all atwitter at the possibility. She walked to Gieo, cocked her hip to one side dramatically, and gave Gieo a thorough looking over. "She looks as fresh and lovely as a spring morning. How is she the possession of a rough and tumble hunter?"

"*Huntress*," Gieo corrected for her, "and my name is Gieo."

"Yo?" Danny asked.

"Gieo," Veronica corrected for him. "It has a 'g' on the front."

The little baby crush, an egg really, not even a peeping baby crush yet, that Gieo had formed for Veronica broke free of its shell and became a full-blown squawking crush in the moment Veronica got her name right without needing direction. She didn't know Veronica, but she knew she was trouble.

"My, my, then you must belong to the one and only Red Bishop," Veronica said. "How times must have changed if she's taking pets. Although with a cute thing such as yourself, she could hardly be blamed."

"Red Bishop?" Gieo asked. Immediately, she felt stupid for the question and the inarticulate way in which she phrased it. For some reason, her brain wasn't working right around the Madame, and her mouth was becoming a blundering accomplice in making her look and feel foolish.

"She must not have told you much of herself," Veronica said. "That's hardly surprising, the taciturn thing that she is. You come by when we're all set up, share a drink with me, and I'll tell you everything you'll ever want to know about our mutual friend." Her slow, lingering cadence and choice of words and phrasing, all spoke of a Southern belle, but she didn't have a hint of an accent. The overall effect of her speech was disarming and hypnotic without intimation that it might be artificial despite the obviousness of the affectation.

"It was good to finally meet you," Danny said with a curt tip of his cap to Gieo. "Now, Madame VV, if you're ready to head out, I've got a few strong men with carts to see to the move. Tombstone welcomes the Lazy Ravens with open arms."

Veronica and her girls departed with a few winks and smiles thrown in Gieo's direction. Before the Ravens had departed fully, Gieo caught a brief glance of Fiona, standing well apart from the crowd, glaring intently in their direction. At first, Gieo suspected the angry glance was meant for her, but as she remained standing still, the glare moved, following someone departing. Gieo tried to follow Fiona's sightline and deduced either Danny or Veronica had done or said something to infuriate the gunfighter.

Chapter 11
Money? Oh, right, THAT stuff

Gieo first tried to catch Fiona in the crowd. For being taller than most, and a strikingly beautiful redheaded former lingerie model, the gunfighter was surprisingly sneaky. When Gieo finally pushed her way over to where Fiona had stood, the gunfighter was nowhere to be found. She thought about following the crowd over to the old courthouse. She'd overheard a few people saying that's where the Lazy Ravens would be setting up shop, but she decided against it until she actually thought through something to say to Veronica; the last thing she wanted was a repeat of the embarrassment of that afternoon. The mystery of Fiona being known by someone in Vegas and the bizarrely ominous alias of Red Bishop were just things she'd have to let go for the moment.

She made her way back to the saloon to see if Fiona had gone home. Sadly, her room was empty and Mitch hadn't seen her come back. Gieo grabbed Ramen and her toolkit from the roof and set up her shop in the saloon to begin fixing tech in hopes of getting her hands on more raw materials to finish the motorcycle. Without another influx of parts and trade goods, she was likely to be out of everything by the end of the week. As it stood, the Wagoneer had already been stripped and the rooftop filing system of salvage was looking rather empty.

The excitement of the Lazy Ravens' arrival spread through the town, along with the word of a formal announcement from Zeke, who had officially begun calling himself the mayor of Tombstone at some point in the last day or so; mayor was a good enough title, but Gieo thought 'feudal lord' fit his behavior better. Both public events did a number on Gieo's business and she ended up sitting for hours in the empty saloon, playing go-fish with Ramen.

Later in the evening, after the excitement of the day had worn off, a few stragglers came trickling into the saloon with broken items. One of the men, a goat herder and cactus harvester, had a tea kettle and electric toothbrush with him. Gieo had combined the two items for a few of the townsfolk in her first week in Tombstone. The kettle's steam power was easy enough to harness with a few paddles and widgets, charging the electric toothbrush for a short time using a copper wire coil. The boiling water was even enough to disinfect the bristles if the owner was so inclined. It wasn't as fun or inventive as the first couple of times she did it, but she couldn't really complain considering it was the only work she'd seen all day.

"What do you have in barter?" Gieo asked hopefully.

The man slapped his dirty palm against her table with a metallic clink. When he pulled away his grimy paw, there was a stack of five silver coins, all about the size of a quarter, with some strange markings on them. Gieo picked up one of the coins and gave it a glance over. They looked minted in a fairly professional way, with an imprint of the wacky Las Vegas skyline—Eiffel Tower, pyramid, Empire State Building, medieval castle, etc.—on one side and the Lazy Raven crest on the other.

"What's this?" Gieo asked.

"Money."

"Oh, right, money." Gieo had almost forgotten what money looked like. Even before the Slark invasion, she'd never really dealt in cash. Debit and credit cards were faster, easier, and accepted everywhere; on the rare occasion she did have tangible money, it was always paper. Coins were interesting in theory, but nothing she'd ever bothered with.

"Will you take it?" the goat herder asked. "They've done away with Slark heads as currency. The hunters are selling their heads for these, and then they can buy fuel with cash. A bunch of us got paid in them for helping the ladies set up their new digs. Then they even bought some cactus from me. They're awful pretty, and it's nice to have the jingle of money in my pocket again."

"Sure, if everyone's doing it, I'll do it too," Gieo said with an edge of sarcasm. "Out of morbid curiosity, what is the going rate for a Slark head?"

"Ten crows—that's what the ladies were calling the coins."

"And how much does fuel cost?"

"Six crows a gallon." The goat herder smiled at being so helpful and liberal with his information. When he smiled, Gieo could see he desperately needed the electric toothbrush.

"Wait, so if the old ration was six heads for fifteen gallons, the rate should only be four crows a gallon," Gieo said.

This comment shot a hole right through what the goatherd had been told. His smile dropped, and he shook his head. "No, it's six crows a gallon, ten per head," he said. "The math works out, or Zeke wouldn't have set it up this way."

Gieo smirked knowingly. Yes, she was sure Zeke had worked it out in his favor; using a little fractional math, it was easy to determine the new rate was a third more than the old system. He'd raised the prices and it would likely be at least a week before the mathematically challenged hunters would notice the difference. But, even when they did finally figure it out, what could they do? Increased profit and tangible assets might appeal to Zeke, but that still couldn't account for everything he was doing lately.

"Yep, Zeke certainly set people up for something," Gieo said. "Your payment is fair. Let's take a look at that toothbrush."

Fiona stalked the streets for hours, hopping mad about Veronica's arrival, angrier still that Danny didn't recognize her, and most importantly, about Gieo being there to flirt her up the second she stepped off the train. Fiona had a nearly overwhelming urge to shoot quite a few people. The desire, which might have had a plentiful outlet in the cultists, found nowhere to turn. The Lazy Ravens took to the street almost immediately upon arrival, and ushered the cultists away. Yahweh had instilled so much fear of non-cultist women in his followers that they fled at the mere blurry sight of the brightly adorned prostitutes, enforcers, and dancers. Then, the Ravens had done something even stranger. They turned their attention to the people who had gathered to see them sweep back the chanting methanol drinkers, and began buying goods off of them with silver coins. The townspeople, none of which were hunters, were grateful for not only the removal of the cultists, but also the reintroduction of money, and so practically heaped goods upon the Ravens.

Fiona had even been handed a single silver piece by a girl who was too young to know who she was—likely sixteen or seventeen from the complete lack of any lines on her face. The girl smiled to her, winked, gave a flirty bat of her eyelashes, and said she'd be happy to do a little dance for Fiona if she found four more of the coins. Fiona fingered the coin during the rest of her aimless walk amidst the dusty streets of Tombstone until long after sundown.

She found herself outside the Lazy Ravens' new home in the brick courthouse with the white pillars out front. It was only about a block or two from the saloon, but, then again, most everything in Tombstone was only about a block or two from most everything else. The ladies were cooling themselves on the steps in the fading warmth of dusk. When Fiona turned off the street to walk up toward the courthouse, a couple of the ladies broke away from the pack to intercept her.

"Sorry, sweetie," one of the women said. "We're not open for business yet." When she got close enough to see that Fiona was a woman and not just a very skinny man, she changed her tune. "Listen, we're not taking applications from the local talent either, so you may as well..."

The other woman quickly elbowed the first in the side, cutting off anything else she might say. "Veronica has been expecting you," she said quickly. "Sorry about the misunderstanding, Red Bishop; Stephanie is new." Fiona didn't recognize either of them, but that didn't really mean anything. She wasn't good with names or faces, and just because one of them knew who she was didn't necessarily mean she'd ever met either of them.

Fiona passed by the two without comment and into the old courthouse. Once inside, she was again greeted by one of the Ravens, but this time the escort, a lovely Hispanic woman in a revealing flamenco dress, took her by the arm and guided her expertly through the maze of the courthouse corridors to one of the judge's chambers on the second floor. The modifications on the courthouse hadn't taken much time at all. What had once been a house of justice and law, had spent some time as a munitions depot during the Slark skirmishes that finally halted their eastward expansion, and then as an all-purpose storage once Zeke took over. To look at what the Ravens had done to it, Fiona would have imagined it was always intended to be a brothel.

Veronica answered the door before Fiona could even knock, pulling her in by two handfuls of the front of her shirt. Fiona found herself shoved back up against the closed door once Veronica had her inside the office turned bedroom. Veronica's lips rushed up to meet Fiona's. Veronica tasted of strawberry candy and slippery gloss. Fiona returned the kiss in the heady, aggressive embrace, nearly forgetting herself in the moment. The complete memory of who she was kissing rushed back to her. Veronica had things to answer for and they weren't going to get answered while making out.

Fiona pushed Veronica away, although not far enough to break her hold on Fiona's shirt. "You've got a lot of nerve coming here," Fiona growled.

"You had a lot of nerve when you left me in Vegas," Veronica growled back. "I'd say this makes us even."

Fiona tried to extricate herself from Veronica's grasp, but Veronica redoubled her efforts and ended up pushing both her hands up under Fiona's shirt to grasp her athletically modest breasts. "You're skin and bones. Life in Tombstone must not be agreeing with you," Veronica said. "I remember when you had glorious breasts and I couldn't feel your every rib." She teased Fiona's nipples until they were solid little diamonds between her fingers. Fiona let her head fall back against the door, nearly knocking her hat off in the process. Veronica knew how to touch her, knew how to make her forget things, and absolutely spoke the truth when she said Fiona had been healthier in Vegas. "Can't your pet cook?"

The mention of Gieo brought Fiona back to reality, and she finally managed to push Veronica away. "Leave her out of this," Fiona hissed.

Veronica stalked away, more amused than hurt. "She's an adorable little thing," she said. "As long as she has a talented tongue, I wouldn't care either if all she knew how to do was lick and suck. What I'm more surprised about is your taking of a pet. Wasn't that one of your primary problems with our organization?"

"There's a big difference between what she and I have and the Ravens' slave trade."

"Of course there is. We only dealt in men."

"Dealt?"

Veronica flopped onto her overly cushioned bed, sinking on her stomach into the marshmallow-esque comforter. She glanced over to Fiona with her lower lip jutting out in a pout. "We discontinued that division when the council ratified a constitution outlawing slavery," she said. "Your little slave rebellion and the money it cost us had a lot to do with the decision, actually. Oh, but don't worry, someone figured out we could make twice as much with indentured servant contracts, so now you're something of a folk hero in Vegas."

"Speaking of, why didn't Danny recognize any of you?"

"How could he?" Veronica let out a cute little giggle, rolling onto her back. "Our human traffickers always wore masks, and he barely got picked up before you broke him out. He probably saw hooded figures, the inside of a boxcar, and then you and your band of rebellious human property making a mess out of my train. You know you broke my heart and cost me a fortune all in the same night?"

"That still doesn't explain what you're doing here." Fiona folded her arms over her chest, trying desperately to hide the fact that her nipples still hadn't calmed down from Veronica's tweaking of them.

"To put it bluntly, we're taking over the west," Veronica said. "Think about it. We could be the ruling class in the strongest new-world country. The Omaha Pact gives us all the food we can handle and then some just to keep us from invading. With all the desert city-states brought under Vegas rule, we could finally move against the Slark."

"You sound like Gieo," Fiona snorted.

"Again with your pet; she must have a talented mouth to have you so smitten. Fuck it! Bring the little crotch-licker along for the ride if you're so hung up on her." Veronica slid from the bed and began the slow process of peeling away her Can-Can dress, turning her back to Fiona in a feint of modesty. "I'm not remotely the jealous type. We could even share her, if you're willing."

"I never said I wanted to come back to the Ravens."

Veronica glanced over her shoulder, arms crossed over her breasts as she let her dress fall away, revealing the fishnet stockings and lacy little thong beneath. "Oh, sweetie, in a few days, you're not going to have a choice."

"I could go east to Texas."

"Gone," Veronica said with a little rise in pitch to her voice. She tossed one of her fingerless opera-length gloves over her shoulder to add a little flare to the declaration. "The Mexicans took it over and then they all died of a series of cholera outbreaks. I think the Slark have their eyes on the land, but they'd need to go through Arizona first, and they can't make that push. Not with Tombstone, Tempe, and Albuquerque in the way." Veronica turned back to Fiona, slowly letting her hands fall away from her breasts. Fiona knew them all too well, with their pert, pink nipples and the crescent shaped scar along the underside of the left breast where Veronica had nearly lost a knife fight in the wild, early days of the Ravens' taking over Vegas. Fiona used to lick the scar, calling it the river of strength that started in the mountains of her courageous heart and wound its way to the ocean of her breasts. It felt like an eternity ago, but seeing Veronica's scar brought it all back.

"I almost forgot," Veronica teased, catching onto Fiona's prolonged stare at her chest, "you're a breast woman. I also noticed your little Korean pet doesn't have a lot going on up top, even with a corset."

"Not breast-wise," Fiona admitted, "but just a little further up, she has more than anyone I've ever met." It was a proud declaration, and one she thought might harm Veronica's ego considering, to that point, Veronica had been the smartest person Fiona knew.

It stopped Veronica in her tracks, but not with wounded pride as Fiona had hoped. She looked intrigued. "Oh, do tell." Suddenly, Veronica couldn't hear enough about the woman she'd been degrading the entire conversation. Her eyes reflected the high-speed gears working behind them, and Fiona knew she'd said too much.

"She's a scientist," Fiona said, unable to stop her bragging, "and a pilot. She built an airship that actually flew, and it wasn't her first."

"I need to talk to this girl."

"Be prepared to have your ear chewed off."

Veronica cocked her head to one side and shrugged. "She actually seemed a little tongue-tied when I met her earlier."

Fiona had never seen anything but overt charisma and spastic charm from the pilot. She'd bombarded Fiona with a million questions, comments, and conversation pieces within the first five minutes of meeting her, and then shoved her hand straight down Fiona's pants within a few miles of their first car ride together; shy and tongue-tied were not normal behavior for Gieo. Veronica read Fiona's face, as she always could, and her eyes widened under the realization.

"I must have really had an impact on her," Veronica said, "one you clearly didn't. Are you losing your touch, love? Time was you had women and men hurling themselves at your feet."

Fiona's hand reached for the door, but didn't even make it to the handle before Veronica caught her wrist. She was fast, much faster than Fiona even, and knew every tell the gunfighter had; after all, she was the one who had taught Fiona the killing trade. Tears, honest to goodness tears, began welling in the corners of Fiona's eyes. She was a child in her former mentor and lover's hands.

"I didn't mean it like that. I know what she's going through, wanting to be possessed by you. Fiona, you still have that effect on me," Veronica whispered, closing the gap between them. "Please stay. My heart shattered when you left."

Fiona inhaled deeply of her former lover's scent, the strawberries that touched everything about her, the desert dust clinging to her hair, and the undertone of familiar sweat coursing beneath it all. Veronica felt like home, felt like safety, felt like letting go.

"You could have come after me," Fiona whispered, not wanting to give in, but knowing she didn't really have a choice.

"You said you would kill me if I tried," Veronica replied with a little laugh. "But I'm here now."

Fiona grasped Veronica around the waist and lifted her. Veronica easily straddled the gunfighter's hips. Their lips met again in an urgent kiss. Fiona struggled to breath past the intense embrace. Veronica was nearly her height and easily matched her in strength and weight as she'd had a much stronger path since their parting. Despite being the one held off the floor, Veronica steered Fiona to the bed with her hips and legs, finally pushing the gunfighter onto her back atop the pillowy bed. Veronica broke the kiss and smiled down to Fiona, running her hands along her exposed stomach and taut abdominal muscles.

"I'm going to feed you up, get you strong again, back to your shining old self," Veronica promised. "In a month you'll be ready to stand at my side when I roll over the entire west coast. We'll make a world run by women, devoid of Slark."

"I'm ready now," Fiona snarled in protest. She reached up, grabbed Veronica by the back of the neck and flipped her down onto the bed, immediately diving on top of her. She ground her hips into Veronica, pressing the front of her leather pants against the thin lacy material between Veronica's legs.

Veronica let out a little groan of pleasure and laughed. She easily reversed their positions, flipped Fiona onto her face, and pinned the gunfighter's right hand behind her back. Veronica's leg found its way up between Fiona's, pressing her knee firmly down against Fiona's ass.

"You're not strong enough to top me right now, let alone rule at my side," Veronica whispered hotly into Fiona's ear. "I don't want to hurt your pride though. Your confidence is sexy and vital for what's coming." Veronica let her go. Fiona gasped in a few deep breaths, having struggled to breathe through the face-full of comforter. "I have a gift for you to use on your pet. It'll help put a swagger back in your step." Veronica strolled across the room, threw open one of her many steamer trunks, and retrieved an item all too familiar to Fiona. She tossed the leather harness with a metal ring and a few buckles onto the bed. The huge, red phallus mounted in the strap-on harness whispered to Fiona of her former life.

She plucked the old friend from the top of the bed and inspected it to be sure it really was the same one. The extra holes punched to fit the straps to her slender hips were right where she'd left them. Even the scratch marks were there from where the strap that ran just above her ass had rubbed against a cement wall when they made good use of the toy in a parking structure in Barstow. They'd fought Slark all day, losing their entire squad of Ravens and the accompanying male slaves. When it looked like it would be the end of them after the aliens had finally cornered them in the shopping center parking structure, they'd done what anyone in that situation might do: fucked like bunnies with the expectation of dying before morning.

They wore urban military fatigues, camouflaged in grays and blacks for their night ops. Aside from a few bumps, bruises, and scrapes, they'd both escaped the catastrophic results of the battle that had claimed the rest of their squad, but their ammunition and explosives were all burned in the act of escaping. The Slark knew where they were, but didn't know they were down to knives and harsh language for weapons. The Slark had lost so many in the chase that they waited for reinforcements as night came on, certain the Red Bishop and White Queen were capable of slipping away if they attacked with so few.

The cold light of the moon mingled with the rosy glow of the various fires burning throughout the city to give a low, ambient light to the parking structure, level three, section D, space 49. Fiona was stressed, as she tended to be, and Veronica was exhilarated, as she tended to be. Veronica had leaned against the cement support pillar, her face flushed with excitement, dusty with a sheen of sweat. She'd produced the strap-on from her pack like it was just another implement of war. Fiona could hardly believe her eyes at the impracticality of bringing a ten-inch dildo to a battlefield. Veronica had smiled through her protests though, and, with her appealing, mesmerizing way, she'd asked, "Is there anything you want to do before we die?"

She'd stripped Fiona before she could put up much of a fight. Their empty ammunition harnesses, shirts, boots, and combat fatigues fell away, creating something of a nest on the concrete floor. Veronica tried again and again to get the harness to fit Fiona's slender hips, finally letting Fiona punch a couple extra holes further in for the buckles using her pocket knife. Even as Fiona was getting used to the sensation of wearing such a thing, something she'd never done before, Veronica was busy mentally checking off things on her list. She pushed Fiona against the pillar, fell to her knees, and began giving the most lurid blow job Fiona could have imagined, taking the enormous, red phallus in her mouth with inexperienced verve. The strap along the back, just above Fiona's ass, scraped and rubbed against the wall with every plunge and sloppy sucking motion Veronica made. There was little in the way of physical sensation to the blow job for Fiona, but the visual, auditory, and energy components shifted her thinking from survival to sexual ends. When Veronica had satisfied her curiosity, she'd climbed Fiona's body, her lips made rosy from the work, an ineffable smile on her face, having checked off something she'd never done and didn't want to die without knowing. "Some of the girls talk about how great that is," she'd said. "I had to know."

"Oh," Fiona had replied breathlessly.

"Was it good for you?"

Before Fiona could answer, Veronica's lips met hers. They kissed, Veronica's mouth still tasting rubbery from the blow job and tingling from the work. Fiona lifted her, spun her in a half-turn to press her back against the pillar, and guided the strap-on between her legs and into her as though she were hungry to accept it. Holding Veronica up, straddling her waist, even with the help of the pillar through every thrust, was exhausting, but clearly worth the effort as Veronica was well on her way to climax before Fiona's strength and energy even started to flag. She came screaming, riding hard, scraping her bare back against the cement pillar, gripping a handful of hair at the back of Fiona's head. Fiona had never seen her so lovely, so happy, and so alive. Before she'd even come down, as though life was the lone remaining half of an orange requiring harsh treatment to drain every last drop of juice, she shook Fiona to attention by the handle of her hair, and locked gazes. There was something wild and primal in Veronica's hazel eyes that had excited Fiona in ways she'd never felt. "I want to try anal," Veronica had said. Fiona's brain refused to process the request the first time, forcing Veronica to repeat herself. "I said, I want you to violate me with that thing—I've never done it, and I don't want to die without knowing if I like it or not."

"Can't you just assume it'll be painful and degrading?"

"Exactly my point!" Veronica had laughed as though the world, and Fiona in particular, tickled her. "When have I ever shied away from either of those things?"

Veronica had dismounted, turned to face the pillar, and bent at the waist. Fiona hadn't the slightest clue how to proceed. Veronica guided her through the process of using spit to lubricate, taking her time, and using a natural angle, which all led Fiona to believe the experiment had spent a lot of time between Veronica's ears before she found a sufficiently dire situation to bring it up. The pre-preparation that involved fingers, stretching, relaxing, and spit took on something of a virginal, sensual quality as Veronica was nervous and thus not interested in it ending right away, and Fiona was in no particular hurry as the act itself wouldn't be doing much for her and she was entirely possessed with the need to not hurt Veronica; after a good deal of very intimate stretching with the three longest fingers on Fiona's right hand, Veronica had declared herself ready. Fiona had followed the further instructions with all care, guiding the springy, red strap-on between the alluring curves of Veronica's ass, using every last drop of her spit possible to ease the process. Stoicism, which was something Veronica had in spades, prevented any verbal reaction from escaping until Fiona was slowly working the toy in and out, grasping the base with both hands for stability. "You're right," Veronica had groaned, "it's unpleasant." Fiona had offered to stop; Veronica told her there wasn't a chance in the world they were going to quit after how much effort it had taken to get the thing in there. She'd guided one of Fiona's hands to her waist, and told her to stop being a wuss about it. Veronica's own hand had found its way to her clit, giving herself a different context for the act with furious, urgent rubbing. Fiona took the demand with tentative care at first, losing a bit of her reticence when Veronica began pushing back against her. Her lover's legendary stoicism mixed a pained edge into her moans of pleasure, but without any other discernable discomfort, although her body told a different story, showing that whatever stimulation she was giving herself was clearly tempered by a fairly intense pain from what Fiona was doing. The red strap-on, though never fully entering Veronica's tight swirl, began sliding easier, and Fiona took that as a cue to increase the speed and depth of her thrusts, until she could feel the trembling, sweat-soaked, Veronica climaxing in a deeply intense and strangely muddled orgasm that left her visibly shaking, forehead rested against the pillar, wet blond hair clinging to her neck and shoulders. Fiona very slowly withdrew the strap-on from her in a wet sucking sound, accompanied by a hiss of pain from Veronica's lips.

"Are you okay?" Fiona had asked.

Veronica's response, which Fiona never forgot, "If you ever tell anyone I enjoyed that, I will kill you." There was an element of jest to it, mostly from the gentle slap of her own ass that Veronica added for effect, but the deeply embarrassed quiver in her voice told Fiona that Veronica had not only not expected to enjoy the act, she loathed herself for how much she'd enjoyed it.

Veronica turned slowly, her face a mask of pleasure with a strange lacing of shame. She caught Fiona's eyes—the primal shine to them had been satisfied. "Do you want to try?" Veronica had asked. Fiona didn't, although she only shook her head, struggling hard to keep any facial expression out of the mix that might indicate how much she didn't. "Good," Veronica sighed. "I could use some vanilla to clear my head." The reciprocity of filling out Fiona's list may have been provincial, but the emotional bond created through Veronica's list added a new level of intimacy that Fiona cherished, even if the sex itself was only athletic and a little rough.

As the sky began pinking with the coming dawn, reinforcements from two different Raven camps rolled back the Slark long before they were in any real danger. Fiona and Veronica were too busy with each other to join the fight.

Fiona returned to the present with a strange, sad longing for the closeness she'd shared with Veronica. They had been inseparable after Barstow. Their falling out, less than six months after the parking garage, took place at the edge of the burning wreckage of a train. Fiona had indeed threatened to kill Veronica if she followed. The statement hadn't severed all of Fiona's emotional nerves as she'd suspected, and secretly hoped, it would. Whatever else Veronica was, she was Fiona's first love. The strap-on, acting as a strange and lurid symbol of their past intimacy, wasn't given as a wanton gift, but Fiona couldn't divine exactly what it meant.

"You want me to…?" Fiona began.

"I want you to do what comes naturally to you, gunfighter."

Chapter 12
Feverish, famished, and frustrated

Fiona left the Lazy Ravens' brothel with a sack containing hundreds of the silver coins and the enormous strap-on from her past. She was rich, not because the coins had an inherent value, but because she knew Veronica would make them worth killing for within a month's time. That's what Veronica did: find desires, exploit them, and consolidate all the vices under her rule. Her Machiavellian approach to controlling a population was the norm in the Lazy Ravens, and Veronica was the best at setting up franchises. Before Veronica had come to Vegas to tame the town, it was Tombstone without Zeke's tenuous control. Methanol cults, slavers, drug dealers, Slark sympathizers, white supremacists, and roving marauders turned the former tourism Mecca into a perpetual war zone. Fiona joined the Ravens just to have a group to watch her back. Within six months of arriving in town, Veronica had brought the entire city of Las Vegas under Lazy Raven control, took over the slave trade and eradicated anyone who wouldn't be brought in line. Immediately after, she reintroduced money, taxes, racketeering, and government. Tombstone was looking to be a softer approach for Veronica—at least, Fiona hoped it wouldn't turn into the slaughter required to tame Vegas.

Fiona walked the streets again, head and heart full of conflicting feelings and thoughts, and weighed heavily with newfound wealth and an old friend. She nearly drew steel when she caught on that she was being followed. Her hand went to her gun, but her tail identified himself before she could jerk it and blow him out of his boots.

"Easy, Red," Danny said, "it's just me."

Fiona relaxed her posture, although her hand remained on the butt of her pistol. Danny emerged from the shadow between two trucks, hands held up, Padres hat turned backward to make his face clearly visible.

"What do you want?" Fiona asked with a little more acid than she intended.

"I saw you come out of the Lazy Raven Nest," Danny said. "That's what they're calling it, I guess." He stuffed his hands in his pants pockets and shrugged like the confused surfer boy she'd known years ago. "Do you think Veronica recognized me?"

Fiona slid her hand away from her gun and took the rest of the striking coil out of her stance. She sighed and shook her head. "I should have known you would put it together."

"My mom only raised three fools, and I wasn't one of them," Danny said with a boyish grin. "If you're making a play for anything, count me to back your hand. There's only a few of us left, but we all remember what you saved us from." Danny took a few steps closer to lower his voice to just above a whisper while still being heard. "I'm also starting to piece together that what you saved me from might also be starting here."

"Veronica says the Ravens are done with human trafficking," Fiona said.

"Maybe she was telling the truth, I mean, you know her better than I do," Danny said. "Do you think she was lying?"

"She can lie to me like breathing and I would never know the difference."

"All I know is the people that Zeke puts on the train to Vegas don't come back," Danny said. "Maybe train tickets back cost too much. Maybe they like it so much they stay. I don't know. I'm not about to hop a train and find out. I've got the wrong plumbing for a position of power and I'm not interested in bondage, if you catch my meaning."

Fiona snorted. "Welcome to the world I grew up in." She turned to walk away, although she only made it a few feet before Danny called after her.

"Are the rumors true?" Danny asked. "Are you the Fiona Bishop from the Victoria's Secret catalogue?"

Fiona stopped dead in her tracks. She thought it was a real secret, something only someone as smart and stalker-ish as Gieo would figure out; she even thought of saying something trite and hackneyed along the lines of 'that Fiona died a long time ago,' but she didn't think she could keep a straight face. She looked over her shoulder and gave Danny a sultry half-smile reminiscent of her modeling days. At twenty-six, her modeling career would have been long over even if the Slark hadn't invaded—what did she care if Danny knew.

"The one and only," she said, walking away.

Gieo was packing up her work for the day when Fiona finally strolled through the saloon's swinging doors. It took everything in her not to leap from her seat to run to her; then, everything in her failed to hold her back, and she went ahead and vaulted the table.

"Are you okay?" Gieo asked. "You've been gone all day and I was worried. Not that you'd get hurt, but that you'd shoot more people on my behalf. You look half-starved and sunburned. Have you eaten today? Did you drink any water?"

"No, I guess I haven't had anything since breakfast." Fiona took off her hat and wiped her forehead with the back of her forearm.

Gieo reached up and touched Fiona's forehead with her hand as soon as it was done being wiped, but before Fiona could replace the hat. "You're burning up," she said. "Were you out in the sun all day?"

"I suppose."

"You've probably got heat stroke." Gieo guided Fiona to a chair, took her hat and sunglasses from her, and began fanning the gunfighter with both. "We have to get you cooled down." Gieo knelt at Fiona's feet and began pulling off her boots.

"What are you doing?"

"You have two options, but both of them involve you getting naked," Gieo said. "You can do it yourself voluntarily, or I can do it against your will, but it's going to happen."

"Aren't you in a frisky mood?"

"Irrelevant," Gieo said. "You wouldn't survive having sex with me in the condition you're in."

Fiona had to admit that was probably true. Her head had started pounding before she even walked in the doors and she was getting a serious case of the spins just sitting. With Gieo's help, Fiona managed to stumble up to her room where Gieo deposited her on the bed and raced around the room to open both windows and retrieve water from the jug next to the nightstand.

"I made fifty of those little silver coins this evening," Gieo said as she busied herself undressing Fiona in the most unceremonious way. Fiona, who had gone limp at some point, just nodded. "Apparently that's only eight gallons of fuel though."

"This wasn't how I pictured this," Fiona said as Gieo pulled off her pants. The cool air on her legs felt good and she began to wonder if maybe the pilot wasn't right about the heat stroke.

"I can tell," Gieo said with a little laugh. "You're not wearing underwear, Lady Firebox. At least I know your carpet matches your drapes."

"I don't have a carpet," Fiona said, trying to laugh through a dry throat.

Gieo inspected the modest amount of almost perfectly straight, flat, red hair on Fiona's mound. It was true. Even in a natural state, Fiona was far smoother than fuzzy and in no places bristly or bushy. "You've got me there," Gieo said. "I have to tame mine or be ready to braid it."

"I'd like to see that."

"Which part? The taming or the braiding?"

"First one, then the other."

Gieo laughed and shook her head. "I think the fever is making you delirious." She pulled off Fiona's t-shirt before depositing her back on the bed. Gieo looked a little sad and contemplative as she stared down at Fiona's naked form causing Fiona to curl around herself in embarrassment.

"Fuck, you don't have to look at me like that," Fiona said.

"You're not taking care of yourself." Gieo knelt beside the bed, dipped her hand in the pitcher of water, and began rubbing her damp hand along Fiona's back. "I'm worried about you."

"You and everyone else."

"I'm not everyone else," Gieo said. "I'm your…something."

Fiona relaxed a little, allowing Gieo access to more of her skin. The water felt amazing and Gieo's hands were delightfully soft. "That tears it, though," Gieo said. "I'm doing all your cooking from now on, and you're going to eat what I say, drink when I say, and not get heat stroke again unless you have written permission from me."

"You can cook?" Fiona asked.

"Oh, sweetie, you'd be hard pressed to find something I can't do." Gieo gave her a little wink and dipped her hand back in the pitcher.

♠♣♥♦

After a long night of keeping Fiona's skin properly wetted, fanned, and cooled, Gieo was awoken by the early morning sun warming her as she slept, half on the floor, head and arms on the bed. Fiona was finally sleeping comfortably after fitfully tossing and turning all night. Fiona had drunk enough water that Gieo thought her stomach might start pooching out, but had never once needed to use the bathroom. Gieo felt Fiona's forehead and found it normal on the side of cool. She closed the windows, pulled the shades, and draped several blankets over the curtain rods to block out all but the most stubborn of light.

Gieo made for the door with the nearly empty pitcher in hand when Fiona awoke and rolled over to face her. A little squeak from the mattress springs stopped Gieo at the door.

"Where are you going?" Fiona croaked. In the dimly lit room, still bleary-eyed and frizzy-haired from a rough night of sleep, she looked far more innocent and sweet than Gieo knew her to be.

"I was going to get you some more water, make breakfast, and see about earning some more of this new money we just got saddled with," Gieo whispered, although she wasn't sure why she was whispering as the only sleeping person in the room was awake and talking.

"Don't bother with the money," Fiona said, rolling onto her back. With her toe, she nudged the bag she'd been carrying the night before, nearly knocking it off the foot of the bed where she'd set it. "Veronica gave me more money than we could use and told me I could have more whenever I wanted."

"Oh," Gieo said. Her mind immediately kicked into high gear. Fiona had spoken with Veronica, exchanged something for money, and had an open invitation to return for another exchange at any point. Of course she did. They must have been friends, good friend, girlfriends even, on-again/off-again sex partners, lovers of epic proportions whose tale could only be captured in classic poems or sappy songs written and sung by multiple Grammy winners! The only role left to Gieo in this play was the jilted, foolish girl who hurls herself into the Grand Canyon as a romantic, but ultimately futile, gesture to prove her unrequited love. The only songs sung about her would be depressing ballads about how she deluded herself into…

"Where did you go just then?" Fiona asked. "You drifted off and kind of stared into space."

"The Grand Canyon," Gieo said. "I'll go make you breakfast."

"Veronica wants to talk to you."

"What about?"

"If I had to guess, I'd say airships."

Gieo took the cryptic message downstairs to the kitchen, filled the pitched with the hand-pumped well water, and set to work looking for something worthwhile to cook. Mitch's new kitchen boy, Bond-O, a great oaf of a man with only three fingers on his left hand, was busy rattling pans and burning what might have once been identifiable as food when she walked in.

"Hey, Go!" Bond-O shouted and waved with a three-fingered hand covered in cornmeal based pancake batter.

She had her doubts about Bond-O's capacity to learn cooking beyond what he had already picked up from baking mud pies as a child, but she would have to try. First things first, she had to get a hairnet on the wild mane of black hair on his head and the equally erratic beard he'd clearly tried to trim at some point using garden sheers—with mixed results from the looks of it.

"I hate to say this, but we're going to have to be kitchen buddies for awhile until the food improves around here," Gieo said with a weary sigh.

"Bond-Go buddies!" the man-child shouted in delight with a big thumbs-up. He popped his batter covered thumb in his mouth, bit down hard, and yelped a little before dissolving into giggles. "Mitts were my cook buddy for awhile before the knife-ccident."

Gieo had no idea why Mitch, or 'Mitts', thought Bond-O would make a suitable cook, but the old bartender seemed to be the only man in town with patience enough to find a use for him. Rumors were that the big lug was a refugee from a state mental hospital, most likely suffering from extreme developmental delay. Having the mind of a five-year-old trapped in the body of a Hell's Angel enforcer seemed a particularly cruel irony to Gieo, although hadn't apparently dampened Bond-O's spirits. At least, she noted with no small amount of surprise, someone had pounded a highly fastidious nature into the gentle giant. He was the cleanest Tombstone resident, aside from Gieo, and still occasionally gave her a run for her money in the neat and tidy department. He'd taken to sleeping in a shed outback, which was quickly cleaned to a shiny polish and decorated in enough brightly colored flower prints and pictures to rival any little old lady's sitting room. Watching him beat eggs with his three-fingered fist, she couldn't help but wonder what tragedy had befallen him before Mitch found him on the side of the road, petting a cow skull, and singing Cher's greatest hits to himself. For better or worse, she was going to be his second kitchen buddy until a knife-ccident or a sudden epiphany of culinary genius on his part separated them.

After several hours, and several near misses with accidents of more than just the knife variety, Gieo had managed to pull together something resembling food from the meager means provided. Bond-O staples like sawdust, rat droppings, and what might very well be fiberglass insulation shredded extra-fine were removed from the menu entirely to be replaced by actual food, which Gieo had to send the oversized fry cook to purchase around town with the fifty coins she'd earned the day before. She returned to Fiona's room by midmorning with a plate of bacon, eggs, stewed tomatoes, and cactus strips in southwest chili sauce.

Fiona awoke at Gieo's return, but didn't seem nearly as interested in the food as she was in the jug of water. She drank greedily and rolled over to go back to sleep. Gieo set the steaming plate on the nightstand and swatted Fiona hard on the rear end with a satisfying thwack. Fiona rolled over without much of a response.

"You're going to eat and you're going to thank me for my astounding patience on your behalf."

Fiona squinted at the food and sniffed the air. She crawled across the bed to get a better look. "That looks like actual food."

"Yeah, and it was neither cheap, nor easy."

"I'm not that hungry," Fiona said.

"You better get hungry, because that food is going inside you one way or the other."

Fiona drew herself up to a sitting position in the bed and pulled the plate onto her lap. She ate quickly without real recognition that the food actually tasted like food. The Tombstone diet of utter shit was a source of pride for most of the hunters; they saw it as a test of their toughness to eat and survive on what would kill a lesser being. Gieo had pointed out how patently stupid that was, but Fiona had only shrugged and said that's just the way it was. Gieo was just about done with Fiona's shrugs and 'whatever's; from then on out, Fiona's apathy would be met with aggressiveness. The food vanished in a matter of minutes. Fiona tossed the plate aside and let out a long, loud burp.

Gieo retrieved the plate and headed for the door.

"Where are you going?" Fiona asked.

"To shower, to sleep, to walk out into the desert never to be heard from again…I haven't really decided."

"Thank you for breakfast." Fiona scooted back in the bed, clearing a little space. "Now come cuddle with me and take a well-deserved nap."

Gieo nearly burst into frustrated tears on the spot. She walked to the bed with mincing steps, pulled off her riding boots, and crawled into place beside Fiona. "Did the mighty gunfighter and huntress just say 'cuddle'?"

Fiona wrapped herself around Gieo in an intimate way they hadn't really ever gotten around to in the week they'd shared the bed upon Gieo's arrival. The comforting position of breathing in the smell of Fiona's skin with her face nestled under Fiona's chin nearly put Gieo into a blissful sleep on contact. Fiona gently stroked the back of Gieo's neck with the very tips of her fingers in idle passes.

"If you tell anyone I said cuddle," Fiona whispered. "I'll have to kill them."

"So only people I don't like?" Gieo whispered back.

"Exactly."

Chapter 13
The history of Vegas chess

By early afternoon, even the makeshift curtains constructed of blankets couldn't hold out the heat of the day. Gieo awoke and reluctantly left Fiona's embrace. Fiona stirred when she slipped away, but rolled back to sleep shortly after. Gieo checked Fiona's forehead to make sure the fever hadn't risen again. Thankfully, the gunfighter seemed to be thermal regulating on her own. Gieo pulled on her boots and slipped downstairs to seek out food for Fiona.

Bond-O and Mitch were trying to work the kitchen together through a lulled lunch crowd. With the hunters free to come and go as they pleased, the town had gone back to being nearly empty during the day. Sandwiches appeared to be on the menu, although with the whimsical approach Gieo had come to know as commonplace with Bond-O's cooking. Anything he had two of could create the outsides while anything that couldn't be counted on to hold together as an outside piece was relegated to filling. Some of the sandwiches seemed like reasonably creative attempts, while others were patently ridiculous. Gieo took two of the pancake sandwiches. The first had a filling of tomatoes and apples, while the second was stuffed with slow-cooked chicken pieces, chilies, and pickled okra. The other, less appealing options seemed to be two slabs of unidentifiable, undercooked meat surrounding cactus strips and ancient powdered donuts all held together with peanut butter.

As she was departing, she waved to the enthusiastically learning Bond-O and smiled; his food contained actual food now at least. The thought occurred to her that Bond-O was a little like Fiona in that both of them were far better off in the new world order. She wondered how many of the survivors of the invasion and the cataclysm perpetrated by man in retaliation were somehow better off than they'd been before civilization crumbled. She was happy that Bond-O would never again know the medicated stupor of a mental hospital and that Fiona could find a useful outlet for her chaos tics. Still, something about the thought nagged at her.

Until she'd seen the upside of the invasion and fall of man for so many, Gieo hadn't ever really thought about exactly what she'd missed out on. The summer the Slark invaded, she was preparing for college at MIT. The world was opening up to her in beautiful ways that spoke of a life on the cusp of blossoming. Now, she was teaching a mental patient how to cook to avoid malnutrition, nursing a dangerously violent woman back to health in hopes of developing a relationship with her, and attaching electric toothbrushes to tea kettles as her primary means of support. The realization settled a sullen cloud over her. She'd had to be a survivor on her own for so long, seeing opportunity in catastrophe for lack of any other option, that she'd never really let herself wallow in what was actually stolen from her by the Slark. She'd grieved for her parents, for her favorite TV shows, for the pop singers she'd liked that were no doubt dead, but she'd never mourned for the loss of the person she was meant to be.

Back in the room, Gieo found Fiona already trying to get dressed. She set the plate of food on the nightstand again, and began undoing all the work Fiona had managed in clothing herself.

"I need to go hunting," Fiona protested.

"The sack of coins at the end of the bed says you don't *need* to do that again anytime soon," Gieo said.

"Okay, fine," Fiona grumbled, "I *want* to go hunting."

"I *wanted* to go to MIT, marry a Wellesley girl, graduate with honors, and work for NASA, but that didn't exactly happen either! So fuck what you want—my list is longer!"

Fiona took off her own shirt and slid back into bed, watching Gieo with wide eyes.

"I'm sorry for snapping at you," Gieo murmured. "I'm going to go get cleaned up and see what Veronica wants." She made it to the door before Fiona spoke.

"I know you've made sacrifices," Fiona said. She didn't say anything else before she started eating, but somehow just hearing Fiona admit as much made Gieo feel a little better.

Gieo took a quick sponge bath on the roof. She dressed in her black and purple saloon girl dress with the shiny, tight top and flowing, ruffled skirt. As with most of her clothes, she'd modified the dress with leather strips to hold widgets, hooks, and necessary gear-workings to have it interface with an airship. She'd actually worn the dress while piloting her second dirigible—it was something of a good luck charm, and it left her shoulders and chest bare in an appealing way. She added her leather top hat, and gave Ramen a pat on the head before heading out.

"Have you thought about a puppy?" Ramen asked in parting.

"It's on my list."

The streets were clear and eerily quiet. Dust eddies, kicked up by the swirling desert ground-breezes danced across Gieo's path. Aside from her own, knee-high Victorian lace-up boots crunching across the remains of asphalt and creaky, metal signs shifting in the wind, there was nothing to differentiate Tombstone from a ghost town. She couldn't put her finger on it, nothing more than a crawling feeling at the back of her neck, but something told her to look over her shoulder before turning the corner at the end of the street. Four cultist men, moving as quietly as the dust eddies themselves, were coming up on her quickly.

She turned the corner and ran.

In the dress, with the high-heel boots, she knew she wasn't going to get away from the swift-moving scarecrows, but she could avoid their limited sight. She crossed the next street up, ran a few buildings down, and ducked into a narrow alleyway between two buildings. The dark, fetid air was several degrees cooler than the street. The smell of dried motor oil and mildew was suddenly overpowered by the stench of unwashed human flesh. Two of the milky-eyed cultists stepped across the shaded alleyway entrance, hearing, rather than seeing Gieo as she tried to slink back into the gap so narrow it could only be walked down single-file. She'd selected the alley poorly and her heart sank when she felt a chain-link fence press against her back. A quick glance over her shoulder told her the fence was not only un-climbable, but, even if she did manage to get over the barbwire-topped, ten foot tall fence, she would just be in a second enclosed two-foot wide gap between the fence and another building.

As little as she knew about fighting, she knew that was her last resort, and so she tried to look as fearsome as possible by crouching and getting into something of a karate stance; she desperately hoped the cultists were foolish enough to believe all Asians were secretly ninjas, Shaolin monks, or karate masters. Before they could even decide who was to go down the alley first, both cultists dissolved into pulpy red slurry from hips to chest. Gunfire, more hollow and thunderous than the metallic shriek and explosion of Fiona's gun, registered, but almost seemed unrelated to Gieo as she couldn't see the shooter. The cultists looked as surprised as she did at the sudden transformation of their midsections into ground meat. Two more powerful gun shots and two more bodies falling let Gieo know whoever had come to her rescue had also finished off the other two cultists following her.

Her mouth was dry and her hands shaky. Slowly, she crept toward the front of the alley, hoping whoever took down the cultists didn't do so with the intention of kidnapping her for themselves. She half-expected to see Fiona in the street; she'd gotten so used to the gunfighter's timely interventions that another would have felt routine. Instead, strolling across the mouth of the gap, brazen as you please, removing two spent shells from the breach of a double barrel, ten-gauge shotgun, was Veronica, wearing a wedding dress modified into prostitution appropriate attire.

"If it isn't Fiona's lovely little pet," Veronica said in her smooth, practiced Southern belle persona. She shouldered the smoking shotgun, cocked her hip to one side, and smiled like an armed and dangerous blushing bride. "I was just about to pay you a friendly visit. Come take a stroll with me."

Gieo gingerly stepped over the felled cultists, shuddering when she felt her boots squish into…she had no idea what it was, but it was red, spongy, and smelled horrible. Veronica offered her free hand to help guide Gieo through the slippery mess, and Gieo gladly took it.

"I'm getting a little sick of being rescued," Gieo muttered.

"If you'd like, I could teach you to fight," Veronica said. When Gieo was clear of the mess, Veronica linked arms with her and guided her to walk down the middle of the street like two old friends on the way to afternoon tea. "I taught Fiona and she's done mighty fine for herself."

"I'm not all that comfortable with violence against people," Gieo said.

Veronica giggled in a girlish titter, squeezing herself even closer to Gieo's side. "Aren't you just the sweetest thing!" she exclaimed. "Why would these blind gentleman want to do you harm?"

"They think I'm the devil and want to burn me at the stake."

"I wouldn't be surprised to find out a precious little thing like yourself had the devil in you, but to think you're the devil incarnate seems like a mistake only blind men could make." She winked as though it were reflex. The conspiratorial nature of the exchange sent a shiver through Gieo.

The affectation, which was ridiculously charming and only amplified by the virginally sexy wedding dress, lost a bit of its hypnotic power for Gieo after seeing Veronica obliterate four people with the limbered shotgun she had slung over her shoulder as though it were nothing more hazardous than a parasol. The strength and dangerous edge that Fiona wore like a shield, armor, and club to bludgeon with, was present in Veronica, Gieo could sense it just beneath the surface, but she wore it like a dirty secret, slutty lingerie concealed beneath pedestrian clothing, kept under wraps for special occasions. Gieo surprised herself a little in the realization that she found both very different types of dangerous women compelling and sexy.

The closer they got to the Raven Nest, the more of a shine the town began to boast. Cleanliness and a feminine touch radiated in ever-increasing waves off the brothel. The nearest few businesses and occupied buildings took to the Ravens' influence readily; the positive nature of the influence was undeniable. Men, gentlemen really, were dressed cleanly, tipped their hats to the passing women, and spoke in cordial tones with one another. An infection of civility had found root in Tombstone, and the epicenter of the spread was the brothel.

"Fiona was always a knife looking from someone to hone the blade with an edge," Veronica explained as they walked. "I supplied the edge and a purpose to the cutting, but her morality drove her to other, less ambiguous, endeavors and I'm sorry to say it created a divide between us that couldn't be easily mended."

"Tombstone seems like an odd haven for someone with morality," Gieo said.

"Make no mistake, vice and turpitude exists in spades here, but there is no ambiguity to it. The four dead men divided into eight parts half a block behind us are a fine example—lousy morals, but their intentions were clear."

Finally reaching the Raven Nest, Gieo couldn't have imagined something so opulent and feminine could even exist anywhere anymore, never mind that it had sprung up in the middle of Tombstone in a little over 24 hours. Women and services were advertised. More than just prostitution, simple pleasures like massages, burlesque shows, drinks, food, and a dance hall were all available for the right price; more decadent pleasures like spa treatments, medical services, and sexual favors were listed for astronomical prices that Gieo couldn't imagine anyone in town could afford yet. The situation, combined with the needs of men, did nothing to dampen spirits as many sought out the simple comforts of female companionship even if it was little more than a dance or a shared drink. Men left happy with contented smiles on their cleanly shaven faces and printed photographs to remember their visit even if they were never touched in the process.

"This isn't at all what I expected," Gieo whispered.

Veronica tittered again and gave Gieo's arm a reassuring squeeze. "The world was ruled by men because they were the first ones to climb to the top; knowing what we know about the world they created when given that chance, why on earth would we let them do it again?" Veronica handed off her shotgun to one of the girls on their way through the front door. The other women, charming song birds all, shot flirty glances, kind waves, and warm smiles in Gieo's direction as they passed through the pleasant smelling halls of the Raven Nest. Gieo had to admit, if this was a picture of the world ruled by women, she couldn't have agreed more.

Their final destination was a sitting room on the back half of the courthouse. It was likely at some point a cafeteria in its original incarnation, but had since undergone a transformation into a hookah lounge, entertainment hub, and tea parlor. Men sat in mixed company with women, joking laughing, sharing pots of tea and pulls from bubbling hookah pipes all while a string quartette of three beautiful women played soft strains of Vivaldi. Veronica ushered Gieo to a reserved table beneath a window, overlooking what had formerly been a parking lot, but which was quickly being turned into a garden of some kind. Something seemed off about the garden at first until she realized the nature of the plants being tended; she didn't know a whole lot about drugs, but she'd gleaned from news programs what marijuana and poppy plants looked like. Superficially, the organization looked squeaky clean, but she imagined many of the hookahs were loaded with hashish or raw opium.

"I have questions for you, as I'm sure you have some for me," Veronica said, folding her hands delicately in her lap. "Please, feel free to start with one of yours to get things rolling. I am nothing if not an open book."

Gieo mirrored Veronica's posture, pulling her knees together, tucking her feet beneath her chair, with her hands folded in her lap. "Why is Fiona called the Red Bishop or Red by some? I thought it was just a hair color thing, but it seems like there's more to it than that."

"It was a hair color thing, in a manner of speaking," Veronica explained. "Our units in Las Vegas were designated by chess board pieces. We had many divisions that I won't bore you with; suffice it to say, red was a division color, and Fiona was placed in it based, in part, on her hair color, but mostly due to her violent outbursts. She rose quickly from pawn to knight to rook and finally to bishop where she likely would have stayed had she not left our organization."

"The parting due to the aforementioned moral ambiguity," Gieo said. "Why would she have stayed a bishop though? Why not promote her to king or queen eventually?"

"There are no kings in the Lazy Ravens; if you've played chess you know how wholly useless Kings are, and that appears to be true of society as well. The positions of queens are difficult to come by and require a versatility Fiona simply doesn't possess. Besides, the Red Queen, who was the only one above Fiona, would have had to die, and Carolyn just isn't the type." A serving girl came around to their table, delivered a pot of tea, two tea cups of fine china, and a small tray of cut star fruit. Gieo almost didn't recognize the exotic fruit it had been so long since she'd seen it.

"What position do you hold?"

"I am the White Queen." Veronica poured a rose scented serving of tea into Gieo's cup first, before filling her own. "White is the offensive side of the board in chess, thus, I am the colonizer while the Black Queen defends our holdings."

"I was vice president of the chess club in high school," Gieo said, immediately feeling silly for comparing an unimportant high school club to the ruling structure of a new world order.

"You'll have to favor me with a game at some point," Veronica said, seemingly unconcerned with any slight the comment might have carried. "I would like to get to know every little thing about you, my dear. The picture Fiona painted was most flattering, if not hastily sketched. The broad brush strokes indicated you are a scientist."

"Physics mostly," Gieo said, "although I'm a quick study of most things mechanical and electrical."

"You are also a pilot?" Veronica took a slow, lingering bite of a piece of star fruit, nibbling down one of the points in delicate bites that completely engrossed Gieo's attention. "That sounds very exciting."

"Dirigibles…airships," Gieo said, "although I would like to put together something faster moving eventually."

"And I would like to help you. Fiona also mentioned that you and I are of a like mind in what should be done with the Slark." Veronica leaned forward a little, giving Gieo more than a passing glance at her cleavage. It was an obvious flirtatious move she'd seen Veronica work with Danny, but there was something undeniably attractive about the posture for whoever it was focused on. "Zeke isn't forward thinking enough for the position of authority he has. I would like to see this township governed by a slightly more ambitious, decidedly female, figure. I would like to push the Slark out of Los Angeles. And, I would like an air force to do it. I was led to believe you might share some of these desires."

Gieo nearly choked on her tea at hearing almost exactly her plan mirrored in Veronica's words. Something in the back of Gieo's head screamed that it had to be too good to be true, to proceed with caution, but, gazing into Veronica's shimmering hazel eyes, she wanted more than anything to believe.

"How do you…I mean, do anything, hold Vegas? Take new places? Attack the Slark? Set up colonies?"

Veronica laid her hand on Gieo's knee and smiled, rolling her eyes as if there was such an obvious answer that the question could only have existed to prompt the response at the right time. "With an army, of course," Veronica said. "The world was left with soldiers, hundreds of thousands of them, without any chain of command, any structure, or any paycheck. Most soldiers are broken, tamed horses, in desperate need of organization and command; we give them what they crave and the pay they deserve. We have soldiers from as far away as Cuba, Canada, Mexico, and El Salvador fighting for the Lazy Ravens, although the primary backbone of our forces is still, and likely always will be, American."

"A few hundred?"

Veronica shook her head. "The last numbers I saw put our force in the neighborhood of fifty thousand."

"How is that even possible? Just to feed and organize an army that big you would have to…"

"…have a government? We do. Taxes, healthcare, regulations, elections, sanitation, water works, foreign affairs, everything you'd imagine a good government should do." Veronica motioned over one of the women at the serving bar, who seemed to be waiting for the summons. The woman grabbed a rolled piece of paper around the size of a wall poster and walked it over to the table. "There are always the ridiculous types that were thrilled to see the government go, and we encourage them to exercise their 'rugged individualism' on whatever worthless piece of dirt they want to go die alone on, but the vast majority of people figured out very quickly that society was the only thing keeping them from a short, miserable life ending in a violent, often disease-riddled, death. These people, the pragmatists, the enlightened, are the ones we welcome, and they live much longer, happier lives as part of something greater. Humans are social creatures and we work best when we work together." On the final two words of the speech, the woman with the rolled paper, unfurled what she carried to show Gieo a redrawn map of North America. Huge swaths of land in the North East, New York, Boston, Washington D.C., the Great Lakes, and surroundings areas were blacked out—lands purged of all life in the great cataclysm that had finally brought down the Slark's technology, destroying nearly everything humanity had as well in the process. The south was redrawn in red as the Confederate States. The Midwest was carved into fragmented pieces, pulled together as the Omaha Pact. In the mountains, the western states, Nevada, Colorado, Utah, Idaho, parts of eastern Oregon and Washington, on up into Montana and Canada was labeled Raven territory. Texas and Old Mexico appeared to be under Mexican control, although in nothing as solid as a country. Arizona, New Mexico, and the surrounding deserts were all labeled Barrier City States. The entire west coast, with an epicenter in Los Angeles where Gieo always suspected the Slark's mother ship had crashed, was labeled Slark territory.

"This is North America as it stands now," Veronica explained. "Mexico was once an ally to the Ravens, a partner to rely on, but they have fallen to disease, and look to be taken soon by the Slark if something isn't done. The Omaha Pact feeds both us and the Confederate States—we are not friends with the Confederates. They are the patriarchy of old unified under the same rebel flag of Dixie from the Civil War. The only thing that remains to be seen is what the Barrier City States will choose."

Gieo could see the Ravens' interest in the Barrier City States. If the Slark did take Mexico, their capitol of Las Vegas would be nearly surrounded on three sides with only Tombstone and Tempe to watch its back. "I don't understand…" Gieo lied. The world was recovering, well beyond what she'd expected, and her little dreams of flying airships against the teeth of the line felt frivolous in comparison to the nation building Veronica was proposing. Gieo suddenly felt like she was standing on the precipice dropping off into the sea or at the forefront of an uncharted world; everything was so much bigger and more frightening than she ever knew. Still, she didn't want to let on that she knew Veronica's true intentions. "What do you need from me?"

"If what Fiona says is true, you could be the mother of the first air force in the new world," Veronica said. "We need you, Gieo. Humanity needs you."

Chapter 14
Mistakes of identity

Veronica sent Gieo on her way with a sack containing at least as many coins as she'd given Fiona. In addition to the coins, Gieo was also given a list of things she might consider doing to ingratiate herself to the Lazy Ravens; most of the items involved making headway on finding pilots, building airships, and turning Tombstone's opinion positive in regards to the Ravens.

Gieo was so busy reading the list she almost didn't notice Zeke storming his way up to the old courthouse. She managed to jump out of the way at the last moment. Zeke didn't seem to recognize her in the saloon girl dress, glassing over her as just another one of the women lounging in front of the brothel. From the clenched fists at his sides and determined lean to his steps, Gieo could easily deduce he wasn't there to take part in relaxation services. As frightening as Zeke normally was, Gieo assumed his manners would have to change in Veronica's company if he wanted to walk back out.

Stephanie, one of the younger girls with a shock of bright pink dyed hair dangling over her face, was to be Gieo's escort back to the saloon on the off chance more cultists were on the lookout for the Asian she-devil. Why the cultists focused on her rather than the three dozen Lazy Ravens was beyond Gieo, and, quite frankly, seemed a little single-minded. Stephanie was a less interesting walking partner than Veronica, apparently more concerned with bitching about Tombstone than actual conversation. She linked arms with Gieo, but did so only out of a sense of duty, keeping her free hand on the Uzi dangling from the shoulder strap at her side. Gieo felt safe, knowing full well Stephanie wouldn't have been chosen if she didn't know how to use the compact machinegun, but Gieo quickly wished Veronica had personally walked her home, if only for the charm factor.

The walk went without incident, and Stephanie took her leave with little more than a nod and an 'it's been fun.' Dinner, for better or worse, actually smelled edible when Gieo walked in through the swinging doors. She began to wonder if Bond-O might be something of a savant or at least a quicker study than she'd given him credit for. She poked her head inside the kitchen to find him busy at the great, black stove, throwing mountains of ingredients into a bubbling cauldron of stew. His immediate concern was stirring in the contents of an ancient bag of jelly beans. As odd as the pile of items next to the stew pot were, they all seemed to be more or less edible, so Gieo decided to let things alone.

"Looking good, Bond-O," she said.

"Mitts have another knife-ccident," Bond-O explained. "Told me to make stew alone. Bond-O was really sorry though."

"Maybe Mitch is just knife-ccident prone," Gieo said with a smile. "When it's ready, can you send up two bowls to Fiona's room?"

"Bond-Go!" he exclaimed with a thumbs up on his three-fingered hand.

Gieo checked Fiona's room only to find the gunfighter not at home. She'd passed her car on the way in, which meant she hadn't gone hunting. Gieo headed to the roof to see if Ramen had seen her, but instead found Fiona at the edge of the roof, beneath the patio umbrella, watching the video feed from the cultist compound. Fiona looked concerned by something. Her gun hand rested on the side of her holster, idly tapping her fingers against the leather in a nervous tic she didn't appear to be aware of.

"Is everything okay?" Gieo asked.

Fiona snapped her head around. Her hand went from tapping to gripping the gun's handle. She relaxed when she saw Gieo. "No," Fiona said through clenched teeth. "The cultists are arming themselves."

"With what? Sharp points on their canes?"

"Guns and Molotov cocktails."

Gieo jogged across the roof to get a better look at what Fiona was talking about. Sure enough, in low-definition black and white, there the cultists were, stockpiling assault rifles and pistols alongside bottles with rags dangling from their tops. As far as nonsensical, insane methanol drinking behavior went, this had to take the cake.

"The last thing this town needs is a couple hundred, half-blind lunatics spraying bullets and hurling firebombs," Gieo muttered.

"I tried to get a hold of Zeke to give him a heads up, but Rawlins said he was out."

"I saw him going into the Raven Nest," Gieo said. "He looked angry."

"Maybe he already knows."

"It looked more like an anger meant for Veronica than a general displeasure with the world at large."

Fiona tore her attention away from the screen where she'd been cataloguing weapon numbers, types, and location. She glanced up to find Gieo leaning forward, one hand on the arm of the lawn chair and the other across the back. The tight-fitting top of her dress had pushed her modest breasts up into a few fingers worth of cleavage. Fiona decided she was more of a quality than quantity type when it came to breasts; Gieo might not have much, but what she did have was pure perfection.

Gieo caught on the gunfighter's adjusted gaze and leaned forward even further. "Do you think they might be hiding some guns in there too?" she said with a wry smirk.

"If you're going to lean over with those things in my face, you can't get irritated when I look at them," Fiona grumbled.

"Who's irritated?" Gieo laughed. "Look, touch, lick, fondle, whatever. The collar I'm wearing might be for show, but I thought I was pretty clear in letting you know I was fine with it meaning possession for real. You're the only one holding you back as of late."

"What if I said I was done holding back?"

"I would say it was about damn time."

Fiona grabbed Gieo around the waist, spun her once, and landed Gieo across her lap. Gieo giggled in spite of herself, and draped her arms over Fiona's shoulders when she came to rest comfortably on the gunfighter's lap. Fiona leaned up and kissed Gieo with an urgent sweetness when Gieo expected rougher treatment. The softness of the kiss, the warmth of the embrace, and natural feeling of sitting on Fiona's lap all combined to melt every nerve in Gieo's body. There were no affectations with Fiona; she was what she was—Gieo really started to like that about her. Fiona's attention left the kiss. Her lips followed, making their way down Gieo's neck, kissing along her exposed collar bones, and finally leaning her back a little to kiss across the top of her modest cleavage. Gieo's skin burned under the kisses; the heat of desire only spread with Fiona's hot breath, pushing the wildfire throughout Gieo's body. She wanted Fiona to have her, right then, right there on the roof, and she couldn't be bothered to care if anyone saw or heard what they were doing.

"Horses, boss!" Ramen came roaring across the top of the roof, his twin propellers kicking up the dust that had collected on the scant remaining inventory.

"Mother fucker!" Gieo shouted in frustration. "I'm already working on getting you a puppy—there's no way you're getting a horse until I see how well you do with a dog."

"Not for me, boss," Ramen said, completely unfazed by the cursing or angry tone to Gieo's voice. "Horses are getting unloaded from the train."

Fiona responded this time. She lifted Gieo off her lap, leapt from the lawn chair, and scooped up the telescope. She ran to the far edge of the roof and looked east toward the rail station. Not only was there another train only days after the first, it was a different train, and it was indeed unloading horses along with another two dozen Lazy Raven ladies. They looked to only be about halfway through a very lengthy process that might stretch on for several hours more.

"I think we know why Zeke was so angry," Fiona said. "The Ravens just broke his monopoly on transportation."

Following the horses turned out to be superficially a simple task. This completely shattered when they were strung together, mounted, and the whole lot rode off with a couple of wagons hauling the tack and hay behind. Keeping up on foot would be a difficult prospect and driving would be over obvious as Fiona was fairly certain the trail her car left could be seen from space. The horses would have to be tracked after dark with the help of Ramen.

Back in the saloon, they found two dozen agitated hunters with Danny as their spokesman. If there were a good half of the cantankerous lot, they were the ones. Something felt off to Fiona, but not in the terms of a lynch mob. Danny came away from the group with twenty-five sets of eyes following him.

"We've got a problem," Danny said.

"More than a few if you've been paying attention," Fiona replied. "What do you have to add to the pot?"

"Zeke came out of the Raven Nest beat to shit," Danny said. "I don't know why he went in there and I don't know why things turned south, but they took their time teaching him a lesson he wasn't eager to learn."

"Shit," Fiona muttered.

"Normally, he'd have the hunters over there to take care of business, but he doesn't have the clout he once did, and getting jack-rolled by a bunch of prostitutes doesn't help his case much," Danny said. One of the other men, Fiona couldn't remember his name, but she assumed Gieo knew it, came over and nudged Danny in the arm. "Me and the boys, we've been talking. We're thinking this new progress is getting hobbled by Zeke's greed. We're thinking maybe you ought to take over as mayor."

"Zeke is a dangerous, wounded animal right now," Fiona said. "He's not going to be predictable or rational again anytime soon, especially not if Rawlins saw you all come in here, and there's no doubt he did."

"There's another problem," Gieo said.

"The cultists…" Fiona began.

"No, not that, well, yes, that, but also fuel prices," Gieo said. "Zeke's fucking you all over with the new system. It takes a little fractional math to figure it out, he picked difficult numbers to cross multiply without a calculator on purpose, but it works out to a pretty big hike—I don't think he counted on anyone figuring out until it was too late."

This news, more than anything else Gieo could have said, set a fire under the gathered men; if they weren't Fiona's men before, they certainly were then. There were a few comments about Zeke's reign needing to end, that he'd held the keys to the pumps for too long, and a few less constructive comments about Zeke's personal habits and appearance.

"There's also a problem brewing with the Hawkins House," Fiona said to quiet the men. "They're arming for something big. I don't know where they got the guns and bombs, but they're better armed than us and have a ten to one numbers advantage."

"The trump card Zeke mentioned," Danny said. "Yahweh must have found the old counterinsurgency supply cache."

"Aside from being mostly blind, the man's from Texas; how would he know enough about Tombstone to figure that out?" Fiona asked.

"I believe I can answer that for you." Veronica strolled through the door with a file folder held above her head. "I was digging through some old records in the courthouse and found out something interesting about our good friend Zeke. It would seem he was born a bastard with a father only added to the records a week later."

"He and Hawkins had the same father," Gieo said, slapping her forehead at the realization. "They've been working together this whole time."

"Yes, that is where I was going with that," Veronica said, not hardly perturbed by her big reveal being spoiled.

"That explains the cache and a lot of the shit he's been putting me through lately, but that doesn't explain the horses or why Zeke just stumbled out of your place after being worked over," Fiona said.

"The Slark fuel is almost gone," Veronica said. "I told Zeke I knew of a way to stretch the remainder and make him wealthy in the process; he was so panicked about the prospect of being left with nothing that he jumped at the chance. I failed to tell him I had every intention of reintroducing the horse to Tombstone long before the fuel was gone. We've been doing it all over the west and it has worked fantastically. He saw the livery train, put the pieces together, and came over claiming I skunked him on our deal. He was lucky we let him walk out after some of the things he said."

"We're with you, Red," Danny said. "Just let us know what you need done."

"He'll go after the horses," Gieo said, "and he'll use the cultists to do it."

"The horses are on their way to the old high school on Gun Club Road," Veronica said. "They're probably already there under as heavy of a guard as we can manage right now."

"Add Mitch's truck with the gun platform from your airship to the defenses," Fiona told Gieo. She turned to Danny and the rest of the hunters. "Go with Veronica and help however you can."

Gieo fell in behind the departing hunters as if to follow them outside to carry out Fiona's orders. When the crowd was sufficiently clogging the door with Veronica on the other side, she grabbed Danny by the back of the jacket and pulled him back inside. Fiona and Danny both gave Gieo a perplexed look.

"The horses aren't the only target," Gieo said. "You don't need Molotov cocktails to kill horses."

"So what else is he hitting?" Danny asked.

"The Slark fuel depot," Gieo said. "He'll likely send a group there to take out the fuel if they can't get to the horses—if he can't have the fuel, he definitely won't want us to. I'm sure Veronica has figured this out too, but isn't saying. If Zeke destroys the depot, she'll have the monopoly."

"Danny and I can handle that," Fiona said. "Go with Veronica and get that gun platform to the high school."

Gieo looked hurt, but walked away to carry out the order. Fiona followed her out the back of the saloon, around the side street to the old convenience store with the mortar shell hole in the side. Mitch's truck was squirreled away in what was left of the building. He had reinforced the walls so they only looked like they would fall in if sneezed on; it was a lovely hiding spot as nobody wanted anything to do with the seeming death trap. It would be a slow crawl, even if Mitch and Bond-O could be found to help in the driving and stoking, but they were likely ahead of the curve on Zeke's plan and thus had the necessary hours to spare.

Fiona's heart was thundering in her ears with every step. She'd been steadily walking away from what she knew ever since she'd met Gieo and now she found herself on the edge of a cliff, miles from the beaten path, with nothing else to do but jump. Fiona caught up to Gieo before she could disappear into Mitch's hiding spot for his truck. She spun the pilot around and pressed her against the cinder brick wall of the crumbling convenience store. She kissed her hard, one arm wrapped around her waist and the other holding her chin to keep her head still through the violent kiss. Gieo moaned into Fiona's mouth, clawing at the gunfighter's clothing with clumsy aggression. Fiona broke the kiss; they stood mere inches apart, breathless and wanting.

"Tell Mitch and the kitchen boy to get the truck out to the high school," Fiona said, her voice flinty with desire, "then come up to my room. I have something to show you." There was no turning back on any of it anymore; she'd jumped in more ways than one, and now she had to find out if she had wings.

Fiona walked away, leaving Gieo gasping against the wall, butterflies of anticipation fluttering through her stomach. The pilot watched Fiona's slender ass and long legs in the brown, leather pants as she walked away. Gieo came to the conclusion that the view of

Fiona walking away was more attractive than Veronica's cleavage-flirtation-posture, especially since Fiona's was a passive beauty while Veronica's only worked while focused.

Gieo ran off to find Mitch with a pronounced spring in her step.

Mitch and Bond-O were steaming their way toward the high school with a couple hunters as escort. It would take close to an hour to get the truck out there, which Mitch was none too happy about as the truck used to have a double digit top speed that it just didn't have with Gieo's new engine plan. It would be nearly unstoppable and wouldn't run out of fuel anytime soon though, which may or may not make up for the 8 MPH cruising speed.

Gieo slipped through the dark, silent saloon, knocking on Fiona's door with a few tentative taps. A sliver of soft, candlelight crept out from beneath the crack under the door. She heard Fiona invite her in. Gieo opened the door to find a dozen or so candles giving the room a rosy glow. Fiona stood near the bed, lighting a handful of candles on the night stand. She was wearing a black, lace-panel bustier with matching lace boy-cut panties and the largest, reddest strap-on Gieo had ever seen. When she was done lighting the candles, she straightened up to her full height, her bronzed body and lovely lingerie glimmering in the candlelight. For an instant, beneath everything Fiona had become, Gieo could see the vulnerable woman she had been before the Slark—the same beautifully exposed quality that had made her fall in love with Fiona before they'd ever met.

"You are so beautiful right now, I could cry," Gieo said. "I thought you didn't like underwear though…"

"For you, I'll make an exception," Fiona said.

"As sweet as this is," Gieo said with a mischievous smile, "I hope you're not planning on taking it easy on me."

"That was never the plan."

Gieo crossed the room to her. Fiona met her halfway. Their lips practically collided; their hands exchanged awkward gropes through clothing. Within minutes, they were both panting, eager, and flushed with excitement. Fiona turned Gieo around until her chest was against the pilot's back, pulled up the front of her skirt, and plunged her hand down the front of Gieo's black cotton panties. Her long, powerful fingers pressed down between Gieo's lips, finding their way inside her, discovering her already warm and wet.

Gieo practically fell limp in Fiona's arms. She rested her head back against the gunfighter's shoulder, rolling her hips against the fingers slipping in and out of her, thrilling at the sensation of the huge strap-on rubbing lewdly against her ass with every motion they made together. Fiona's free hand came up to her breast, massaging it through the tight material of the top of her dress, teasing her nipple until it strained to poke through the fabric. Gieo reached up and pulled the front of her dress down, freeing her breasts to sit atop the folded material, giving Fiona full access to her hard, little nipples.

"Are you ready?" Fiona whispered hotly in her ear.

"Don't ask," Gieo moaned, "just take."

Fiona pressed her hand against the center of Gieo's back and bent her over the edge of the bed. Gieo managed to get her hands out in front of her to prevent bouncing awkwardly. With her feet still planted on the floor, legs straight, and ass in the air, she thrilled at the sudden shift to being entirely vulnerable. Fiona flipped up the back of Gieo's skirt, grasped her underwear by the waistband, and pulled them down to knee level, preventing Gieo's legs from parting entirely. Surprisingly, she knelt first behind the pilot, her hands making their way up the backs of Gieo's legs, puzzling until Gieo felt Fiona's tongue thrust into her from behind. Fiona's darting lapping and occasional full plunges sent warm shivers across Gieo's skin, adding to an arousal already on the cusp of overwhelming.

At the edge of begging, Gieo finally felt the enormous, bulbous head of the strap-on press against her lips and then it was inside her, slipping easily into her, filling her up in a way she had positively ached for. She practically screamed in joy at feeling Fiona's hands on her hips, not realizing until that moment, how much she'd wanted to feel Fiona from this exact position; it wasn't her first time for this type of treatment, but the only other time was far too short and too long ago to remember as anything but fantasy. Gieo gripped at the sheets, buried her face in the bed, stifling her passionate moans as the strap-on slid in and out of her in long, beautiful strokes, big on the edge of too big.

Something about Gieo's posture irritated Fiona. She positioned her legs outside Gieo's forcing them in together, creating an added edge of tightness and resistance to thrusting the strap-on into the pilot. To prevent any further gasps or moans of pleasure from being lost into the muffling bed, Fiona grasped the back of Gieo's collar and pulled it back, yanking her head up. Gieo gasped at the rough treatment more in pleasure than discomfort. Forced to let every sound of her bliss float out into the air, Gieo found she was more vocal than she'd ever remembered. Hazy memories of the peyote night filtered back—she was a screamer when it came to Fiona. The delicious, filling thrusts of the strap-on pressed down against her g-spot, sending shockwaves through her system with every hard push Fiona made. Gieo was screaming, barely able to mix Fiona's name into the jumble, begging for more, begging for harder, begging for faster. Fiona, to her credit, met every request by redoubling her efforts until Gieo was dead certain she would never walk right again, and wouldn't even care to try. A rolling orgasm, weeks in the making and fucked right out of her with astounding energy, buckled her knees and sent an undulating twinge down her legs.

Fiona, satisfied with her handiwork, lay across Gieo's back, leaving the strap-on fully buried inside her, to kiss Gieo lovingly on the back of the neck. She released her hold on the collar, letting Gieo's head drop to the bed in an exhausted flop. Gieo focused on the sweet hereafter, determined to remember everything about the moment with Fiona's breasts pressed against her back, feeling ridden hard and put away wet, all with a deep satisfaction on more than just the sexual level.

"This might just be because I've never been fucked like that, but I think I'm falling for you," Gieo said. She felt something cold and wet drop on her cheek. It took her a moment to figure out it was likely a tear.

"If one or both of us doesn't make it back after tonight, I want you to know, ever since I met you, you've made my life worth living," Fiona whispered.

Gieo reached out to find Fiona's hand on the bed beside her head. She interlaced their fingers and gave her hand a hard squeeze. The dire need and speed of the night's events prevented true processing of exactly how dangerous of a proposition it all might end up being. In the contemplative moments after earth-shattering sex, all the doubts and fears came rushing in.

"We both have to make it," Gieo said with steely determination. "You have to do this to me at least once a day for the next twenty or so years. I've already mentally scheduled it."

Fiona slipped from her. The absence of the strap-on inside her and the gunfighter on top of her felt a little lonely to Gieo; she immediately wished for the return of both. She rolled onto her back and pulled up her underwear. She stared up at the ceiling with a little smile playing across her lips—she was going to be deliciously sore tomorrow, and looked forward to the physical reminder of their night together.

Chapter 15
Dust-up disrupted

It had taken Mitch and Bond-O so long to get the truck moving that Gieo was able to catch up at a slow jog mixed with a brisk walk. She climbed aboard and hooked herself into the gun platform ready to spin the gyroscopes atop the boiler on the bed of the truck should the need arise. She didn't imagine anyone would attack the truck with the enormous quad gun manned; besides, the thing's engine sounded like the thunder of the gods, belching steam and smoke to match. Bond-O, wearing a leather apron of his own, thick work gloves, and goggles worked the bellows and pumps required to keep the engine at top performance while Mitch drove, shouting directions out the back window to keep the easily distracted chef on task. Bond-O waved up to Gieo when she scrambled onto the truck—the two empty fingers on the glove of his left hand waggling comically with the wave.

The sun had long set by the time they rolled up to the old high school. The hastily built ramparts, gun platforms, and barriers around the dusty brick buildings spoke of an anticipated attack from all sides. The horses had been moved off the playing fields into the gymnasium to give them an iota of protection. A few of the Ravens directed the truck into a position in the dead center of the primary firing line. The cultists would be on foot, coming from just about anywhere, but the hunters would need something flat and smooth enough to drive over. Gun Club Road would be the only entryway for them, funneling them right into a hornet's nest of firepower with Gieo's quad gun at the center.

Gieo unhooked herself from the turret and hopped down to find Veronica waiting for her. Veronica gently cradled Gieo's face in her soft hands, smiling brightly to her. Before Gieo could ask what was going on, Veronica was hugging her tightly. She smelled of strawberry candy and clean linen. Her arms were strong, but the hug held the softness only inherent to hugging another woman; Gieo rested her head on Veronica's shoulder to savor the sensation she had almost forgotten existed.

"You're so brave to join us," Veronica whispered to her. "We won't forget this."

"I can't fight," Gieo said.

Veronica pulled the hug back to arm's length and cocked an eyebrow.

"I can shoot the gun," Gieo said, "but I know I couldn't shoot at people."

"Then I won't ask you to." Veronica smiled and touched Gieo's cheek. "Does the bartender know how to operate it?"

"No, and it wouldn't work to teach him anyway," Gieo said. "The turret has to hook into clothing, and the dress I'm wearing is the only clothing I have with me that will work."

"Clever way to keep the Slark from using any of your salvaged weapons since they don't really wear clothes," Veronica said with a smile that shot pride right through Gieo. "Can you teach Stephanie how to fire it?"

"Of course, but I don't want to just sit idly by while…"

"Don't worry about that," Veronica said. "I know just the thing for you. Find Stephanie, get her situated, and then come see me at the top of the front steps."

Finding Stephanie was an easy proposition. Many of the Ravens had dyed hair, but Stephanie seemed to be the only one in the area who favored pink. She was standing a post at the edge of the rampart with two other Ravens who were doing more chatting than guarding.

"Hey, Gieo," Stephanie said as Gieo approached. "Good to see you again." The affected smile Stephanie wore said it was indeed good to see her, but the blank stare in her eyes said she couldn't care less.

"How are you at handling big guns?" Gieo asked.

The other two women in Stephanie's guard duty snickered a little under their breath.

"What's that supposed to mean? I handle them just fine," Stephanie snapped. "I don't know what you heard, but there are other reasons someone might choke on…I mean, you throw up on one guy and suddenly…"

"No, not at all what I meant," Gieo said quickly cutting off any further explanation. "The gun pod on the back of the truck." Gieo pointed to it looming above the firing line. "Veronica wanted me to teach you to use it."

"Oh," Stephanie said, still letting the information sweep away her indignation. "OH! I'd love to!" She grabbed Gieo by the hand and dragged her toward the truck.

"There's just one problem." Gieo eyed the revealing outfit Stephanie was wearing with a creeping sense of doom. "We have to switch clothes. The turret is something you have to hook into to operate."

Stephanie stopped pulling her, turned to get a good look at Gieo's outfit, and smiled her approval. "That's a cute dress," she said, "no problem." Stephanie shifted directions and began pulling Gieo toward the school buildings. One of the trailer classrooms sitting a bit apart from the main body of the school was being used as a changing room by many of the Ravens who apparently had been pulled from work without being given a chance to change clothes. The beautiful flowers of women who entered exited in military fatigues and body armor. Gieo's spirits rose when she realized she would be wearing desert camouflage instead of Stephanie's chemise.

Once inside, Stephanie quickly slipped out of her outfit. The crisscross front lace chemise with attached garters and opera-length stockings came off with practiced grace. She unzipped her platform-heel go-go boots as well and held out the skimpy outfit for Gieo to take.

"I thought I could wear one of the uniform things," Gieo said, eyeing the outfit with disdain.

"You're not a Raven," Stephanie said. "Uniforms are only for members."

Gieo weighed the options of shooting cultists and hunters with the quad guns or dressing in prostitute wear—it was a close one, but she decided the chemise would be less traumatizing long term. She and Stephanie were exactly the same size and nearly identical dimensions, which was no doubt why Veronica had chosen her.

"Okay, fine." Gieo unzipped her dress, realizing more than a few eyes around the makeshift dressing room immediately drew to her.

The visual attention and knowing smiles only increased from the other, half-dressed women after Gieo had shimmied into the black, lace chemise, stockings, and boots. She was fairly certain her nipples were visible through the dainty material and her cotton panties had seemed a little bigger when they weren't the primary thing covering her lower half.

"Do I need the collar too?" Stephanie pointed at the spiked collar Gieo was still wearing.

"Not, that's…something else."

"Oh, I completely understand—I wore one for awhile too. You look great, by the way," Stephanie said, her eyes finally smiling with her mouth. "Let's go get that gun rolling!"

Back at the firing line and the truck, more eyes followed Gieo with more smiles and even a few snickers. Gieo pushed it out of her mind and focused on teaching Stephanie how to hook herself into the turret, which clasps went to which hooks on the clothes and how to use her feet to rotate the gyroscopes for elevation and lateral movement. Stephanie was a quick-study, picking up precise targeting movements with near mastery in just a few tries. Gieo surmised that Stephanie might have been lousy at blow-jobs when it came to big guns, but she was shaping up to be Annie Oakley when it came to firing them.

After Stephanie was fully situated, Gieo found Veronica at the top of the main entry steps at her makeshift command post. Veronica was the first to actually laugh at Gieo's clothing; the infectious laughter quickly spread through the rest of her officers. Gieo felt like crawling out of her skin in embarrassment, and seriously considered storming off. As though reading the furious blush and antsy feet, Veronica quickly snagged Gieo's hand and pulled her into the midst of the officers.

"I didn't know whether or not Stephanie was going to haze you," Veronica said. Her affectation, the polished Southern belle minus the accent, had completely vanished as though it had never even existed. In her normal speaking tone, she actually sounded a little Creole or Cajun although drastically faded with time, distance, and willful effort. "I know it might not feel like it, but this is a sign of respect and interest."

"Interest…?"

"Have you been getting smiles and friendly glances?" Veronica asked.

"Yes."

"That means the ladies approve of Stephanie's choice to invite you in," Veronica said. "If your hazing wasn't welcome, someone would have told you off by now. I promise, I really thought she would just give you one of our uniforms—she's normally such a truculent little thing. Our sumptuary customs are a little backward from what you might think; you're wearing the true uniform of the Ravens right now, and, I might add, you're wearing it very well. You could change, if you wanted to, but I'd think of it as a personal favor if you didn't right away." Veronica gave Gieo's shoulder a gentle squeeze.

Gieo's embarrassment dissolved under the compliment. The officers smiled and nodded their agreement, only adding to her blush. She felt a strange sense of acceptance that she'd only really ever felt at science and math summer camps. Growing up, she was too much of a lesbian to fit in with other Orange County Asians, too Asian to fit in with other Orange County lesbians, too smart to fit in with the weirdos, and too weird to fit in with the braincases; such was the otherness created by her race, sexuality, eccentricities, and 200 IQ. She found acceptance at science and math summer camps for the extremely gifted. Most of the other outcasts there were just happy to be free of the oppression they lived under during the rest of the school year that they couldn't care less that Gieo was a lesbian—they all had their own idiosyncrasies born out of their genius and her sexuality wasn't even that odd by comparison. She'd counted on college to be the next chance she would have at recapturing that acceptance, but that was all six years and an alien invasion removed. Standing in the midst of so many beautiful, talented, intelligent women, it felt like the power structure that had once been so oppressive had been flipped on its head, leaving Gieo to stand on the top, finally able to see the sun.

"I'd like to be one of you," Gieo said.

"Oh, honey," Veronica said, "you were born one of us." Veronica slipped her arm around Gieo's shoulder and guided her over to a tall, brawny blond wearing a lab coat over her military fatigues. "This is Dr. Davidson, White Bishop and chief medical officer of our cell. I think you and her could help each other a lot. Dr. Davidson, this is Gieo, White Rook and air force commander."

"Please, call me Silvia," Dr. Davidson said, taking Gieo's hand to shake it. "Let's get started on some water purification systems, an electrical grid, and sterile areas for medical work. I could use a fellow egg-head to get this place up to speed."

Gieo smiled up to the angular face of the tall doctor; it all sounded like heaven to her.

♠♣♥♦

Fiona and Danny strolled the perimeter of the gas station turned Slark fueling depot for the tenth time as the sun faded in the west. He had his Winchester 30/30 across his shoulders with his wrists draped over opposite ends. She knew, like her classic pose of leaning against the wall, that the posture he was in afforded him almost an instantaneous jump of the rifle into firing position; she'd taught him well.

"So, are you in love with that Gieo girl?" Danny finally asked, breaking the silence they'd been walking in for the last hour.

"I don't know," Fiona said, "probably, although that hardly matters since I've been in love before and that didn't exactly pan out."

"Before was Veronica?"

"Yep."

"You ever been in love with a man?"

"Nope."

"Bad luck for me, I suppose."

"You need a psychotic redhead in your life like you need a flesh-eating virus."

"Must be the lack of options making me talk crazy." Danny chuckled.

"Must be."

"Did I ever want you before the Slark invasion," Danny said. "I used to spank it to your catalogues twice a day when I was in junior high."

"That particular affliction seems to be going around," Fiona said. She glanced at him out of the corner of her eye—a little chaos tic caught her off guard. "Do you still think I'm beautiful?"

"You saved my life, kept me from slavery, and taught me a trade," Danny said. "I'm going to think you're beautiful when you're old, toothless, and weather-beaten because yours was the first face I saw when I peeked out of that boxcar. You were standing on the hood of your car, under-lit by fire, hair blowing in the wind—best night of my life. I actually thought I'd died and gone to heaven seeing as there was no rational reason my fantasy woman should be dressed up like a samurai cowboy, saving my life." Danny gave her a long look over out of the corner of his eyes and nodded. "Objectively speaking, yeah, you're gorgeous."

Scampering footsteps across open ground drew their attention to the gas station. In an instant Danny's rifle was in his hands and Fiona's Colt was out of its holster. They both relaxed when they saw the grease monkeys running over to them.

"Are you two here about Rawlins and the blind fuckers?" the lead grease monkey asked.

Fiona slipped her gun back into its holster and straightened her posture. She'd never actually heard one of the grease monkeys talk; it hadn't even occurred to her that they could, but just chose not to. A sick, post-apocalypse, worst-case-scenario part of her had thought they'd had their tongues cut out or something.

"You guys talk?" Danny asked, indicating she wasn't the only one.

"When we want to," one of the others said.

"You're two of the nice ones," the leader said. "You never hit us, always gave us a tip, and never called us names just for doing what we had to, so we thought we'd give you a heads up that the Slark fuel's about gone."

"Yeah, we've pieced that together," Danny said.

"Oh," the leader looked crestfallen until something dawned on him. "Did you know that Zeke told Rawlins to come back here with his posse of methanol drinkers after the sun went down?"

"Told him to wait for the signal," the one who had spoken earlier added. "That they'd know what to do if it came."

"That gives us the when and who," Danny said.

"Thanks," Fiona said. "You boys best find another place to sleep tonight. If this goes sideways the fueling depot won't be more than a black smudge on the world come morning."

"Thanks, miss," the leader said, "we'll do that."

As the grease monkeys jogged toward town, Fiona overheard one of the boys grumble, "I told you Zeke was going to kill us."

The desert sky in the west was painted red, pink, and orange with the last of the sun falling below the horizon. Fiona glanced back to the gas station and turned a slow circle. The Jefferson Davis Memorial Highway, or what was left of it anyway, would be the quickest way, but Rawlins was no fool. She pointed down 10th street, which bisected the highway creating the corner the depot sat on. It was seldom used and wouldn't arouse any specific suspicion if methanol drinkers were seen on it.

"That'll be where he comes from," Fiona said. "If we camp out in the cluster of houses across the street, we should be able to pin them against the station, which'll prevent them from using the fire bombs for fear of blowing it while they're still in range."

"Ambush hunting is just my style," Danny said.

Getting positioned with good sightlines for shooting and good cover for being shot at didn't take long at all, and soon Danny and Fiona had the gas station in their sights with the trap ready to be sprung. Dark came on slow, as it tends to in the dog days of summer, creeping across the sky with agonizing reluctance. More irritating still was the fact that Rawlins wasn't remotely punctual. The air was already turning cold when he finally pulled into the station's roundabout with ten armed cultists dangling off the back of his tow truck. Rawlins had it in his head that he and Fiona were heading for a bedroom at some point in their future and she had it in her head they were heading for a dust-up. Fiona grinned with grim satisfaction about the chance to finally prove him wrong and her right. Rawlins barked orders to his cultist minions who carried out the commands with all the stealth and accuracy of blind lunatics with brains burned by too much sun and years of wood-alcohol consumption.

"Do we wait for the signal?" Danny whispered to her.

"What'd be the point?" Fiona replied. "The sooner we clear them out, the sooner we can get out of here. Swing around to their right, using that fence as cover if they pinpoint our hiding hole."

"You got it."

Rawlins, the only one of the bunch with vision enough to know what good shooting sightlines were, kept himself mostly obscured from the street side of the station while most of the cultists milled about as though their blindness also prevented them from being seen. Fiona and Danny picked out their targets from the cultists wandering closest to their ambush position, and fired almost simultaneously. Even in the dark and open air, it was impossible to tell where the shots had come from. Two cultists dropped at the edge of the formation. The rest panicked and took to spraying every direction they could find in wild swings of their assault rifles.

In the ensuing chaos, Danny and Fiona took two more.

From his position, guarded by the hood of his truck on one side and the driver's door on another, Rawlins picked out the position the second shots had come from. He shouted to redirect the cultists. The methanol drinkers, driven almost deaf by their errant firing, didn't appear to hear Rawlins. Danny sprinted from cover before Fiona could grab him, picking his way along the fence line to flank their position when two of them stopped to reload. Rawlins finally got control of them in the moment of silence and redirected them to fire on Danny.

Fiona popped from her hiding spot and dropped the two who were drawing a bead on her partner. Rawlins was out from his truck with his pump shotgun in hand, making for Danny's new position. Fiona shot at him, winging one of the cultists with the first shot and killing a second outright when Rawlins ducked behind him as a human shield. Fiona snapped down the front of her Colt to yank the spent shells. Loading new slugs from her bandolier belts took an eternity. She heard Rawlins' shotgun report; she heard Danny's Winchester return fire. She snapped her gun back together and looked up from her work of reloading just in time to see Rawlins catch Danny with a blast on the run. Danny stumbled a few steps and dropped into the dusty side yard of one of the houses.

Fiona burst from her cover, putting down the remaining two cultists with well-placed headshots. She stormed at Rawlins with her gun leading the way. He spun his shotgun on her, recognized who he was about to blast, hesitated one moment, one moment too many, and Fiona blew his trigger hand clean off at the wrist.

She covered the rest of the gap between them. He'd fallen to his back, abandoned the gun as valueless without the requisite two hands to operate it, and clutched feebly at the gushing stump that was once his hand. She stepped over him, leveling the massive barrel of the Colt Anaconda directly at his forehead.

"You hesitated," Fiona said, her voice icy as death.

"I couldn't shoot you," Rawlins said. "I love you. I've loved you since I saw your picture in that catalogue." Rawlins looked away from her. His face was loosing its color quickly as the life drained from him out of his destroyed wrist. "I always knew I'd be shot dead someday, but I never thought it would be you doing the shooting."

"Because you're fucking stupid." Fiona pulled the trigger, exploding the back of Rawlins' head across the gas station tarmac.

She ran to where Danny went down. She hoped he had just been winged. He was a young man, twenty maybe, if anyone would be in good enough shape to bounce back, it would be him. When she saw his body still prone, the rifle just out of reach, her hopes changed to having just enough time left with him to say goodbye. She grasped his coat and rolled him gently onto his back. He was dead. The heavy shot had taken him directly in the heart. He was probably gone from his body long before he even hit the ground. Fiona sat hard on the long, dead grass stained with Danny's blood and cried. She hadn't cried since Vegas, hadn't really allowed herself to, hadn't really had a reason to, but with Danny gone … the last evidence that she'd ever done something good with her life … she couldn't stop from crying. She cried until her throat hurt, until she hiccupped painfully. And even then, it didn't feel like enough.

The sky lit up with blinding, white flares, not above the gas station or the outskirts where the old high school was, but right above the north end of town. The disorienting strobe flares held in the sky like balloons. They weren't Zeke's signal or something the cultists were using to enhance their lousy night vision. No, she hadn't seen them since Barstow; they belonged to the Slark. She could already hear the clattering of their crawlers in the distance.

Fiona scooped up Danny's rifle and ammo belt and ran for her car.

Chapter 16

Trust in honor and a lack of options

Fiona roared away from the front of the saloon north through the heart of the city. If she could reach the Slark when they were still in the ruins of the Mountain Road suburbs, she might be able to turn them east toward the high school rather than let them hit the undefended, unsuspecting town while every armed person was away. The cataclysm on the east coast had destroyed anyone in the Slark community above blue collar status; their advanced military tactics were gone, as were humanity's, leaving them with undisciplined troops led by the strongest, but seldom smartest, of their soldiers. Tricking them into calling off their attack to chase a car they might know well was a long shot, but a logically sound one.

Fiona's car, when pushed to the limit, was more than capable of getting ahead of the formation, lighting up the night sky with its flaming trail to make sure they'd know exactly which way to follow. The Slark were still picking their way cautiously toward the town through the sparse homes held in the northern hills when she pulled up to the ruined edge of Cactus Road. She slipped from the car, sitting on the top of her door, leaning across the roof with Danny's rifle. In the flickering strobes of the Slark flares, she found a target and fired. The shot, a long one, missed the head of her prey, but clipped one of its legs. The resulting panic caused by the Slark's wound spread through the line. She flicked the lever-action and fired again, this time finding center mass, plucking an uninjured Slark from its perch on the side of the centipede-like vehicle. This time, the Slark scanned the area and found the sniper in question. Fiona considered levering in another shell to take out one more, but didn't see the need for it; they'd spotted her and shifted their attack in her direction. She slid back into her car, gunned the engine, and launched into the expanse of open desert between Cactus Road and the high school.

The dust, brush, and errant rocks would tear up her car, there was no avoiding that, but if she was lucky, if she picked her path right, she could make it to the high school before mechanical failure stopped her. She heard smaller rocks, the trunks of sage brush, and other unidentified objects of density ricocheting off her cattle-catcher, several making it through to bounce along the undercarriage. She hadn't struck anything to flip the car yet, and was beginning to feel a little cocky about her chances when she spotted her first cultist. She veered to the right, heading a little further north to find the edge of the formation only to discover several more cultists. When the options became slow to the point of turning entirely north or try to weave between the blind men and women, she chose the latter, hit the gas, and left an easily tracked trail right through the middle of the cultist army. Though not really trying very hard to avoid clipping stragglers, as her only real concern was not plowing into a group large enough to stop her car, she ended up missing everyone entirely, finally emerging on the other side with the well-lit high school beckoning her in.

The Raven defense line recognized her car, a small blessing considering the shit-storm the night had turned out to be, and a few of the women quickly rearranged the barricade to form an opening large enough for her to drive through. She hit the hole with her car on its last legs. She wasn't sure what she'd sucked into her air intakes, but she could imagine it would take the grease monkeys a day's work or more to get it all back out. When it didn't look like her car was going to make it all the way into the compound, several of the women jogged over to give it a push, letting it come to rest in the faculty parking lot.

Fiona slipped from the car with Danny's rifle in one hand and his bandolier in the other. Before she could even fully shut the door, Gieo pounced her, knocking Fiona back against the car. The pilot was dressed differently, smelled faintly of a foreign perfume, and stood several inches taller than Fiona remembered her being, but none of that mattered. She squeezed Gieo tight with one arm and kissed her full on the lips. The pilot threw her arms over Fiona's shoulders and returned the pleasure.

"What are you wearing?" Fiona asked when their kiss fizzled in its own time.

"The Ravens' uniform, apparently," Gieo replied, flush with excitement both sexual and cerebral.

Before Fiona could respond, Veronica's voice rang clear and loud out into the desert night, amplified by the loudspeaker system liberated from the top of the scoreboard.

"Zeke, Yahweh, or whoever is in charge of this encroaching band of blind fuckers who are suddenly illuminated clear as day," Veronica shouted. "You've got Slark behind you and light enough on you to make you easy targets for my sharpshooters. Turn back now, take your chances with the Slark, and I can promise my girls won't paint bull's-eyes on your backs. I doubt the aliens will give you the same courtesy if you keep heading in this direction."

"You would feed us to these bastards?" Zeke shouted back without aid of a bullhorn. "Where's your honor and humanity?"

"My honor's the only thing that made me promise not to shoot you in the back," Veronica replied. "As for my humanity, I left it in the same place you left yours when you came out here to kill us and murder our horses. Good luck, and don't even think of retreating in this direction."

Unintelligible shouts came out of the cultist formation. They were still a hundred yards off, but would come no further. The makeshift army of a couple hundred blind men and women armed with machineguns turned back, walking toward the flashing strobe flares, with their useless, milky eyes illuminated in the light they couldn't see.

Fiona made her way toward Veronica who was already on her way over to the car. The roaring engines of several of Zeke's hunter vehicles, formerly coming closer along old Gun Club Road, turned away, fleeing for the desert. Fiona assumed whatever hunters Zeke had retained at his side had no interest in seeing what would come of Tombstone when Slark were added to the turmoil. They would run, hope their cars had enough fuel to reach another free city state, and wait to hear if Tombstone fell.

Fiona wasn't certain of the reception she would receive from Veronica, and so tensed before the blond commander of the Ravens reached her. Veronica pulled Fiona into a warm embrace, holding her with relieved affection.

"You are a wonder, my love," Veronica whispered into Fiona's neck.

The compliment and the title felt strange as if the words were ill at ease with each other considering the source. Fiona returned the hug, but not the words.

"You've taken Gieo from me?" Fiona pulled away from Veronica's embrace, briefly gesturing to Gieo's outfit, borrowed from Stephanie.

"She came to us willingly," Veronica protested. "She wants to be one of us."

"Didn't you see the collar?" Fiona asked. "It's not up to her."

Veronica folded her arms over her chest and scoffed. "Did I miss something, or didn't you just drive your car into our protection? As far as I'm concerned, you never stopped being one of us."

Fiona clenched her teeth so tightly the muscles in her jaw began to twitch. Veronica, for her part, seemed aware of the gunfighter's anger, but not remotely fazed by it. "It isn't up to you," she finally said.

"Don't you get it?" Veronica snapped, taking a step to get right into Fiona's face. "We win. Women survived, and now we get to make the world right. Our leaders, our scientists, our generals who sacrificed themselves to even the playing field with the Slark were 90% men. The smart, capable, women survived because those idiots didn't trust us with that kind of power. Now we're the only ones left with intelligence enough to claim it. We'd be no better than the moronic, bi-gendered Slark if we ignored that advantage. Not all women have the strength and willingness to kill that you have, and I won't let them become human property of regressed men simply because you don't like my methods."

"Even if that means making slaves of anyone who doesn't like our rules?"

"What the fuck do you want from me?" Veronica said, her voice rising to a shout. "I didn't come up with the idea, I didn't own slaves, hell, I never even took a pet, unlike you. More importantly, we don't even do that anymore. We're new to running shit and we had to be ruthless in taking control or we would have ended up property again."

Fiona suspected, but didn't know for certain, if the feeling of being property or less-than men was universal to all women, but she knew she'd felt it and she knew Veronica had too. Ruthless was a good word for what the Ravens were, but ruthless also made sense for the things they'd had to accomplish without protection of law or society. At one point, Fiona had understood and agreed with what they were doing. Ideological differences over slavery were kind of foolish to cling to when it was already abolished and was also part of American and human history as well, and she couldn't very well walk away from those things on principle.

"They tore it down…" Fiona muttered.

"…so we could build it back right," Veronica finished for her. It was the mantra and identify friend/foe or IFF of the Ravens, used to identify one another in the dark during the firefights that would forge New Vegas; it was truth, as the Black Queen had explained, but also came to embody safety and the knowledge friends were near. Veronica leaned forward, her lips nearly reaching Fiona's before Gieo's hand could interject between them.

"Whoa, lips off my woman," Gieo said, holding her hand firmly as a wall in the middle of the kiss. Energy of a strange, nervous quality filtered through the crowd. Some of the Ravens giggled, some looked away, some took a step forward as if to back their commander's play should she lash out at the pilot, and other simply stood, mouths agape, unable to believe Gieo's temerity.

For a strange, confused moment, Fiona didn't know who Gieo was talking about. Part of her immediately responded in jealousy, assuming Gieo was calling Veronica her woman and warning Fiona away. She didn't fully realize what was meant until Gieo wrapped her palm around Fiona's face and pulled her attention to look down at the pilot.

"Don't…don't kiss her," Gieo said, tears welling up in the corners of her eyes. "Don't be with her…be with me."

Fiona traced her fingers along the edge of the spiked collar around Gieo's neck. When Gieo pulled her hand away from Fiona's mouth, she found her smiling. "I am with you," Fiona said.

They held each other close and walked away under the scrutiny of dozens of stunned eyes.

Fiona leaned against the side of her dusty car, watching Veronica sitting on the steps of the main entrance with her shotgun draped across her lap. She had the same look that mixed sorrow and rage in equal parts that she'd had the night Fiona had betrayed her. The train Fiona had attacked all those years ago was Veronica's even if the cargo wasn't. Fiona could lie to herself, claim she didn't know for sure if the slaves were Veronica's or not, but it wouldn't do any good; she found out the truth during the planning phase and it hadn't changed her actions one bit.

The sound of gunfire from the cultists and zaps from Slark weapons held solid much of the night, only pushing into the east, away from the high school, at the approach of dawn. Maybe Zeke was better at organizing blind people to fire in the same direction than Rawlins was, or maybe the Slark really were frightened of blind people. Regardless, when the clatter of machinegun fire finally dissipated just before daylight, the last few pops of rifle reports sounded to be a quarter-mile farther away than when the battle had started.

Gieo slept soundly in the passenger seat of Fiona's car, wrapped in a borrowed military blanket and the security of knowing Fiona had stood in front of the entire assembly of Ravens and chose her. Fiona glanced over her shoulder, through the windshield to make sure Gieo was still asleep before making her way across the quiet grounds of the high school to Veronica.

"I thought you would have forgiven me by now," Veronica said softly. "I forgave you a long time ago."

"This isn't about being angry with you," Fiona said. "I knew you weren't a slaver…" The next words stuck in her mouth, not wanting to be spoken for fear it'd open up an old wound long since healed. "…I was afraid of you. That's why I threatened you not to follow; that's why I left."

"Afraid of me…why?"

"I was losing myself in you to the point where I couldn't even tell anymore where you started and I began," Fiona said with an icy edge to her voice. "You have a way of colonizing more than just cities. You colonize people until they think and act the way you want them to." The look that flashed across Veronica's face told Fiona she'd never even considered this side of herself. The vulnerable, lonely part of Veronica, left over from before surfaced for a moment. Fiona knew Veronica was like Gieo in so many ways, including the taking of a new name. In that vulnerable moment, Veronica became Tanner Delacroix again, the Baton Rouge tom-boy, named after her grandfather and raised as a son by a single father and four older brothers who didn't have the time or inclination to understand the female gender. Fiona was the only one Veronica had ever told about her past; she carried the weight of the secret as a precious treasure.

"I never wanted to colonize you, or own you, or…" Veronica trailed off, fighting back tears, visibly angry at herself for their very existence. "I thought there would be time for us to come back together. I didn't think you'd find someone else—didn't think there was anyone in Tombstone you'd want."

"I picked her up from an airship crash a couple months ago," Fiona explained. "Up until then, you would have been right."

"I guess I waited two months too long to come back for you." Veronica stood from the steps, slid two fresh shells into the breach of her over-under shotgun, and snapped the barrels back into place. In the rising sun of the earliest of dawns, she returned to the Amazon goddess Fiona knew her to be. "If you wanted me to, if it would have made a difference, I would have crawled for you, from Vegas to Tombstone on my hands and knees for your forgiveness."

Fiona smirked and shook her head. "I never liked you on your hands and knees."

"Best for both of us then that I didn't try." Veronica brushed past Fiona, rallying the Ravens around her to begin the stretched-skirmisher formation into the desert to see who had won the night and who was going to be cut down as the victor.

Fiona woke Gieo with a kiss and a light tickle of her ribs. The pilot came out of sleep with a faint smile and bleary eyes meant only for Fiona. "The Ravens are heading out to survey the field," Fiona told her.

"I'll come with you." Gieo slipped from the car, wrapping herself in Fiona's denim jacket to keep out the early morning chill.

Fiona held out Danny's old rifle and the bandolier of shells. "Take this," she said. "You'll need to be armed."

Gieo slipped the ammo belt over one shoulder to settle it across her chest and took the offered rifle with great reverence. "This is…"

"Danny's."

"Where is he?"

"Still dead, I would imagine."

Fiona walked away to end the conversation, forcing Gieo to jog a little to catch up. They fell in with the Ravens' formation near the officer cluster at the center of the line, walking a few paces off from Veronica. As much as Fiona had hated the idea of returning to the fold, she found the familiar warmth of walking a battlefield with her sisters-in-arms compelling and wonderful. She smiled to Gieo, who smiled back as if she understood how special such camaraderie was.

They came upon the Slark bodies first. Slowly, corpses of cultists and a few hunters found their way into the mix, although the numbers were decidedly skewed toward more Slark dead than human. More often than not, the Slark were shot in the back, which lent some credence to the theory that they were afraid of blind people. Fiona scanned the ground, hoping she would be the one to find Zeke or Yahweh's body, but neither appeared to be among the dead.

The crawlers, three of the twenty-yard long centipedes with gun platforms, had broken down in the midst of the retreat. A few smoke trails rose off the vehicles indicating they likely had suffered serious damage when the humans overtook them. There were no living cultists in sight.

Zeke, splattered green and red with the blood of his own multiple wounds mixing with the shed blood of his enemy, was busy about mopping up the last of the Slark with his bare hands. He grabbed by the neck one of the few Slark left alive and hurled it over one of the front legs of the nearest crawler.

"You see this rock, you ugly bastard?" Zeke shouted in the Slark's face, spraying the lizard-man with angry spittle. "You traveled a thousand light years just to get beat to death with this rock!" Zeke smashed the rock into the Slark's head again and again, long after the twitching, scaly form had gone slack. He dropped the rock and his most recent prey and began searching the ground for another wounded Slark to finish off with hands-on violence.

Fiona actually found a small kernel of pity lodged in her heart for Zeke in that moment. He was alone, reduced to the only emotion he had left, and fighting with rocks for lack of any other weapons at hand. His pride was stripped away, leaving him bare to the world. To add to the vulnerability, one of the shoulder straps of his Slark-skin overalls had snapped at some point in the fighting, likely cut by the same claws that left four bloody streaks across his shoulder, exposing one of his nipples to the world. Veronica made her way calmly over to Zeke; Fiona jogged to catch up.

"Where are the cultists? Where's your brother?" Veronica asked, leveling the muzzle of her shotgun at Zeke's protruding belly.

"They left when the battle turned against the Slark," Zeke said breathlessly. "I got the signal off though; your Slark fuel is long gone."

Veronica looked to Fiona who only shook her head.

"Rawlins is dead," Fiona said. "The depot is safe."

Zeke's head dropped with the acceptance of his grim fate and utter failure.

Fiona scanned the battlefield around them, piecing together from the wounds the Slark had suffered that Zeke had finished the job by himself, mostly with bare hands, battling two dozen of the aliens when both sides had long since been stricken unarmed. The Slark were right in calling humanity beasts; Zeke may as well have been a grizzly bear in the midst of a kindergarten class for all the fight the Slark were able to put up against him without their precious technology. A strange sense of pride came over Fiona in knowing Zeke's triumph of strength was a human triumph.

Veronica seemed to have other questions for Zeke, but Fiona brushed past her, took Zeke's face in her hands and looked into his eyes, searching for some sort of explanation. "What happened to you?" Fiona asked. "Where'd this rage come from?"

Zeke's head became heavy in her hands as he finally relaxed. "I was there, at the battle of St. Louis," he murmured. "My National Guard unit came in to reinforce the army regulars. When we pinned the Slark against the Mississippi, they took to eating prisoners. When their reinforcements came through and surrounded us, we resorted to eating our own dead." Zeke stiffened as the memory passed through him. "Nothing I can do to them will ever be enough."

"What about your brother?" Fiona asked her voice dropping to a soothing whisper.

"Bill's my brother and all, but he never had both oars in the water," Zeke said. "He had his church and followers long before the Slark showed up. He caught on every end of the world theory there was for twenty years or so—I guess he finally got his wish when *they* landed."

"I wish I could offer you a warrior's death," Veronica said, "but quick and painless will have to do." Veronica grasped Fiona's shoulder to pull her away from Zeke.

Instead, Fiona stepped in front of Zeke, shrugging off Veronica's hand. "Look around you; look at what he's done," Fiona said. "We took his town. We took everything he had but the fight left in him. And even then he fought for the same goal we all have. Let him go."

The other gathered Ravens looked around in much the same way Fiona had when she first came upon the scene. They all came to the same conclusion about what Zeke had done in the closing moments of the battle. They nodded their agreement with a few even uttering whispered support of, “The Red Bishop is right” and “Let him go.”

Reluctantly, Veronica lowered her gun. Fiona released Zeke. The once merciless potentate of Tombstone scrambled away with only his life and the clothes on his back to shield him from the harsh world.

“That was a mistake,” Veronica hissed to Fiona so softly only the two of them could hear.

“I owed him,” Fiona said. “I can’t fully explain it and I have no idea why he did, but I know he shielded me from the other hunters when I first came to Tombstone.”

“Be that as it may, if there are consequences for this,” Veronica said, “they’ll be mine, not yours.”

A sharp stab of guilt struck Fiona dead-center in the chest—she knew it too.

Chapter 17
The squeaky wheel gets greased

Gieo settled the head of the strap-on between Fiona's drenched lips, pausing a moment to admire the beautiful way in which she wrapped around the red toy. Gieo grasped Fiona by the waist, and gently rolled her hips forward to press the enormous red phallus into her. Standing at the edge of the bed, with Fiona laying sideways across, her hips nearly falling off the mattress, Gieo was at the perfect height to do all sorts of naughty things to the lanky gunfighter. Of course, as much as Gieo was enjoying her practice at wearing the giant toy, Fiona seemed more than passing preoccupied. Gieo stopped her slow, rolling thrusts and pinched Fiona on the upper thigh.

"What was that for?" Fiona snapped out of her engrossing thoughts.

"You pull my hair sometimes when you fuck me," Gieo said. "I thought I'd try pinching you."

"I thought you liked when I pulled your hair."

"I love it, but I don't like when you're a million miles away when I'm trying to return the favor."

Over the past month, since Zeke's banishment and the disappearance of the cultists, Gieo and Fiona were averaging a minimum of three or four sexual encounters a day. Their active social calendar also coincided with an active business calendar. Instructors from the Ravens took the train down from Vegas to help instruct the remaining Tombstone hunters in horsemanship and cavalry tactics with Fiona as their designated leader. As more units became available, recon patrols increased to track Slark movement and increase the halo of safety around the city. Fiona began spending most of her time on her horse or in her head worrying.

"I'm just a little overworked is all," Fiona said. "Don't you feel that way sometimes?"

Gieo shrugged and shook her head.

"You wouldn't, would you?" Fiona rolled her eyes. Fiona might have called her a liar if Gieo didn't make everything look so damned effortless. She had a dozen projects to juggle, a workload twice or more than anyone else's, and never turned down a chance to teach or offer advice when asked, which was increasingly often. To add to the obscene amount of work Gieo was doing in building an air force, finishing her motorcycle, creating a power grid for the town, setting up a distillation processing plant to use agricultural waste to create ethanol fuel, and a dozen tinier side-projects, Gieo was also mastering the strap-on in ways that not only left Fiona walking a little funny the next day, but threatened to rival her own technique with a few more weeks of practice.

Gieo pinched her thigh again. "Watch it, lover," Gieo said with a smirk. "From this position I can flip you over and know exactly what is up your ass, because it'll be me." Something sparked in Gieo's mind and it immediately translated to her face. She smiled coyly and began rubbing her hands over Fiona's stomach. "Actually, that sounds like fun…wanna try?"

"I have it on good authority it is unpleasant and embarrassing," Fiona said.

"That's a shame." Gieo stopped rubbing Fiona's stomach. She leaned back far enough to slip the strap-on out of her and set about removing the harness. "Since you refuse to enjoy sex and won't cower under the threat of unpleasant and embarrassing sodomy, dare I hope you'll tell me what's really wrong if I simply ask?"

Fiona propped herself up on her elbows and gave Gieo a long look-over with her eyes narrowed to sultry slits. "You know, your breasts look amazing in this light…"

"You can lick them if you want…" Gieo stomped her foot and shook her head. "Stop trying to distract me. What is going on in that tangled mess of wires between your ears?" Gieo finally slipped the strap-on off her hips and tossed it onto Fiona's stomach with a hollow thump and a tiny splat when the wet head whapped against flat skin.

"I'm worried about Veronica," Fiona said, looking down at the huge red dong resting just north of her bellybutton. "She was right about the consequences thing. If Zeke is going to come back, he's going to come back after her. I should have let her kill him."

"Baby, there's no way Zeke survived out in the desert with no supplies after fighting all night."

"He's too much of an asshole to die that easily." Fiona flopped back onto the bed and rested her hands above her head, staring at the ceiling pensively. "I also can't figure out why Zeke shielded me when I first came to Tombstone. I wasn't even really sure he had until I said the words out loud and made them real, but knowing now that he did, I have a powerful craving to know why."

"I'm about to finish my bike today," Gieo said. "I'll go scour the desert for his corpse, haul it back here, and you can interrogate it to your heart's content."

"How do you make it look so easy? Why aren't you tired and irritable like the rest of us?"

"Superior Asian genes, my bad-ass purple hair, and the love of a crazy woman."

"Blow me, Stacy." Fiona absently lifted the strap-on from her stomach and waggled it in Gieo's direction.

A silence hung in the air where Fiona had expected a giggle. She tossed aside the toy, pulled herself up into a sitting position, and looked to Gieo with concern.

"Is that why you call Veronica by her real name sometimes? Familiarity or control?" Gieo asked.

"What are you talking about?"

"You call her Tanner," Gieo said. "You don't seem to notice you're doing it, but she lights up like Christmas every time you do. It's only when you think you two are alone, and never more than once at a time, but I've heard you do it."

"A little of both, I suppose," Fiona said. Denial would be pointless; Gieo was nearly impossible to lie to and Fiona simply didn't have the energy to even try. "It feels like a special secret, knowing real names. Sometimes it just pops out."

"Bullshit," Gieo growled. "With her, you use it all sweet and tender. With me, you're mocking me or making a harsh point." Gieo pulled on her modified cargo shorts with elaborate tool belt functionality throughout, and began buttoning up the blouse she'd pulled open, but left on, when they'd started.

"That's not fair." Fiona hopped up and made to put an end to Gieo's hurried re-clothing efforts. "When you told me to pick, in front of everyone, I picked you." Fiona reached out to take Gieo's shoulder. In a blur she was spun around by her arm, her legs kicked out from under her, landing face first on the bed with a little bounce and squeak. Gieo was immediately on top of her, pinning Fiona's arm behind her back.

"When did I forget how to fight?" Fiona muttered.

"Veronica has been teaching me judo," Gieo explained calmly.

"And this is how you chose to tell me?"

"This is how I'm getting the point across that you need to treat me better no matter how tired you are."

Fiona couldn't decide which was wounded worse in the exchange: her pride at being so easily flipped by her much smaller, formerly-helpless girlfriend or her relationship prowess in that Gieo not only thought Fiona hadn't been treating her well, but that she also kind of agreed. Fiona didn't want the apology to sound coerced, although she wasn't sure how she would manage that considering Gieo pretty much had her helpless. "I'm sorry," Fiona muttered into the blanket. "I will try not to let my work make me distant, I'll stop calling Veronica by her real name, and I'll only call you Stacy in the sweetest and loving ways."

"And I get to try anal with you."

"Giving or receiving?"

"Giving!"

"You're going to have to go ahead and break my arm then."

Gieo released Fiona and sighed. "Fine, I accept your apology without the last condition."

Fiona sat up, rubbing her sore wrist, shoulder, and elbow in various alternating orders. "Why is that even in your head?"

"My natural and insatiable curiosity, I suppose. Hell, I built a robot who knows how to lie just to see if I could," Gieo said with a little snort. "I get curious and have to know if I can do something."

"Then wouldn't it make more sense for you to be on the receiving end?"

"Forget that," Gieo said. "It sounds unpleasant and embarrassing."

♠♣♥♦

They parted on friendlier terms than Gieo might have expected from the steep decline the conversation had taken. Fiona went off to the corral to see to the evening patrols, and Gieo headed up to the roof to sort the last few boxes she had of traded valuables, which she was eager to disperse and be rid of.

Ramen, who was the only one Gieo could trust with the overseer position, guided the work on the three dirigibles being built in the old park. The park apparently had never had much grass, and the community buildings ringing it in on the one side had long since stood empty. As with most things nobody else saw value in, the Ravens repurposed it all and had the open expanse functioning as an airship dry-dock in short order.

Gieo sifted through the dusty milk crates with no real aim in mind. She was still a little sexually frustrated from the fight that derailed her thrice daily getting laid, and none of her projects had the intrigue to distract her. Cowboy boots on the roof drew her eager attention, only to dash it when they belonged to Veronica.

"The ships are coming along," Veronica said. She was dressed in skin-tight black ropers, black cowboy boots with the jeans tucked in, a white tank-top, and a black Stetson. Her blond curls bouncing around her slender shoulders remained the only trapping that had once been her Madame Façade.

Gieo gave a non-committal shrug and returned to her sorting. She'd begun to figure out Veronica awhile back. Her colonization routine wrested power from whatever male hierarchy existed through the guise of sexual meekness and availability, which was why the Ravens had been so tarted-up in the first place, and then pulled the rug out as soon as they found their control. More than that, the fields of drugs were only partially grown for medicinal purposes. The remainder was spread among the handful of Tombstone men who had been vocal about the change in leadership. With the endless search for a dragon or Mary-Jane as their new goal and the Ravens as their only access, the vocal objections turned into hazy support. When the drugs could no longer be purchased through goods or coin, the five or six dozen men who had formerly despised the Ravens came willingly to know indentured servitude to pay for their fix. Gieo rightly suspected it would be a lifetime sentence, albeit one shortened by drug use and overwork.

"We still need pilots," Veronica said, strolling toward Gieo in a meandering path.

"We'll need to train them then," Gieo said. "Start scouring your ranks for spatial awareness and math skills, and I'll start writing the curriculum."

"Fiona will find us a target long before we have trained pilots." Veronica's shadow, long in the lateness of the hour, cast over Gieo, stretching all the way to the edge of the roof.

"Since I can only fly one at a time, I'm not really sure what you want me to do about that." Gieo stood up and turned to find herself only inches from Veronica. She smelled strongly of strawberry candy or lip gloss or shampoo or all of the above. Her wicked smirk, dazzling hazel eyes, and intimate proximity set Gieo's head spinning a little.

"I was thinking of a recruitment flight," Veronica whispered. "Juarez survived Mexico's bout with disease to become a free city state. Of course, it could be brought into the Raven fold with a little show of military might."

"Why not just run your prostitution and drug-ring scam on them?"

Veronica laughed and ran the backs of her fingertips down Gieo's cheek. "There is no universal tool to work every problem," she said. "If you can believe it, Juarez is even less civilized than Tombstone. They'll bend, but not from drugs or charm."

"There are no pilots in Juarez," Gieo said. "You're only after the slave labor."

"I'm after soldiers," Veronica corrected her. "Vegas is stretched thin right now trying to repel attacks on Reno and Bullhead City. There are five thousand Mexican regulars and former drug cartel foot-soldiers in Juarez. They could easily be turned to shock troops to help us break the line at Old Yuma."

"One airship is hardly going to scare them…you do realize you're standing really close to me, right?"

"You stopped being a pet a long time ago." Veronica reached up and snatched the front of Gieo's collar before she could even react. "Why are you still wearing this?"

Gieo had never seen someone move so fast; she could only imagine how deadly Veronica would be in a straight up gunfight. Regardless of being taken by surprise, Gieo refused to show a reaction. "It's a sex thing," she said with a gloating smirk. "Fiona likes tugging on it when she fucks me." There was no doubt in Gieo's mind that Veronica was a top to end all tops, but something about the way she moved, or eyed Fiona, or a quality even less tangible, told

Gieo she liked to be on the receiving end of fucking even if she liked dictating all the other terms of sex.

If the verbal blow landed, there wasn't any outward sign of it. Veronica smiled, a little crooked on the right, and pulled Gieo closer by the collar until the pilot could feel her breath when she spoke. "That sounds like our girl—she liked to pull my hair."

The circumstances were different, the comments more overt and the threatening overtones far more obvious, but Gieo quickly recognized the situation as the typical back-biting girl-style fighting. Veronica wouldn't physically attack Gieo when she could use snarky words to cut her emotionally; Gieo had really hoped that part of her life had ended with high school. In the past, she'd internalized her hurt, become quiet, sullen, and paranoid about every whisper behind her back that might be another jibe at her expense. It hadn't worked. Like blood in the water, the other girls had taken her castling as weakness and pressed forward with their stabbing her in the back. Gieo took a page from Fiona's operating manual and did something crazy instead.

As quickly as she could manage, which was far slower than Veronica's grab, Gieo reached up, snagged a handful of Veronica's blond tresses, yanked her head back, down, and to the right, and planted a wet, somewhat slobbery, kiss directly on her strawberry flavored lips. After she was certain her point was made with the unpleasant, almost virginally inept kiss, Gieo released Veronica's hair and wiped off her own lips with the back of her hand.

"Fancy that," Gieo said triumphantly. "I like to pull hair too!"

Veronica had long since lost her hold on Gieo's collar to stagger back a step or two. She raised her hand as if to wipe off her mouth, but stopped short, and regained an iota of her composure. The mask was shattered though, and they both knew Gieo had unbalanced Veronica's position.

"That's hardly a traditional judo move," Veronica said with a little laugh.

"You're hardly a traditional teacher, I'm hardly a traditional student, and this is hardly a traditional…" The rest of Gieo's tirade, which she really thought was building to a nice crescendo, was cut short when Veronica clipped Gieo's legs, spun her in a three-quarters circle, slinging her almost to the rooftop floor, bringing her to rest perfectly over a knee.

Gieo was a little surprised to find herself bent over, but more surprised at how easily and quickly Veronica had dropped to one knee without making so much as a thumping noise against the roof. Veronica had her sufficiently wrangled with a hand on the back of her collar and another resting on her lower back. Gieo's initial assessment of the situation as being simple emotional attacks and girl-fighting was apparently something else entirely, or maybe it wasn't, maybe all the girls who had been so horrible to her in high school had done so out of repressed, lesbian sexuality and desire; Gieo doubted it could account for all if it, but she began to wonder about a few cases in particular.

"If I'd met you first, I would have had you in my bed and on a throne next to me from our first night together," Veronica said. "Funny how the world works to rob me of the woman I love and give her over to someone I'm unerringly drawn to. No, funny isn't the word…"

"Who says I would have wanted you?" Gieo said, somewhat forced from her entire weight being supported over a single slender knee beneath her midsection.

Veronica pulled the back of her collar up and gave Gieo a hard swat on the behind. The sting of the slap and the tug on her collar were shockingly familiar and taboo at the same time. Gieo hated herself for liking the differences in how Veronica stole one of Fiona's routines.

"Say you wouldn't have and I'll let you go." Veronica's hand went from the spank to a gentle caress along the backs of Gieo's legs. Her fingers were soft, talented, and delicate like porcelain on lace.

"I would have," Gieo muttered. In the moment after, she could have kicked herself for not lying were it not for the difficulty of such an act in such a position.

"You're so like me, yet so…" Veronica's hand made its way up between Gieo's legs like a knife, thumping hard against her at the top, rubbing meaningfully at the warm, wet, unfinished business of earlier that afternoon. Gieo, almost as a biological imperative, moaned in response. "…sweet. I envy this niceness you've managed to retain through everything." Veronica had stopped rubbing on the word sweet, which made Gieo nearly scream in frustration, but began again when she lulled in describing her thoughts. Gieo demanded that her body stop enjoying being rubbed through her shorts, swore she liked Fiona's rough hands to Veronica's delicate ones, and prayed Veronica had no intention of stopping again. "You are quite possibly the last nice person left on the planet. It's almost unimaginable that you would let me do this to you."

"I don't have a choice," Gieo whimpered.

Veronica's hand stopped. "Ask me to stop." Gieo remained silent. "Or, ask me to keep going."

There were parts of Gieo that said the words, all but hurled them from her lips for Veronica to stop, but that wasn't what she said. In a voice she hardly recognized as her own, Gieo heard herself say, "Please, keep going."

Veronica did as requested, pressing the edge of her hand against the slit between Gieo's legs, finding the hard dot of her eager nub with the knuckle of her thumb, and teasing it back and forth, up and down, through the material of her shorts, sending much anticipated shockwaves of pleasure through Gieo's body. Gieo panted, gasped, and pulled ever closer to climax, head held up and throat slightly strangled by the collar that was to make her Fiona's alone.

"Did you want me when you first saw me?"

"No," Gieo said between moans. "When you saved me from the cultists, I saw something dangerous in you that I liked. It frightened and excited me."

"I'm getting a little sick of hearing how much I scare women," Veronica said, letting a little slack on Gieo's collar to make talking and moaning a little easier.

"I'm not scared for the reasons Fiona is…" Gieo had to pause in her speaking, had to pause in thinking as a whole when she finally came, in a low, earthy moan ending in a satisfied hiss tempered by a tinge of shame. Veronica slowed her rubbing and released her hold on Gieo's collar, letting her head dangle near the floor. Idle, delicate fingers stroked the sensitive hairs and skin at the nape of Gieo's neck in a lovely way that sent tingles to match the shivers of her orgasm.

"Then why?" Veronica asked softly.

"Because I want to be you."

Veronica helped Gieo to her feet and scooped the pilot up in a delicate, surprisingly romantic embrace that left Veronica's hand at the nape of Gieo's neck, never relenting on the gentle caresses that felt so heavenly. Veronica kissed Gieo lightly on the lips, gave her a final squeeze, and walked away without another word.

Chapter 18
Riding out for the territories

Fiona waited at the makeshift corral that was once the high school football field. The last patrol of the day came galloping in just before the sun dipped below the horizon. Fiona held the gate for the twenty odd riders and walked it slowly closed when they were through. Stephanie rode as the captain of the unit, although Fiona had wanted Cork in charge; Veronica insisted on Ravens in every position of leadership, leaving Cork as the official second without hope of promotion. Cork, a former Texas Ranger—of the lawman kind, not the baseball playing type—was a natural leader, a skilled horseman, and a crack shot with pistol, rifle, and shotgun; Fiona had plans to utilize those talents regardless of Veronica's decree.

Cork handed off his gelding to one of the stable boys, who had formerly been a grease monkey, and loped toward the stretch of fence Fiona was leaning against. He had the swagger and lean body of a man half his age with the weather-beaten rawhide of a man twice his years or more. His salt and pepper, handlebar moustache blew in the wind after he came to rest against the fence beside Fiona, taking on a stillness only broken by the breeze through his facial hair.

"Ten," Cork said in his low, even voice. "Glad we don't have to lug heads anymore."

"Since my goal is clearing space you'd only want to exaggerate down if you were going to at all," Fiona said. "Is Stephanie pulling her weight?"

“She doesn’t weigh much.”

Fiona smirked. “Was that a joke from stoic Cork? I thought you got your nickname for how quiet you were.”

“I only ever talk to you, ma’am,” Cork said. “You’re the only one of these ladies that wouldn’t shoot me for a wrong word or misstep.”

“I don’t know about that. Stephanie might even be sweet on you if you talked more.” Fiona nodded in Stephanie’s direction. She was currently barking orders at the remaining hunters, verbally chasing them into rank and file, demanding an accounting of all rounds spent. *She might not be a hunter, but she certainly cuts to the quick as a disciplinarian*, Fiona thought.

“Sounds like fraternization.”

“It does at that, but I’d feel a whole lot better about the merger of Tombstone and the Ravens if people started getting along,” Fiona said. Silence hung between them for a time. Fiona could sense Cork’s imminent departure to finish tending his weapons and mount—he had that potential energy look about him like a loose rock ready to tumble. “I want to start sending some smaller patrols east.” She hadn’t fully worked up the nerve to say so just yet, and her voice rose when she did, but she also didn’t want him to walk away and have to call him back. It was a ludicrous statement and she was hoping Cork wouldn’t piece things together.

“Nothing east of here but dead Mexicans,” Cork said.

“It’s the direction Zeke went.”

“I see.”

“I’ll mark it down as a sub-patrol of five when Stephanie is leading one of the larger columns in the west.” Fiona turned to look at the old Texas Ranger, waiting until he finally nodded. “Pick four of the best and keep your head on a swivel. Zeke’s craftier than any Slark.”

“I’ll do just that. Good evening, ma’am.” Cork tipped his hat and began swaggering back to the stables where the rest of the hunters were conglomerating.

Fiona pulled herself away from the fence, mounted her roan mare Tyra, and set off toward town at a brisk trot. She had a patrol of her own in the morning and a craving like hunger rising between her legs that she desperately needed Gieo to tend to before bed.

♠♣♥♦

Gieo paced the rooftop until sunset and then paced a little longer for good measure. She was starving, thirsty, and overheated, but she couldn't allow herself to deal with any of those things until she figured out what she was going to do about her infidelity.

Veronica was such a chaotic, dangerous figure; Gieo wished she would go away and stop making things complicated. Immediately after thinking that, she hated herself for it. Veronica was only partly to blame for what happened.

There wasn't even a good reason for it, not that Gieo believed there ever was a good reason for cheating, but in this particular case it was downright unconscionable considering her sexual needs were more than handled and her relationship with Fiona was rocky, but relatively stable. Excuses she wouldn't have bothered with, but she wished she at least had an explanation worth anything. All she could come up with was that something about Veronica got inside her head and crawled around. Superficially, Veronica was every girl who had ever made Gieo's life miserable, all grown up into exactly the type of successful, powerful woman she always thought they would grow up to be—but that wasn't the real Veronica. Underneath there was something insecure and vulnerable—something that Gieo shared with her. She suspected Veronica knew what it felt like to be an intellectual outsider, to live among a population neither capable nor interested in intelligent conversation, and to feel crazy sometimes for seeing the world in such drastically different ways than everyone else. Veronica was a fellow genius and Gieo couldn't help the kinship of outsiders inherently felt between them.

It wasn't until she'd nearly forgiven Veronica and herself for what they did as almost inevitable that she stopped to consider Veronica's motivation. If her true goal was to get Fiona back, the plan seemed likelier to earn them both a bullet. It couldn't be as simple as that, but the thought did raise concerns. Exactly how dangerous would Fiona be if the news was broken when she was armed…? Gieo briefly entertained the notion that getting shot by Fiona might not be a bad way to even the scales; this was quickly dismissed by the memories of what Fiona's .44 magnum did to people.

Gieo's thoughts were cut short when Ramen helicoptered in from the airfield on his twin rotors. If a robot could look self-satisfied, that was exactly what Ramen looked. For just having a couple of antennae and visual sensory apertures to emote with, he did a remarkable job of expressing himself.

"We're a week, maybe two, away from having a completed fleet with the big daddy set up for you and me, boss," Ramen said. "This'll be the shortest time between flights for us and the first time we'll have escort ships and planes—actual planes!"

Gieo stopped her pacing and glanced over to the hopping little robot. "What are you talking about?"

"Crop dusters!" Ramen fluttered a few feet off the ground in his excitement, sending clouds of dust away from the rooftop. "Someone found half a dozen crop dusters at the old airport and we're retrofitting them to burn ethanol. Each escort dirigible will be able to launch real fighter planes!"

"I have no idea how to fly something like that and no prayer of teaching anyone else," Gieo grumbled. "It's such a good idea though and all we'd need to do is find one pilot with half a brain to explain it." Gieo shook her head and groaned in frustration. "But I can't even think of a way to start looking because Veronica is pushing to enslave the town of Juarez and I cheated on Fiona this afternoon. My brain is a little too full with girl-trouble right now to divine an answer to a sudden need for crop-dusting pilots."

"You cheated on tall boss with blond boss?"

Gieo nodded; Ramen let out a low, somber whistle.

"Did you kiss her?"

"Sort of."

"Feel her up?"

"Not really."

"Lick her in inappropriate ways or places?"

"No, and it's weird to hear you talk like this."

"So what *did* you do?"

"Let her yank my collar and rub me through my shorts," Gieo said, a little too loudly. "Why am I even telling you this? I need to be figuring out a million things and none of them are easy!"

"Let's take a step back, look at the list of things to do, and find an easy one that you can fix right now." Ramen clattered over on his two mini-crawler legs, and placed his little omni-tool hand on Gieo's wrist. "Like you're always programming me: be solution oriented."

"Fine, okay, something easy…" Gieo thought for a moment. "I'm hungry. We can fix that."

"Sure we can, boss!" Ramen hopped over to the crate Gieo was sorting earlier and fished through to the bottom, coming up with a brown, plastic packet easily identifiable by anyone in the post-apocalyptic world as a meal-ready-to-eat, or MRE in military acronym-speak. The surplus, dehydrated, vacuum-sealed meals were designed to survive ages and possibly even nuclear explosions. They tasted horrible, made promises on the labels that the withered remains of food inside could never hope to keep, and required boiling water to make edible, but they were plentiful, almost completely immune to spoilage, and theoretically they were scientifically designed for maximum nutrition.

Gieo took the offered MRE and stopped short of tearing it open. On the packet, near the bottom where a blank line usually indicated the MRE was surplus that was never delivered to the military, there was a designation number. Whoever had traded the MRE to her had taken it from an actual military unit. The insignia was rare on its own, but the actual designation of the unit was downright baffling—the 76th Space Control Squadron of the Space Wing at Peterson Air Force Base in Colorado. The MRE had belonged to a missile command soldier, and quite possibly an astronaut.

"Where did we get this?" Gieo asked in a hushed whisper.

"From the Colorado hunting party staying here when we first arrived in town," Ramen explained. "They traded us a bunch of those for an old winch we got from installing a tape deck in Jackson's Wagoneer, which we then got a partial spool of chain for when we parted out the…"

"The men in the hunting party," Gieo interrupted, "were any of them wearing any old military clothing? Search back through your visual databases."

"Almost all of them at one point or another," Ramen said. "I'm surprised you didn't notice."

Gieo tried hard to remember what the burly mountain men looked like. If she mentally gave them a shave, cut their long manes of hair, and put them in flight suits rather than the heavy coats of trappers, she could almost picture them as the soldiers they once were.

"We had a whole hunting party of pilots and astronauts in town a few months ago and we didn't even notice," Gieo muttered. "I guess we can wait and see if they come back."

"Or you could just go see them, boss. They left the coordinates to their hunting lodge with me in case you ever wanted a change of scenery—it's outside Fort Carson. You were too busy making eyes at Fiona to notice, but they seemed really interested in having you work for them."

"That's something like 800 miles away," Gieo said, "across a bunch of free city state territory. It'd take weeks to get there on horseback if I got there at all."

"You could take your motorcycle and fuel up in Albuquerque. Word around the Ravens' camp is they've already tamed that city state."

"If I found already-trained pilots, there wouldn't be any reason to press Juarez…"

Cowboy boots thumping up to the roof snapped Gieo's head around. Fiona emerged from the roof access door looking dusty and a little bashful.

"If you don't need me anymore, I'm going to power down now, boss," Ramen said, powering down immediately after without waiting to see if Gieo did in fact need something else from him.

"I'm really sorry about being so distant earlier," Fiona said. "You've kept your personal stuff and work stuff separate so well and I should try to follow your example."

"Really, that's not…"

"No, let me finish," Fiona said. "You were right. I do need to treat you better and I'm planning on starting right now. Let's head downstairs and I promise my whole world will be about you until sunrise."

A wickedly barbed sea-serpent wound its way through Gieo's intestines and stomach threatening to turn her inside-out with anxiety. If she were a slightly more terrible person, she thought she might have taken the offer and then hopped on her bike the next day to drive to Colorado with or without telling Fiona before she left. Of course, if she were that kind of person, she assumed she might just be able to go her whole life without ever telling Fiona the truth. Veronica was right about her though; she was too nice.

"I did, or, rather, had done to me, what I'm fairly certain will be considered cheating in your eyes," Gieo blurted out.

Fiona's face went from blushingly excited to stricken. The transition sent a hot poker right through the center of Gieo's chest.

"Explain," Fiona croaked.

"Veronica came up here being weird and insulting, I kissed her, but in a really gross way to make her leave me alone, and then she flipped the switch to flattering," Gieo rattled off quickly in a single breath, hoping to get the entire explanation out before Fiona could respond. "She kind of spun me into a really vulnerable position and started rubbing me, but only through my clothes, and I kind of came."

"She asked you to ask her to keep going…" Fiona said. It should have sounded like a question, but nothing about the way she'd said it could make it anything other than a statement of unadulterated fact.

"Yes."

"And you did."

"Yes. How did you know?"

"Because that's what she does." Fiona didn't sound angry or look like she had any intention of shooting anyone or anything. Gieo desperately wished she would yell, threaten Veronica, or pistol whip the both of them while calling them every name in the book. But she didn't. She simply stood there with that stricken look on her face, twisting the fireplace poker rammed through the center of Gieo's heart. "The only question was going to be how you were going to respond."

"I think I know why I did it if you'll just let me explain…" Gieo took several steps toward Fiona, tears welling up at the corners of her eyes, blurring her vision.

"I don't suppose that matters now." Fiona held out her hand, keeping Gieo at arm's length. "You should probably go ahead and sleep up here; I see you've still got your tent set up."

"I might have to go to Colorado tomorrow," Gieo said, trying to throw everything she could at Fiona to keep her from going downstairs without her. "I'll have to leave really early, so we should talk about this now, before I have to go, since I might not come back."

"I suspect you'll make it there and back just fine if that's what you want," Fiona said. "If I don't see you before you leave tomorrow, have a safe journey."

Tears rolled down Gieo's cheeks. The cold, hollow way Fiona was speaking cut her more deeply than any explosive, violent reaction could have. There was a weary-resignation hanging off Fiona like a wet blanket and it made Gieo ache to her very core to know she was the one who put it there.

"I love you so much," Gieo said between sobs.

"I know you do," Fiona said. "It was never a question of that." She turned and walked back downstairs, closing the door behind her with a soft click that made Gieo flinch.

Chapter 19

Uncomfortable memories and departures

Fiona spent much of the night failing at sleeping. As the sky began to gray, she abandoned the project of rest, and dressed for the day. In the wee-predawn hours, Tombstone was as quiet and empty as a church. The sun would bring birds, buzzing insects, and the clamor of preparation for war, but in those small hours when the sky was only gray, not yet bringing the golden light of early morning, Fiona found a moment of peace. The livery, a new instillation within the city appropriately housed in the fabled O.K. corral as was its original intended purpose, was a short walk from the saloon. She picked up Tyra, brushed her, saddled her, and rode out for the stables.

The warmth and light of dawn hadn't fully settled over the desert by the time she trotted up to the old high school, but activity was brewing nevertheless. Cork and his riders were already saddled for their patrol. Fiona tipped her hat to the four hunters turned horsemen, who saluted her military style in return on their way out toward the rising sun.

Fiona veered her mare away from the main stables to where her car still sat, a month after its fateful drive across the open desert to lure the Slark away from the city. A thick layer of dust clung to it, leaving her to wonder if it would ever drive again. Nobody had even bothered pulling the tumbleweeds or brambles from the intakes. With a single finger, someone had drawn a heart on the driver side door in the dust. The heart's lines weren't completely clean, indicating it had probably been a week or more since its etching, but Fiona suspected she knew who had drawn it. It was the sort of thing Gieo would do.

Fiona dismounted, tied Tyra off on the spoiler at the rear of the car, and took a slow walk around her former vehicle, inspecting the sorry state it had come to. Though her original intent had been to survey damage, she continually returned to the heart to question its existence as though somehow she would be able to tell for sure if Gieo had drawn it or what it might have meant if someone else was the heart's artist. She heard Veronica ride up long before her thoroughbred came into view. Peppermint, Veronica's horse, was a colossal gray stallion of racing stock with an antsy stance and form-perfect gallop. The horse had a havoc personality and Veronica only encouraged her mount's aggressive proclivities. Tyra, who was not in season but recognized Peppermint's virility, strained against her tie-off when Veronica trotted up to where Fiona was standing.

"You're antagonizing my horse," Fiona muttered.

"There's a lot of sexual tension going around these days," Veronica said brazenly.

"Gieo told me what you did."

"I assumed she would," Veronica said, "but that's not why I'm here."

"I don't care why you're here," Fiona growled. "That's what we're talking about."

"Fine, what do you want to say?" Veronica turned Peppermint in a few slow pirouettes to take down some of his energy. She snapped her head around with each slow rotation to keep her eyes on Fiona. "Because I've got nothing to say on that topic."

"You couldn't leave it alone?"

Veronica shrugged.

Fiona saw red. "Do you even want her or are you just trying to spoil her for me?"

"What was good enough for you isn't good enough for her?" Veronica snarled. "Maybe you're forgetting what made me drop Carolyn in a hot minute to sew myself to your side? Are you mad at her because she's following in my footsteps or are you mad at me because you wish you hadn't blazed the trail in the first place?"

Anger drained out of Fiona like a rain barrel punctured at the base. She'd forgotten, somehow she'd forgotten. The trick she'd always blamed on Veronica was the one she'd invented. Before Veronica had done it with Gieo, before she'd done it with Beth, before she'd done it with Suzy, Jessica, Dylan, and half a dozen other girls, Fiona had done it to her. The collars, the dominance, the asking to be asked, it was all Fiona's creation. Veronica had used it to make certain points both to Fiona and Carolyn, but it originated with Veronica over Fiona's knee, betraying Carolyn and setting their whirlwind romance in motion with cheating as the norm.

"Both," Fiona whispered, "but mostly the latter."

"You're a racehorse with blinders on," Veronica said, her demeanor visibly softening. "You're going too fast to see and unable to look back at the chaos you're leaving in your wake. I won't deny the damage I've done or my part in the betrayal, but this little trick of seduction was yours."

"I know, I know. Let's say I owe you this chance, let's say I owe her the chance to choose, what are we supposed to do now?"

"We give her time to think," Veronica said. "If she was to do it on a knee-jerk, no pun intended, she'd pick you without hesitation, but that's not what you want, is it?"

Fiona shook her head. She'd laid the choice out for Veronica all those years ago, made it a hard choice to refuse, and put a short fuse on the powder-keg of a situation, but she'd still respected the choosing process. Ultimately, Veronica had picked her, had thrown Carolyn away without a second thought, and Fiona always had a doubt about Veronica's loyalty because of it. She didn't want the same specter haunting her relationship with Gieo, but at the same time she desperately wanted to have a relationship with the pilot and letting her choose might mean giving that up.

"She'll be gone for almost a week," Veronica said. "Give her that time and we'll ask her when she comes back."

Fiona nodded her agreement, but couldn't hold her tongue. "What do you really want from this? I don't believe you're after Gieo to have her for your own and I don't believe you're doing this just to fuck me over."

Veronica gave a tug on her reins bringing Peppermint into a stock-still stance that Fiona hadn't thought possible for the tightly-wound stallion. "I want everything," Veronica said in such an even and earnest tone that Fiona didn't doubt it for a moment. "I want her, I want you, part of me still wants Carolyn. Even now, even when I'm reshaping the world as I want it, I know I can't have everything. Still, I want you to know, my preference would be to have both of you. She's not that kind of girl and you're not one to share either of us, so I guess we'll just have to let it sort itself out."

From everything Fiona knew about Veronica, and she knew her very well, it was the truest thing she'd ever admitted. It was an impossible dream, but Fiona knew it was an honest one the moment she heard Veronica say the words. "What did you come out here to talk about?" Fiona asked, wanting to put conversational distance between herself and the hard truths brought down on her by their exchange thus far.

"Carolyn is coming in on the train today with two thousand infantry," Veronica said. "You need to find her a hard target within a day's march. We're resuming open hostilities with the Slark."

"With Los Angeles as the ultimate goal?" Fiona asked, knowing full well what the answer would be.

"With eradication of the invaders as the ultimate goal."

"I've been thinking about something Gieo told me and studying the maps she pieced together during her years of attempted flights," Fiona said, "and I think I have a target bigger than anything taken down since the cataclysm."

Veronica's eyes lit up like the desert sun. "Show me."

Gieo had spare Slark fuel, plenty of water both for drinking and steam powering her motorcycle, MREs, and Danny's old Winchester. She was as ready as she could make herself for the 800 mile trek to find pilots. Sitting on her bike behind the saloon, scarf pulled up over her nose and mouth, goggles fitted over her eyes, and helmet strapped securely over her braids, she couldn't bring herself to kick the engine over and take off for the mountains.

She wanted Fiona to come say goodbye.

Before the sun could even rise high enough for Gieo to consider it a late start, she spotted Fiona on her roan mare, riding out with her patrol of twenty-five, heading northwest toward the ruins of Tucson. Gieo silently wished Fiona good luck and cranked over her bike's engine. The heavily modified Indian motorcycle whirred to life like an alien abomination that combined a steam locomotive and a fighter jet, making Gieo exceptionally happy she'd decided to wear ear plugs.

Getting used to the bike's speed was a risky proposition. She wanted to take it slow, get a feel for the experimental technology, but the bike wanted to find its upper limits and then possibly push right through them. As Gieo shot out of Tombstone, she realized the bike was going to win that argument and possibly many others. The oversized, solid-form rubber ties, which each weighed nearly as much as she did, created weight enough to hold the bike to the ground, crushing rocks and debris without the slightest hesitation, but in no way strained the engine's remarkable power output. The bike's gyroscopes with counterbalances made controlling the motorcycle almost effortless, which was a feat in itself as the bike probably had a curb weight of nearly a ton. Gieo dipped and leaned into the corners, and the bike responded like a receptive lover.

She blew through the rubble that was once St. David and clipped the edge of Benson on her way to the remains of Interstate 10. Benson, which had been reclaimed by a handful of Cochise Indians, required a sharp turn through drastically decayed streets. Gieo pulled off the maneuver with grace and ease, much to the surprise of the collection of women on the side of the road, pressing corn tortillas beneath the shade of an old gas station awning. She waved briefly to them and gunned the motorcycle, flying up the ramp onto Interstate 10.

Even with the massive shocks she'd fitted to the bike's frame, the constant vibrations of the engine and the road combined with the motorcycle's impressive girth to set an ache to her hips and thighs, along with a numb behind. The crumbled remains of Deming, already washed away by the desert and neglect, left little hint of how to get to New Mexico 26. Gieo slowed the bike, against its protests, and wound her way through the ghostly streets until she finally found the general direction of northeast. The empty buildings, abandoned houses, and sandblasted remains of cars were chilling up close, and made her nervous wondering if one of the countless broken windows might hold a sniper waiting for just such an opportunity. Piloting across the desert was easier, and less lonely with Ramen in accompaniment; driving across the barren landscape was unnerving and far scarier than the prospect of having her airship shot out from underneath her.

Deming passed without incident though and she found what she believed, by solar navigation, to be NM 26. The road itself was difficult to discern from the surrounding desert, which had crept across the asphalt to reclaim the land. In more than a few stretches the only hint she had that she was even on the right track was the narrow corridor where sagebrush wasn't growing and the occasional milepost marker. On the open road, she found the motorcycle's engine, almost entirely air cooled, required a fairly high speed to keep from overheating. Her slowed search through Deming had apparently come dangerously close to swamping the bike. She had another change of highway to do at Hatch, and she wasn't eager to find out if her motorcycle was going to heat spike if she couldn't find her way to Interstate 25 in a timely fashion.

Hatch, which should have held the same nothingness of Deming, not only wasn't in ruins it was actually thriving to some degree. Plants flourished, trees provided shade, the roads were maintained, and people gawked at Gieo as she slowed her bike to pass through. A few of the Hatchians even waved. Aside from her motorcycle, the rest of the town appeared to be functioning just fine with horse traffic, even forcing her to dodge around a few buggies in the road. She desperately wanted to stop and see how they had managed to exist in the desert, but couldn't risk overheating her bike only to find out they weren't as friendly as the town made appearances to be.

After crossing a couple bridges over a few dirty canals, which explained the town's ability to flourish, Gieo noticed her motorcycle was beginning to struggle with overheating. A slow drain of water on the system exited via steam runoff valves into cooling coils which would eventually require time to let the steam condense back into water, which could take hours in the desert heat, or she could refill from the water supply she carried with her. If she was being honest with herself, the bike wasn't the only thing getting too hot and needing a drink.

Once on Interstate 25, the bike calmed a bit, slowly dropping off its temperature as the constant flow of air let the massive engine breathe easier. There was a reservoir nearby, although Gieo hadn't the faintest notion of how she might get down to it, or if it indeed had any water left. The other option was to continue on to Truth or Consequences and see if they had water and a shady place to rest. As far as symbolic destinations went, she thought Truth or Consequences was about as perfect of a location as there could be. She'd told the truth to Fiona and had no idea how dire the consequences were going to be, but, like the town, she decided she may as well roll the dice and see.

By the time she reached Truth or Consequences she was starving, boiling in the saddle, and fairly certain her legs, hips, and ass would never again know full sensation. The city itself, which stood somewhere between Deming and Hatch in condition, contained a few scarecrows of people far more afraid of the sound of the Slark engine in her bike than she was of them. She was clearly human, but none of the people in the decrepit buildings seemed to want to know anything else about her. She slowed briefly, enough to get her bearings, and then pushed the bike, which by that point was bellowing steam and making awful noises, toward the Elephant Butte reservoir. The weather-beaten signs guided her in reasonably short order to the state park landing. Water was harder to find with the dam effectively reduced to rubble by who knows what. Gieo brought the bike to a stop beneath a massive picnic table enclosure that had somehow survived the years. The water would be a short walk over open enough ground for her to see back up to her bike if necessary.

Lowering the bike's pod legs to hold it in place required manual cranking as not enough water remained in the system to run the hydraulics. Out of the saddle, everything in her body screamed at the change of position. Her lower back ached, her legs felt like jelly, and her butt was numb beyond anything she could have imagined. She unhooked the two brass reservoirs on the sides of the bike and began her slow trek down to the water. Without a functional dam to hold the reservoir, much of the lake had leaked out, leaving her to walk a fair distance over sun-baked lakebed before finally reaching the water. Along the way she passed the bleached remains of trees, rocks, and even giant skeletons of great catfish two or three feet in length, picked clean by scavengers and left to turn to dust in the desert sun. Gieo peeled off her helmet, scarf, goggles, and boots to stand with her feet in the cool water, leaning down occasionally to splash handfuls of the lake over her head, face, and neck. The afternoon sun caught on the water's surface, creating shimmering patterns over the bluer than blue lake.

When she'd brought her internal temperature down enough for comfort, she shielded her eyes from the sun to gaze out over the beauty of the lake, not natural specifically considering it was a man-made reservoir, but natural enough. She felt like a pioneer or explorer, two feelings she'd never considered the value of but suddenly really enjoyed. If she had one wish, it would be that Fiona could share the feelings with her. Of course, she would need two wishes to transport Fiona there and also grant her forgiveness.

Gieo settled her goggles back over her eyes, slung her helmet and scarf over one shoulder and set to refilling the bike's water tanks. The great brass canisters were ludicrously heavy when filled, and Gieo found the hike back up the hill a good deal harder than the one down. To add to the difficulty, the numbness that had gripped her lower body retreated like the waters of the lake, only to leave her with profoundly inflamed muscles not used to the type or vigor of the exercise of riding such a massive motorcycle over such long distances. Nearly to the bike, with most of her cooling-off work entirely undone by the hike back out of the lakebed, she spotted movement under the awning. She dropped the canisters beneath a hickory tree without a second thought and slid the Winchester from her back.

Her heart thundered in her ears with every step as she crept up toward the awning. She levered a shell into the chamber with slow, deliberate movements as not to be heard, and made a wide arc around the shaded area to flank whatever was investigating her bike. Deer, she prayed for it to be deer, or maybe a coyote, or even a feral dog. Or if it had to be humanoid, let it be a Slark, she could shoot a Slark. Her heart sank when she stepped onto the cement area holding the two dozen picnic tables. It was a human. A man to be specific or, at least, what was left of one. His tattered rags and jumbled collection of worn containers like fanny-packs and makeshift satchels, spoke of a scavenger's life on the edge of ruin. Gieo stepped from the cover of the picnic tables and held the rifle out not in a threatening manner, but sideways to show she didn't have intention of shooting him.

"Hello there," Gieo said.

The man leapt nearly out of his skin, and more than clear of the bike. The sharp, wild look to his eyes told her he wasn't a methanol drinker, but nor was he in possession of a complete deck of mental cards. He backed off, mumbling under his breath, words meant only for himself, at a pace Gieo couldn't have kept up with even if he spoke loud enough and directly to her.

"I don't want to hurt you," Gieo said, "but I can't let you strip my bike either." She dropped her voice to the most soothing tone she could manage. Noting, with some surprise, that she sounded a little like a TV anchor when she tried to be calming.

The man showed no outward understanding of what she was saying; his conversation with himself completely engrossed him. He was backing away as she slowly walked forward, and his posture didn't seem particularly threatening. He walked with something of a limp in his right leg, and repeatedly brought withered, leathery hands up to his scraggly beard to pick at something she couldn't quite make out. As she got a better look at him, she realized he was a hair above a skeleton in girth, possibly thirty or seventy years old from how sun-beaten and hard time had been on him. More than anything she just wanted to help him, feed him, give him water, or something reasonable to wear. She'd never seen anyone so downtrodden and frayed; it all cut right to her nurturing, altruistic instincts and triggered them all.

"What's your name?" Gieo asked. "Do you have a name? Mine's Gieo."

The slow walking and talking act brought her to within reach of her bike and put him off the edge of the picnic table area, standing just inside the shadow cast by the awning in the late afternoon sun. His conversation with himself continued, unabated by anything she said, without the slightest sign of becoming intelligible.

"Are you hungry? Thirsty? I have some food with me if you'd like," Gieo said.

The man's conversation with himself came to an abrupt end, and his hands, the gnarled, skeletal claws that they were, shot down to one of his many belts, and quickly drew a battered old 9 mm pistol. She swung the rifle out of the non-threatening pose and brought it to her shoulder. Every tendon in the man's gun arm, visible beneath his overly tanned skin, tensed to pull the trigger. The world slowed, Gieo fired first, the rifle bucked in her arms, and a modest wound opened on the right side of the man's chest with a spray of blood and gore blasting out the back across the hardscrabble ground behind. He crumpled like so much old newspaper, never dropping his gun, but never firing it either.

Gieo was practically panting in the brief aftermath. A few birds, flushed by the sound of rifle fire, scattered from the tree she'd dropped the canisters under. She flicked the lever action and slowly crept between the remains of picnic tables to find the downed man. His feet came into view first, still and dirty, then his skinny legs clothed only in rags, then his stomach and chest, working furiously at shallow, agonizing breaths. He was talking to himself again, although much slower now, but still unintelligible, struggling to form the words amidst his strained breathing. Before she could even reach him, his shallow, labored breathing came to a slow, whimpering end with a frothy bubbling of blood exiting the hole in his chest.

Gieo's trembling hands set aside the rifle, leaning it against the post of the awning. She sat down hard on the edge of the cement, gripped her knees to her chest, and cried. A strange feeling, something long forgotten and buried, came rushing back. It contained guilt, which made sense, and of course shame, which was appropriate, but also something else, something she'd thought she would never feel again after feeling it her first time. She was fifteen when she'd experienced it, with a boy, the only boy she'd ever been with, at aerospace camp, when she was still trying desperately to prove to herself and everyone else that she wasn't gay—she'd lost her virginity to him. His name was Jared Bae, and he too had been trying to prove he wasn't gay. In the embarrassing, painful, and humiliating act between them, they both managed to verify to themselves and each other, unequivocally, that they were both indeed homosexual. The loss of her virginity and its accompanying innocence was a horrible, aching loss for a fifteen-year-old girl, and she'd only consoled herself in her purity's passing with the firm understanding that she would never have to experience it again.

Staring at the lifeless body of the man she'd shot, the loss of an innocence she didn't even know she had crushed her anew.

The foolish, impetuous, and scientifically motivated part of her brain demanded that she inspect the man's weapon to prove to herself that it was either him or her, that necessity, like in that dormitory room with Jared Bae, had forced her actions. She pried the weapon from the man's limp hand only to find the gun was all but fused together from time, grit, and neglect. She couldn't force the slide back or even pull the rusted clip out, never mind the fact that the trigger had broken off at some point. He could no more have shot her with his extended finger than that gun. Like before, when she felt forced into unbidden action, she'd made a mistake and lost her innocence to yet another man, but this one wouldn't be better off for the discovery.

Part of her wanted to know who he was. Part of her wanted to give him a proper burial. Part of her wanted to shrug it off as an aspect of survival in the new world as so many others around her seemed able to do. But these parts were not to be listened to. She dropped the pistol next to the body. She slipped her rifle into its holster along her back; it wasn't Danny's anymore—he was dead and she'd killed with it. That rifle belonged to her as much as she belonged to it. With the refilled tanks refitted to the bike, she left the reservoir in her rearview mirror, knowing she left a part of herself there when she did.

Chapter 20
Yahweh sightings and things to come

Fiona didn't need to be told what she was looking at. At the edge of Drexel Heights, in what used to be the collection of single-story buildings and mobile homes of Mission Valley at the southern end of Tucson, the methanol drinking cult of the Hawkins House had made its new home. Through the scope of the high-powered hunting rifle borrowed from one of her riders, she estimated their numbers to be close to a hundred. It was difficult to make out from the distance, but she suspected she saw Yahweh walking among them.

"What do you want to do?" Claudia asked.

Fiona handed back her Marlin 270. Claudia was petite, roughly the size and dimensions of Gieo, but French Canadian to the very core with big, round, blue eyes, pale skin, and naturally curly black hair held back in a ponytail. As adorable as she was singing French love ballads on stage during burlesque shows, Fiona knew her to be a crack shot with the black-stock Marlin and a talented tracker of the open desert. As a number two for her patrols, Fiona felt fortunate to have Claudia.

"I can't justify the losses we might take or the bullets we'd burn wiping them out," Fiona said.

"They're in our way, no?" Claudia shouldered the rifle and looked down the low bluff across the sage and Joshua trees as though she were plotting attack patterns and cover.

"They are, but they're not dangerous this far from Tombstone and they're not going anywhere." Fiona slid back down the other side of the bluff to where the rest of her riders waited in a holding pattern. Claudia reluctantly followed. "Carolyn is bringing in two thousand army regulars. If these cultists need to be moved, the Red Queen will move them. It's enough right now to know where and how many there are."

"Your patience surprises me, Commander," Claudia said with a coquettish smirk. She adjusted her black, CSOR beret with the maple leaf and dagger insignia. "From what I had heard of you, restraint was not your forte."

Fiona had her doubts about Claudia actually being a former Canadian Special Operations Regiment commando, but there was little doubt she knew enough about explosives and small arms to fake it. The beret fit her perfectly too, which lent some credibility to the story. She was right about Fiona's restraint though—it wasn't something she'd shown in the past.

"From what I heard, Canada didn't allow women in combat," Fiona replied, bringing a light chuckle from the riders near enough to overhear the jibe.

"Perhaps not, but this has been remedied since, no?" Claudia slung her rifle over her shoulder and vaulted into the saddle of her horse like a sprightly pixie sniper. "If you must know, I am the daughter of a commando."

"Your father is still alive then?"

"This I cannot say, but I would be surprised to find he is not. What of your own father? Did he die in the invasion of Los Angeles as so many did?"

"I sure hope so," Fiona said, bringing another, more nervous chuckle from her gathered riders.

"Then for your sake, I hope he did," Claudia said with a little smile and a wink. "It would seem we have other patrol concerns more pressing at the moment, Commander." She nodded to a dust trail across the open desert to the south.

Fiona led her column out in that direction, over a second rise, close enough for Claudia to get a good look at what was kicking up the desert floor. Sighted in through her scope, Claudia let out a low whistle. "You will call me a liar when I tell you what I see," Claudia said. "A Slark patrol is chasing two wagons driven by methanol drinkers."

"I'll call you a liar if you're proven wrong," Fiona said. "Regardless of who the lizards are chasing, they're on our land and need to learn it." The riders let out a whoop with this, and Fiona led them on a charge across the desert, kicking up their own cloud of dust, thundering hooves at a gallop on an intercept course.

Fiona rose up in the saddle, letting her legs absorb the shocks of the galloping, flattening her back to run parallel to Tyra's. She was out ahead of the formation, tucking her head into the wash of her horse's mane, keeping tilted enough for the air rushing past to go over her hat, rather than knocking it off. She was coming up on the two wagons quickly. They'd lost the road to charge wildly into the desert. Fiona spotted the Slark crawlers beyond the wagons, gaining ground quickly. She shot past the startled dozen or so people divvied up between the two wagons, riding close enough to get a good enough look at them; Claudia was telling the truth—they were all sporting the chipped up marble eyes of methanol drinkers.

Closing on the Slark, who hadn't anticipated anything but easy pickings, Fiona pulled her pistol and gestured with it to split her formation, narrow it out, turn it into two waves that would pass on opposite sides of the two crawlers. She veered left, leading the first cluster of twelve in a line along one side of the Slark formation. Leveling her pistol at the driver of the lead crawler, she fired. The pistol bucked in her hand and the shot landed, albeit a glancing blow that took a chunk out of the lizard man's right side. A few shots from carbines, sub machineguns, pistols, and rifles rippled in from behind her, finishing off the driver and the obvious gunners along the sides.

The second crawler, in a much better position to defend itself, took a few shots at Fiona's riders. They missed her, and she got a couple more shots off, taking one more Slark before clearing the formation, but she heard the thumping of a rider going down behind her and knew they'd made at least one solid hit. Their focus on Fiona's wave left the second crawler vulnerable to Claudia's charge up the other side with the remaining twelve. She slowed in the attack, taking full advantage of their exposed backs, to all but wipe out the Slark on the second crawler.

Fiona led the remains of her charge in a sharp turn, allowing Claudia's loop to swing around the outside before both waves could turn back on the Slark formation. The remaining dozen or so of the lizard men had abandoned the shot-up crawlers and were scattering to the desert, dropping to run on all six limbs when they fled. Fiona led her group up the same side Claudia had cleared, but in the opposite direction, fanning her formation out with a chopping gesture of her shiny Colt Anaconda. The lone Slark who had made it the farthest reared up when she barreled down on him, raising his strange looking rifle to fire. Fiona never gave him the chance. She leaned in low along Tyra's side to present a smaller target, focused down her arm, and fired, blowing the top part of the Slark's head clean off.

Her riders on both sides of the formation finished cleaning up the last of the Slark, even sending a few of the fastest to chase down the stragglers who had fled at the first sight of the dust cloud on the horizon. Fiona turned her attention back to the wagons, which had stopped to see about the outcome of the battle; this was damn peculiar behavior, as far as Fiona was concerned.

"See about the wounded," Fiona barked to Claudia as she rode past, heading in the direction of the wagons. In all the excitement of battle, with her heart still racing and her hands still tingling, Fiona couldn't remember how many shots she'd fired. Her gun may be empty or it might be down to a couple more shots; she couldn't be sure and neither would be good news if the cultists on the wagons turned out to be unfriendly toward their rescuers.

As she neared, she noticed the wagons had taken some fire from the Slark, and hadn't faired too well in the exchange. The survivors looked frightened of Fiona and her approaching handful of riders. A quick count of those left alive in the wagons revealed ten: four women, four children, and two teenage boys. Three men were dead or dying in various defensive positions on the wagon, and Fiona suspected a fourth had been thrown at one point or other.

"Why aren't the Slark afraid of you anymore?" Fiona demanded, unsure if the cultists even had an answer to that question. "What are you doing out here in a couple of rickety wagons?" she continued before hearing an answer to her first query.

A matronly woman, the one who had been driving the lead wagon until the team of two very old horses had nearly dropped, stood from the bench seat, and turned her sightless eyes in the direction of the voice addressing her.

"The demons haven't feared our holy sacrifice since the battle outside Tombstone," the woman said. "Their fright subsided quickly when battle was upon them and we would have been overcome were it not for the Prophet's brother. Some escaped and no doubt told the rest that they had nothing to fear of the sightless. We have been hiding and fleeing from them ever since."

"Slick tricks can only get you so far, it would seem," Fiona said, but immediately regretted it. People did far more foolish things for a slim chance at survival in the early days of the Slark invasion and she couldn't fault the efforts that had apparently served these cultists well for six years just because it finally stopped working. "If they're giving you so much trouble, why roam around in the open during the day?"

"We are fleeing the Prophet's care," the woman said. She had a worn, tired look about her. Fiona might have guessed forty or fifty, but the oddly smooth quality of the skin on her neck said she was young turned prematurely old by a hard life; her real age was probably a lot closer to thirty. "He can no longer protect us. The apocalypse he promised has come and gone, but the Lord did not send for us. We are hungry and need shelter. We had hoped to find the Prophet's brother victorious and once again offering protection in Tombstone. Did he return to his post?"

"He lost and was sent packing into the east," Fiona said. "Tombstone is under Raven control, so I doubt you'll find much there to your liking."

"We will accept Raven rule," the woman said. One of the teenage boys stood from the wagon to protest, but the woman wheeled around and caught him with a harsh backhand across the cheek before he could utter a word. She reached out with the other hand, fumbling blindly for a moment, and caught him by the front of the shirt before the strike could send him tumbling out of the wagon. Fiona was more than a little impressed at the woman's alacrity considering her blindness and awkward footing. "I'll not see you and your sister starved or killed by demonic invaders," the woman hissed at the boy, who was obviously her eldest son. "If we must sacrifice our faith for food and protection, then so be it."

Claudia rode up in the midst of the exchange. She gave the cultists in the wagons a confused glance, but didn't really seem interested in what drama was unfolding amongst the blind. "Karen had her horse shot out from underneath her," Claudia said. "I think her leg is broken. Francisco was shot in the arm, but he says he is okay; I think he is lying and likely to die if he does not let someone help him."

"Dump the bodies out of the wagons," Fiona said, "and load Karen and Francisco into them. See about getting a splint on Karen's leg and a tourniquet on Francisco's arm—we just need them good enough to make it back to town."

"These cultists, what would you like me to do with them?" Claudia asked.

"We're taking them with us." Fiona felt the creeping sensation of someone watching her, then another and another. The low rise she'd started her charge from held a new army, more than enough to cause a problem for her, with Yahweh at the head. "The world is an irritating place when old enemies just keep resurfacing to get in the way of more important work being done."

Claudia noticed in much the same time Fiona did. She hefted her rifle to her shoulder and sighted in on Yahweh's chest. "I can make sure he does not resurface again," Claudia said.

"No, with wounded in tow, our horses lathered, the element of surprise long gone, and much of our ammunition spent, he wouldn't be the only one not resurfacing," Fiona said. "We move out; Francisco and Karen won't survive a fight and we can't leave them. If he follows, then you can put a round in him and we'll all have a lovely Alamo moment."

Claudia reluctantly lowered her rifle. "Mark my words, Commander, I will be the one to kill that man for you."

"Let's hope you don't have to do it today." Fiona kept her eyes on the rise as they departed slowly, keeping riders at a walk to guard the wagons' front, rear, and sides. The cultists watched them leave, but did not pursue. As the sun began to set, and the column pulled well out of firing range, the silhouettes of the cultists retreated from the rise. For a brief moment, Fiona considered sending Claudia back to take out Yahweh in the last of the light, but it felt risky. As little as Fiona thought of Yahweh, she knew he wasn't stupid; Claudia might have an easy time of it, or she might ride into a trap, and she was too valuable to risk on a solo mission with a fairly trivial goal. If what the cultist lady said was true, Yahweh was already losing his chips and had a lousy hand of cards.

♠♣♥♦

Albuquerque had taken the hardest hit in the state. Gieo knew this, knew they'd had an Air Force base that the Slark no doubted wanted gone in the early days of their invasion, but couldn't imagine a way a city could rebound from that level of destruction to rise again as a free city state. As far as she knew, the city had gone from being the largest metropolitan area in New Mexico to a graveyard for half a million people. As she drew nearer to where she should have been able to see the skyline, all she saw was the ruins and craters left by the invasion. The entire south, where she assumed the Air Force base was, had been reduced to the obliterated dark side of the moon. Makeshift signs guided her to the west to use the detour around the ruins as all freeways through the city were long since destroyed with little hope of ever being rebuilt.

The eerie feeling she had driving through Deming was compounded a thousandfold through what remained of Albuquerque. The handmade signs along the detour became thicker, clearer, and the buildings they surrounded became sparser. Strangely, the sparseness was orderly, not the destruction of invasion, but of organized scavenging. Someone had done a fantastic job of dismantling everything in the area for building materials. The closer she got to the city state, the more stripped the world around her became. Her long, winding loop through the ruins of South Valley finally deposited her on Interstate 40 to head northeast. As she neared the Rio Grande River, she spotted the Albuquerque free city state, rising like a walled fortress of old, around Grande Heights and Villa De Paza.

Gieo was exhausted and numb both emotionally and physically. She was eager for rest and a chance to process the day. Her motorcycle was again coughing steam and nearly at the redline for temperature from the slow detour, and she had to practically will it up to the city's massive gates. She'd expected Ravens to be manning the checkpoint and defensive walls, but instead found what looked like normal United States Army. Two men, clean shaven, in full desert camouflage, armed with M-16s stopped her at the gate. She hand cranked down the pod to brace the bike and waved away the steam fogging up her goggles. They flanked her on either side, although didn't seem all that suspicious or threatened by her.

"What business do you have in Albuquerque?" one of the soldiers asked.

Gieo reached into the front pocket of her cargo pants and pulled out a letter of introduction from Veronica intended for the White Bishop in charge of Albuquerque. She handed it to the soldier who read it over quickly before handing it back.

"Wait here," the soldier said. He left his partner to watch over Gieo while he went to the guard booth, hand cranked an old World War II radio to life and spoke briefly into it, doing more listening than talking. He returned in short order, motioning to the men walking posts along the top of the forty-foot defensive wall, which was actually quite marvelous close up. The huge, steel gates slowly wound open, apparently pulled by engines on the opposite side. The soldiers waved Gieo through without another word.

The interior of the free city looked like a combination of the formerly upscale neighborhood, American southwest pueblos, and a medieval city of Europe. Gieo's bike argued with her all the way through the gate, and only made it a few blocks in before finally cutting out and quitting on her. She'd run dry or too hot for too long and the bike wouldn't be moved short of time to cool or a good dousing with cold water. She lowered the pod legs again, removed her helmet and scarf, and fell forward against the handlebars to cry. She didn't care that the people walking the streets around her stopped to stare, that the very professional looking soldiers patrolling the street might think she was weak or simpering; she had an upset stomach full of agitated nerves and crying seemed like a fine release, at least for some of them. She was tired, hot, dirty, and painfully alone with thoughts she hoped she would never have to deal with. Her crying might have continued indefinitely were it not for a gentle hand on her shoulder. She snapped her head up from the handlebars. Crying into her goggles had the obvious consequence of filling them with water. She yanked them free of her head and wiped at her eyes with the gritty back of her gloved hand, which only served to further irritate the already enflamed skin around her eyes.

The woman who had touched her shoulder was a towering Amazon, black as the ace of spades, with an impressive head of dreadlocks, and a powerful set of musculature on her lofty frame. She was dressed in khaki shorts, hiking boots, and a tank-top looking a little like a nature show host. She was flanked by two U.S. soldiers who actually stood several inches shorter than her. Her skin, which was the most beautiful shade of shiny ebony, was lined in dozens of places with white scars, which she apparently wore clothing to accentuate, rather than conceal. Something about her face was kind and a little wild.

"You're the rider from Tombstone the gate mentioned?" the woman asked, knowing full well who Gieo was. Her voice was rich and smooth with a worn edge that put her age at likely over forty.

Gieo sniffled and offered the woman the letter from Veronica. She took it but handed it off to one of her guards without even glancing at it.

"Do you have a name, girl?" the woman asked.

"I'm Gieo," she replied. Getting out of the saddle the second time was harder than the first, and Gieo actually nearly toppled over, requiring a little steadying from the Amazonian woman.

"Take your time," the woman said. "A bike like that must rattle every drop of blood out of your legs on a long enough ride." She smiled showing off the whitest, straightest teeth Gieo had ever seen. By standing next to her on the sidewalk, Gieo guessed the khaki-clad woman to be almost six and a half feet tall.

"It's been a really long day," Gieo said weakly.

"I can imagine," the woman replied. "I'm Alondra McMichael, White Bishop of Albuquerque."

Gieo returned the smile, feeling the warmth of the woman's protection stretching over her. There was something powerful and confident about Alondra that spoke of a cunning yet caring natural leader. Gieo was infinitely pleased to see this side of the Ravens.

As they walked the streets, Alondra insisted Gieo take her arm for support as needed. Gieo gratefully accepted gaining more than physical support from the gesture. The city she saw on their brief walk toward Alondra's home spoke of a size and scope Gieo didn't think existed anymore with an order that almost felt like old times.

"How many people live here?" Gieo asked.

"Our last census estimates put it at around seven thousand," Alondra said. "Not counting the fifteen-hundred soldiers."

"Yeah, about them…" Gieo nodded in the direction of one of the soldiers flanking them.

"You've no doubt heard about the fracturing that took place on the plains in the late days of the war with the Slark," Alondra said.

Gieo shook her head. After Orange County fell, she and her family had fled east without thought to anything beyond survival; the only thing she knew about the war with the Slark was the U.S. and her allies had lost, but made sure the Slark went down with them.

"Well, the military rallied nearly everything they had left on the great planes, outside of Cedar Rapids, to make a final push against the Slark's great crawler battalions. You remember those certainly, the walking cities of firepower that they had before the cataclysm?" Alondra asked.

Gieo remembered, could still hear their great clanking legs, as long and tall as city streets, swinging overhead while the bombs and fire rained down from the platform hundreds of yards above. It was months into the war before anyone even knew what a Slark looked like as they had used the great crawlers almost exclusively. It wasn't until three missile frigates off the coast of Alaska actually brought one down that humanity learned what they were fighting was lizard men from space.

"The army fractured. Many of the men abandoned their post, followed Brigadier General Mackenzie who would become a warlord, and fled south toward Texas and Mexico to begin a guerilla war," Alondra continued. "Those who remained fought the Slark valiantly and lost. The Ravens have been picking up the pieces ever since. Finding soldiers still interested in fighting is surprisingly simple. Once a soldier, always a soldier, eh, boys?"

"Oorah, ma'am," the two soldiers said in unison.

"Most of the men here are army regulars from one place or other, but my personal guard is Marine Corps. My father was a leatherneck, my husband was a leatherneck, and my son was a leatherneck," Alondra said with a noble sadness. "There's something powerfully special about the Marines."

Gieo didn't need to ask. She could infer from Alondra's tone and use of the past tense that the three men mentioned were no longer living. Next to Alondra, Gieo felt small, with small problems, small emotional burdens, and small goals; greatness, she surmised, had the ability to do that.

"Why the defensive walls?" Gieo asked, eager to be away from the topic of dead Marines.

"After the fracture, Albuquerque had some problems with raiders from the aforementioned warlord. The walls were built out of necessity, and when I arrived, I reinforced and manned them," Alondra said. "The raids have stopped. I don't know where General Mackenzie went, but he's long since abandoned his attacks on the west now that the Ravens have moved in. For the time being, I sit, build, and wait to hear when we move. I had hoped that's why you were here, but you're no messenger."

"I'm on my way to Colorado in search of pilots," Gieo said. "We're building an air force in Tombstone."

Alondra laughed loud, long, and hard, so much so that her Marine entourage laughed with her. Gieo waited out the laughter, but felt a little insulted by its boisterousness and length.

"Veronica is a madwoman," Alondra said, "but I guess that's the type of thinking the Ravens have always taken a shine to."

They strolled up the walkway of a large, two-story, stucco home with a riverside view. A lovely cactus garden lined what used to be the front lawn. The Marine escort left their company at the front door.

The interior was dimly-lit and a good ten degrees cooler than outside. The American southwest décor continued throughout, mixing native and Spanish influences both in architecture and decoration. Alondra led Gieo to a side guest room down a seldom used hallway. The room had an honest to goodness bed, a bookshelf filled with old Louis L'Amour books, and a bathroom opposite the walk-in closet.

"Get showered, cooled off, and come find me on the back patio when you're ready to eat," Alondra said.

"Showered?" Gieo asked with unabashed hope.

"Hot and cold running water," Alondra said. "This is civilization, after all."

Gieo barely waited for the door to close before running for the bathroom, stripping off her clothes with every step.

Chapter 21

It's all uphill from here

It had been close to six years since Gieo's last shower. Sponge baths, tub baths, and bathing in lakes and streams were all effective enough to get the job done, but there was something delightfully decadent about a shower that she just didn't appreciate until after it was gone. She ran the water cold first to wash away the grit and sweat of the day. Once her skin was cooled and cleaned in a way it hadn't been in six years, she turned the water knob for hot, finding the simple pleasure she'd almost forgotten existed—hot water from a shower head. For the first time in ages, she stepped from a shower clean and refreshed. If civilization had any argument for its existence, a shower was it.

Indoor plumbing really seemed like a fanciful world that included movies, the internet, and cable TV. Standing in the tiny bathroom, wrapped in a towel, still dripping wet, Gieo tested the handle on the toilet. It flushed. She nearly burst into tears of joy right then and there. All the nervous energy of the day combined with the things she'd long since forgotten about missing, and she found herself on the edge of hysterics at something as simple as a shower and flushing toilet still existing somewhere. Part of her, a very loud, vocal part of her screamed that she should live in Albuquerque; she would be infinitely more helpful to the Ravens if she could take a shower and use an indoor bathroom. Something Alondra had said to her snapped her from her delusional thoughts.

She burst from the bathroom and quickly got dressed in repeatedly-patched and leather-reinforced blue jeans and a white pleasant blouse. In bare feet, her purple hair with increasingly long black roots still wet, she padded through the house to the back patio. The smell of a summer barbeque greeted her long before she could find her way onto the Spanish-style veranda. The patio's plank trellis held tomato plants and an entire herb garden in hanging pottery. The sky was painted in vibrant pinks and oranges traditional of sunsets in the desert. To the east, down the hill, a handful of men in waders were standing in the river, fly fishing to add their bait to the whirring insects brought out by the coolness of dusk. Alondra stood at the edge of the lowest tier of the tile patio. Smoke from the massive black grill scented the air with cooking meat, vegetables, and hickory. Gieo's focus melted into the beauty of the scene and the familiar smell from suburbia of a backyard barbeque. She nearly broke into tears again.

Alondra came walking up toward the house with a tray of grilled food, steaming even in the warmth of the New Mexico evening. She pointed with her grill tongs to a mosaic-top metal patio set. Gieo made her way down to the circular table surrounded by four chairs and took her seat at one of two place settings. Alondra set down the tray, resting the tongs across the barbequed chicken pieces, tomatoes, and corn on the cob. She took her seat across from Gieo and smiled with those brilliant, white teeth.

There was so much about Alondra that spoke of an eternal youth. Her body easily could have belonged to a nineteen-year-old athlete, as could her skin, but her eyes, hands, and voice spoke of an age and experience well beyond a possible number. Gieo found herself far more in awe of Alondra than attracted to her, although her undeniable substance and wisdom were beautiful yet imposing qualities.

"You have indoor plumbing," Gieo said, unfurling one of the cloth napkins to drape it over her lap.

"Most Raven cities do," Alondra said. "The basic components of our oldest technologies survived the cataclysm and people who knew how to put them together and make them work aren't difficult to find if you exchange protection and food for their expertise. Las Vegas's very existence is owed to human arrogance and technological triumphs. This is even truer now as the Raven capitol."

"Then why doesn't Veronica bring these things to Tombstone?" Gieo asked. Even at her workshop her water had been drawn from the earth by a hand-pumped well; her bathroom had been a spade and an old camping toilet as she didn't really know how to create an outhouse. It really irritated her that Tombstone could easily be another Albuquerque but wasn't.

"Veronica is a colonizer," Alondra said with a little chuckle. "Her mentality is conquest and control. According to her, hot showers, flushing toilets, and a reliable electrical grid only serve to make people soft. To be honest, she would be far better served in the Red set, but Carolyn isn't about to relent her position as queen, and so Veronica took over the Whites."

"Why aren't you the White Queen?" Gieo asked. "You're clearly better suited to creating civilization than she is."

"I appreciate the compliment," Alondra said, "but creature comforts and stability are only part of the job. Albuquerque was quite literally dying for aid when I arrived with my soldiers. Being raided by Mckenzie and the Mexicans for several years will make any protection look appealing. Not all surviving cities are so eager to rejoin a centralized government. Veronica is a master at knowing what each city needs and how to accomplish it. I'm more of a city planner for a populace that will readily welcome me."

"If Tombstone knew what you did here, they'd fall all over themselves to welcome you," Gieo said with a smirk. She scooped food onto her plate, offering to do the same for Alondra who nodded her acceptance of being served. "Why didn't you read my letter of introduction?"

"I'd rather get to know you in a more natural way," Alondra said. "The bike you rode in on is a marvel, and one I assume you built yourself or you wouldn't have driven it across the desert alone. Tell me, why have I never heard of you?" Alondra leaned forward on the table, tenting her fingers under her chin and looking at Gieo as though she were the only woman in the world.

"I'm kind of new to the Ravens," Gieo said. "Before that, I was alone in a workshop and fortress of my own creation. I'm just now realizing exactly how big the world still is."

"What made you rejoin society?"

"Someone special picked me up after my last airship was shot down." Gieo had wanted a more grandiose motivation to share, but the simple fact was she'd wanted Fiona.

"What's his name?" Alondra asked, an intrigued sparkle rising in her onyx eyes.

"*Her* name is Fiona," Gieo said.

The little sparkle rose into a genuine flash of an epiphany. "Her last name wouldn't happen to be Bishop, would it?"

Gieo nodded.

"That explains a lot," Alondra said. "There are two lesbian Queens in the Ravens. One is Carolyn and the other is Veronica; Fiona was a swirling, destructive force in Las Vegas who came close to spoiling our unified front by pitting Carolyn and Veronica against each other for her affections." Alondra took a bite of chicken, chewing it thoroughly before continuing. "Maybe you can explain to me what is so spectacular about her, because you gay girls can't seem to keep your hands off that daffy redhead."

As angry as Alondra's glib description of Fiona made Gieo, she had to admit it was probably one of the kinder she'd heard. She had an inkling to Fiona's turbulent past with the Ravens, but had never really been in a position to hear more of it from someone who wasn't directly involved.

"What exactly happened between Veronica and Fiona?" Gieo asked, trying desperately to keep her voice even and calm.

"I think it'd be best if you directed that question to any of the three involved," Alondra said. "Suffice it to say, you've walked directly into the middle of a complex love triangle half a decade old. I will tell you this: you're not the first girl to get pulled into the tangled mess between them."

They finished dinner with a scant discussion of things to come, their plans for the future, and a promise for Gieo to return through Albuquerque on her way home. The topic of Fiona and Veronica didn't arise again as Gieo couldn't imagine Alondra would speak more on a topic she'd already put to bed.

Gieo slept fitfully despite the relative opulence of the guest room. Her mind wouldn't let go of the new enigma of Fiona and Veronica's relationship including a tangled mess and another woman whose name Gieo had heard, but of whom she knew little else—Carolyn. She didn't trust Veronica and she was beginning to wonder if her trust for Fiona might be misplaced. Exhaustion pushed back against her whirring mind, knocking the complex thoughts aside long enough to put her into a deep sleep where she found harsh nightmares of the man she killed. His face kept coming back to her, the bubbling frothy blood of his sucking chest wound boiling out of the bullet hole in endless streams while his conversation with himself continued unabated. She felt the unwarranted weight of something left undone crushing her chest and only realized before waking that she'd wanted to know the man's name for a reason she could neither describe nor understand.

She awoke feeling sick and harried as though her sleep was spent running. To add to this strange sensation, her body rebelled against the exercise and long ride of the day before. Muscles and joints that had never ached before were making up for lost time. Getting out of the comfortable bed was difficult and getting dressed a painful proposition. She found she'd slept far later than she'd intended. Midmorning had come and gone with the heat of the day already pushing toward its apex. Gieo packed, found something to eat, and left Alondra's home.

On the quick walk back to her bike, she grew accustomed to the pain in her joints and muscles. Word had apparently spread about her rank within the Ravens as the soldiers she passed saluted her crisply. She saluted in response, taking a shine to the novelty of it all. Back at her bike, she found a water spigot on a nearby building, and wonder of wonders, it functioned. She filled the brass water tanks on her bike and set off. The guards at the gate waved her through without fanfare.

The road north was an easier ride than anything thus far. The temperature dropped as the elevation rose toward the mountains, allowing the bike to run cooler once Gieo adjusted the manual choke to accommodate the rarified air. The ride up into Colorado ran smoothly with Interstate 25 passing over most of the ruins of small towns without fully dipping into any of them. As Gieo suspected, when she got closer to Fort Carson and Colorado Springs, the landscape changed. War clearly had taken its toll on the infrastructure, but to Gieo's surprise, there were handmade signs along alternate routes guiding her to the northwest and Woodland Park. The damage Albuquerque suffered paled in comparison to the obliteration the Air Force Academy and Fort Carson undertook during the war. The landscape went alien, glassed, with nature's recovery slowed by the toxic weapons the Slark used. Gieo followed the signs, often having to drive over the glazed ground blown clean from the heat of explosions.

Towering trees, sylvan wilderness, and the natural splendor she'd hoped Colorado would hold began to take over as she pulled onto the winding road up toward what the signs called "Space Mountain." Cars along the sides of the roads were pulled off by a wrecker and stripped of valuables. The signs of life were not necessarily good signs as Gieo saw it; Alondra's warnings about barbarians, separatists, and marauders hadn't fallen on deaf ears and Gieo couldn't even be certain what the Colorado hunting party had truly wanted with her. Options being what they were though, she had to try.

The signs guided her in straight and true, and soon she found herself pulling up to a five-star resort hunting lodge. Log cabin bungalows and a beautiful three-story A-frame main lodge with windows running from top to bottom rose almost perfectly from the great lodge pole pines and Douglas fir trees. The hunting party, many of which she vaguely recognized, were about their business, working on general maintenance or domestic duties. Surprisingly, a handful of women and a few children were even mixed into the group. Gieo slowed her bike, coming to a stop well out of the edge of the roundabout driveway for the main lodge, and pulled off her helmet and scarf. A few of the burly, bearded mountain men came strolling down the way. The lead man, who wore his sandy blond hair and beard long but kempt, waved to her.

"As I live and breathe," the man said, "if it isn't the tech expert of Tombstone."

Gieo waved back and slowly lowered the pod on her bike to hold it in place. They seemed friendly enough and the presence of women and children gave the entire lodge a look of domesticity as though it were a sociable camping trip and not an attempt to rebuild society after an alien invasion. As the men got closer, Gieo slipped from the saddle, stretched her back and tried to force a smile, although she was tired, sore, and not in a particularly good mood.

As the four mountain men neared, Gieo could see they were unarmed, smiling, and looking as affable as could be. Of course, they were all over six feet tall and brawny so it wasn't as though any of them would have to be armed to do her harm. They smelled gamy and odd, not necessarily a bad smell, but something peculiar and ancient, harkening back to the days when men ate only the wild animals they could kill and wore the pelts of the hunt.

"I'm McAdams, if you don't remember," the blond man said. "Come on up to the lodge and I'll introduce you around."

Gieo glanced to the undercoat the man wore beneath a bear pelt, recognizing the insignia. "That would be Major McAdams, wouldn't it?" Gieo asked.

"Once upon a time, I suppose, but that part of my life is over now."

"It doesn't have to be," Gieo said, this time with a genuine smile.

♠♣♥♦

After making it back to town without incident, Fiona handed over the wounded to the town's rebuilding hospital and the cultist defectors to the Military Police division of the Ravens. They would likely be questioned about information that wouldn't be valid or important in short order. Yahweh wouldn't stay put knowing the Ravens had his address, but there was likely other, subtler bits of information the cultists could give in exchange for amnesty and a place in the new society. The MPs would know how to ask and what was and wasn't valuable; Fiona hadn't the temperament, training, or inclination to even try a cursory investigation on the ride back despite the chattiness of the women in the wagon.

The following day, Fiona walked through her random duties without much focus or attention. Her head was in something of a fog, wandering back and forth between missing Gieo intensely, despite it being two days since her departure, and worrying about what Yahweh might do now that his protection from the Slark had faded and his stability in the alliance with Zeke was long gone. To add to the concerns about old enemies resurfacing, Cork's patrols, which shouldn't have found anything, found evidence of Zeke being alive in the form of decapitated Slark on the border between Tombstone's region and what used to be Old Mexico. Further complicating everything, Stephanie's patrol to the south had hit major resistance, indicating the Slark were well on their way to flanking the southern border of Raven territory. Toward the end of the day, with a head full of concerns, the weight of the world on her shoulders, and a heart aching for someone she'd pushed away, Fiona found herself on the roof of the saloon, looking to feel closer to Gieo.

A distant whistle and chugging of steam power drew her attention to the station across town. She wandered over to the telescope still set up at the edge of the roof and sighted in to see what was going on. Carolyn had arrived, the red banners of the disembarking Ravens told as much, and with her were thousands of army regulars in their desert camouflage, trucks, artillery, teams of oxen to haul, and hundreds more horses. Fiona would have to take a meeting at some point with the Red Queen who hated her with good reason. The information Fiona had given to Veronica was quickly turned into a plan that would only function if Gieo succeeded in bringing back pilots, which was a glaring hole Carolyn would no doubt point out.

Imagining that Gieo would not succeed set a stone in the pit of Fiona's stomach. Failure didn't necessarily mean death, but there were a whole lot more failing options with mortal ends than ones without. Her bike could break down in the desert leaving her stranded to die of thirst, or wreck and kill her outright, or marauders, or kidnapping, or Slark, or any other number of awful things. Fiona could kick herself for letting Gieo leave alone or even leave at all.

"Something wrong, tall boss?" Ramen asked. The little robot's voice startled Fiona to the point of nearly jumping out of her skin, although the fright showed through on the surface as little more than a twitch of her gun hand.

"I'm worried about Gieo," Fiona said, trying to calm her thundering heart.

"I am too," Ramen said, "but not for the same reasons you are."

"How's that?"

"Gieo's a talented survivor, more so even than yourself," Ramen said. "Think about what it must have taken for her to live alone all these years while trying concurrently to break the Slark line. Getting to and from Colorado in one piece won't be a problem if she puts her mind to the trip, but you've given her some reasons to doubt."

Fiona leaned against the low wall at the edge of the roof and folded her arms over her chest. "Is this more robot nonsense? What are you even talking about?"

Ramen fluttered up from his sitting position and scuttled on his little crawler legs closer to Fiona. "You're the first real girlfriend she's ever had," Ramen explained. "She may seem self-assured and confident in what she's doing, but she doesn't really know the first thing about relationships before or after the invasion. Begging your pardon, tall boss, but you've really done her a disservice by not guiding her better."

The tiny, brass and copper robot, who looked a lot like a jumble of kitchenware welded together, was making all kinds of wicked sense to Fiona. It was all crystal when Ramen laid it out for her; Gieo's mistakes, their communication issues, the thunderously strange behavior exhibited in the relationship seemed reasonable in the light of this being Gieo's first and only real relationship. People didn't get to skip the awkward, clumsy, ill-informed couplings of teenage years—they just got to postpone them to later in life if they were unlucky, but like with all inevitabilities, they had to happen. Fiona had known true relationships, love, and even cohabitation within a commitment both before and after the fall of humanity. It was absolutely preposterous to expect Gieo to understand the intricacies of any of it without a single real point of reference. The technical cheating of being seduced by Veronica was completely comprehensible if Fiona thought of Gieo as an innocent fifteen-year-old girl, which, in relationship-experience terms, was what she was. Gieo, like all inexperienced girls, could easily have her head spun by someone attractive and worthwhile making her feel wanted and important; Fiona could remember the feeling and the stupid things she'd done to recapture it all the way through her teenage years and even, at times, into her early twenties.

"I am so fucking stupid," Fiona muttered.

"You believed she was brilliant in all things," Ramen said. "She goes out of her way to make people think that of her. You can't be blamed for believing what you both wanted you to believe." Ramen clattered over to Fiona, placing a little clawed robot hand on her knee in a strangely reassuring gesture. "What matters now is what you're going to do to fix things. Be solution oriented, as Gieo always says."

Fiona looked down into the robot's faintly glowing eyes and smiled. "You're right, and I'm going to start by telling Carolyn that Gieo will succeed in bringing back pilots and that we should prepare for Veronica's plan as it stands."

"Great, I think, but that's not really what I meant, tall boss…"

"I know, but it's important nevertheless." Fiona glanced around the rooftop and came to the second part of her plan in short order. "I want Gieo to move here officially, and not on the roof, but in a real home, with me."

"That's more of what I was thinking, and I can help you," Ramen said with a happy little flutter of his helicopter rotors.

Chapter 22
Dreams of a melancholy past

Carolyn was the voluptuous earth mother of the Red chess set when Fiona performed her grand betrayal and lit-out for the free cities. The years had done little to change this. She still wore the flowing sun skirts, bare feet, and peasant blouses she always wore, still had the full hips and chest of the strikingly fertile, and the bright orange hair held in a thick braid down her back. Fiona didn't know why she thought a few years would make such a difference, but it clearly hadn't in more ways than one. Carolyn's gold-flecked brown eyes still smoldered when they landed on Fiona, and her smoky, rich voice still cooled when she spoke of or to the gunfighter. The chain of command didn't require her to speak to Fiona, as she'd said, and anything she had to hear she could hear from an equal in Veronica.

Why the hell Carolyn had forgiven Veronica, but not Fiona remained a mystery.

Fiona had taken her leave for the evening when Carolyn made it abundantly clear she need not be there for the debriefing of the plan she and Veronica had devised on a target Fiona had found. She didn't argue, knew there would be no point in it, and so retired to her room for an early rest. Despite her physical exhaustion, sleep was difficult to find. Morning came as though a blink of an eye was all the sleep she'd taken, but rather than rising with the sun trying to force its way through her shades, she decided the patrol roster could be ably handled by Stephanie and Cork for the morning rides, which she wasn't meant to be a part of anyway, and she returned to sleep in hopes of catching up on some much-needed rest.

The dream wasn't a perfect recollection of the past, mostly because Fiona knew she was dreaming, although not in the controlled sort of way she might have liked. Bill's Gamblin' Hall in the middle of the Vegas strip was where the Ravens had set up their earliest headquarters during the gang wars that would decide who controlled Las Vegas and eventually the entire mountain west area. The Flamingo still had the shifting advertisement on the front of the building for the Osmond's live show, which was one reason Fiona knew it to be a slightly-askew dream. She remembered the advertisement from her trips to Vegas before the invasion, but also remembered it never working quite right after. Something had gone wrong with the billboard-faced building after the electrical grid went down, and nobody cared to fix an advertisement for a show that no longer ran for two singers who likely didn't survive the invasion or the aftermath.

The guards at the door, two women armed with AK-47s, nodded to her as she entered the casino. The Old West decorations of Bill's gaming floor were tempered by survival restocking, moving the defunct gambling apparatuses into backrooms to be disassembled for possible useful parts while concurrently clearing floor space for ammunition, weapons, and foodstuffs. By that point in the gang war, the Ravens controlled most of Vegas and had already restored much of the electrical grid, although not to its full-gaudy past, using the abundant solar panels and turbine fields popular in the Nevada desert. Some whispered of taking back the Hoover Dam, but that would be years in the making.

At the time of the dream's recollection, North Vegas was still a smoldering pit from where Nellis Air Force Base had been wiped off the map and Southeastern Vegas in the Henderson and Boulder City areas was still controlled by a conglomeration of biker gangs known as the Winged Cobras, a combination of the Hell's Angels and another group Fiona guessed to have been snake oriented. The writing was plain on the wall for all to see; the Ravens had won the war for Vegas, collected the most stragglers from the military bases in the area, and would eventually rise to prominence with their chess set model of leadership and willingness to profit from human trafficking.

The Red set still made their home in Bill's Gamblin' Hall while the Whites moved to the Bellagio across the street. The Black set, the true rulers of Las Vegas and the source of all stability with the Black

Queen Ekaterina, made their home in the black pyramid of the Luxor on the other end of the strip. The rumors were Ekaterina had brought the model of the Ravens' leadership over from the Russian Mafia, and that her father had once been a crime boss in Moscow with plans to pass his empire on to her, but Fiona didn't care much for the rumors. What Fiona knew about Ekaterina could fit comfortably in a thimble and that was how she wanted to keep it; the Raven Queen was strong, smart, ruthless, and ambitious—beyond those things, Fiona didn't want to know what had gone into forging a person like Ekaterina.

It wasn't odd for Fiona to head to Carolyn's room. As a Red Rook at the time, she was given ample access to the hierarchy, but her goal, her expressed purpose for being there, was one that could have potentially cost everyone involved a great deal. In the haze of her dream, Fiona couldn't remember why this tryst was so dangerous, but thrilled at the risqué sensation restored by the memory. She knocked their secret knock on the penthouse door: twice in the center, once on the frame, twice more at hip level.

Carolyn opened the door, grasped Fiona by the front of her t-shirt and pulled her inside. The Red Queen was beautiful, matronly, and fertile looking in all the best ways. She was what Fiona imagined a pornographic version of Mother Nature might look like, although she assumed the pornographic part existed strictly because Carolyn did mostly pornographic things when they were alone together. Carolyn pressed her sumptuous body against Fiona's letting her feel the warm, soft curves, the excited heaving of her breasts as she breathed heavily with anticipation. How this idealized version of motherly and womanly had come to be the head of the chess set meant for war and blood, Fiona could never understand, but the incongruity of her position with her appearance hadn't once prevented Carolyn from displaying dazzling competence as the Queen of Battle.

Fiona kissed her, wrapping her hand through the thick braid at the back of her head to control the depth of the kiss. Carolyn responded by grasping Fiona's ass roughly with both hands, pulling her in closer to grind lewdly against the gunfighter's leather-clad legs. They were about the same height, although Fiona peaked at forty or fifty pounds lighter than Carolyn at her lithest, and the Red Queen used this advantage to full effect. Fiona was lifted through the kiss by the hands on her ass, and she allowed herself to pull up from the ground, wrapping her long legs comfortably around the shelf of

Carolyn's ample hips on the narrows before they tapered into her slender waist. Fiona kept her upper body bent enough to hold the kiss while Carolyn walked her across the room to the bed, depositing her on the tangle of sheets and blankets in an unceremonious flop.

Many of the other girls and even a few of the male soldiers collected by the Ravens viewed Carolyn as the great mother, the heart and soul of the organization, the maternal influence watching over them. This was made all the more real as Carolyn had a son, a stoic little boy named Frankie after the author of his mother's favorite book, who all but worshipped the greatness of his mother, while coming to represent the power of the Red Queen to not only survive but effectively raise offspring in the aftermath of the invasion. But Fiona saw Carolyn in no such light as her own mother had long since soured her on the entire concept of what maternalism was. Instead, Fiona saw in her something greatly sexual and womanly, which were traits mostly ignored by the others. This ability to see her maternalism as inherently sexy endeared Fiona quickly to the Red Queen. Only one other, a fellow malcontent without a solid reference for mothers, saw things the same way as Fiona, but in the heat of the moment in the recalled dream, Fiona couldn't be bothered to even think of this other's name.

Standing above Fiona at the foot of the bed, Carolyn slipped her billowing blouse off over her head slowly, revealing her mountainous breasts held pertly in a satiny cream-colored bra. She had the type of breasts Fiona imagined would look grandiose regardless of the garment or position. Her skin, which had formerly been white with a dappling of freckles, had tanned to a deep bronze, as had most people's out in the desert, leaving her with an exotic glow in juxtaposition to her bright orange hair. Fiona slid to the edge of the bed to sit with her legs spread around the standing Carolyn. She wrapped her arms around Carolyn's hips, pulled her close, and kissed hotly across her soft stomach, up onto her breasts, burying her face in the warm luscious mounds. This was what Fiona remembered most about Carolyn and what made the dream such a heartbreaking reminder of something she'd lost and might never have again; the warmth and comfort she derived from pressing her cheeks into Carolyn's chest was an act so pure and honest she always felt cleansed after doing so.

Carolyn parted before Fiona was ready, lifted one of her legs to plant her foot on the outside of Fiona's hip, and slowly pulled up the hem of her beige sun skirt. Fiona immediately shifted her focus to the curvaceous leg beside her, kissing along Carolyn's inner knee, up her inner thigh, along the smoothest, softest skin as the leg's width grew, until she could see, smell, and almost taste the bright red fire between Carolyn's legs. Carolyn hated underwear, wore it only when absolutely necessary, and seemed to thrill at the ease of access it granted. Fiona pressed her face into the orange curls, seeking out the soft, wet folds of her lips just beneath. Carolyn's strong fingers interlaced into Fiona's hair, her hips rolled and writhed at the instant attention, and her breathing sped from anticipatory panting to eager gasping. Fiona licked, suckled, and tongued under the direction of Carolyn's hands in her hair until her face glistened and shone with the dew of her lover's pleasure. Carolyn's orgasms were shallow, rapid things, like bunnies jumping across the surface of her skin, and could go on as long as Fiona could manage or Carolyn could stand. In this case, Fiona felt the dream diverge again from reality. Her younger self, in truth, had quit long before Carolyn had wished it, but in the dream, Fiona had pressed on until Carolyn could no longer endure the mounting, tingling pleasure. In both cases, Carolyn ended up thrown onto the bed, with Fiona crawling up her to share a kiss. Carolyn loved the taste of herself on Fiona's lips, wrote poems about the shared intimacy of the act, and always demanded passionate making out after Fiona had gone down on her.

Fiona obliged with a long, deep, adoring kiss, pressing her tongue and lips against Carolyn's more with the goal of passing on the slippery wetness to her than an actual kiss. When Carolyn had tasted all the interior of Fiona's mouth had to offer, she licked at her chin, nose, and cheeks to tongue off the rest.

With their kiss shared, Carolyn laid back, her eyes shining with the afterglow of true satisfaction, her lips pink and wet from the aggressive kiss, and her skin flushed red across her cheeks and nose. Staring at the ceiling over Fiona's right shoulder, she said the words Fiona had struggled for years to forget. "I love you in ways I could never love her."

Fiona awoke with an angry jolt, sitting straight up in bed. She was aroused by the dream and her heart was racing, but it was all crushed under the weight of what she'd finally remembered. She was the problem. Wherever she went, she was the problem.

Despite the Ravens' strict rules about drug use, Fiona had used what they grew to control the populace as recreational fun or self-medication depending on the day or her mood, leaving her with, at best, a patchy memory of her time in Vegas. Despite the fanciful concoction of revised history Fiona had created over the years, she couldn't change what had actually transpired. Her often drug-addled, arrogant, younger self hadn't seduced Veronica until after she'd heard those words from Carolyn. And, as far as Fiona knew, Veronica still didn't know that Carolyn was cheating with Fiona long before the ultimatum Fiona gave Veronica that nearly split the Ravens. Somehow, Fiona had forgotten entirely her brief, intense relationship with Carolyn. A combination of shame, drug use, and time had buried the indiscretion until seeing Carolyn again brought it back to the surface.

Carolyn had every reason to hate her. Fiona was a betrayer, a cheater, a liar, a jilter of honest proclamations of love, and a cruel, unthinking thief. She hadn't loved Carolyn, certainly not in the deep, abiding sort of way Carolyn loved her, and so she'd stolen Veronica, whom she did love, and expected the world to accept her wisdom as its own. In retrospect, Fiona knew the only thing that kept Carolyn from killing them both, was a trueness of love and spirit that neither Fiona nor Veronica possessed. Veronica was the only other to see in Carolyn what Fiona had; she doubted Carolyn could have trusted the affections of anyone else after being betrayed so thoroughly by both Fiona and Veronica.

Worse than the guilt Fiona felt over what she'd done to Carolyn was the terrible fear that Gieo might learn of what Fiona really was and not want her anymore. She came to the grim reality that there were still too many people alive who knew of what she'd done for Gieo to never find out. Fiona would have to tell her and hope.

Gieo was beginning to wonder if maybe Tombstone and her own workshop were the only places left on the planet without comfortable beds and running water. She awoke to a chill in her room in the main hunting lodge. The evening before had been productive, after a fashion, although the woman she had hoped would be her biggest supporter turned out to be the biggest obstacle to getting the pilots to return to Tombstone with her. McAdams' wife Charlotte, a stern woman with tightly pursed lips and premature gray in her chestnut hair, hadn't wanted Gieo to stay any longer than was necessary and certainly hadn't wanted her to take the military men back to war.

The night before, they drank pre-war beer, exchanged flight stories, and ate dishes derived from every creature the Rocky

Mountains could provide long into the night without much headway ever being made toward the Air Force pilots joining her cause. Much of what transpired was more than fuzzy in the cold light of dawn as Gieo's Asian lineage gave her nothing in the way of alcohol tolerance and her petite size left little territory to spread so much beer over. She'd tried her best to keep up, to show herself an equal to the true pilots, but ultimately only succeeded in getting unintelligibly drunk with a splitting headache and mouthful of cotton the following morning as her reward.

Gieo wrapped herself in the quilt from the bed and made her way over to the sliding glass door that led to the second-story balcony. She parted the curtains and eased open the door. Out on the balcony her bare feet crunched over a fresh powdering of snow frozen by an early frost. True to her hopes, the cool, mountain air did have a reinvigorating effect on her hung over mind.

She slid the door closed behind her and made her way out into the rarified mountain air. She'd forgotten autumn was coming to everywhere but the desert and the high Colorado elevations had sped the cold in even faster. She heard another door slide open and a similarly quilt-wrapped woman stepped out onto the balcony a few rooms down. Gieo glanced over to find it was Charlotte. Clutched in the hand not holding together her quilt robe, she carried a mug of what smelled like tea from the steam wafting across the space between them.

Gieo offered Charlotte a wan smile, which wasn't returned.

"Why do you insist on carrying my husband back to war?" Charlotte asked without so much as a good morning.

"We never stopped being at war," Gieo replied.

"He'll go no matter what I say," Charlotte said with a quiver in her voice that nearly cracked Gieo's heart. "I think it's what he went looking for when he took the hunting party on a tour through the free cities."

"I don't want to cause any rifts." Gieo turned and stepped over to the edge of the side railing to come as close to Charlotte as the separate balconies would allow. "I won't use your kids to try to change your mind, but don't you want to live in a world free of the Slark? Don't you want a chance to rebuild without wondering if those giant crawlers are going to come rolling down those mountains to wipe out everything you've built here? Your husband and his friends are special men, brave and talented in ways that could make a difference." Gieo's feet began to burn numb from the cold and she shifted to just one to give the other a rest. "Look, this is all stuff I brought up last night, and stuff you probably already knew. If he's going to leave anyway, wouldn't you rather he left with your support? Parting on bad terms when one person might not be coming back isn't good for anyone." Gieo's voice wavered at the end, though not intentionally, but she saw that the verbal shake had accomplished far more than her words in persuading Charlotte.

"Fine, then promise me they'll come back," Charlotte said, her voice and demeanor noticeably softer.

"I always do, and I've never had this much support or experience on my side," Gieo said.

"It'll take them awhile to set things right to leave again, and a few days to get there," Charlotte said. "He's a good man in a world with precious few left. Bring him home to me when this is over."

"I will, Charlotte, I promise," Gieo said. She didn't want to make the promise she couldn't possibly assure, but simply saying the words strengthened her own resolve to make them true and had a profound effect on Charlotte who finally smiled to her.

"Of all the people to come looking for my husband, I'm glad it was you," Charlotte said. "Come inside and I'll feed you before you head back."

Gieo stepped back into the room with her feet freezing and her hands shaking. She had her pilots, had the blessing of the matron of their little society, and could return to Tombstone with her promises fulfilled. Still, all she could think of, all she could want, was to return to Fiona and be forgiven and loved again.

Chapter 23
Homecomings are a mixed bag

For a brief, hopeful moment Claudia's frantic knocking on the door made Fiona think Gieo was home. The second straight day of sleeping in probably didn't help her muddled state. Fiona pulled herself from the relatively comfortable embrace of the bed and stumbled to the door. Halfway across the room slumber fell away enough for her to realize she would have heard Gieo's motorcycle if it was really her even though the energetic knocking was at the right height and with the right vigor to be Gieo. Claudia stood on the saloon's upper landing flushed with excitement when Fiona threw open the door.

"I have found him for you, Captain-my-Captain," she said. "The cultists were located by my morning patrol."

It took Fiona a moment to remember why Claudia should be so excited about the find. The little sniper had promised to be the one to kill Hawkins for her. Fiona couldn't bring herself to disappoint the girl by letting her know she didn't care one way or the other if Hawkins died. It was a Raven objective though and one worth pursuing.

"Does Carolyn know?" Fiona asked, rubbing the sleep from her right eye with the heel of her palm.

"I brought it straight to you," Claudia said. "Should you want to handle this without her knowing, this is a triumph she can learn of after the fact, no?"

"Yes, we'll go on our own for now," Fiona said. "Pull Cork and his boys off the afternoon ride. The five of us can take care of things just fine."

Claudia might have been concerned by the peculiar request if she was more of a company woman, but Fiona knew a kindred spirit when she saw one; the French Canadian sniper and singer was one distasteful event from jumping the Raven ship entirely, just as Fiona had been. The small number of riders must have spoken to Claudia's ego as well, indicating an assassination job and not one of wholesale slaughter. Watching Claudia jog away after a crisp salute, Fiona wondered if maybe it wouldn't be easier to let her take the shot and cleave the cult's head. Some questions still remained in Fiona's mind and Hawkins was one of two living people who might have the answers.

Fiona dressed quickly to find Claudia, Cork, and two former Texas Rangers waiting on horseback outside the saloon. Claudia handed her Tyra's reins and Fiona mounted. The five rode south, guided by Claudia along a winding trail cut by twenty or so riders earlier that morning. They spoke little. Cork didn't need to be told where they were going and the two men who had once formed a Slark hunting trio with him knew to follow his lead with the dogged loyalty of the best Labrador. They broke away from the well-patrolled areas around Bisbee and Lowell heading southwest into the open desert. The midday sun beat down on them with brutal strength and resolve. The creak of leather, clank of tack, and clomping of horse hooves beat out the music of the hunt as the riders strung out to a staggered line. They crested a rocky rise with Claudia and her ebony pony leading the charge.

Across a shale flat, likely on the side of the border that once was Old Mexico, one of the Slark's giant walkers had gone down, likely broken from the cascade wave that destroyed the vast majority of technology on the planet. The six-legged walking weapon platform had tilted face-first into the desert near a small, natural spring lake creating an enormous expanse of shade beneath the tail end jutting at a near 45 degree angle. Living in the shade and likely inside the ruins of the old Slark monstrosity were the remaining cultists. It looked as though the handful of families who had fled on the wagon, only to be saved by Fiona's riders, weren't the last to abandon the cause. Their numbers appeared to be cut again in half by desertion.

Fiona drew up alongside Claudia with Cork flanking her on the other side. The afternoon sun struck at their backs, making them difficult to discern amid the rocky bluff they'd approached from.

"From here, I can get off a shot worth writing home about," Claudia said. "Should they give chase, we can keep out of their visible range and make short work of them."

Fiona considered the reasonably domestic scene below. At the great distance, it was impossible to tell whether the Slark vehicle was convenient shade or served some other purpose. Fiona took binoculars when Cork offered them and scanned the target area. Few families remained and the staggering men of the cult were doing far more than simply existing beneath the shade. Slark weapons, fuel, and technology were already pulled from the wreckage, organized across the open desert floor. Regardless of what Fiona might have liked to do, the find was too good to leave in the hands of the cult, with or without Hawkins.

"Spread out around the ridge," Fiona said. "Keep the sun at your back and wait for my signal." Fiona dismounted her horse, handing off the reins to Claudia.

"What is the signal?" Claudia asked. "Better still, what is the plan?"

Fiona cryptically patted the Colt Anaconda on her hip and began her walk down the craggy slope to the shale flats below. Her heart was thundering in her ears and the heat off the bleached desert floor threatened to boil up through the soles of her boots with every step. She held her hands up in the universal sign of surrender when she thought she was close enough for one of the cultists to divine who she was. Her estimation of their vision was off by a few dozen yards as they didn't spot her until she was almost completely upon them. Passing within the halo of scavenged parts, Fiona began cataloguing their salvage. Out of the corner of her eye, she spotted a blast shield used by a gunner port on the Slark vehicle, likely removed for its possible use later as a firing position cover. She stopped close enough to the blast shield for comfort and waited for the cultists to come out the rest of the way, which they did in short order, armed to the teeth and rightfully antsy about her sudden appearance.

Hawkins could have ordered her shot on sight, could have made things an easy choice for all involved, but to Fiona's relief, he held back the firing line of the forty or so remaining cultists to parlay with the seemingly vulnerable gunfighter.

"The Lord works in mysterious ways, and so it would seem does the devil," Hawkins said, emerging from the center of his milky-eyed defenders. "Yet again, you have found me, and yet again, you do not finish what you started." His Texas twang fit oddly well with his bombastic way of speaking.

"You can skip the proselytizing, Bill," Fiona said. "I know who you really are and know your brother."

"Half-brother," Hawkins corrected her. "This is about Zeke then?"

Fiona shrugged and offered a little grin. "Isn't everything?"

This actually brought an equal smile to Hawkins' weather-beaten face. "You, more than anyone else, understand the conundrum that has been my life since the end of days. Very well, gunfighter, tell me what you would know of our mutual friend and enemy?"

"He shielded me, likely shielded us both when we arrived in Tombstone," Fiona said. "Being family, I can understand why he protected you, but I can't piece together why he would help me."

"You give blood too much weight with my brother, but you are not far off. The reasons are one in the same," Hawkins said. "I was of use to him, a foil to play off of, and a private source of power to draw from when the time was right. So too were you. We were both hammers to use against the people Zeke feared."

It sounded reasonable, precisely like something Zeke would do, but it didn't make any sense when held up to the facts. Hawkins and his cultists were an excellent implement against the people of Tombstone to keep them unified and under Zeke's control, but it didn't follow who Fiona would be a weapon against.

"Who would I be a hammer…?" Fiona knew the answer as she was speaking the words. Veronica would have come down on Tombstone with the wrath of a thousand Arizona suns if anything had befallen Fiona in exile. She was leverage with the Ravens to keep Tombstone a free city. If the Slark fuel supplies hadn't begun to dwindle, their arrangement might never have altered.

"I *see* that you have pieced it together," Hawkins said. "You were the cherished gem of the Ravens' most feared queen and Zeke convinced the city only he could keep them at bay by keeping you alive. But he did not count on the treachery of women."

Her question more or less satisfied, Fiona felt the conversation had gone on too long for her peculiar mental affliction. "You're more like your brother than you know," Fiona said coolly. She jerked her Colt, thumbing back the hammer as she brought the enormous gun to bear on the surprised crowd. She'd blasted the two men flanking Hawkins before they could even raise the AK-47s in their dusty hands. With a short half-spin step to the right, she knelt in behind the shield, glancing over her shoulder in the process just in time to see Hawkins' head explode from a well-place sniper shot.

The remaining entourage of cultists opened fire. Their bullets ricocheted off the shield like hail off a stone. More rifle-fire poured down from the ridge, collapsing the line of cultists as they tried to flee. Fiona looked to the left of the shield, and then to the right. One cultist made to flank her on the right, but caught two slugs from her revolver the moment he came into view. Another rushed the left side of the shield, hoping to catch her off-guard. She swatted aside the muzzle of his rifle, stepping inside the weapon's unwieldy reach, and buried the enormous barrel of her pistol in his chest. She fired, setting his shirt ablaze, and hurling him backward onto the desert floor.

With the retreating of footsteps fleeing her, Fiona took that moment to slide back down the shield's scalding face to reload. Careful, deft fingers removed the casings of the five shots she'd used. She tucked the spent brass in her side satchel before reloading from her bandolier. By the time she'd finished the chore of reloading, the rifle fire from the ridge had tapered off to lone shots, picking at the now fortified cultists. Fiona pulled herself away from the edge of the shield directly back and waxed her vision around the outside to the right to see where the defensive line began and ended. As she'd suspected, they rushed to the right, leaving her left entirely free.

Taking a deep, calming breath, she rushed out to her left, finding the next cover on the run. She slid in behind a large crate of metal bric-a-brac. Again, bullets pelted the salvaged Slark technology harmlessly. A few shots from the ridge found their mark on the freshly exposed targets. The cultists, aggravated to stupidity by the snipers on the ridge, foolishly turned their attention to firing wildly into the waning sun. Fiona spun out from the left side of her new cover, walked with her gun-hand extended, sighting down the length of her arm as each shot presented itself. From the perfect flanking position, she was able to roll up their line, felling five more before her gun clicked empty and the cultists swung their attention back to her. She ducked around the edge of the crawler's leading leg as the bullets whirred past her on either side.

Reloading the second time was far more difficult than the first as the gun was heating up under constant use and her fingers were growing tingly from the adrenaline of combat. She completed the task in what felt like an eternity, but was likely less than thirty seconds. Fire from the ridge hadn't remotely run out of targets when she resumed her onslaught. Two cultists burst from around the leading edge of the crawler in the vain hope of catching her off guard. She shot both down mid-stride with the second in line gripping the trigger of his assault rifle to spray bullets across the ground as he stumbled through his final few steps.

If what they were doing could be called a plan, it relied entirely on the cultists remaining on the defensive. Fiona readied herself to make another rush, but emerged from her cover into the teeth of a counterattack from the cultists. She fired instinctively, killing the first two in line. The third of a dozen or more making a charge on her position had a pistol. She heard the pops, felt the agonizingly sharp stabs of bullets biting into the flesh of her right thigh. A shot from the ridge cut her attacker down, but the damage had been done. She stumbled, bouncing off the side of the Slark crawler. She tried to cover her own retreat, but the pain and shock of being shot staggered her aim and her remaining two shots sailed off into the open desert to land miles from their intended targets. She was clicking on empty chambers when she managed to drag herself into the alcove created by the crawler leg's mechanisms.

She dropped her steaming gun into the collected silt to clutch at her wounded leg with both hands. When the clutching failed and she pulled back only bloody palms from the free-flowing wounds, she changed her tactic to a tourniquet hastily constructed from the leather strap of her satchel. Tightening the strap carried with it an agonizing ache almost on par with the original gunshot wounds, but stemmed the flow nevertheless. She retrieved her gun from where she'd carelessly tossed it, blowing the silt out of the barrel with quaking lips. Reloading this time was a colossal task with trembling fingers made slick from the blood smeared across them.

Rearmed, she steeled herself for the monumental pain awaiting her when she tried to regain her feet. As prepared as she thought she'd made herself, getting up onto her good leg nearly threw her back to the ground. Standing on her remaining shaky leg, she felt like throwing up from the pain. Without the aid of adrenaline and endorphins, she knew she would have ended up right back on the ground; even still, her stance was a tenuous position.

The cultists pressed their advantage, rushing to the edge of the gap when they had regrouped enough for another charge. Fiona felled the first, winged the second only to have him finished off by a blast from the ridge. The third managed to get off a few wild shots before being taken down by a hale of bullets from Fiona and the snipers. Bullets bounced around inside the narrow metal alcove, nipping twice at the free edges of Fiona's denim jacket, but never finding her flesh. No answer she'd managed to pull from Hawkins was worth the shit-storm she'd kicked up in the aftermath; regretting her impetuous stupidity was something she'd once excelled at, but increasingly loathed.

She hobbled for the entrance knowing full-well she was a dead woman if she remained trapped in the single-entrance alcove. She burst, or at least as much of a burst as she could manage on her gimpy leg, from the alcove with her gun blazing. Adrenaline shot through her with the first bullets biting at the sand around her feet. She found targets, fired, missed some, hit others, and continued limping on throughout. She was almost back to the buried crawler leg when she felt something wet, hard, and hot thump her on the left shoulder. She spun under the impact and went down on her right side. Her gun tumbled from her hand, lost in the effort to catch herself. It took a moment to realize from the tatters of her jacket and shirt what had happened. She'd taken a reasonably close blast of birdshot on her left side. If the fool had bothered to load his shotgun with any grade higher, he likely would have dissolved her from the waist up. As it was, the pellets meant to fell small game birds hurt like hell, but were all likely close to the surface.

Fiona crawled to cover using her right arm and left leg, leaving her wounded right leg to drag behind her while clutching her numb left arm against her chest. Sniper fire continued from the ridge, but accompanying it was the sound of hoof beats thundering across the shale with the clatter of carbines. The remaining cultists, of which there were very few, scattered only to be cut down by the three riders.

The world began to go fuzzy around the edges. She was fairly certain Cork had taken up her defense. She heard him say her name. She felt the empty shells from his MP-5 falling on her like rain. The world refused to come back into focus and she fell into darkness against her will.

Gieo passed through Albuquerque with only a pause for lunch and a short meeting with Alondra. Knowing the roads she would travel and the capacity of the bike, she had little doubt she could make the trip in one day if she kept her speed up. She asked Alondra to show the pilots from Colorado every courtesy as pilots of the Ravens and military men when they passed through. Alondra assured her it would be done. As a parting comment, Gieo mentioned the possibility of moving the fledgling air force to Albuquerque in the not too distant future, but Alondra said it was far likelier they would find themselves in Las Vegas. The cryptic statement, spoken without leaving the door open for further inquiry, left Gieo with questions Veronica likely wouldn't answer, but Fiona might if they were on speaking terms upon her return.

Passing Truth and Consequences took everything in her not to turn off to drive down to the reservoir. She wanted to know if the body was still there, reasoned she might have enough time to bury him properly, or at the very least investigate further to find out who the man might have been. Her handlebars never wavered as she rocketed past the ruins of the town. The scavengers would have had their way with him by then and even if they hadn't she had no tools to dig with nor did she think it truly mattered who he was. Knowing and burying wouldn't bring anyone peace and so she rode.

The day wore on and her body rebelled against the riding. She stopped but once to refill the tanks from the jugs she brought with her and only when the bike was already at its coolest, cutting the rest time down. The desert sunset painted the sky pink and gold as the day slipped away into dusk. Bats, eager to feed on the nightly insects, took flight even before the red orb of the sun had fully passed beneath the horizon in the west. Gieo pulled into Tombstone with the lone goal of lying down for several hours with none of her limbs anywhere near each other.

The town was a kicked hornet's nest with none of the hoopla intended for her return. The scout from one of Fiona's rides—Gieo recognized her as Claudia—spoke animatedly to Veronica, who looked like the spigot for her blood had been left to drain. Gieo lowered the pod on her bike in the middle of the street near the makeshift airfield in the park, and nudged her way through the crowd to where Veronica was standing. From the murmurs among the gathered Ravens, Gieo pieced together that Fiona had found the remains of the Hawkins House along with a newly discovered giant Slark crawler. As Gieo pushed her way into the inner circles, the stories about Fiona's condition became graver.

"Cork says she's as stable as he can make her but that she shouldn't be moved by horse," Claudia was finishing her report to

Veronica when Gieo came within earshot. “If she’d just told us what she was planning we could have…”

“You couldn’t have done anything differently and she couldn’t have told you what she didn’t know herself,” Veronica cut her off. “She probably didn’t even know what she was going to do until after she’d done it.”

“She calls them chaos tics,” Gieo said, adding the only piece of information she had to the conversation. “What happened?”

“She’s been shot,” Veronica said. “We’re preparing a truck to go get her with the Slark fuel we have left. Hopefully they can refuel at the crawler when they…”

“Forget that.” Gieo was already past Veronica and on her way into the makeshift airfield. The smallest of the dirigibles was functional for flight but still unarmed. “Ramen!” she shouted. The mechanical fluttered off the saloon roof and whirred down to her side. “Get the *Little Monster* ready to fly.”

“You don’t even know where she is,” Veronica said, following to protest.

“That’s why I’m taking her with me.” Gieo jerked her thumb in Claudia’s direction. “We can be there and back before you even get a truck to her.”

“How many can you take with you?” Veronica asked.

“What? I don’t know, ten maybe, but we need the room to carry her back.” Gieo walked briskly around the airship stoking the furnace while Ramen filled the water and fuel ports.

“You’re not bringing them back,” Veronica said. “They’ll stay behind to secure the wreck site for our use until we can get a salvage team out to it.”

“Sure, whatever,” Gieo said. “Petites only and no heavy weapons or machinery. We need to save on weight for fuel and speed.”

Veronica turned to organize her team as quickly as possible. Gieo nearly collided with Claudia when she made to remove several of the armor plates from the starboard side.

“I am sorry,” Claudia said. “I tried to protect her.”

It seemed a strange concept to Gieo that Fiona might need protection, yet not strange in the slightest that Fiona would make it obscenely difficult for someone to do so; the incongruity was at once comfortingly familiar and rather depressing.

"Veronica is probably right," Gieo said. "If she wanted to be protected, she wouldn't have gone out of her way to make it difficult. Apologize by helping me get her back."

"Then we will fly to her like avenging angels!" Claudia said with infectious glee.

Gieo replied with a weak smile before returning to the armor plating. She couldn't be sure if she'd need it or not. She vaguely knew where the antiaircraft defenses were, but didn't know where she was going yet. Regardless of the destination, the cargo was worth the attempt and she wouldn't bother slowing enough to offer a good target until she was safely back in Tombstone with Fiona.

Chapter 24

The first flight of length with a landing

Hooked into the *Little Monster* as it steamed across the twilight of the desert sky, Gieo couldn't bring herself to tell the eleven passengers that she hadn't really ever landed an airship after a lengthy flight. If there was good news in that dire track-record, it was the fact that she had walked away from every crash landing thus far.

Claudia's directions were toward the south, which was another mixed bag. Gieo didn't know if the Slark had antiaircraft batteries in Old Mexico, but she also didn't think they would after comparing her own map to the one Veronica was using. It made sense that the defensive line was to the west as it appeared to be the direction of the border between humanity and Slark.

Without weapons or armor, the *Little Monster* made good time. Pre-invasion blimps had a top speed of around fifty miles per-hour; Gieo's dirigibles didn't have to bow to the FFA and ran on steam powered engines burning Slark fuel. Her sleeker, smaller airships cranked across the sky with more alacrity than anything Goodyear or MetLife could manage. At a top speed of close to seventy, the *Little Monster* zipped through the encroaching darkness followed by a thrumming whirr and a vapor trail from the steam engines.

"Your ships breathe like living things," Claudia shouted to be heard over the engine bellows.

"Ramen thinks so too, which I always thought was weird since it's actually a lot closer to a flying train." Gieo shifted forward in the harnesses holding her in the glass ball at the front of the cockpit to keep her field of vision clear on the ground below her. A smart antiaircraft battery would wait until she was past to fire on her knowing evasive maneuvers wouldn't be able to begin until after the first shell was fired if they did.

"What do you keep looking for?" Claudia asked. "We are still a ways from the target zone."

"Don't tell the others, but I tend to get shot down a lot," Gieo said.

"How much is a lot?"

"I think the last time I had a flight that didn't end in a crash was on Jet Blue."

"What do we do if we are shot down?"

"Learn to fly by flapping your arms, I suppose," Gieo said. "The safety measures for this ship haven't even been built yet, let alone installed."

"You are my kind of crazy," Claudia said. "Cork said he would set fires so we will know him in the dark. Watch for those."

No sooner had Claudia said the words than Ramen's voice buzzed through from his perch atop the front nose of the dirigible. His words came through the ship's telecom with a crackle. "I can see a ring of fire burning a few miles ahead, boss."

"Let's bring her in," Gieo yelled into the cone microphone above her head. She downshifted the great gears of the propeller engines resulting in a rumble and shudder running down the length of the ship. Adjusting the angle of the wings, the drag along the top guided the narrow vessel down toward the ground in a shallow dive. Their airspeed dipped to match a landing approach in the vicinity of the technical specs of what Gieo thought would be a good landing speed for a ship she'd designed but had never landed.

The ship banked into a half-orbit over the downed Slark crawler to let Gieo pick the landing zone she liked best. The shale flat offered plenty of even and smooth ground to set down the dirigible. She pulled back hard on the two main levers guiding the wings, bringing the airship to a jerking stop above the landing zone she'd selected. Spinning two wheels on either side of her feet with the peddle handles on the valves, she lowered the landing struts. Steam hissed from the release valves along the sides of the cockpit as the blimp lowered slowly to the ground in a remarkably smooth landing. As soon as the *Little Monster* had settled onto its six extended legs, the Ravens threw open the two doors on the sides and poured out.

It took Gieo a few moments to lock down the blimp in its landed position and more than a few moments to unhook from the various straps, clips, and gadgets required of the pilot. She slipped out of the hatch on the bottom of the pilot's bubble, landing on shaky legs. She hadn't realized exactly how adrenaline-inducing a landing was; getting that jolt of excited energy made sense during a crash, but seemed out of place for a textbook perfect settling of the blimp.

She raced to catch up with Claudia. Three men were already carrying a makeshift stretcher toward the airship. The urgency in their steps spoke of time not having run out. Gieo met them halfway. Fiona was battered, her face was pale, but she was awake and alive. Gieo ran to her side and took her outstretched hand.

"You came for me," Fiona said.

"I figured this would be the only way you'd be glad to see me again," Gieo said, struggling to hold back the joyful tears of stress and relief.

"I was being stupid," Fiona said cryptically.

Cork held Gieo back as the other two men loaded Fiona into the belly of the dirigible. "She's lost a lot of blood," he said. "If she goes into shock now it'll be the end of her."

"Got it, don't scare her," Gieo said. She took another step to leave, but Cork pulled her back again.

"Give her this back." He held out Fiona's Colt to Gieo, handle first.

Gieo took the gun and slipped into her own belt. Something about the way the old ranger said the words and offered the pistol told Gieo it was an important gesture for her to even be given the gun. She threw an arm around his narrow shoulder and hugged him close.

"This is all going to be okay," Gieo said. She didn't know why she said it. The words didn't offer her any cold comfort, and she doubted the old lawman needed her reassurance. Still, she needed to hear her own voice, devoid of confidence as it was, saying the important words as a matter of superstition.

The flight back started as uneventful as the flight out. Gieo couldn't decide whether it was luck, divine providence, or a matter of her not actively looking to get shot down that made the difference. Regardless of the source of her good fortune, she was excessively thankful. Claudia kept Fiona company while Gieo tried desperately to keep her eyes to the desert floor and her focus on the controls when everything in her body screamed to check on Fiona. Things became slightly more interesting beyond the halfway point when the low-fuel indicator light came on.

Gieo had fueled up with a rate of consumption in mind that probably wasn't realistic and hadn't even thought to try fueling up at the Slark crawler. Their excessive speed to that point, along with having no idea how much fuel could be consumed in a single landing, had really depleted what little she'd put in the tanks. One thing was certain: continuing on at the current pace wouldn't get them to Tombstone.

"Are we slowing down?" Claudia shouted through the puffing and rattling noises of the dirigible.

"We're running low on fuel," Gieo shouted back over her shoulder. "We have to slow down to conserve."

"Do we have enough to make it?"

Gieo didn't really have an answer for that. The dirigible likely wouldn't crash when the boiler finally ran dry. She could always jettison the engine, lock off the gas valves, and gently float down to wherever, but they'd be completely at the whim of the wind and Fiona would almost certainly die as they might end up in Texas before they touched down in what would probably be a fairly violent landing.

"We have to," Gieo finally shouted back. She dropped altitude and speed to find the optimal efficiency, recalculated their arrival time, and cursed herself for every added minute that might mean Fiona's death.

By the time the lights of Tombstone came into view, the *Little Monster* was struggling. Every agonizingly slow breath from the bellows seemed like it would be the last as the refractory period lengthened each time. Gieo turned off all but manual control to the wings which required her to hand-crank the metal flaps to make them move. The gears and gyroscopes aided some in the work, but she was sweating and exhausted with limited control. Slowed airspeed was a problem on her approach. The dirigible was aching to be on the ground and was about to drop from the sky to prove it. Her arms were so tired that she had to use both hands to adjust one wing and then the other into the proper landing position. The blimp listed and she nearly lost control in the process. She'd heard takeoffs and landings were the most dangerous times during air travel. Considering her airship was struggling to either drop nose-down on her or capsize entirely as she was adjusting the wings, she had to modify her former disagreement with that position. Under Gieo's instruction, Claudia operated the manual levers to lower the landing struts. She got the last one down an instant before the *Little Monster* hit ground, scraping a little across the asphalt before coming to a complete stop.

She touched down in Tombstone to excitement. She wondered how much more fevered the pitch would be if the Ravens knew how close it was to a crash. Medics came and took Fiona the second Claudia opened the doors.

"It might be hard to see with her life still dangling the way it is, but this was a win," Veronica said to Gieo as they walked briskly to keep up with the medics. "The cult needed to go away and this giant crawler find might fuel us for awhile."

"That'll mean less than nothing to me if she dies," Gieo snapped.

"This isn't the first time she's been shot up and it likely won't be the last." Veronica grasped Gieo's arm and spun her back around. "Call it temporary insanity on my part, but that might be the last time you're going to fly and certainly the last time you will without armor or crash safety measures. I'd sacrifice an army of Fionas to keep you alive; you're that important to our chances."

Gieo's anger burst through her like a firestorm. She launched her arms out and gave Veronica a hard shove to the chest. "I would die a thousand times for her," Gieo said, knowing it was a crazy statement, but not caring in the slightest. "I got your fucking pilots. In a few weeks, you'll have everything you need, and you can stop pestering the both of us." She didn't know why Veronica let her go after the obvious breach of protocol and decorum.

She wouldn't find out until days later what overtones the conversation really held.

It was a couple days before Fiona fully exited the morphine haze following the surgeries and blood transfusions required to remove all the birdshot and two 9 mm slugs from her body. Once the control of her medication was left to her, she immediately quit the opium haze in favor of the roaring pain left over from her wounds. She wouldn't tell Gieo why, but the pilot had her suspicions about Fiona's former life including a pretty stout drug habit. Staying in the clinic wasn't a matter of choice as she was restricted to bed rest by order of Carolyn.

As tearful and awkward as she'd expected her reunion with Gieo to be, it actually held a far steamier side. By the time her faculties had fully returned, it was early morning and the hospital's hallways and rooms were silent. She waited for a few hours until the sun came up and with it came Gieo. The pilot seemed anxious about Fiona's return to lucidity. She came when Fiona beckoned her over though, and didn't resist in the slightest when Fiona pulled her down with her good arm and kissed her passionately as though it were all the kissing she would ever get.

Gieo had tried to apologize again but Fiona had taken all the blame that was hers. It all seemed so trivial and petty in hindsight to hold onto the tepid grudge over an arguably gray area betrayal after Gieo had so bravely flown to save her. Fiona said they were more than equal when everything was weighed and measured.

After a few more days of chatting, reading, and playing chess to pass the time, Fiona was sick of books, sick of the hospital, and knew Gieo had all but given in to playing with her eyes closed to keep the chess matches interesting; she needed to get out, wear real clothes, and feel the desert sun on her. More than that, she had an impossible ache for Gieo that couldn't be effectively satisfied while bedridden in a hospital.

Perhaps Gieo sensed her needs or perhaps Gieo's own needs ruled her actions in a similar fashion, but no sooner had Fiona thought about fleeing the hospital to find sexual release than Gieo showed up with the implements, formerly carried by a nurse, to give Fiona a sponge bath. The basin of water, sponge, soap, and now a razor, which the nurse hadn't bothered to offer, took on entirely different connotations when Gieo walked them into the curtained-off area of Fiona's hospital bed.

The act of receiving a sponge bath carried a shockingly helpless sensation; receiving one from Gieo made Fiona's urge to be in control screech to be heard. The pilot made a good faith effort to be professional in her ministrations—at first. She undressed Fiona from her hospital gown, took special care to bathe and shave smooth the exposed areas of her very long legs, minding the bandaged portion of her right upper thigh. When she stopped at the top of Fiona's now glistening, smooth legs, she held the razor thoughtfully and offered Fiona a mischievous smirk.

"Do whatever you like with that," Fiona heard herself say, although she barely recognized her own voice through the lusty, flinty quality it had taken on.

Gieo deftly slid the razor around the softest areas between Fiona's legs, leaving only a bright red landing strip along her mound with an arrow at the end pointing directly down. A pilot needs guidance sometimes for landings, Gieo had informed her. Fiona wholeheartedly agreed, especially when Gieo's lips made their way down the freshly shaven mound, along the arrow's route, to plant vigorous kisses across the top of Fiona's smooth, aching lips. Fiona's fingers found their way into Gieo's purple hair, grasping at the four thick braids with no particular goal in mind other than to translate her desire through touch as Gieo's tongue flicked at her sensitive folds.

Quiet and stoic in the face of passion were two things Fiona had once prided herself on. Of course, the nurse who came storming in on the scene said Fiona was disturbing everyone within earshot, which called into question the silent quality Fiona once prized. Gieo tried to apologize, but it was all for nothing after she asked for a little privacy to finish things up; the nurse clearly couldn't tell whether she meant the sponge bath or the tongue bath, and decided neither would be appropriate. Gieo informed the nurse, in no uncertain terms, that the request had been a pleasantry, and unless she wanted to watch or offer tips, she should probably leave. The nurse stormed off, and Gieo immediately lowered her head back between Fiona's legs.

The gunfighter's shock was short lived, and any sense of decorum went directly out the hospital's dusty windows when Gieo's lips and tongue found their way back to their work. They'd already been found out, and Fiona couldn't be bothered to try to keep quiet any longer, not that she'd done a very good job of it in the first place. Fiona was desperate in her need; Gieo's mouth found its way to the ecstasy button, and that was all it took to momentarily drown out the residual pain from her gunshot wounds. Fiona's climax brought the nurse back, this time with reinforcements. She tugged at Gieo's braids to get her to stop.

The pilot popped her head up with a satisfied smile, licked her lips, and informed the nurses that their patient appeared to be feeling much better.

Fiona was unceremoniously discharged from the hospital shortly after.

Gieo, who was rather sick of the saloon, sick of the rooftop, and spoiled by Albuquerque's opulence, had asked for and was given a house of her own on Safford Street. The little blue house had a white picket fence, a willow tree in the yard, and a hitching post for horses outside the fence.

The side of the house, formerly a yard long since gone to dirt, held space enough for the borrowed buckboard wagon Gieo used to transport the still gimpy Fiona. Inside, the work Gieo had put into restoring the place was evident, but so much was still left to do. Fiona found a seat in one of the living room chairs and waited while Gieo flitted about trying to find implements of comfort to settle in the gunfighter.

"You don't have to fuss over me," Fiona said. "I'm just glad to be out of the hospital."

"I found a cane while I was cleaning and…"

"I doubt I could be persuaded to use it."

They sat in silence for a moment, Fiona awkwardly positioned in the chair to provide the least amount of stress on her still-healing limbs and Gieo leaned back against the great wood-encased television, likely a holdover from the 70s, with her arms folded over her chest. A few birds chirped in the willow tree outside and insects buzzed under the dusty boards of the porch and clumps of dried grass clinging around the house's foundation.

"You're the reason I started shaving my legs again, you know?" Fiona said.

"Ditto." Gieo smiled.

"Cork came by the other day," Fiona said. "He mentioned you had my gun."

"It's in your gun belt, upstairs, sitting on the chest at the foot of my bed." Gieo pulled herself from the edge of the TV and knelt beside Fiona. The gunfighter was wearing a linen skirt, her cowboy boots, and a tank top. She looked far more feminine and vulnerable than Gieo could remember seeing her, at least, in person. Gieo rested her hands on Fiona's smooth knees and gave them a reassuring squeeze. "I'd like you to stay with me, at least while you heal. The kitchen here is amazing, the bed is soft, and I can take care of you."

"What happens when I'm done healing?"

"Whatever you like," Gieo said quickly, having anticipated that very question with every rehearsal of the conversation she tried in her head.

"You're a good deal quieter than before you left for Colorado."

Gieo narrowed her eyes as though studying the faded floral pattern on the arm of the living room chair. She pursed her lips and let a low whistle escape between them. "I killed my first man," Gieo said, startled that she'd modified the statement with the word first. "Outside of Truth or Consequences, he came at me, he had a gun, I thought it was real, and I shot him." Gieo looked down, giving the chipped and worn hardwood floors equal scrutiny, hiding the embarrassing tears welling at the corners of her eyes. "The gun wasn't real," she said, chaotically rubbing at her eyebrow with two curled fingers as though it itched something fierce, more of a nervous tick than dealing with any real discomfort. "He was just some crazy, probably harmless drifter, and I shot him for being too close to my bike."

"Of all the things in this world, this is what I wish I could have protected you from," Fiona said, resting a reassuring hand on Gieo's shoulder. "It'd be trite for me to say it gets easier when I hope you won't have to ever again, and it'd be disingenuous for me to tell you the man was dangerous when I don't really know if he was and you wouldn't believe me anyway. But I can tell you that you'll survive this."

"It just doesn't match the person I thought I was," Gieo said, finally turning her attention back to Fiona.

"The things we dread don't have to change us for the worse," Fiona said.

Gieo rested her head on Fiona's leg, feeling the hand on her shoulder shift to caress the back of her neck. "I love you," Gieo whispered into the clean, soapy scent of Fiona's skin.

"I love you too, Stacy." Fiona spoke the words with a touching crack at the end.

Gieo felt an overwhelming surge of indescribably good emotions combining the best parts of relief, acceptance, and of course love all in one wave. She was in the middle of working up the nerve to start pushing up Fiona's skirt to resume what she'd started earlier and pour some of her flourishing emotions into the gift of physical pleasure when a frantic knock came at the door. The knock and exuberance were so like Gieo that she almost mistook herself for being on the porch for a moment.

"Come in, Claudia," Fiona shouted.

The door flew open and Claudia burst in with a wildfire set behind her ice blue eyes. "The pilots are here," she said breathlessly. "This is going to happen; we're going to break the Slark line!"

Chapter 25

Learned domesticity and advanced military tactics

Over the next month, leading into the cooler days of autumn, Gieo and Fiona lived in relative domestic bliss. The promise Gieo made to take care of Fiona, to nurse her back to health, reversed on her as Fiona became the domestic goddess, sending Gieo off to work at the makeshift aeronautical training grounds with a packaged lunch and a hot breakfast. This was hardly the role either had expected for Fiona, but the simple happiness she found in keeping the house, cooking food, and relaxing, *actually* relaxing and not just what she'd called relaxing in the past, had a remarkable livening effect on her. Slowly, through good food, ample sleep, and reduced stress, the shine to Fiona's diamond returned and she began to resemble the global beauty she'd once been. Her gunshot wounds healed remarkably well leaving only a slight limp in her right leg that she was confident would fade completely with time.

To keep herself busy, Fiona took up loading brass, first her own, and then others when she'd filled every .44 magnum casing she had. The delicate, repetitive nature of the work was soothing for her, sitting at her worktable in the spare room, looking out the window from time to time at the willow tree's dangling limbs blowing gently in the breeze. Part of her began to forget what the town outside of their shared house was really like. Claudia, Stephanie, Cork, Mitch, Bond-O, and Veronica all made occasional visits, but they seldom spoke with Fiona about anything other than the chores that had been occupying her mind anyway. Cork had been the first to mention Fiona's roles within the Ravens having been usurped by Stephanie, and Claudia confirmed that Fiona was no longer to be a part of the battle plan. Fiona didn't care. She'd waged her war against the Hawkins House in the name of the Ravens and felt she'd earned the break.

Lying in bed with the midmorning light pushing its way through the thin, faded drapes of their bedroom, Fiona casually inspected the scars on her shoulder from the birdshot. The fairly clumsy removal process had left her with scars that looked vaguely like white leopard print on her tan skin. She rather liked the design.

Gieo was still asleep in the huge bed next to her. She'd tangled herself in the bedding until her left leg was free, as she always did. Fiona admired the exposed leg for a time.

The pilot brought out a particularly perverted lust in Fiona. In all her past relationships, she'd been fairly passive in accepting whatever line her partner chose to draw in the sand when it came to kink, but with Gieo, the darkest parts of Fiona's mind worked all on their own and every thought she had was to push that line a little farther down the beach. Gieo stirred awake, rolled over and smiled to Fiona in the euphoric state achieved only by waking up without an alarm clock.

"What are you thinking about so intensely?" Gieo asked dreamily.

"That you seem to activate the kink center of the slutty lobe of my brain," Fiona said.

This gathered up every scrap of Gieo's attention and woke her up in more ways than one. She slithered across the bed closer to Fiona with her eyes sparkling lustily. "You do the same for me, but I need specifics about what you've been dreaming up this time," Gieo said. "Otherwise I won't be able to keep accurate ledgers and all. It's a matter of good bookkeeping."

Fiona bit her lower lip before she relented; the reticence seemed necessary to convey she was not overly wanton with her fantasies. "In the interest of good bookkeeping then, I was thinking about how sexy it would be to do things to you while you're flying—all hooked into the airship harnesses, helpless."

"That could be dangerous," Gieo said. "I love it!"

"Now all we have to do is steal one of the airships," Fiona said, adding a suggestive eyebrow waggle.

"We'll have to do it soon," Gieo said. "I'll be officially grounded next week to give more flight time to the pilots actually flying the assault."

"I'm sorry."

"They should ground McAdams while they're at it," Gieo said with a huff. "He's smart, has forgotten more about aerial combat tactics than I will ever know, and he's twice the pilot I am even after just a month of training in the airships. He's like a big, brawny, bearded version of what the Ravens seem to think I am."

"So why don't you tell them all that?"

"Because then they'd ground him too and we'd both be miserable." Gieo nudged her way even closer to Fiona until she could idly trace her fingers along the dotted scars left by the shotgun. "Flying is incredible and I can imagine McAdams has been missing it even more than I have. The last time he flew was the war, and it didn't sound like that went too well."

"Let's talk about something happy then." Fiona leaned in and gently placed a few hinting kisses along Gieo's outstretched arm. "Tell me about a recent product of your kinky center in the slutty lobe of your brain."

Gieo laughed weakly and smiled. "Anything and everything," she said. "I came to the conclusion quite awhile ago that I'd be hard pressed to find a limit to what I would do for you or let you do to me. You have a blank check to my body, Red."

It had been months since Fiona was last called by that nickname. Something about Gieo accidentally using it as a familiar term set off a different line of thinking in Fiona's brain that had, to that point over the last month, been largely dormant. Zeke had called her Red when she'd first arrived in Tombstone; it was a nickname she'd had most of her life, but only had meaning among the Ravens. On its own, she could chalk it up to coincidence, but it also reminded her of something Hawkins had said to her right before Claudia had blown his head off—she was the cherished gem of the Ravens' most feared leader. Now how had Zeke known that when she'd first arrived in Tombstone?

"No, no, no, no, no," Gieo said quickly. "Wherever your brain is going, it can wait." She snuggled in closer to Fiona to kiss her on the neck to no avail. "Seriously, you could put on the strap-on and see how many things in this house you haven't bent me over yet, or vice-versa, or both!"

"How did Zeke know who I was when I came to Tombstone?" Fiona asked of no one in particular.

Gieo groaned and let her face slip down until her cheek rested on Fiona's chest. "I don't know," she grumbled. "I'd claim it doesn't matter but Cork told me to tell you the other day that he has reason to believe Zeke is operating out of Juarez now."

"What?! Why didn't you tell me?" Fiona squirmed far enough back from Gieo to look her in the eyes. She knew she had that old crazy look she always got that was kind of frightening and chaotic; Gieo had told her about it, and informed her it was one of those things that made her a little scary. Fiona had been trying not to make that face anymore.

"Let's see," Gieo said. "I came home and you were up on a footstool dusting the crown molding wearing those khaki shorts I love. You'd also caught your t-shirt on a nail at some point so I could see your bra—the white lace one with the butterflies. After that I was a little distracted with tearing your clothes off. What does it matter anyway? It's not like you can waltz into Juarez to find him, and even if you could, what would you do then? You're the one always saying he's the only man who could out draw you."

"I don't know," Fiona mumbled. "Find answers, I guess."

"Again with the answers! To what end?!" Gieo hopped up onto her knees on the bed, hands in front of her in a pleading gesture; Fiona was always a little surprised when Gieo demonstrated exactly how agile she was.

"There's something about him," Fiona said. "He's a survivor in ways that amaze me and he…was actually really nice to me most of the time; you don't understand how rare that's been in my life. Most of the time when people were nice to me, they wanted something—he never seemed to. Plus, he went with the army during the fracturing and managed to survive the assault from the crawlers; I don't think a man like that would be able or willing to let go of something like what happened with Veronica."

"Wait, the fracturing?" The phrase sounded familiar to Gieo although she couldn't immediately place where she'd come by it.

"Yeah, the big split in the army before the Battle of Mt. Vernon," Fiona said.

"Outside Cedar Rapids?"

"Yeah, I guess."

"He was probably a Raven," Gieo said wearily. "Alondra told me most of her soldiers came from the survivors after the fracturing.

That must be how he knew about you, knew how the Ravens worked, and knew how to contact them when things got tough. He was probably one of Alondra's old soldiers who left to run his own life."

Fiona flopped back onto the bed and stared at the ceiling. "I really should just tell you whatever it is I can't figure out," she said. "It takes you five seconds to piece together things that stump me for months. Sometimes I feel so stupid around you."

Gieo slipped across Fiona's lap, straddling her waist. She was wearing just pink cotton boy-cut shorts with no top. She'd begun dressing that way for bed when they moved into the new house, stating it was how she was most comfortable; Fiona pointed out most women wore a top with no bottoms, and Gieo pointed out most women didn't have a peculiar phobia about something crawling inside them while they slept. Gieo assured Fiona she knew how ridiculous such a fear was, but, then again, so were her fears of spiders and zombies. In the morning light, her breasts were perky and flatteringly lit by the sun creeping in through the drapes, Fiona had to admit Gieo might be onto something.

"Yep, you're just a big moron," Gieo said. "I keep you around for your looks and willingness to shoot people. You're like a cardboard cutout of yourself with a gun and trip-line attached." Fiona had the predictable response of trying to buck Gieo off. Not surprisingly, Gieo was remarkably difficult to unhorse, as it were. Fiona struggled, Gieo's legs tightened around her, until Fiona had worked herself nearly to the point of biting. "I'm kidding," Gieo finally said. Her face was flushed from exertion and lit up by a satisfied smile. "You're the only one who thinks you're stupid, which, ironically, is kind of stupid."

"I'm surrounded by geniuses," Fiona said angrily. "A little self-doubt is only natural."

"You're surrounded by geniuses in Tombstone?" Gieo asked with a sharp laugh.

"Okay, maybe not Tombstone at large, but between you, Veronica, and Zeke, I've had a hard time not feeling stupid."

"Come on, bad points of comparison, and considering how many stupid mistakes the three of us routinely make, you probably shouldn't give us anywhere near as much credit as…" Gieo kind of trailed off. Her hands made their way along Fiona's chest, pressing the t-shirt Fiona had slept in around the shape of her breasts. "This month of healing time has done some wonderfully healthy things for other parts of you as well. I mean, not Victoria's Secret cover things yet, but still…"

"Those were mostly padded pushup bras scientifically designed to create cleavage," Fiona said.

"Not in my head they weren't." Gieo smiled. "Anyway, my point is, most of the time around you I'm fluctuating wildly between nervous wreck and horny school girl. I loved and idolized you before I ever met you. You feel stupid around me? Imagine how I must feel whenever I'm around you."

"This is the less competent version of you?" Fiona asked incredulously.

"Yep, when you're not around, I float stuff with my mind."

"Then what would you say I'm supposed to do?"

"You can start by learning to let things go. If Zeke wants to set up shop in Juarez, who cares? If he was a former Raven using what he knew of the organization to survive, who could blame him? There's no census data on this for obvious reasons, but from what I've seen, the Slark hit males, soldiers in particular, the hardest; it makes sense that the ones who are still alive are likely good at surviving and lucky as hell."

Fiona doubted it would be as simple as all that, but she did like the sound of it. "What do we tell Veronica?"

"What do we ever tell Veronica? Nothing," Gieo said. "She'd probably use it as a fresh reason for us to waste our time attacking Juarez when we have a real target in the west. Speaking of the devil, we have a meeting with her and Carolyn this evening."

"Why?" Fiona sighed.

"I made the mistake of mentioning how much better you were feeling. I think they've got a commendation or something for you for wiping out the Hawkins House," Gieo said.

Fiona made a move to extricate herself from beneath Gieo, but the pilot pushed her back down. Gieo's face, which to that point had been all smiles and mocking laughter, took a serious shift that set Fiona at attention.

"All joking aside, you know I think you're wonderful, right?" Gieo asked. "You're beautiful, smart, charismatic, good at what you do, and completely fearless—I'd build shrines to you if I didn't think it'd creep you out. The only real problem you have that seems to be causing you the most misery is that you're completely unable to let go of things that upset or confuse you."

"For you, I'll work on letting go of the past," Fiona said. She'd long since gotten used to having people speak of her in glowing terms; Gieo's compliments, while heartfelt and sweet, weren't anything Fiona hadn't heard before. What did stick out to her, and what really made her love Gieo all the more, was the one constructively critical note at the end; it spoke of an honest concern for her well-being that was rare in the rest of her admirers.

Gieo smiled with such contended warmth that Fiona wanted to frame the moment and hang it on the wall for the colder months to come.

"We should get dressed and start walking. As much fun as it'd be, I don't think we should try riding with you on the handlebars of my mountain bike," Gieo said. "Besides, I owe Ramen a puppy and I heard Jeffers' mutt had a litter a few weeks ago. Maybe we can see him on the way."

"Why don't you get a horse already?" Fiona asked. "I could teach you to ride."

Gieo wrinkled her nose in response with an embarrassed tint of pink rising in her cheeks. She'd fixed up the old mountain bike found in the house's shed specifically so she could avoid having to ever use a horse; when people asked, she'd claimed it was closer to riding the modified Indian motorcycle she'd become synonymous with, but the real answer was far more provincial.

"I'm afraid of horses," Gieo said.

"If I'm going to work on letting things go, you're going to need to work on the list of things you're afraid of."

"Fine," Gieo said, "I'll consider taking riding lessons."

"I was thinking you could start sleeping completely nude, but that works too."

"Like my underwear has ever been an obstacle for you." Gieo writhed a little on top of Fiona, rolling her hips lewdly against her, knowing full-well what affect the warmth of her skin and the pressure down on Fiona's most sensitive areas would have.

"If we're walking, we should get started now," Fiona said, adding an impish grin, "but you're in big trouble later."

Chapter 26
No times like old times

The walk was longer than Fiona expected, although not longer than she should have, considering Gieo rode her bike every day. By the time they reached the heart of what could be considered the population, her leg was stiff and a little achy. She assumed the injury could stand some exercise to fully heal, but she still told Gieo with increasing frequency that they might need to find a ride back. Gieo, for her part, replied with the always-declined offer to go find someone to give them a ride while Fiona rested.

The day was cool enough to not raise a sweat on Gieo while they walked, but Fiona had a sheen from painful exertion by the time they strolled up to the Ravens' compound. Fiona had strapped on her gun, but she hadn't really felt the twinge of nervous energy she might have even a few months ago when the Ravens were still new to Tombstone. The town had clearly changed for the better under their rule even if it did so to the detriment of a few select citizens, Fiona among those who had to give up some personal liberties for the stability of all.

Toward the end of the walk when the patrols of Raven soldiers increased, Gieo took Fiona's hand in hers. As strange as the intimate gesture felt at first, Fiona did not pull away. It was her left hand, which probably explained why Gieo practically insisted upon walking on her left side. It wouldn't hinder her draw should she need her gun, and so Fiona let the familiarity stand for the moment. As they walked through the gates of the Raven compound, Gieo released her hand unceremoniously.

They were shown into Veronica's office on the second floor. A refreshing breeze blew in through an open window occasionally ruffling, but not displacing, paperwork on the desk. Fiona didn't know for certain if the paperwork was a holdover from the desk's likely long deceased owner or something belonging to Veronica. Paper was far rarer and more valuable than it likely had been since the Middle Ages. If there were still paper suppliers somewhere, Veronica would be the one to know how to be supplied by them.

Veronica stood in the corner with her back to the door, looking down out the window over the opium and marijuana fields in the back of the converted courthouse. Opium, which grew readily in the desert, was uncovered while the marijuana had protective netting and a network of irrigation tubing running above it. She was dressed in the gray and black military fatigues of the Ravens with her pistol backward-slung on her left hip.

"When Carolyn gets here, we can start handing out the bad news," Veronica said. She turned her head slowly, the afternoon light catching her features, making her look both tragically beautiful and achingly sad.

"Like Christmas, I would imagine." Fiona sat down at one of the chairs, stretching her right leg out in front of her to rub the sore muscles of her upper thigh around her freshly-healed bullet wounds.

"Yep," Veronica said, "we're all going to get something."

Gieo felt a little adrift in the strange familiarity between the two women. She'd spent a considerable amount of time with Veronica over the past few months, but she hadn't developed anywhere near the rapport that Fiona and Veronica seemed to have implicitly.

Gieo and Veronica remained standing when Carolyn arrived. Her matronly curves were poured into a similar uniform to Veronica's although, while it looked fairly dashing on the lither White Queen, the uniform looked almost pornographic on the curvaceous Red Queen. Carolyn navigated the office as though she owned the room, building, and state in which it was all contained. She took no notice of the three inhabitants on her arrival, cutting a straight course to the leather executive chair behind Veronica's desk. She sat calmly and finally acknowledged those assembled.

"Fiona," Carolyn said coolly, "the Ravens appreciate your continued service above and beyond your duties in the elimination of the Hawkins House despite the extreme personal risk." It was clear from the strange cadence with which she spoke and the formal tone of the language that it was a missive handed-down from a command structure above her. "Your pay will of course continue through your convalescence that will no doubt stretch beyond the coming engagements."

Fiona snorted and shook her head. "Like you'd want me on that ride anyway."

Carolyn ignored the comment, turning her attention next to Gieo. "McAdams and his key officers are entirely too valuable to send on the current mission. Command of the air group will revert to you. Make any arrangements necessary to accommodate this change."

Gieo's elation was hardly tempered by Fiona's quickly shouted objection of a very primal, "No!"

Again, Carolyn ignored Fiona, instead turning her attention to Veronica. "I will be taking the full army group north after we break the Slark air defense line to roll up any further antiaircraft batteries in the area. This should open a large enough gap in their defenses for the return of the air group and hopefully leave a gateway for future incursions into their territory. Once we've cleared some space, we will be returning to Las Vegas."

"I suppose you'll be wanting the airships we've built too," Veronica huffed.

"Don't be ridiculous," Carolyn said with a dismissive wave of her hand. "McAdams and the other top officers are already on their way to Las Vegas to begin building a real air force. Your blimps will be used as reconnaissance scouts for the south."

"You don't mean for me to stay here?" Veronica's posture changed from practiced nonchalance to visible agitation in the span of her sentence.

"You will remain in command of this southern observation post until it is deemed unnecessary by Las Vegas," Carolyn said sternly. "There are still plenty of Slark and marauders coming out of Old Mexico and we need an early warning should a southern push begin."

Carolyn was so matter-of-fact, so downright flippant with everyone in the room that Gieo felt like reaching out and slapping the motherly redheaded commander. Glancing from Fiona to Veronica, Gieo assumed they were all in agreement on that position.

"Thank you for your time, ladies." Carolyn stood, and with the same business-like approach carried out in her entrance, she quit the room, leaving the three occupants stunned-and-poorly from the news.

"What just happened?" Gieo asked quietly.

"We were all just royally fucked, that's what," Veronica growled.

Fiona had slumped left onto the arm of the chair, using her left hand to prop her head up as though it were too great a weight for her neck at the moment. "The war is restarted and we're not going to be a part of it," she muttered.

"What are you talking about?" Gieo said, trying to insert some levity into the conversation. "I'm going to be commanding the squadron for the attack on Bakersfield's refineries. This is the biggest operation since the cataclysm. Everyone keeps saying so."

"She thinks you'll fail," Veronica said. "If she thought this was going to work, if she thought you would live through it, she wouldn't have pulled McAdams. But even if you do manage to pull it off, she's planning on putting your dirigibles on a shelf out of the way while she develops a real air force with real pilots."

Gieo looked from Veronica to Fiona for confirmation of the assessment. Fiona was only shaking her head in apparent disbelief.

"We could leave," Gieo said, trying desperately to shift gears. "You did it before."

Fiona sighed. "There are no free cities left except Juarez, and we wouldn't be welcome there. Anywhere else in Raven territory, we'd just be arrested and hanged for desertion."

"That's insane!" Gieo protested.

"The Ravens were built on the model of the Solntsevskaya syndicate," Veronica said flatly. "Insane is their modus operandi." Veronica returned to her desk and bent over to pull several manila envelopes from one of the bottom drawers, shunning the chair that Carolyn had so recently vacated. "Sadly, for Carolyn, so is backstabbing." She offered the envelopes to Fiona who took them without question. "Give those to the people named on the outsides with the operation phrase, 'listen to the wind.' An affirmative reply will be, 'under the fire-red sky.'"

Fiona smirked, rising slowly to her feet with the envelopes tucked under her arm. She gave Veronica a conspiratorial salute.

"What's going on?" Gieo asked as if the room had just turned upside down on her.

"Carolyn is a conniving bitch with an axe to grind against Fiona and me; your crime is keeping lousy company, I suppose." Veronica explained. "There's no way I wouldn't have a plan ready on the off-chance she decided now was a good time to take revenge on the lot of us."

Fiona guided a very confused Gieo out of the room with new errands on the itinerary. Back outside, away from potentially prying ears, Gieo leaned in close to Fiona and asked, "What was that all about?"

"My relationship with Veronica started a little before hers ended with Carolyn," Fiona explained. With a deep breath, she continued with the part she'd never admitted to anyone. "My relationship with Carolyn ended at almost exactly the same time." She hoped Gieo wouldn't view the whole tangled mess as something distasteful or overtly despicable, which, of course, it was both. "Veronica and I were able to watch each others backs fairly effectively afterwards…"

"Until you left," Gieo interrupted.

Another realization Fiona hadn't even spent time in the same county of—when she'd left Veronica she'd also left her alone with Carolyn's retribution. "Yes," Fiona said, the old feelings of being the traitor rebounded onto her. "Regardless, I wouldn't want to try to match nefarious plans with Veronica. She thinks in terms of years and branching eventualities. Whatever she has in these envelopes was being set up before Carolyn ever boarded a train."

"Can we trust Veronica?" Gieo asked.

"We can trust Veronica to look out for Veronica," Fiona said. "As luck would have it, we're directly tied to her in this."

"Do you have any other evil ex-girlfriends I should know about?" Gieo asked.

"These two aren't enough for you?"

Gieo laughed and nudged Fiona with her shoulder. "At least I understand now what Veronica meant when she always said she thought you were into breasts," Gieo said. "Carolyn must have terrible back problems after lugging those melons around her whole life."

"Melons," Fiona rolled the word around her mind and mouth. "Yeah, that's the word for them. But I'm just as much about personality and yours is definitely the biggest and best I've seen."

"Flatterer," Gieo said. "You finish up with the envelopes; I'm going to go get a puppy for Ramen."

They kissed briefly and parted company with a promise to meet back at the saloon when their individual errands were completed. Gieo glanced back over her shoulder to the gunfighter as they walked in opposite directions only to find Fiona glancing back to her.

The reciprocity felt nice.

♠♣♥♦

Fiona had kept her cool to the best of her ability in the office, but after she exchanged a final glance with Gieo and disappeared around the corner, she was fuming mad and entertaining the notion of burning down the whole operation to keep her lover from the poorly supported mission. It took all the self-control she had to turn left at the end of the street to head for the makeshift airfield rather than go right over to Carolyn's office and do whatever felt natural, which almost certainly would involve treasonous violence. As sides to be on went though, being on Veronica's was a good place to be, and Fiona had to trust in her former lover and friend's cunning as she had so many times in the past.

When she reached the airfield with the dirigibles and planes about ready to fly, Stephanie came out to greet her. It was a true greeting, one of genuine interest and warmth. Fiona produced the envelope with Stephanie's name on it and all the warmth drained from her.

"Listen to the wind," Fiona said.

"Under a fire-red sky," Stephanie replied as she took the delivered message. "That'll be it then."

"Are you allowed to tell me what's in it?" Fiona asked.

"I don't see why not. If Veronica thought you'd stab her in the back, she wouldn't have had you deliver it, and even if someone forces the news from you it'll be too late." Stephanie tore the flap from the envelope and dumped a collection of dirigible schematics into her free hand. "We've been skimming the salvage from the Slark crawler wreck. It's supposed to be crated to head back to Las Vegas for Carolyn's use, but we've been warehousing sealed crates full of rocks instead. She'll see the train off before she heads out on the mission thinking all the salvage was claimed by her to be used by her and McAdams later on when in fact she'll just be in possession of the world's largest rock collection."

"How could she not know?" Fiona asked.

"All her people are soldiers. They don't know anything from salvaging," Stephanie explained. "All the techs and engineers are loyal to Veronica. Once Carolyn's soldiers oversaw the protection detail back to the warehouse, our people switched out the goods for rocks and took the real Slark salvage out the back."

"Not that I can't appreciate the joke at Carolyn's expense, but what does that have to do with the envelopes?"

"Months ago, when we first started building the dirigibles, Veronica asked Gieo what she would do if she had Slark tech to repurpose. These are the schematics Gieo drew. That's what our patrols have really been looking for—another big Slark score to build the airships Veronica really wants and Gieo could make nearly invincible." Stephanie turned the schematics to show Fiona. The drawings and diagrams didn't mean a thing to her, but they looked sufficiently convoluted and definitely in Gieo's hand to prove their legitimacy. "Nobody dared hope we'd find a score as rich as the crawler you and Claudia took. When we started pulling pieces, Veronica kept prompting Gieo to update her wish-list."

"How did she know Carolyn hadn't intended to use the Slark salvage for the airships all along?"

"We didn't, at first," Stephanie said, "but when they wanted to start crating it, Veronica had a fairly good idea what was about to happen."

"And now…?" Fiona asked, less and less surprised by the foresight in Veronica's plan.

"We've been planning for this all along," Stephanie said with a mischievous grin. "It'll take less than a week to retrofit the Slark tech to the dirigibles and planes. I don't know what is in the rest of the envelopes or who they're intended for, but if you deliver them I'm assuming all our bases will be covered." Stephanie saluted Fiona, turned on her heels, and walked back into the giant tents covering the airship field.

Fiona walked on with her gimpy leg growing increasingly fatigued and achy, but with four envelopes still to deliver.

Before the sun set, before she was due to meet back up with Gieo, Fiona was exhausted, her leg was a four-alarm fire, but she had delivered the remaining orders to Claudia, Cork, a Hispanic woman at the pilot compound, and a final missive to a message rider who had clearly been waiting for the drop, riding a prepared horse to the northeast immediately after receiving the package.

On her way back to the saloon, the pain in Fiona's leg eased. She was working within one of Veronica's plans—it warmed her with confidence. Gieo was in front of the building, just off the plank sidewalk, gifting a scrappy, brindle mutt to Ramen, who looked as elated as a rattling little robot could manage.

It was a weird world, Fiona surmised, but infinitely better for her than the one it replaced. Gieo began walking toward her when Fiona was spotted, but couldn't hold her pace and eventually jogged, throwing her arms around Fiona's shoulders. Fiona responded by wrapping her arms around Gieo's waist to lift her into the hug.

"I'll always have your back, lover," Gieo whispered to her.

It felt good to have someone say the words and mean them.

Chapter 27

Oil!

The work of the week, slow at first with Carolyn and her men still in town, sped to an efficient clip when the Red Queen and her army of military men struck out for the west with the rising sun at their backs. The march of Carolyn's battalions, even with wagons, a brief train ride, and horses would be long, arduous, and would be taken slowly to leave them fresh for fighting when they hit the teeth of the line Gieo had mapped through her many failed flights. With the town clear of all but those loyal to Veronica or Fiona, the Slark salvage came out of its various hiding places mapped by Cork to make its way onto the makeshift fleet. The handful of pilots from Colorado, spurned by McAdams and the Raven command, quickly saw the truth of their situation and threw their lot in with Veronica's plan as their best hope for survival. Many still believed McAdams couldn't possibly have known about Carolyn's treachery before his departure to Las Vegas; Gieo agreed with their assessment of the man, but she secretly wondered what he might have been offered. Regardless, her vow to Charlotte to bring her husband home safely was on his own head now.

The airships, which had once looked flimsy and ill-conceived, blossomed into full-blown weapons of war with the addition of the Slark armor, armaments, and structural support. Turning their former technical superiority back against them seemed like lovely poetic justice to Gieo as she surveyed the complete sky armada of three airships and seven planes. Each of the smaller dirigibles could launch two modified crop dusters while the biggest monster, the one she would pilot, boasted three biplanes in accompaniment.

"I'm not one for worrying about others," Fiona said, stepping beside Gieo on the scaffolding around the airship field with its now open top.

"No, you seem to like making people worry far more," Gieo replied. She leaned against Fiona's shoulder with her arms still crossed over her chest. "Ramen would like you to take care of his puppy while we're away."

"What did he end up naming it?" Fiona asked.

"Shrimp Ramen," Gieo said. "To be honest I'm surprised he even managed to come up with that. Programming creativity into an AI is nearly impossible."

"You seem to excel at impossible," Fiona replied, wrapping her arms around the diminutive pilot. "If you don't come back, I will come looking for you."

"That'll show me," Gieo said.

The rest of the afternoon and evening continued with preparations. Gieo angled for Fiona to take her home for a little going away fun, but Fiona flatly refused, demanding they wait until after Gieo came back.

As Gieo was set to board the largest of the dirigibles for their departure, Fiona gifted her with the shifting knob from her car, promising it had luck in it. Gieo barely managed to hold back tears when she leaned down from the access ladder to kiss the lanky gunfighter goodbye.

Once inside the cockpit of the *Big Daddy* as it had come to be known, Gieo hooked herself into the various pulleys and gyroscopes necessary to fly the dirigible effectively. The knob to lower the weapon systems into place was a thread match for the knob Fiona had given her. She replaced the blank black ball with the silver skull from Fiona's old car.

The airships lifted off into the inky night sky atop the cheers of the collected throng of Tombstone residents. Their proscribed course and pace would put them at the Slark line the following morning, 10 AM if all went well, when the sun would be at their backs and their ships difficult to find in the light. Gieo turned the three dirigible squadron to the northwest in a slow, droning arc.

Fiona stood by, holding Shrimp Ramen idly against her chest, watching her lover go off to war, hating herself as much as anything for all the times she put Gieo through what she was experiencing in that moment.

Gieo had heard pilots were a cocky breed, and the handful of gunners and pilots she was taking with her on the *Big Daddy* certainly fit that description. Some were the Colorado military men and some were Raven trainees—regardless, they all saw themselves as a breed apart, one meant to rain fire from the sky onto lesser beings. Seeing the dust of Carolyn's column nearing where Gieo knew the Slark line to be, she figured they were about to find out what kind of pilots they truly were. It was the same antiaircraft battery position she'd assaulted in the spring when Fiona had come to her rescue after being shot down. There was symmetry to the whole thing that felt fated.

The dirigible formation slowed to wait for the ground force to make their assault. It wasn't a sneak attack as the dust cloud from the marching column could be seen for miles and the blimps, though difficult to spot when backlit could clearly be heard, but rather it was an overwhelming force with air support. Even from the great height and distance, Gieo could make out the streaking trails of rocket propelled grenades being launched by Carolyn's two battalions. The fight was over quickly. The soldiers fanned out, rolling back the Slark defenses, and then just as easily detonating the antiaircraft weapons with loud popping explosions. The radio crackled with a soldier's voice, letting Gieo know the gates were open.

She kept her formation tight, dove low, and pushed the three dirigibles to their top speeds as she shot through the opening created so easily by 2,000 human soldiers obliterating fifty or so Slark spread over half-a-dozen emplacements they believed were well-kept secrets. The support force, the overwhelming majority that was to push back the 2,000 humans would take awhile to muster, but was undoubtedly on the way. This was the reason for the low approach, and Gieo, once on the other side of the battery she had once assaulted alone, spotted a second column of dust and exhaust on the horizon of the counterattack to be made by the Slark. She turned her formation on an intercept course.

The Slark, who had long forgotten what human air power might be capable of, and who had never seen the likes of the Slark technology laden airships, stopped in their tracks to gawk at the encroaching blimps rather than scatter for cover. Gieo cranked the alarm handle above her head and to the right, letting her gunners know they were up. She grasped the silver skull knob gifted by Fiona, and pulled it down, dropping the main weapon systems into place along the sides of the dirigible's carriage. *The Big Daddy has its big hammer out to do some big smashing*, Gieo thought with no small trill of joy running through her stomach.

Fire from the various weapon pods along the flanks of the airships rippled through the hull as all gunners found targets and range on the unsuspecting Slark column. Explosions from high-impact shells set off a cascade of secondary detonations as the minor crawlers took several direct hits. The high-pitched whine of Gatling guns followed, peppering the desert floor with tens of thousands of rounds, obliterating the Slark foot soldiers where they stood. Gieo sighted in along the center of the column, bringing the *Big Daddy* in low, and released the payload of cluster bombs specifically intended for the purpose. The grape-bunch bomblings dropped from the belly of the great airship in a slow hale, suddenly breaking up by shaped charges in the center of the bundles to spread the baseball-sized phosphorus bombs out to cut a white, fiery swath of destruction. What remained on the periphery was easily mopped up by the *Little Monster* and the *Hard-Paw* flanking the larger airship.

"The board is clear, Red Rovers," Gieo said into the cone of the radio receiver by her head. "We're on route to target."

"Good luck, *Big Daddy*," the ground forces replied.

It would be close to nightfall by the time they reached Bakersfield and they would have no such ground support or advantage of the sun at their back when they attacked the refineries that fueled the Slark war machine. Regardless, Gieo felt confident the element of surprise would remain theirs, and the fields would be ripe for the picking. She recalculated her fuel consumption, gained altitude, and returned to the proscribed course she'd laid out that would weave around any possible population centers.

"If you want to catch some sleep, I can wake you if needs be, boss," Ramen's voice crackled down the wire. He was in a far more protected encasement in the nose cone than he'd ever been with far more control over the systems on the ship than ever before. As unique advantages went, Gieo was glad she'd spent the years to develop such a friend and partner in crime.

"I think I'll do just that," Gieo said, fairly certain she wouldn't be able to sleep even if she wanted to despite not having slept in more than twenty hours. Pulling herself up into the cocoon, a similar mummy-style sleeping compartment to the ones on space stations, which was added to the design by McAdams and his crew, she found herself lulled into a gentle slumber by the thrumming of the airship as it winged its way toward the final target. If all went according to plan, the trip including the turnaround, would only take two days, but it was made abundantly clear to her by the military men that 24 hours of sleep deprivation significantly impaired a pilot's capabilities. Ramen dissembled the order through the tiny air formation to put the pilots to bed.

Gieo dreamed deeply of flying among the clouds free of an airship or wings, dancing atop the moonlit mountains of the sky, unable to see the ground through the cloud cover below her feet, and an ocean of stars above her. The serenity of the dream was shattered before she could even truly process the splendor created by her subconscious.

"...2% theory applies to both sides!" Ramen was screaming to her.

She was already dropped back out of the armored core of the ship into her pilot's sling, given precious little time to hook back into the necessary apparatuses. Her hands were slowed by the lingering remnants of sleep. It took her a moment to realize what Ramen was saying. She'd had a theory that the cataclysm only boasted a 98% effective rate, leaving 2% of the world's technology reset, turned off, visually no different from that which was destroyed, but still functional with a new power source. Size and complexity appeared to amplify the cataclysm's effect, as was probably the intention, but she didn't know for certain until that moment that the Slark had found ways around this hypothesis just as she had.

Well before the target zone, lumbering out of the ruins of Edwards Air Force Base in defense of the Bakersfield oil fields and refineries, was one of the colossal crawlers favored by the Slark for city obliteration. There was something profoundly off about the fifty-story tall weapon platform. It was belching diesel smog and lacked the sprightly quickness she remembered them having.

"We have to launch the fighters, sky-captain," the commander of the *Little Monster* said across the short-wave radio.

"If we launch them too early, we won't have them for the oil fields," Gieo replied.

"If we don't launch them, we won't make it to the oil fields," the *Hard-Paw* captain replied.

"Both of you launch yours," Gieo said. "I'll hold mine in reserve until we need them. We may not find a landing zone between here and Bakersfield to re-mount them though, so they should make for the rally point at Red Rock Canyon once they've spent their payloads."

The green lights on the copper-plated dashboard let Gieo know the captains were both in an understanding of the changed plan. The tell-tale hum of airplane engines filled the air as the four fighters descended from their holds on the escort dirigibles.

"Look how slow it is. We can go around, boss," Ramen said. "We don't have to fight this thing."

"Are you kidding me?" Gieo asked with a triumphant tone. "Let's show this thing the teeth of our new airship and send a real message to the Slark." She ran the wings out, diverted power to the main thrusters, and rolled the airship into attack formation, eyes set on the target of the crawler's forelegs. She'd seen how someone had taken down the smaller crawler their salvage came from, and had a good feeling it would work even better on one of the biggest in their arsenal.

Gieo painted the shoulder joints on the arachnid legs along the front with a laser sight. The gunners let fly with everything they had, putting the full weight of their fire on the tiny red dot of light beamed down from the nose of the *Big Daddy*. The fighters made their first pass along the top of the crawler, striking at a dive, and releasing their payloads into what was widely agreed to be the weakest part of the crawlers. There appeared to be no appreciable effect, although the retaliation fire from the crawler was far too slow to catch up to even the slowest of the four modified crop dusters. Without Slark fuel to run, it appeared the goliath crawler was a shadow of its former self, but Gieo figured that left them about even considering modified crop dusters were hardly F-22 Raptors.

Targeting lasers, which required a completed circuit to fire, painted all three airships on the first pass. Gieo could only imagine the shock and dismay of the Slark crawler captain when the lasers refused to fire. The Slark armor plating prevented closing of the firing circuit, which made friendly fire incidents between Slark technology impossible; apparently the U.S. military had worked tirelessly before the cascade to try to unlock a way to armor human machines in a similar way, but could never work out what element the Slark used. Gieo rightly figured out Slark armor contained metal not present on Earth, likely by design. Putting together what she knew with what

McAdams knew, and it was an easy jump for her to hypothesize that the Slark beam weapons, the most feared among the Air Force pilots as they required no traditional lock-on, no flight of a missile, hit with unerring accuracy even when fired at supersonic jets, and had near infinite range, would not work on the thunderously slow dirigibles if armored with Slark salvage.

The first pass crippled the front leg, but failed to break it free. Gieo knew they wouldn't make the mistake on the second pass of trying the beam weapons again. The fighters covered their long turnaround for a return trip, still unable to do any real damage to the crawler, but more than capable of drawing clumsy fire away from the drifting airships.

On the second pass, Gieo lit up the target again, directing all fire from all three dirigibles onto the already damaged leg. The crawler had ground to a halt, no longer able to pull the wounded limb up despite obvious attempts to. Gieo knew the salvaged diesel engines they were using, likely robbed from trains, couldn't boast anywhere near the torque of a Slark engine; what might have been a minor setback before the cascade was apparently a debilitating wound with the inferior human technology powering the crawler. Their fire found its mark, but so too did the Slark retaliation. Rockets, provincial and not too dissimilar from human designs, which were hardly used by the Slark in the first contact war, struck home on the *Hard-Paw*. The airship floundered, listed to the starboard side away from the formation, caught fire, and descended to the quickly darkening eastern desert.

"Fighter formations alpha and beta, forget the cover for us," Gieo shouted into the microphone cone, "go cover the crash site against recon crawlers."

The planes broke formation, circled back on their path, and pushed hard to keep up with the already dwindling fire of the descending airship.

Gieo pressed the attack still, coming in close enough to use knives, wishing desperately that she had included a weapon for herself, but trusting in her gunners to finish what they'd started. Relief and elation washed over her when she saw the leg pull free, broken on too many moorings, and finally dropping from the crawler like a felled tree. They pulled away with the clangs and knocks of solid fire weapons bouncing off their armor. The *Big Daddy* drew most of the fire along its armored underside, deflecting all attempts with a shrug and a puff from its great bellows.

Gieo couldn't see the crawler's tumble. Her focus was on the sky above, gaining altitude, but she heard it, suspected people in Tombstone probably heard it. The sound was unlike anything she could even have imagined. The crawler went over face-first and sounded for all the world like a thunderstorm comprised entirely of cars loosing its fury on rocky ground. The creak and whine of metal failing compounded hundreds of times over only broken up by the hollow drums of minor explosions.

"Do we finish them off?" the captain of *Little Monster* asked.

"Not a chance," Gieo replied. "We've knocked them down and lost more than we could afford in the process. Continue to target and let them choke on their defeat."

The high of victory hadn't remotely worn off the crews of either of the remaining airships. Their jubilation was tempered only by the loss of a third of their squadron and the unknown fate of the four fighter pilots who had left to ensure their possible safety. Only after the completion of their mission could they even consider searching deep behind enemy lines for survivors.

Bakersfield had suffered greatly during the war not only for its proximity to the Air Force base, but also because of the concentration of oil refineries it boasted. Only two refineries remained intact and the Slark had apparently made good use of both. The hellish red light of dusk, tainted by the smog put out by the inefficient fuel refining process completed by the inexact hands of the Slark, guided the airships in for the attack on the major production plants of diesel fuel. Gieo could see the Slark scrambling below, but heard no air raid chirping that served as the Slark's audible warning signal, nor did the popping of antiaircraft shells greet them. The goliath crawler had been the first, last, and only defense of their oil production and processing with the estimation it would be more than enough. They descended upon the Slark as Gieo had suspected they would—unlikely conquerors flying improbable ships to attack an impossible target once guarded by a nearly godly defender.

Gieo launched her remaining three biplane fighters and watched the conflagration begin. The Bakersfield refineries, likely the only source of diesel available to the Slark outside of the weak Los Angeles production centers, dissolved under the withering fire put out by the streaking biplanes. Explosions rippled across the landscape, plumes of flame reached into the sky to shocking heights, and the Slark fled their barely understood fuel plants like rats from sinking ships. Gieo watched this all from a safe height, waiting in a holding pattern in a ship of her own design, satisfied that she'd finally finished what she'd labored for years to accomplish.

"Impossible is a word to be found only in the dictionary of fools," Gieo whispered to herself, quoting another unlikely diminutive military leader who had dared, like her, to take on the world.

Chapter 28

A final betrayal before the storm

Fiona's time without Gieo was spent sick with worry until she found some consolation in the bottom of a bottle. Mitch was happy to pour for her while Bond-O was happy to keep Shrimp Ramen busy with kitchen scraps and wrestling gentle enough for a puppy.

Trouble boasted a smell for all the initiated warriors of the world; this scent of impending turmoil came rolling in, chasing the setting sun, as the bats were taking wing for their dusk feeding. Fiona could feel it like the heavy air before a storm and it brought her senses back from the brink of tequila oblivion. She was up on her feet before she even heard the first engine. The handful of hunters and Ravens in the saloon found their feet as well, practically sniffing the air like wolves on the hunt. Engine noises rang through the encroaching darkness.

Armed and ready, Colt in hand, Fiona made her way to the front windows in time to see the first of the motorcycles tear through the empty streets. They weren't hunters looking for Slark heads; they were marauders in search of more complete prey. Before Fiona could stop him, Cork was out the front door of the saloon, wading into the midst of the invading bikers. Fiona moved to back his play, moved to pull him from the fire as he had pulled her in the assault on the Hawkins House, but held at the threshold of the still swinging doors. They knew him, stopped to speak with him, and let him pass unmolested, out of sight in the direction they'd come, on what were obviously important errands. The betrayal stung Fiona initially, followed by blinding rage.

Her anger was quickly interrupted by the sound of rifle fire as the bikers got their first taste of Raven tenacity. They had no doubt come seeking women, beautiful, supple, young, and scarce in the desert, but had found the Ravens weren't easily captured or exploited, not when they had guns so close to defend themselves. Fiona turned to find the remaining four hunters in the saloon less focused on the boiling war in the streets but almost entirely engrossed in what she was doing.

"Cork says not to hurt you," one of the men said.

"Sit it out, have another drink and we'll all just wait for the firing to stop," another continued.

They were advancing on her with one hand on their guns and the other held out like they were approaching a spooked horse. Fiona glanced to Mitch, who stood in a state of ambivalent hell, bottle at the ready, seemingly unsure of the plan he'd signed on for once it came to actually enacting it.

"You aren't one of them," Mitch croaked around a throat made dry from stress. "You're one of us. Things'll go back to the way they were and it'll be like it never happened."

"Like hell…" Fiona raised her pistol on who she guessed to be the fastest of the lot. Her shot was spoiled when the man sprung half a dozen holes and tumbled over a table in the thrall of the machinegun victim's dance. The other four struck similar poses of surprise at being shot and fell as well without Fiona or the four hunters getting a single shot off.

Stephanie stood on the railing of the second level with two other Ravens, smoking assault rifles in hand. Fiona turned her rage on Mitch. She stormed across the plank floor with long-legged strides, her Anaconda brought to bear on the bartender.

"Now, Red…" was all he managed to get out before Fiona put two holes in his chest. The smoking wounds in his shirt poured frothy blood while the bottles behind him caught the escaping slugs and chunks of his ruined back.

"Get his truck out on the street," Fiona growled to Stephanie as the Ravens stormed down the stairs to join her. "I'm done being burned by betrayal for the week and ready to do some burning of my own."

Out the back of the saloon, seeking out the Kodiak's hiding place, they heard the war begin in earnest. What sounded like relatively little resistance initially seemed to have hardened against the marauders the closer they got to the Raven stronghold, no doubt clashing against Veronica's defensive plans that would allow a few hundred Ravens to holdout against a few thousand invaders. But hold out for what, Fiona wondered.

Fiona and her group of Ravens found Mitch's truck hidden in the derelict store next door, but quickly learned Gieo had already stripped bits and pieces from it including the boiler, likely without Mitch's knowledge. The gun would still work, but without the truck to drive it about, they would need the targets to come inside the building and stand against a wall for it to do any good.

"Damn it," Fiona grumbled.

"Bond-O push trucks for fun," a meek, quiet voice spoke from behind them. "Bond-O push truck for you."

Fiona's initial reaction was to tell him absolutely not, to tell him to hide, but she knew that, without Mitch, Zeke's new rule wouldn't be kind to Bond-O and he had every right to participate in the fight for his own existence. She nodded. Stephanie mounted the gun, hooking herself into the familiar gyroscopes, and the remaining two Ravens took up defensive positions on either side of the simpleminded fry cook at the front of the truck.

The truck lurched, moving slow with the meaty shoulder of Bond-O pressed against the front bumper and grill. Finally, it nosed out toward the opening in the wall and began to pick up steam toward the street. Fiona stood on the running board, open truck door behind her, steering with her left hand, gun in her right. They would be an easy target to find, but a hard one to reach.

With the open street before her, Stephanie didn't want for targets. Motorcycles, ATVs, and trucks were pouring into the city, bristling with weapons and hard men. Stephanie started with the closest bundle and worked her way out. The quad gun, meant for obliterating heavily armored vehicles from the undercarriage of one of the medium-sized crawlers, ripped through the marauder column like a chainsaw through tinfoil. Bodies and vehicles alike exploded when the peculiar green shells struck them—it was the bad old days of the alien invasion all over again with deadly Slark technology obliterating effectively defenseless men.

When she swung the gun to one side, the Ravens shifted their focus to the other to cover her back. They crawled down the streets, sweeping clean the invaders from Juarez in a wash of Slark firepower. The truck's initial speed, which was barely above noticeable, continued to slow until Bond-O was finally too tired to continue, leaving them stranded, still several blocks from the Raven stronghold around the courthouse.

"Bring back help," Stephanie shouted, never leaving the trigger of the guns alone as she found target after target. "We'll hold here until help arrives. We can't let them get this gun."

Fiona made it only a few steps away from the stranded Kodiak before the marauders made their first successful counterattack. Rocket propelled grenades struck first, missing the heart of the gun platform. Fiona found herself flat on the ground, covered in dirt and shattered asphalt from the street. Her ears were ringing and her mouth tasted like blood. She could hear the rhythmic drumming of the quad gun, but little else. She turned her head as though underwater, slowly to see the ruined bodies of the two Raven guards and the massive, shrapnel-riddled corpse of Bond-O at the burning front of the truck. She tried to stand, but couldn't keep her feet. A motorcycle shot past her from behind, nearly clipping her in the process. She found her gun amongst the rubble and retrieved it.

She glanced up to Stephanie just in time to see a hurled harpoon strike her dead center. The motorcycle with the wire tether still attached shot past the truck, ripping the diminutive dancer from the gun platform, bouncing her off the wall of the building on the far side of the truck. Before the bike could drag her further, Fiona raised her gun hand and blew the driver out of the saddle with a well-placed shot. The harpooner on the back of the bike kicked over the handlebars when the bike turned sideways, bouncing hard across his neck, bending his head back at an unnatural angle before he came to rest in a tangled mess a dozen feet farther down the road from the bike. Fiona jogged as best she could around the truck to find Stephanie's lifeless eyes staring up at nothing in particular. The steel spike jutting from her chest had likely killed her on impact; a small miracle Fiona could hope for.

The Ravens were making their push out from the stronghold, bolstered by Fiona could only guess what. Explosions rocked the city, fires spread, and soon the motorcycles were in full retreat. Bodies, both men and women, littered the street as Fiona stumbled toward the sounds of rifle fire and explosions. So engrossed were the attackers in attempting to defend themselves against the Raven push that Fiona nearly stumbled into the back of one of their hastily constructed defensive positions behind a scuttled SUV.

A handful of Juarez marauders were being directed in the construction of a barricade by none other than Cork. Before they noticed her, before they even had a chance to glance back over their shoulders at the sound of her scuffling boots, Fiona had put the five Juarez men down with near point-blank shots. She swung the gun on Cork and clicked on an empty cylinder.

"This wasn't how I wanted it," Cork said, raising his sub machinegun. "I couldn't take the abuse from…" was all he managed before a sniper's bullet cleaved his forehead from his body.

Fiona snapped her head around in time to see the outline of a diminutive sniper in a beret scampering across the rooftops away from the sweeping fires chasing her through the city. She couldn't say for sure why, but she felt it would be the last she would ever see or hear of Claudia. Something about the French Canadian woman spoke of an urge to be free of her situation and nothing would provide cover for her escape like a city-ending catastrophe.

Fiona ran the arduous process of reloading her gun with shaky hands and redoubled her efforts to find the Raven line. A second wave of engines was roaring toward the city and she suspected the counterassault would likely be rolled back—she had to be on the right side of it before that happened.

She rounded two more corners without incident before she found the street blocked by an overturned bus set ablaze. The sounds of battle were moving away from her again to the southeast. She glanced around to find the closest, tallest building that wasn't already on fire. She kicked in the front door and bolted up the stairs. A ladder and hatch granted her access to the roof of the two-story office complex. One street over, the Ravens assault was collected around the tip of the spear; at that sharpened point was Veronica with an assault rifle mounted grenade launcher. She was the source of the explosions and her entourage the source of the gunfire.

Fiona recognized the El Camino barreling down on the cluster of women, knew the spikes of the blue and white hunter's car, and didn't need more than one try to guess the driver. Veronica clearly recognized it as well. Her grenade missed by just enough to spare the car but not let it keep its wheels. Zeke's ride tumbled through the right side of the Raven formation, crushing and mangling bodies as it came to rest against a wall. Fiona didn't wait to see the rest of the fight; she had to be in it.

Back down the ladder, down the stairs, onto the open street, she raced to reach Veronica in time. The hollow thunder of shotgun fire echoed through the night in two quick bursts and then nothing. Fiona sprinted onto the street she'd seen Veronica knock out Zeke's car. The accompanying Ravens were either dead or injured, littering the streets with the charred victims they'd already gunned down. Among the fallen, Fiona found Veronica's familiar form.

Her former lover was already gone. Fiona cradled Veronica's lifeless body, lovingly stroking the well-known features of her angelic face, kissing the blond hair, now streaked with blood, that she'd so often ran her fingers through. She couldn't have said to that point what she might have wanted from her manipulative ex, but seeing her dead, knowing she would never again hear her sing or speak, Fiona simply wished Veronica had the chance at some peace in her life before she met the violent end she seemed to know was waiting for her all along.

"The head's severed, Red," she heard Zeke shout from down the street. He was staggered, injured, leaning heavily against the wreckage of his car with a ghastly wound to his right leg. "They'll crumble without her, and we both know it. All you have to do is sit it out, and you can take your rightful place by my side as the ruler of this town."

Fiona gently laid Veronica to rest on the pavement. She rose, sliding her gun back into its holster. "Is that what this is about? Setting me at your side?"

"You're like the daughter I never had," Zeke said. "You're like me more than you're like them! Can't you see that?"

"I don't hate them," Fiona spat back. "I just wanted to be free."

"Join me and you can carve freedom from the world however you like," Zeke said. "I'll carve it in blood right along with you. What are you going to do otherwise? You're not fast enough to kill me and you know it."

"You've told us both that for so long—I'm itching to prove you a liar." Fiona stepped into the middle of the street. Zeke hobbled to mirror her stance, holding only his shotgun at his side.

Fiona's heart thundered in her ears, the world of fire and smoke swirled around her as though she weren't even a part of the destruction, the eye of her own fiery storm. She pulled first. Zeke was faster; his gun was up, pumped and ready before she could aim. He pulled the trigger as if he knew the result, knew what was about to happen with grim certainty. The shotgun clicked on empty.

"Now you know," Zeke whispered.

"Now we both do."

Fiona fired. The bullet burst through Zeke's neck, severing a handful of major blood vessels. He spun to the ground, spraying his car with a fresh coat of red.

Fiona felt a sense of completion wash over her when she saw him fall; they'd misread her, they'd all misread her, not just Zeke and Cork, but Veronica too. The only person who hadn't misread her was flying a possible suicide mission at that moment and Fiona was dead set on making sure she had a landing zone to come back to. If she was lucky enough, clever enough, and good enough, she might have time enough to process what had happened; if she couldn't muster enough of those three things, it wouldn't matter anyway—luck, cleverness, and skill would just be another three corpses in the streets.

The remaining Ravens rallied around her. They made a push to eradicate the invaders, breaking into strike teams, coming back together when they met large resistance, fighting in the effective fashion that had won them Las Vegas. Reduced to scavenging ammunition and weapons from the fallen, the Ravens finally lost their edge in street-to-street fighting. The Juarez marauders were too much, finally pushing the exhausted and injured women from the heart of the city to put them on the run.

In the wee hours of the night, Fiona led the two dozen or so Ravens that remained to the replica street formerly meant for tourism. The marauders outnumbered them by a thousand or more by that point and little remained of the town to even fight over anymore. Capturing Ravens alive, which was no doubt what the Juarez men had been promised by Zeke, proved to be nearly impossible. The hardened women, fighters of Las Vegas all, had no fear of death and took to the grave anyone attempting to set chains on them. More than a few had already blown themselves and their captors to smithereens with a hidden grenade when capture seemed imminent. In Vegas they'd called the suicidal grenade a trump card—Fiona had hoped to never see another trump card played again, but even still, she knew she would pull her own pin if the time came and knew this to be true for the remaining women who stood with her; it might be too late for them, but it would send a clear message to Juarez in a final act of bloody defiance—don't fuck with the Ravens.

The marauders would find them soon enough. They would fight. They would lose. They would take as many with them as they could. But they likely wouldn't see the entire sunrise. With their defensive line set, Fiona waited for the inevitable attack. From across the ruined city, the marauders charged, escorted by motorcycles and pickups, armed, dirty, screaming, and bent on ruin. Before they could reach the effective firing range of the Ravens, three whirring engines roared overhead. Machinegun fire tore through the approaching marauders as a trio of biplanes dove down the length of their formation.

Fiona's gaze shot skyward just in time to see the *Big Daddy*, *Little Monster*, and a hobbled *Hard Paw* along with their accompanying fighters setting up for a weary attack run on a defenseless enemy. As the bombs, shells, and Slark weapons rained down on the fleeing Juarez men, Fiona pulled her hat from her head and waved it at the largest of the three dirigibles, hoping Gieo could see her among the survivors.

The airships and the escort fighters skimmed through the smoke of the fires that had consumed Fiona's birthplace and former home. Fiona couldn't remember having left the town during childhood, but a distinct part of her was glad to finally be rid of the place, even at the extreme personal cost exacted for its demise.

Chapter 29

A new old life

When the ruins of Tombstone were swept clean by Gieo and her air force, Fiona followed the dirigibles to the last landing zone available to them: the old high school football field. The gunfighter and gear-head met and embraced, simply holding each other in shaking arms. There would be time for more, a lifetime if both had their way, but in that glorious moment all either of them needed was to be held.

With what little remained of the town in shambles, and what few survivors long since fled, the handful of Ravens and returning pilots set to work sifting the remains. They buried their dead as best they could, sought out what little food and water stores might remain, and began what would likely be a fruitless search for horses. The casualty rate amongst the townsfolk was surprisingly light; Fiona guessed Cork had warned them away when she was drinking.

Fiona found small combat boot footprints near where Gieo had stored her modified Indian motorcycle—the bike was gone. Any number of Ravens could have taken the motorcycle, but Fiona suspected Claudia was the only one who knew precisely where it was. The little sniper had earned the chance at something else, and Fiona hoped she would find it.

Burying Veronica was an ordeal for all the Ravens present, but struck Fiona with an emotional cataclysm that she hadn't even felt when her mother died. The regret of sparing Zeke all those months ago after the Slark attack sat heavy in the center of Fiona's chest; she knew it would likely be a permanent wound and welcomed the reminder of what she'd lost.

Before the sun could set, when the direness of the situation began to settle over the fifty or so remaining Ravens and pilots, talk turned to Las Vegas. Without Veronica, without means to sustain themselves, there was no reason to squat amidst the ruins of Tombstone or toil in the rebuilding of what had already been relegated to a pointless listening post. In addition to Fiona and Gieo, who had absolutely no interest in Las Vegas, there were several others among the survivors who expressed desire for another option.

This phantom alternative, to which nobody could brainstorm even a remotely reasonable notion of, came in the form of a vehicle column out of the northeast. The dust cloud on the horizon spoke initially of alarm, but that quickly faded when binoculars provided confirmation that the vehicles were marked as Raven. Veronica's gift from beyond the grave extended in the form of Alondra's soldiers, rushing to Tombstone's aid, perhaps a night too late, but in time to preserve those who survived. The rider, Fiona recognized her as the one she'd given Veronica's missive to, stood at the front of the column like a conquering hero returning home.

The orders for the Marine Captain in charge of the expeditionary force were to assist if possible in any way the White Rook Gieo saw fit. Gieo instructed everyone to scavenge whatever they could from the ruins, refuel the airships with every last drop of Slark fuel they could find, and then the whole of them would return to Albuquerque. The Captain, who had initially seemed a little glum about missing out on the obviously exciting combat of the night before, took the orders as an opportunity to complete his mission without taking losses—an acceptable substitute considering Alondra's dislike of casualties among her men.

Nothing was going to feel like victory to Fiona at that moment, but the escape provided by Veronica postmortem could suffice as catharsis in a weary moment.

Gieo spent the better part of an hour in the shower of Alondra's guestroom that she and Fiona were sharing until their accommodations could be arranged. She switched the water from cold to hot and back again half a dozen times just because she could.

She scrubbed, shaved, and exfoliated her skin until the water slid off her like silk over glass. Fiona had already been through the bathroom on a similar errand, but hadn't tarried under the stream of water even half the time Gieo was planning.

Heaven was the only worthy reward for the Asian sky Napoleon and that was precisely what Gieo felt she was given. Wrapped in a towel with her purple hair, grown out nearly to solid black, still wet from the shower, she exited into the bedroom to find Fiona sprawled across their bed. The warm, afternoon sun creeping through the Venetian blinds set lines along the gunfighter's long, shapely legs. Gieo's heart caught in her throat at the sight of her lover dressed in a black Victoria's Secret silky pushup bra and boy-cut panties set from the Angel clothing line Fiona used to model.

"I thought you didn't like underwear," Gieo whispered.

"It's growing on me," Fiona replied, "and I know you do. I thought you deserved a reward."

"We both do." Gieo tossed her towel aside, slid onto the bed, and met Fiona halfway for a long, powerful kiss that would have taken her legs from beneath her were she standing.

The End

Check out the continuation of the Raven Ladies series with:

Available now from
Day Moon Press

About the Author

Cassandra Duffy spent most of her childhood being precocious, which stopped being entertaining or impressive when she grew into an adult, at which point she had to start being precious. After being an outcast child prodigy it was no surprise when she graduated from one of the many fine University of California schools a year early to follow her girlfriend in a cross country move.

Two of her greatest prides are being a true California girl and author of some highly naughty things. She is a dutiful partially-Asian daughter who is beloved by her fairly traditional Korean father who thinks having a gay daughter is just fine as long as she keeps playing coed flag football. She is a stereotypical younger sister, and an adoring aunt of a hilarious little boy. Being a modern techno-freak, gamer-girl, she spent most of her childhood dreaming of being a video game designer, but changed her mind and brought her dreams of world building and story-weaving to writing unique romance novels.

Cassandra is a gleefully monogamous girlfriend to an earthbound goddess who was once her high school bully, but has done a magnificent job of making up for all the school girl nastiness ever since. When she isn't being an avid fang girl (vampire fan girl) or tormenting people in online gaming, she lives and writes in Winter Park, Florida with her partner and soul mate Nichole and their two cats: Dragon and Josephine.

Made in the USA
Middletown, DE
30 September 2016